I0636809

Even After

Mary Catelli

Published by Wizard's Wood Press, 2025.

EVEN AFTER

First edition. May 1, 2025.

Copyright © 2025 Mary Catelli.

ISBN: 978-1-942564-75-1

Written by Mary Catelli.

Chapter 1—The Mirror Tells Tales

From the highest tower in the finest castle in seven times seventy kingdoms, dressed in violet satin and bedecked with gold and amethysts, Queen Augusta Gloriana looked out the window, at flourishing fields and pastures and forests, and at the prospering city below, and gave an exasperated sigh.

She should have known that among all the people she might see on the road, King Ogier was the last, since she had seen him descending toward an inn in the city.

"There is no use sending the men-at-arms. He just stands them drinks."

The ladies-in-waiting murmured their assents. She never listened, they knew, but she noted silence.

The queen swept from the room, not having to look back to know they followed, and down the stairs, dark from the lack of windows and from stone the color of a thunderhead. She fumed. It would be one thing, though folly, if the king were a drunken simpleton to drown his sorrows at his brother's death, but he was merely a reveler who had no better use for his time.

Except for breeding horses, he was willing to do that. Her breath came out in a little huff.

Maidservants, curtsying, scurried from her path, and she swept by.

And on top of King Ogier, she had—Princess Biancabella.

She had tried. She had tried to raise her daughter to be strong and willing to do what was needed, and tenacious enough not to turn from her way, but Biancabella listened when her mother talked about a court of justice—and still she was unshakable in the thought that it should render justice at whatever cost to her own mother.

When she tried to teach her magic, Biancabella looked blankly back.

Augusta Gloriana's lip curled. Though only, of course, after she had made it harder for Biancabella to have her tongue bound and her eyes blinded by magic—as if a stupid girl child, who refused to learn magic or do what was needed, needed to be free of the spells—as if she should not show her gratitude for the ability to see through spells by her obedience.

Now Biancabella flitted about the castle, looking *anxious* all the time. Fussing in the garden as if they had no gardeners.

After all her schemes, all her plots, all her hard work, this was her reward. Trying to pull this all together with no more aid than she had—

It was little consolation that at least no princely entourage came toward the castle, seeking to woo Biancabella. It would come in time, and she would have to deal with the prince when he arrived. Perhaps she might face a whole procession of princes, each one more *princely* than the next.

To think she had once thought that she could marry Biancabella off to the prince who might rescue Snow-White and saved herself the trouble of dealing with him with enchantment.

She swept into the courtyard.

At the castle gate, Ottoline looked sour. Her dingy brown but carefully arrayed hair hid, as best it could, the patch where her right eye should be, and she wore gold jewelry and a red velvet gown, but she looked sour above all.

Augusta Gloriana snorted. Herbert must be in the inn as well. Ogier might be standing on the table and singing songs, but Herbert would already cheerfully snore under the benches.

Then, Ottoline had, after all, been of aid to her—now and again—though the other woman did get to be a princess, not a queen, and so suffer so much less of the burden of her husband's folly and ineptitude.

"I will get Herbert as well, if you like."

Ottoline nodded and looked no less sour. "He wants to hunt. I will go east with him. I will visit the woods without his realizing."

Augusta Gloriana nodded. That might actually be of aid. "If I need more herbs, I will send you word."

#

Biancabella peered from the window, while trying to hide in the shadows at the same time. Her heart beat harder, as if she were a child seeing a chance to steal apples from the orchard, and she could not calm herself.

For once, for once—she stole down corridors and up stairways (feeling like a little girl at her games, instead of being nearly full grown) until she came to the oaken doors, black with age, of her mother's chamber. For a moment, she listened. Silence reigned. She slipped open the door and stepped within. The chamber was hung with tapestries in crimson and purple, and deep blues and greens, showing forest scenes of strange monsters, but it was empty.

Her breath gushed out in relief.

She slipped through the rooms to the mirror her mother had showed her once, when trying to persuade her that nothing was better than to master witchcraft and spells. For a moment, she looked at her reflection: pallid, thin, colorless, and anxious, her hair blond but so pale it looked white—unlike the splendid gold of her mother's.

She could not be beautiful, she told herself in a moment of panic. Certainly never so beautiful as her mother. She had nothing to fear, Meg had just been fussing over her when she said she would be more beautiful than her mother—Lady Regina had been severe about it, telling Meg that even a nursemaid should not be so silly, but Lady Regina was often severe, she wanted Biancabella to be a perfect princess for the kingdom's sake.

She drew a deep breath and told herself that it did not befit a princess, least of all one nearly of age, to step aside from the prudent path, and that Lady Regina, that sagacious lady, had not actually said that she would not be so beautiful as her mother.

She needed to know. To know many things.

Biancabella straightened. She did not need to ask who was fairest of them all. With her half-sister gone—before Biancabella's birth, even—her mother was still that. And that was not what she needed to know.

"Mirror, mirror, on the wall, how can I be safe when I am tall?"

Her words rang out clearly enough. Silence followed.

Her reflection looked back at her, and she felt a fool. Her shoulders slumped. She should know better than to trust what her mother said. Especially since she had already grown to nearly her mother's height and used it only to rhyme.

The reflection blurred a little, as if mist crept into it. Biancabella swallowed. That was no trick. The mist thickened, swirled about, did not quite lose all form, and was again a face, however vague. A face, that for all its vagueness, was not hers. Moments later, a serene face had formed. Its gaze swept over her, and then the eyes closed.

After a moment, a long sigh came from the mirror. "You are not Snow-White."

"I am her sister Biancabella, and I have heard what happened when she was more beautiful than my mother."

"As you grow to be. Though not yet." The mirror's voice was cool and even, and Biancabella flinched. "Fortunately for you that you are older than she was, as you grow into it. She was seven years old when she was that beautiful. You must have a decade on her."

"It's only fortunate," said Biancabella, "if I can change it. She was—eighteen? when my mother finally caught her. I want to be safe longer than that."

"She wished to be safe longer than that. That is harder that it seems to you."

"There must be something I can do," said Biancabella.

"Do you think you can run away to another castle? Live for a time as a scullery maid, hard though that work would be, and then sweep away the prince at a ball?"

Biancabella opened her mouth and closed it. She could find the gowns to bring with her. She could most likely find a castle with an unwed prince. She did not think she could escape her mother that way. She had heard the tales where the witch came and tried to murder the princess after she had her firstborn child.

The mirror, its voice cool and clear, its eyes still closed, swept on. "Do you wish to know what your mother can do? That is a long tale."

Long? thought Biancabella. The maidservants could tell in minutes about Snow-White, and the queen's jealousy, and how hiding with the dwarves had kept her safe but only for a few years. She bit her lip. She wanted safety, not to hear a tale. Still, listening might be wiser if it would leave her wiser than before.

The mirror's voice chilled. "Do you think it is just your sister? Do you think your mother had no more wickedness than that? To curse your sister and *nothing more*?"

Biancabella took a step backward.

"Do you think your mother—and your aunt—alone spread misery?"

"No," said Biancabella, her voice thin. "I have seen others visit, late at night. When my father and the rest sleep, and see nothing. I see. My mother would not hide them from the people of the castle if they meant well."

The mirror fell silent.

"I wish to know how to be safe from them *all*."

"Do you wish for the sun, the moon, and the stars as well?"

"Only if they will help protect me." In the silence, Biancabella pressed on. "Or tell me which path I should take. To travel for seven years and wear out six shoes of iron would do no good if I do not know where I should go."

Slowly, the mirror opened its eyes.

"If I knew enough, it might protect me."

"It will not," said the mirror. "Your sister did her best, but it did not suffice."

"She did not ask you what she could do." Biancabella leaned forward. "I ask."

"Be fortunate. Be very, very, very fortunate. There is no other way. There is nothing in your power to do that can save you. Many a prince, many a princess have tried, and failed."

It couldn't, it couldn't—she had nowhere else to go if the mirror could not help her. She needed its help.

"There must be something they did," said Biancabella.

"I can not tell you. There is no way. She could hide the castle you sought from you."

Biancabella stared at it for a long minute. Then she closed her eyes, tightly. After all her scheming and watching—

She found her voice. "Can you tell me *anything*?" Perhaps—perhaps she could learn something that might help.

The mirror's voice went on, smooth and cool. "Though I have the power to see far, over kingdoms and ages, there is much I do not know, and much that I know that I can not say. But what I *can* tell you is that I have seen many strive, and most fail. If you knew what I knew, you would know how hopeless it is."

Biancabella's heart began to beat not so much faster as harder in her chest. It drummed. Perhaps the mirror did not know what it knew.

"Then tell me."

The mirror paused.

"Tell me enough to make me wisely not strive for something only fortune can bring me."

Minutes passed. Her heart drummed on. She wondered if the beat would keep her from hearing her returning mother. Who might have a huntsman kill her in the woods for trying to usurp her magic.

Slowly, the mirror said, "I can tell you who your foes are, and how they will imperil you. If you wish to hear that."

Biancabella nodded. Perhaps, if Heaven blessed her, she could take that knowledge and find a way to safety. "I do wish it. It will make me wiser." It was not certainty, she could only hope—but still her heart beat harder and harder in her chest.

The mirror's voice grew dry. "It is not like telling you how to break the spell by nothing more than venturing east of the moon and west of the sun, where only the north wind can bear you. I can not tell you that I have no answer, but that I can send onward, to my sister, who might know—for I have no sister. It will be a long tale, and of little profit save in quenching hope. Do you truly wish to hear it?"

Biancabella, in spite of herself, grimaced. The mirror waited, calmly. A minute later, she nodded, however jerky the motion.

"I will tell you—but not now. It will take too long. Look over by the tapestry of the green dragon."

Biancabella obeyed. A door stood there.

"Come to me at dawn, and there will be an hour of safety where I can tell you what you need to know. I do not know how many mornings I will need, but for that hour, we will be safe every morning."

Biancabella nodded again. Her heart was still hammering.

The voice turned wry. "And actually, your questions do not have to rhyme."

#

Augusta Gloriana swept up the last stretch of the road, with the king and the prince reeling, singing some foolish song, behind her.

"Lavender's blue, dilly dilly, lavender's green!" caroled Herbert. Off-key, noted Ottoline from the gate's shadow.

"When I am king," sang Ogier, "dilly dilly, you shall be queen." Augusta Gloriana rolled her eyes. Ottoline's eyebrow went up. She was queen. If she wanted a *king*, she should have chosen more wisely. Dressing herself up in purple and gold did not make Augusta Gloriana any more dignified than any old fishwife prying her drunkard husband loose from the tavern.

She swept up to the gate and within, as if she could overlook Ottoline like a beggar.

"If you kept Biancabella under control," growled Ottoline, "we could actually use the garden to grow the herbs."

Augusta Gloriana swept on, and Ottoline glared after her.

Better yet, she could have raised the girl properly, to aid them. As it was, Augusta Gloriana should keep a better eye on her, or the brat would fall in love with a gardener's boy. Augusta Gloriana might claim that if the boy were a prince in disguise, she would keep off any attacking army, so that he could not save the kingdom and win Biancabella, and if he were truly a gardener's boy, she could have him sent off on a quest, and ensure that he never returned—but Augusta Gloriana had bungled enough that she should know she might bungle that.

Ogier and Herbert were still approaching the gate and singing together, their arms looped about each other's necks.

"If you should die, dilly dilly, as it may hap,
You shall be buried, dilly dilly, under the tap;
Who told you so, dilly dilly, pray tell me why?
That you might drink, dilly dilly, when you are dry."

Ottoline shook her head. She could believe that, at least. Before the men reached the gate, she walked into the garden. Some herbs could be grown here, despite the prying eyes. She would be ready to brew remedies for whatever trouble Augusta Gloriana was about to stir up for them. Really, the other woman prided herself so much on being queen.

Biancabella came running down stairs. Ottoline blinked and wondered where the girl had come from. Then, with a shrug, she turned away. Did it matter? Did anyone care what Biancabella did? Did even she care, or know why she did it?

She was glad that she had never borne a useless child. If Augusta Gloriana had not learned from history, she should have learned from Mistress Laurenza's brats.

#

Her aunt worked in the garden. Biancabella drew a deep breath to steady herself. Her hands were shaking, and now that she had reached the outside, she wondered that she had not fallen flat on her face going down the stairs.

Her breath came out in a laugh. It did not sound steady to her own ears. She closed her eyes and forced her breath in and out. To walk in the garden to calm down—it was still a prudent notion, she just had to avoid Ottoline. She inched toward the gate.

For all her welter of thoughts, it proved easy enough. She picked the path by the castle wall. Ottoline, absorbed in the plants, did not look up. Biancabella crept along like a little mouse. Ottoline seldom cared enough to notice her, she remembered. And now Ottoline had no more reason to think her worthy of notice than before.

She still crept along until a hedge of roses hid her from view. And from the window's view.

Her head bent, her breath gusted out, and her hands went up to cover her face. This had to work. It had to. If the mirror despaired, it did not mean it was so wise that its knowledge could not be used to escape.

Her heart hammered again, and she forced her breath in and out. It had to help.

Her governess would remind her of the witch who had skulls on posts all about her cottage, except for one, and how she would threaten a prince with putting his skull on the last post. Which meant that every prince who came before had failed. His skull had ended up on a post. "And do you think, Your Highness, that every one of them was an ignominious fool, such that a princess need not concern herself about failing that badly?"

She heard footsteps, softly, on a path and looked sharply up. A kitchen maid was briefly visible as she went to gather lettuce or herbs or some such for the meal. She did not glance over.

Still, thought Biancabella, if she had to collapse, it would be wiser to do somewhere more secret. Then she would not have the misfortune of having the servants tell her mother.

As her governess also told her, it was amazing, even unfair, how much more fortunate people were when they were prudent and diligent and courteous.

She walked. She managed, prudently, to walk no more quickly than she usually did, but her gaze went over the flowers without seeing them. Or noting any weeds. She felt glad that no one spoke to her. How her mother would jeer if she learned of her abstraction.

Ottoline still stood over flowerbeds when she returned, and so she circled about her, to continue to walk. There was no point in trying to sew until her hands were steady enough to not betray her, and to make her stitching worth its while.

Perhaps she would learn how to win her way to a castle, and even with the job as a scullery maid, she could still bring three ballgowns. She could after all—

She stopped.

The mirror had said that her mother could hide the castle from her, but she couldn't. Her mother had given her the power to see through such spells. The mirror had not known that.

Her lips closed on her lower lip, worrying it. The mirror might not know what it knew, but she would have piece together what it meant.

A bee buzzed over the hollyhock before her. She drew a deep breath, and smelled the sweetness of it. Slowly, she began to walk about the garden again, this time noting the roses in vivid pinks, the lilies in gold and white, blue larkspur and violet lavender.

It would be pleasant to plant without concerning herself with her mother. And she could wait to speak with the mirror. She waited for seeds to sprout and plants to blossom.

A bee came up to buzz about her skirt. She waited for it to be certain that she was not a flower.

This was the part of the tale that the books always passed over lightly. Like a prince traveling past thrice ten kingdoms.

The bee buzzed off, and she watched it fly, with more purpose than she had in walking about the garden. She stood for a moment longer in the sunlight. Until the mirror told her its stories, she could not usefully read in the library.

She should pack. Or perhaps merely consider which clothes to pack, so as to be ready, and make no decisions on the day. She picked her way across the garden. Perhaps she should pack a ball-gown to make her mother think she looked for a place as a scullery maid.

Then she shook her head. Her mother would not think such a thing.

#

The night sky had barely paled, with hundreds of stars still gleaming and the horizon just visible, when Biancabella finished dressing herself in a simple gray gown. She put on a darker gray cloak with a hood that, pulled over her head, left her face in shadow. It was a fight to keep her hands steady enough, as her thoughts veered between the possibilities of what the mirror could tell her, and whether the knowledge would be useful.

For a moment, Biancabella wished that she knew a henwife, or a talking red calf, that she could consult instead. Then she reminded herself that such an advisor, in all the tales, only told the princess that, for her safety, she had to run away. Snow-White had run away and not been safe.

By the time she climbed the stairs and slipped into the empty and silent room, the sky had grown charcoal gray. She sat before the mirror, catching only a glimpse of her own face as she did. She folded her hands in her lap, remembering when she had sat for her first lessons, of letters and numbers. Her tongue touched her lips, and she spoke. "I have come to hear your tale."

For a moment, nothing happened. Then, again, the face rose out of the swirl of mist. Its gaze seemed to look out at the horizon, without a glance at her.

"First, you must know the history." The voice was quiet, reflective. "That is where the tangles sprung. You would have to undo them all before you would be safe."

Biancabella swallowed.

"Once upon a time, a king and queen had for many years longed for a child, and had none. One day, the queen came upon a cottage where an enchantress lived, with her eleven beautiful daughters." The voice was almost meditative. "When the queen spoke longingly of how she had no child at all, the enchantress told her to go down a certain path and bathe in the forest pool there. She did, and a talking frog told that within a year, she would have a daughter. And so she did: a newborn princess. They invited the family of enchantresses to the christening, but a sorceress who was not of that family was not invited.

"The baby was christened Anna, and the enchantresses gave her all sorts of enchanted gifts. The sorceress swept in, at what she thought was the end, and cursed her to die on her eighteenth birthday. A curse would fall on her when first she touched a spindle.

"Then she swept off. She did not know that one enchantress there gave another gift: that the Princess Anna could be revived from the dead. But did not tell how that would happen.

"After she had laid the curse, the sorceress felt pleased with herself. All the more when the king and queen had kept Anna from so much as seeing a spindle for many years, so that when she chanced to see one, curiosity had it in her hand within a moment, and no one found her in the attic where she lay like dead.

"After a time, the sorceress saw the lands that had been the king's—they were quite troubled and wild. Pleased, she wrapped the tower in roses that would cruelly tear anyone who tried to get within, and set them to bloom in beautiful colors, like banners to celebrate her victory.

"Then she went to enchant a king to marry her, one who could seize the lands that had been Anna's father's, and she took the name of Augusta Gloriana—"

Biancabella's breath eased out.

"She persuaded him to marry her, though he already had a son, nearly grown, whose name was Carlos. He went hunting many a time. One day, an old witch was angry that he had ridden by her cottage, she thought him too noisy.

"So she cursed him to be unable to marry anyone but Anna asleep.

"Soon after, he went hunting and came to the castle, which had all but fallen apart, and was all over-grown, with oaks in the great hall and birches in the kitchen, and roses, roses everywhere. He found a few skeletons among the roses, too. But he found a set of stairs was sound, the roses did not move as he climbed because of his curse, and at the top of it, he found the attic where Anna lay, the spindle in her hand. Surprised that so richly dressed a maiden had so common a spindle, Carlos reached out to take it, and Anna, with a start, woke up.

"When they talked, he realized that his father had conquered her kingdom, when there was no heir, but he promised to keep her safe.

"After a few years, Augusta Gloriana realized that though her stepson went hunting more than ever, he never returned with game. For indeed, he and Anna had married, and she had borne two children, but he did not dare bring them to his father's attention, though his son Helias and his daughter Margarethe were as beautiful as the day—and almost as lovely as their mother—and he loved all three of them dearly.

"So she laid a curse on him. He fell ill, and feverish, and babbled of his Sun and his Pearl and their lovely mother. Soon she realized his bride was the Anna she had cursed. She sent a secret messenger to Anna, telling her that Carlos had sent for Helias. Anna protested the claim, said that her husband could send for all three, if any, but the messenger told her that the prince's orders must be obeyed if he had to bring guards to enforce them.

"As soon as Augusta Gloriana had her hands on Helias, she handed him over to a cook with orders to butcher the boy and serve him up for the prince's dinner. The cook hid the boy, at his home, and served up a young kid instead, and the prince ate it.

"The next day, she sent for Margarethe as well, and though Anna protested such secrecy again, soon she had her. The cook hid her, with her brother, and served up a young lamb, which Augusta Gloriana served to the prince."

Biancabella shivered.

"The next day, Anna came to see what had been done to her children, and why they had not returned. Both of them ran to see her, and Augusta Gloriana saw them. She had them all clapped into a tower—all the three, and the cook and his family—while she had a pit built and filled it with snakes and toads and all sorts of poisonous creatures. But she neglected her curse while she had that done. When she had them all led out as prisoners, to be thrown into the pit, Prince Carlos rose from his bed and came upon them. She realized that she had been found out and threw herself into the pit. They thought she had been killed and devoured, but in truth, she had turned herself into one of the snakes.

"There she lay on the cold earth and watched as the king rejoiced in his beautiful daughter-in-law and grandchildren and never guessed that his son had tried to hide from him—he thought it had been the stepmother he had feared."

Biancabella's eyes narrowed. They had gotten free of her. Still—

"She managed to *slither* off while they lived happily ever after."

"But—" said Biancabella, and then bit her lip.

"Yes?"

She needed to know, she reminded herself. "She was a sorceress. What protection did they have against her? She could have turned them all—" She waved her hands in the air. "—into doves. Or ravens. Or *something*."

Silence reigned. Biancabella's heart hammered. Surely the mirror could not be such a fool as to miss such a weakness. Surely there was some reason why it only affected her mother then. Augusta Gloriana had put Anna to sleep and made Carolus deathly ill.

The mirror spoke gravely. "Often the curse has a weakness so that it can break once laid. And often it has another, of *when* it can be laid: the witches, the enchantresses, the sorceresses—or the wizards or sorcerers—must act at the right time. Great changes are dangerous for such openings. Marriage and birth, and leaving home."

Biancabella nodded, but her thoughts raced.

"Anna and Carolus were not safe before two children were born. First, you would have to pass through a time of great peril. That was far from the worst your mother did."

She faced a time of great peril whatever she did or did not do. "But if I were cursed to never meet my mother again—"

"How seldom curses are that useful," said the mirror. "And that one was unasked for. You can not ask for a curse. And that one, in truth, would protect you not at all. Listen, and learn."

She was here to learn. Biancabella swallowed and nodded.

"Once in the woods, no longer a snake but brooding over how the curse's failure had wronged her, Augusta Gloriana saw a prince riding along, bearing enchanted oranges. He brought them to a fountain, where he cut the first orange open. A canary flew out and asked for water.

"She knew the spell. She dried the water up before the prince could give the bird it and so rescue the princess. The canary flew off and was captured again by the witch who bewitched her. When he tried with the second, and the third, at different fountains, Augusta Gloriana dried them up too, and the other birds were once again captured.

"The other witch, Mistress Laurenza—" Biancabella shifted at the name; it seemed familiar to her. "—was grateful because the canaries had been her daughters, transformed. She said she would help Augusta Gloriana at need. Augusta Gloriana was glad that she had kept such ungrateful daughters and such a foolhardy prince from happiness while Mistress Laurenza suffered—but she was not content."

Biancabella snorted, softly.

"One day, a woman with only one eye fled through the woods, menaced by wild animals, and using witchery on them. Augusta Gloriana defended her against them, driving them off, and saved the one-eyed woman. Then she learned the other woman's name was Ottoline."

Biancabella's breath came out in a huff.

"Ottoline told her sad story: once upon a time, her mother had taken the place of another woman by turning herself into the woman's shape and turning the woman into a sheep. She had persuaded the husband to kill his wife as a sheep, and roasted it for their meal, but the woman's daughter Leni had not eaten any mutton, and had buried the bones. This meant she lacked power over her. The witch gave birth to Ottoline, but when she tried to work Leni to the bone, Leni had gone to the grave, where a birch grew, and gotten her dead mother's help.

"Then the king of the land declared that he would hold balls, so that his son could choose a bride from his land, and the witch thought no more of Leni than to keep her from the ball. She dressed Ottoline in blue and gold before she threw peas into the ashes of the hearth and told Leni to pick them out before she returned, or it would be the worse for her.

"What she did not know is that two doves flew from the birch and picked out the peas at once, and then the birch shook down on Leni a dress of copper-red. Leni had dressed at once and gone to the ball. The prince had taken no heed of any other lady at the ball, least of all Ottoline—but when it was near ending, Leni fled and got back to the hearth before the witch returned to find her gone. Ottoline had known no more than anyone else that it was Leni, but as she told Augusta Gloriana, she was certain that the lady's slippers had been enchanted, and very angry that her mother had not done as well for her."

Biancabella twitched.

"The prince insisted on another ball at once. This time, the witch threw peppercorns into the ashes, but the doves picked them out as quickly, and the birch gave her a dress of silver. The prince had set guards all about the ball to catch her when she fled, but her slippers were indeed enchanted, and she outran them all.

"For the next ball, the witch tried poppy seeds, but the doves were just as deft, and the birch's gown was gold. This time, the prince had set no guards, only spread pitch over the steps where Leni had fled. When she fled this time, one of her slippers was caught, and she had to hobble home on half an enchantment. The witch found her swiftly enough to guess.

"Then the prince declared that whoever could bring him the other of the pair of golden slippers must be his true bride. The witch had taken a look at the one he had, and conjured up its twin. But when she brought it and Ottoline to the prince, Leni had whispered to him to bring her to the church. So the prince took Ottoline off as if he were taking her as his bride, and went to the church. As soon as she stepped into the churchyard, Ottoline turned to stone, and the shoe in her hand dissolved into bark. Leni took out the true slipper and showed him. It did not dissolve in the church.

"The prince took Leni home and married her. Within a year, they had a child, a beautiful boy. The witch, who had been so pleased at Ottoline's wedding, went to see her first grandchild and walked by the church. There, she saw the stone and realized that she had been tricked. In a rage, she freed her daughter and went to the castle. There, she turned Leni into a deer and drove her off. She put Ottoline into her bed, and was well pleased.

"But the baby started to wail and be discontent. The prince asked a wise woman what he should do. The woman took the baby to the forest and called to his mother. Leni came and shed her deer skin, and nursed the baby. The prince saw this and burned her skin. She was terrified, but the wise woman told them to go back to the castle. The witch and Ottoline saw them coming and fled into the woods. With such haste and so little care that Ottoline's eye was poked out by a branch."

Biancabella nodded. This time, after only one child had been born. She had to reckon such things.

"That would not do. That would not do at all. They had set out through the wood and found another kingdom. There, the witch her mother had bewitched another husband, a widower with a son and daughter, Ivan and Anushka. She tried to work her stepchildren to the bone, so Ottoline would inherit all, but they fled her into the forest. The witch, wise to them, bewitched the streams there. They came to one, and it murmured that whoever drank of it would be a wolf. Ivan was thirsty and wanted to drink, but Anushka dissuaded him—he would tear her to pieces! The next one murmured that whoever drank of it would be a bear, and Ivan was thirstier yet, but Anushka dissuaded him again, because he would tear her to pieces. Finally they came to one murmuring that whoever drank of it would be a deer. She told him that he would flee her, but he still drank, he was so thirsty, and then he was a deer. But he did not flee.

"So they lived in a hut in the woods for many a year. But one day the king came hunting there. The deer heard it and longed to join in. His frightened sister told him that the huntsmen would kill him, but he would not be still, and finally, she let him go. All day he ran about the hunt and suffered no harm, and when evening came, he went back to the hut and called to Anushka to let him in again.

"The next day the king hunted again, and this time, the deer was injured. With evening, he went back to the hut, slowly enough that the king could follow. So the king heard him call to his sister.

"The next day, Anushka did everything she could to dissuade the deer, but he told him that he had not been injured enough to be caught, and the hunt was wild in his blood, and so he left the hut again. The king gave orders to his huntsmen that they were to hunt the deer relentlessly, but do it no harm. In the afternoon, he went to the hut and called to her as her brother had.

"He gave her a great fright, but begged her to forgive him, and come with her deer to his castle. Within a few months, he and she married, and within a year, she gave birth to a son. The witch heard and fell into a rage. She had thought them eaten by beasts. She took Ottoline and went to the castle, where they threw Anushka out the window, into a lake, where she drowned. The witch put Ottoline in her place, with magical disguise, but found that she could not hide that she had lost her eye. So she told the king that she could not stand the light, she was weak after giving birth.

"But a servant saw a white duck swim up to the window that night, and Anushka climbed through the window and nursed her baby. The servant thought she dreamed it, but it happened again the next night, and she told the king. So the king went to the room in the night, saw Anushka climbing in, and seized her so that she could not flee. Then he seized the witch and Ottoline and had the witch burned, which turned Ivan back into a man again. Then he drove Ottoline out into the forest so that wild beasts would eat her up. That was when Augusta Gloriana found her."

The mirror sighed.

Biancabella bit her lip. She had heard these tales. She had learned them well because Lady Regina would not leave off her history lessons until she had mastered them. But not like this.

Again, after the child was born, she noted. Then she quailed at the thought of finding a husband and letting him know that such peril awaited him.

"Augusta Gloriana felt grieved for her, to have twice won her way to such a regal position only to lose it again, and told her own story. Ottoline felt grieved for her, to lose her crown so, and to see her revenge for the insult wiped away. When Augusta Gloriana proposed that they work together to deal with such shamelessness, and told how she had kept the prince from carrying off the three canary-maidens, Ottoline agreed.

"They used their witchery to find a suitable time and place to stop such things. They found a beautiful maiden, a merchant's daughter, Elinor, who was forced to do the housework by her stepmother and stepsisters, in a kingdom where the king had ordered all the maidens to a ball, that the prince might choose his bride."

Biancabella let her breath out slowly. "They don't do that much."

"Not anymore," said the mirror. "This was among the reasons. The stepmother poured peas into ashes and ordered Elinor to pick them out, and dressed up her daughters for the ball, thinking that without Elinor there, they would be the fairest. An enchantress who was her mother's friend came to Elinor, dressed her for the ball, and sent her off with a carriage. The prince chased after her and caught her, and brought her back to his court as his bride.

"So Augusta Gloriana cursed the enchantress to not be able to find Elinor. Then, she and Ottoline arrived as two who were seeking a witch and told everyone that Elinor had come from their country, where she had killed her whole family, and that she had bewitched the prince. They got them to burn her at the stake, and the prince was imprisoned in a tower in hope he would recover his wits that her curse had muddled. In the end, at his father's insistence, he had to marry one of her stepsisters, or be imprisoned forever as one in the grip of a curse that so muddled his wits that he was not safe outside the tower.

"They were well-pleased with themselves, that one of those insolent little snips of a girl, and some wretched prince, had not inveigled their way to happiness while the two of them—three with Mistress Laurenza, having to confine her wayward daughters—suffered.

"So they looked about the kingdoms, and they found another witch, whose name was Mother Magda. She was strengthening spells, to keep her dear daughter Snow-White-Fire-Red safe in her tower. She had had a sister, who had adopted a poor baby from a thief of a woman, who had stolen her parsley—she had called the girl Parsley and raised her so tenderly, better than the girl's own mother would have—kept her in a tower to secure her safety, the only way in and out was climbing Parsley's hair—and then this shameless prince had come and seduced the girl away, and when her sister had pursued them, Parsley had thrown things after them to make obstacles, magic she had *stolen* from the sister, to make a forest, a mountain, and finally a flood—and that had *drowned* her sister. Parsley and her prince had run off and married, and were now rejoicing over their child. Why, she had heard the shameless Parsley say that when she saw the prince below, calling to her with the same words her foster mother had used, she had decided that since he said the right words, she could let up a handsome prince as well as a cruel old witch. After all her foster mother had done for her!"

Biancabella considered, coldly, that she would need to marry a prince herself. No gardener's boy, no peasant's youngest son, could bring her safely to another kingdom. Her father was not Carolus's, to give such a bridegroom welcome.

"So the two of them agreed to help Mother Magda with spells that would let her ensure that a person could not see what she wished that person to not see—such that no insolent little prince would see the tower.

"Alas for them—" The mirror's voice was dry. "By the time they were done, Snow-White-Fire-Red had already run off with a prince. Mistress Magda cursed him to forget her, but Snow-White-Fire-Red broke the curse, and so they lived happily ever after. The witches could only rage at this monstrous ingratitude."

Biancabella fought down the impulse to nod. Her mother would have been learning every time these things happened. And they had already ruined Elinor.

"Soon after that, they found a warlock by the name of Boney. He had been caught in a dungeon of a princess, Marya Morvena, and kept there, forever thirsty. When he managed to win his freedom, by tricking her husband into give him water, he carried her off as punishment. When her husband chased after, he spared him twice for the water, and a third time, chopped him to pieces.

"Except the husband had three sisters, who had already married, and to three men who could turn into an eagle, a hawk, and a falcon. When the husband sought his wife, he had passed by the castle of each couple and left with them a thing of silver: a fork, a spoon, a knife. So his brothers-in-law saw, from the tarnishing of the silver, that he had died. They found his body and used magical herbs to bring him back to life, and they told him how to get the help of wolves and bees and birds as well.

"Then he sneaked back to his wife, and asked her to ask Boney how he had gotten so marvelous a steed. She told Boney she was afraid some robber would carry her off, and his horse would not be enough to save her. So Boney told her how he had gotten it from a marvelous and ancient witch.

"The prince slipped off to that witch and kept her horses for her. They tried to run off, to the fields, to the clouds, to the woods, but the husband got the bees, and then the birds, and then the wolves, to herd them back, and was able to claim his horse as a reward.

"Not only did the husband manage to run off with his wife on that horse—his horse told the one that carried Boney that it should throw Boney and crack his skull open! And it did! So the two of them rode off on those two horses, and despite all they had done to Boney, lived happily ever after." The mirror smiled, coolly. "They bred those two horses—and the one your uncle, Prince John, stole was a descendant of one of them."

Biancabella blinked. She had heard the stories, the snippets rather, but to know for a fact that it was her uncle who had taken the horse. . . was pulling her thoughts away. She had to remember the small company that gathered with her mother some nights, and one man in their number.

Her tongue touched her lips. Then, the mirror had said that they met him after this.

"If Boney had not kept his heart outside his body, that would have been the end of him."

"What a pity," said Biancabella, dryly.

The mirror nodded. (And very odd it looked, thought Biancabella.) "It was a long time before he could restore himself, as it was. Far too late for him to avenge himself on Marya and her husband, or their children, at that.

"Having heard this tale, all three of them lamented his fate, and felt ill will toward the witch who had given that husband his horse. They learned that the same witch had cursed the prince who ran off with Snow-White-Fire-Red: cursed him to be unable to marry anyone except her. They were furious. They cursed the land about her so she could see no one, and no one could see her. That would be the end of her ruining the plans of her fellows, so they would be miserable while some feckless prince and princess rejoiced.

"They banded together, then, and formed a circle. Augusta Gloriana, Ottoline, Mother Magda, Boney—they even lured Mistress Laurenza away from her canary daughters. They pledged to aid one another and never give to any prince or princess, peasant lad or merchant's daughter, shepherd boy or goose-girl, or anyone whatsoever, anything that would help break one of their curses or damage one of their schemes —even if it meant they could not curse someone."

That—would make fighting them harder. Happenstance was far easier when they did not plot and plan.

Biancabella's voice shook so badly that she stopped and tried again. "Are you telling me that they have managed ever since?"

Silence lasted several minutes. Biancabella tried to steady her breath. The light had not grown much—and she realized that clouds were moving in. She could not track the time by how bright the day had grown. She forced herself to take a deep breath and asked whether it was wise to leave.

"Always, but the hour grows near when they will wake. You would be wise to leave. And wiser to never return."

#

The sun had risen past the windows, and so the library lay in silent shadows. Daylight enough to read by, and so Biancabella moved about the books.

She had found a chronicle with Carolus's stepmother's name. Augusta Gloriana. A right royal name, she supposed. Her mother could have chosen it after hearing the tale.

If she did not trust what the mirror said, she told herself, she should run away at once.

She stood in the center and scowled. They would not keep the stud book for the horses in the library. Perhaps she should look for a book on which prince it was that Snow-White-Fire-Red had married.

"Biancabella."

Biancabella blinked, and looked over at Lady Regina, in the shadows at the door.

"A surprise to find you here. You were seldom more than dutiful about your studies."

"I was curious," she said. "Someone mentioned a princess called Snow-White-Fire-Red, and I wondered—" Words caught in her throat. She had never lied to Lady Regina before.

"Why, that is a strange princess to wonder about. I do not think that you are akin to her. But—" Lady Regina frowned. A minute later, they looked through a set of books, and half an hour later, Lady Regina had turned up that Snow-White-Fire-Red had married Prince Janos.

"Without being a princess herself," said Lady Regina. She closed the book. "Wise for a princess to remember that a prince, or a king, has choices."

"Yes. It is."

Both of them froze as Queen Augusta Gloriana swept in. She looked them coldly up and down.

"This will not do. No matter how little she learned in her lessons, she has passed the age of the schoolroom. *What* will it look like if some prince comes to woo and finds her still at her books like a girl too young to marry?" She waved her hand on the door. "Leave. Both of you."

#

The sky outside was black and filled with stars. Even the faintest stars still gleamed. Biancabella huddled into her cloak.

"Mirror, mirror, on the wall," she said. Croaked, more like, she thought, and hoped the mirror would understand her.

Slowly the face appeared.

"If some prince fell into my mother's power, and she gave him impossible tasks," said Biancabella, "would she let me see him? So I could tell him what to do?"

"She," said the mirror, "would not let *him* see *you*. Thus you could not tell him. But you could watch him fail. And die."

Biancabella closed her eyes. She had never heard of any other tale where the heroine could sit at home and learn, and yet triumph.

"I do not want to give you false hope," said the mirror.

"It is not your concern to trouble yourself with whether I hope," said Biancabella. "Or whether it is false hope or true. It is your concern to tell the truth, just as it is my concern when I speak. Or anyone else's. That neither my mother nor any of her cohorts try is their shame."

For a moment, the mirror seemed to smile a little, and Biancabella flinched. Just so her mother smiled when she was about to dismiss Biancabella as perhaps being a little clever.

"I tell you the truth," said the mirror. "As I told your mother about your sister's beauty. As I may tell your mother about your own beauty in due course. Perhaps it would be better if you did not know. Your father did not know. Or your Uncle Herbert."

Biancabella let her breath out in a huff. "They knew. It wasn't that they were frightened off by a pillar of stone telling that one route would mean that they would suffer hunger and thirst, the second, that they would die, and their horses would live, or the third, that they would live, but their horses die. They just stopped at an inn to carouse and decided it was better than saving their own father."

It was amazing what her father would admit to when drunk enough. It was amazing what she could listen to when others did not realize she was in the garden.

Though, she had to admit, it was not amazing that the one thing they clearly admitted had to do with an inn.

"They didn't know to not shoot at the fox," said the mirror.

Biancabella blinked. Fox? The true story of how Prince John had been the actual one to find the golden bird—and the horse, and the Princess Sophia—had leaked out in bits even before Snow-White had fled, but she had never heard of a fox.

At least in that tale. "Any prince who does not know to not shoot at a beast he meets on the way is a fool," she said primly. Sometimes they could threaten the beast and be rewarded, though she had never liked those tales, but to shoot at the beast was folly.

After a grave moment, the mirror said, "I will tell you the truth when it gives you false hope, for I always tell the truth. I can not force you to heed me. You will judge by your own judgment whether it is wiser to stay or to go, but you will judge more wisely if you know whom you face."

Biancabella closed her eyes for a moment. "Tell me."

"They—this circle—looked about the land to see what allies they could gain. They found a witch, a Mother Trude, lamenting her fate. Her sister had sent to her her two little stepchildren. She had set the boy to carry water in a sieve and the girl to spin, but they had bribed her mice and her wrens with bread—and the mice had spun the flax, and the wrens had told him how to stop up the sieve with mud so that the water could be carried. The next day, when she set the boy to chop wood and the girl to weave, they had bribed her cat and her dog with ham. The cat had sat at the loom and ruined all the mice-woven thread and then had given them her magical handkerchief and magical comb, and the dog had told them how to escape. Her birches had gone to block their way, and the children had bribed them with a ribbon, tying it on the branches, so the children had fled away—and for this treachery, all the beasts and the trees had scorned her, saying the children had done more for them than she ever had. When she gave chase, the children had used the magical kerchief to make a river, and then the comb to make a tangle, and getting through was not in time—the children had gotten away. Worse, her sister had had to flee for her life."

The mirror looked at her sharply. Biancabella looked back. Her father would not make her mother fly for her life if she returned from a wicked witch and told how her mother had sent her there.

The mirror went on. "They could only commiserate with her plight and have her join their circle. They advised her to be rid of the traitors, both beasts and trees, and she did. Then they taught her some spells, to make food more plentiful, so she could use it to bribe as the children had. She was more pleased with that, but she had no use for it *quite* yet.

"Soon after, they heard of a neighboring land, where a king had walked by night, and so heard three sisters speaking of what they would do after a marriage: one, if she could marry the king's baker, would feed all his court with one loaf of bread, so that none of them would feel hunger after; another, if she could marry the king's butler, would give drink to all his court with one cup of wine, so that none of them would feel thirst after; and the third, if she could marry the king, would bear him three marvelous children, two sons and a daughter, with stars on their foreheads.

"So the king married off the older sisters to his servants, and they did as they had said. Then he married the youngest and awaited the birth of the marvelous children."

Biancabella frowned. She had heard of three siblings with stars on their foreheads. But, she told herself, the tale was far from done.

"They went and spoke fair to the sisters, who were bitterly jealous at how much higher their sister had wed. When the babies were born with stars gleaming on their foreheads, the sisters took them, put in their place three black puppies with white stars on their foreheads—Ottoline provided them—and threw the children in the river. The king, in revenge for his wife having deceived him, had her imprisoned in a tower.

"They were all pleased at how they had foiled such a nothing of a girl being happy when they were miserable. Ottoline was so pleased with herself that when she saw seven brothers fumbling a bucket in their haste to get water to christen their sister, and their father, thinking their slowness meant they were playing instead, cursed them to be crows, she granted him his wish. They all went flying off, cawing, and a neighbor who saw it told their parents."

Biancabella winced.

"Ottoline did not keep close watch," said the mirror gravely. "Years later their sister freed her bird brothers, and Ottoline did not notice."

The mirror met her gaze. The tip of Biancabella's tongue touched her lips. She had to concede that her mother would not track her as an idle fancy, and so would never forget her.

"But sixteen years later, they did hear a tale of how three beautiful siblings, two boys and a girl, with stars on their foreheads, appeared in the land. They were all but full grown, now—the children had floated down the river and been rescued by a virtuous enchantress, who had named the older boy Jean, the younger boy Pierre, and the girl Isobel. She raised them up, told them what had befallen their mother, and gave them gold that they might return to their father's kingdom and buy a fine house, and so come to their father's attention.

"With that much gold, they bought the house of an enchanter and all his enchantments with it. Though they had never heard of these strangers before, people visited them, lured by the enchantments, and came away wondering at such marvels, and most marvelous of all the two boys and a girl with stars on their foreheads.

"Mother Magda would not have it. She went to the sisters, the children's aunts, and told them these were the children, and they all went to the house and shook their heads over it: true, it was lacking little, but it did sorely need the Dancing Water. Mother Magda so enchanted Isobel that she could not rest for longing for the water.

"So Jean went looking for it. He met a hermit on the way, and when the hermit asked, he told him he was going for the Dancing Water.

"'You go to your death, my son, but if you go on this way, there is another hermit, older than I. Ask him for aid.'

"Jean went and found the older hermit, who likewise could say nothing more than he went to his death, but sent him on to a third hermit, older than them both, with a beard that flowed down like a mountain stream.

"'The danger is not little, my son, but the Dancing Water you seek is up this hill. You will come to a gate guarded by two giants. If the giants' eyes are closed, do not go in. And again, if the gate is open, do not go in. When the giants' eyes are open, and the gate is closed, go boldly forth, push the gate open. Then you will find the Dancing Water.

"He thanked the hermit, and went up the hill, and saw the gate open and the giants' eyes shut. So there he stood and waited. An hour later, the gate shut, and the giants' eyes opened. Then he went boldly forth and pushed opened the door. Within was a bowl with the Dancing Water. How it leapt and jumped! But the brother did not stare, only went and picked it up, and then carried it off and showed each of the hermits in turn, and bore it off to Isobel, who exclaimed much over it and gave him a score of kisses for his love for her.

"But her aunts heard of his success and how the wonder of it had increased their fame. Soon the king would hear of them. They went to Mother Magda, and she devised another plan. They went and admired the Dancing Water, but—still, one thing was lacking. She did not have the Singing Apple. And Mother Magda enchanted her again.

"Jean, already knowing the way, set out again. The hermits told him that it was even a greater danger than the other, but the last told him that if he went into the castle as he had before, and went on, to the door opposite, he would find himself in an orchard. The ground would be all littered with apples like jewels, but he must not touch one. He must go to the central tree and pick the apple there.

"So he watched the giants and the door as he had before, and walked into the orchard, and did not touch the fallen apples, but went straight to the tree and picked the apple. As soon as it was in his hands, it began to sing, and it sang all the way back to the house, and everyone marveled at it, and Isobel gave her brother two score kisses.

"So the aunts returned to Mother Magda, who made another plan. This time, they told Isobel that she lacked the Bird of Truth.

"Jean set out again. This time, the last hermit told him he should pass through the orchard, and come to a garden beyond where the Bird of Truth, white as snow, would perch on the brink of a fountain, and where many statues stood. Whatever the bird said, he must ignore it, and pull loose a feather, which he must dip in the fountain and use to brush water on all the statues.

"All the rest Jean obeyed, but at the fountain, the Bird of Truth said to him, 'What are you doing here? Do you not know that your father is a king, and your mother is a prisoner in a tower?'

"'What?' said Jean, and turned to stone.

"Many days later, Pierre and Isobel waited anxiously for him, until Pierre said that he must see what had befallen him. He followed what his brother had told him of the way and found the three hermits, who warned him of falling into Jean's peril, but the last also told him how to go in. He managed to hold his tongue when he saw that one statue was Jean, but when the Bird of Truth told him what it had told Jean, he cried out, 'What?', and was stone like his brother.

"Isobel grew more and more anxious, and Mother Magda and the aunts more and more pleased. Finally, Isobel went after her brothers, and they hoped that would be the end of the three of them. But she heard the same directions as her brothers, and when she reached the garden, she held her tongue when the Bird of Truth told of her father and her mother and pulled loose a feather. As soon as she anointed all the statues, they came to life, and her brothers gave her three score kisses for her love for them, and she bore back the bird with her brothers, and soon their house was the wonder of seven kingdoms."

Biancabella scowled in thought. The enchantress would be hard to find.

The mirror rolled on with the tale. "At which time, Augusta Gloriana heard of it. She came and berated Mother Magda: she should have told her, and she would have used the spell to bewilder the children so that they would not see the hermits and so would perish, but she would retrieve the matter for her.

"Finally, the tales reached such a pitch that the king himself went to see, and he told himself that were it not for the puppies, he would think these his children, and the Bird of Truth proclaimed the truth and asked him if he ever heard of a woman giving birth to puppies. The king sent for his wife to be taken from the tower and brought to the house.

"Then, Augusta Gloriana arrived. She told many a story, of women who had given birth to a creature half-hedgehog and half a man, to a pig, to a spring of myrtle, and the Bird of Truth had to admit they were true. She told the king that the children had enchanted themselves to look like the children his wife had promised him, and her enchantments bewildered him so he would not listen to the Bird of Truth.

"But the Dancing Water and the Singing Apple rose up and filled the house with the apple's song, and the water's dance, so that it was hard to seize the children and their mother. They fled into the night. Soldiers pursued them, but the Bird of Truth flew all about and threatened the soldiers with the truth about them, so they all got away.

"And lived in poverty, but not harmed by either the aunts or the circle. Only, Augusta Gloriana set spells so that they could never again see either the hermits or the enchantress who raised them.

"One day, Jean went seek his fortune. Perhaps they could prove to their father that they were his children. So he wore a cap that hid his star, and he found a job where he could work, and his master gave him three sheep in payment at the end. He set out again, driving them, to sell them, and met a man who had three dogs. This man told him that one was named Pepper and would tear to pieces any man or beast it fought, and one was named Salt and could always bring him food, and one was named Mustard and could bit through iron and steel, and he would trade them for Jean's three sheep.

"Jean thought it was a good deal and did so, and had Salt bring them food to eat before he went on. After a time, he came to a town all hung in black. He asked what it was about and heard that a dragon had come and demanded the king's daughter Helena, and there was nothing to do but give her up. A knight of the king's, Red Henry, had promised to fight the dragon and save her, but no one believed that he would manage, so fierce was the dragon.

"Jean asked where the princess would be given to the dragon, and went there, a hillside with a forest on one side. Soon after, they brought Princess Helena, and Red Henry strutted like a bantam cock beside her. But as soon as they had chained the princess in place, and left, Red Henry scampered off, saying that one death was better than two.

"Then Jean came out of the woods with his dogs and assured her he would help her. Helena said he should flee for his life, but Jean only sent Salt for food, had Mustard eat up her chains, and when the dragon came, set Pepper on him so he was torn to pieces. Helena gave him a hundred kisses, which knocked his cap askew so that she saw the star. He told he was on a quest, but would return in three years to marry her."

Biancabella bit her lip. Jean and Helena were common names. Many a prince and princess bore them. She had read more than one account of a Prince Jean and a Princess Helena.

"As soon as he and his dogs left, Red Henry came out and told Helena that he would kill her unless she said he killed the dragon. Soon after the king's people returned and escorted them to the castle with great rejoicings. Red Henry said he had killed the dragon, and Princess Helena asked her father if he doubted his honesty—but that she had sworn an oath not to marry for three years if she were delivered, so that she could give thanks for Heaven for her deliverance, and the king said they must respect her oath.

"Now Jean searched all about, for the hermits, or the enchantress who raised him, or anyone else who could help him, but near the end of the three years, one of the men whom Isobel had freed from being a statue came to him and told him the enchantress had sent him: he was under a curse, and would never see the enchantress again, nor would he ever win his father's throne. He should return to Helena and marry her, and be happy."

Biancabella's heart started to hammer harder.

"So he went to return. But Boney had looked to enchant Helena and heard of how the enchantress had evaded the spell. He told them all, and Mother Trude went to Red Henry and gave him some willow withies, which would cage Jean, and told him how to find him on the road, with the king's castle in sight, all adorned for Princess Helena's wedding the next day.

"With the willow withies, Red Henry trapped Jean in a cage, and though Pepper tore Red Henry to pieces, Mustard could not get Jean out of the cage. So Jean sent Salt for food. At once Salt went to the king's table and grabbed some food. Princess Helena recognized the dog at once and ordered the guards to follow it. They found Jean trapped in his cage, and Helena pulled off his cap to show the star and said that this was her bridegroom who had slain the dragon. One wedding guest was an enchanter, who freed Jean, and Jean only sent word to his mother and brother and sister before they held the wedding of Jean and Helena, and they celebrated it for three whole weeks.

"As soon as it was done, the dogs came to Jean and Helena and said to Jean, 'We waited only to see if you would remember your family, having won to your fortune. Now we will go.' They turned to birds and flew off. But the couple lived happily ever after, and Isobel and Pierre married great nobles of the land and lived happily as well."

Biancabella clapped her hands to her face. She had noticed the names, but told herself she was dreaming. "But—but—" She stared at the mirror. "They were my great-great-grandparents! Helena and Jean!"

"Yes," said the mirror. "It would be wise for you to bear that in mind. Helena and Jean have both paid the debt of nature, but you are still here. She might, like the stepmother and half-sister, throw you into the lake so that you turn into a duck."

"A duck? That might be safer than staying here," said Biancabella. "Ducks are disenchanted. If they escape—but it has been so long!" She stared about the room. What they had done to her kingdom had been only a few years of that. "They must have had time to do so much evil."

"And they have," said the mirror. "After the enchantress saw Jean when he could not see her, Augusta Gloriana was at pains to enchant each and every one who could help any young lovers, as soon as she heard of any, so that they could not see the lovers." The mirror smiled. "You will find that does not work on you yourself *quite* so well. Your mother had high hopes of you, to teach you in her ways."

Biancabella's nose wrinkled. "In *that*?"

"In that. But while it is not quite an hour—"

Biancabella blinked and looked about. The windows showed glimpses of a sky ablaze with reds and pinks.

"—I do not think it wise to get half way through a tale and end. Go. Go now. And return on the morrow."

#

In the sunlight, Biancabella walked about the garden.

Her mother had no interest in it. She supposed, now, that a sorceress was not a witch and did not use herbs the way a witch would, and Ottoline must be much the same though she showed some interest, less as the years passed.

She had taken charge of it so young that at first her orders had been humored rather than obeyed, but as she had grown older, the gardeners had taken her more seriously, and she had helped with her own hands as it was planted with flowers in delicate shades: roses and heartsease, and lilies and so many others. It flourished about her, the black stone of the walls making the pinks and creams and dainty blues all the more vivid, and the flowers filling the air with sweetness.

She wished she had work to do in it, to spend her time to at least a little profit, but—she did need the time to think.

The pond spread before her. For a few minutes, she stood at the bank and looked at her reflection: pale, wan, insipid. Perhaps—perhaps she could stay forever. Perhaps she would not be fairest of them all. The mirror had not said that, and Lady Regina had denied it.

But she might be, and her mother could always drive her out, as she drove Snow-White.

Or a prince might come to woo her, when her mother would hate it.

She could not stay safely.

"I can not stay safely for three years, three months, three weeks, and three days," she whispered, "listening the mirror. Without a prince to watch over, who will wake at the end."

A breeze pulled at her skirt and hair. She could take her three finest gowns and flee to be a scullery maid, but that would be conceit. A princess being worked to death and starved had to flee at once. She was in no such peril. Yet. She could take time to make a prudent judgment of her case and learn all that she could.

A bumblebee alighted on a pink lily. Biancabella sighed. She could set out. Perhaps she might find an enchantress or a wizard to aid her, since the mirror had said she was not quite so bound by the spell. Still, she would need considerable aid. She would have to stop them all and not just her own mother and aunt, since their circle was bound by such oaths that they would all hate her.

The bumblebee flew off from the lily. Perhaps she should flee now.

She had visited the mirror two mornings in safety. That was no promise of future safety. She had not gone to rob a giant three times, climbing an enchanted beanstalk, but going back to the mirror again and again and not expecting to be caught would be as foolish as that thief.

"Without," she said, "even the excuse of being sent by a king." Then she blinked and looked about. No one had heard her. Even a yellow butterfly fluttered over pink roses as if she had not spoken.

She sighed. Still, not only were there no balls and no prince here, she did not doubt that if she found work as a scullery maid in another castle, and then did dance at three balls and marry a prince, her mother would plague her when her first child was born.

And—she had wandered all around the garden three times.

She grimaced at the count, turned, and walked to the door below the solar. Lady Regina would sit there and sew. And she had sewing of her own.

When she climbed the stairs, Lady Regina and the other ladies looked up, smiling. Then they froze for a moment before their smiles vanished, and they scrambled to their feet.

Biancabella turned and joined in the general curtsy to Queen Augusta Gloriana.

Her smile looked no colder than before Biancabella had heard more of her story.

"I have been most negligent of you, my daughter. At your age." She shook her head.

Biancabella wondered if she planned a ball. Or, more likely, a tournament. Her mouth dry, she wondered whether her mother could begin a war to lure out a princely suitor in disguise. Then she scoffed at herself. Her mother would not want her to marry, any more than any other princess. She did not want to see her and some prince happy.

"To have a governess still will make princes and kings think you are still a child. It is an insult when you are nearly old enough to marry. I should have thought of that before I found you in the library."

Lady Regina curtsied again. "Of course, Your Majesty. A governess has failed if her pupil does not leave her care." Her voice was smooth, but her face was white.

#

Most of the ladies went to help Lady Regina pack. Biancabella sat in the solar and sewed. The few ladies remaining whispered among themselves, but Biancabella carefully kept her gaze on her sewing, without a glance to any of the women.

When one started to murmur about what an odd thing she made, she said, her voice flat and imperious, without looking up, "I am too old for a governess to school me."

Many more murmurs followed. She did not listen.

She could not pack, not now, when she would be seen, and she had already chosen what to pack. Therefore, she would sew.

#

It was the same hour, but the sky was far darker, with many stars hidden by clouds. Biancabella kept her hand on the wall as she crept up the stairs and felt very small. She carried what she had sewn, a carefully made bag, and its strap weighed down on her shoulder.

She could have said that with her mother talking about marriage, she wanted to be ready for a journey.

When she slipped out the top door into the room, she could barely see her own reflection in the mirror, but as soon as she sat, the mirror swirled, and the face appeared at once. That, she could see clearly.

"I am pondering what I can do with your knowledge," said Biancabella.

"I could tell you much," said the mirror heavily, "but it would take days and weeks. I could tell you something of their other allies—"

"Take half your time to tell me," said Biancabella. "After that, I have a plan."

The mirror blinked.

"There are eight in the circle. I think. But I have seen them gather to talk here, coming through the garden in the twilight." Her voice turned meditative. "I thought I dreamed it because no one noticed them."

"I doubt it was a dream," said the mirror.

"Aren't there many, many, many evil people about?"

"Many," said the mirror. "But those who do not work wizardry, they do not think much of. The aunts who egged on Isobel—Red Henry—Elinor's stepsisters and stepmother—they did not think much of them. Once they were done with them, they were done, and the stepsister who married the prince ended up locked up in a tower." Its voice grew dry. "You know what happened to Red Henry."

Biancabella nodded slowly.

"As for the others—you know what they think of the witch who gave the prince a horse and cursed the other prince to marry Snow-White-Fire-Red. The others, witches and wizards and ogres, were not all so—unhelpful as that, but Augusta Gloriana and Ottoline often curse their ingratitude, folly, and laziness. You may have to deal with others. But you might be safe if you could deal with the circle. Whom you have seen. If that is, it were feasible to deal with them."

Biancabella frowned. "Ottoline and Augusta Gloriana, with two old crones and a middle-aged woman in a feather gown. And a man all lean and sinewy, with ragged hair that stuck up—"

The mirror's face nodded. "Boney."

"One man wore a crown. And one was a little, wizened man."

The mirror nodded, more deeply. "Soon after Jean's wedding, the circle gathered in the forest to discuss what had happened, for good or for ill."

"Did they hear animals talking of what they had heard over the last year?"

"No," said the mirror, with a smile trying to creep on her face. "They did not meet at midsummer. But a little, wizened, twisted man came out of the woods and jeered at them all for throwing the babies in the river, as if they were certain of their drowning—and wasting them.

"Whereupon Mother Trude taunted him back and told how he would win children by helping their mothers go to the ball, or by doing magical spinning to make them look like marvelous spinners—but he was always losing the children he had won when their mothers guessed his name. Or he would gain a girl baby, and then catch a king and demand his firstborn son under a riddle, and then the boy would come—and steal the girl away.

"He stamped his foot, and Mother Magda rushed in to soothe: tell them what had happened, and they would help. They had great interest in keeping some insolent lass from cheating an honest sorcerer. All they asked in return was that afterwards, he would help them when they needed to prevent such mischief against themselves.

"He gave them a great harrumph, but told them how it was true that he would win the babies, only for them to cheat him, again and again. They promised their aid, and he went to a tavern and coaxed a miller into bragging that his daughter Jill could spin hay into gold, and the king heard of it.

"So the king seized her and locked her in a tower filled with hay, and ordered her to spin it all into gold, or he would cut her head off. Jill wept for hours and hours, and near midnight, the wizened little man appeared and offered to do it for her, if she gave him her first-born. Desperate, she agreed. So he spun and spun and spun, and it was all gold.

"The next morning the king married her without so much as asking her. Nine months later, she had a baby boy. That day, the wizened man appeared and told her that unless she guessed his name in three days, he would take the baby.

"Desperate again, she sent all over the kingdom for names. A huntsman carrying her orders went through the woods of a night, and saw a bonfire where the wizened little man jumped about and said how she would never guess that his name was Rumpelstiltskin. He told Jill, who rejoiced. When the wizened little man appeared, she guessed Jack, and then Tom and finally Rumpelstiltskin. He told her it wasn't. She fainted, and when she came to, the baby was gone.

"The king was enraged. His councilors, knowing which side of their bread was buttered, told him that the spinning must prove she was a witch, and she must have killed the baby for her witchery. They agreed that she should be taken into the woods and killed. The king gave the order to the huntsman, who took her off into the woods. Far, far off, to another kingdom, where he married her, and they lived in the woods. All the circle was pleased, more or less, though Jill and the huntsman were happy."

In the silence after, Biancabella said, "And that's seven."

"Some time after—after other foul deeds—a wizard named King Drakos played cards with a young man, named Ian. After Ian had already won all his money, King Drakos made another bet.

The bet was that the young man could marry one of his daughters, against all the money. The young man won.

"And worse—King Drakos laughed at him and told him that he could get her only in his own kingdom—but when Ian set out to find her, he found an enchantress who told him to go to a lake, and steal the swan-skin cloak of one of the maidens who bathed there, and give it back, so as to get her to guide him to the wizard's home.

"She was Vasilisa the Wise, King Drakos's daughter. She told him if he would pledge to marry her and take her away from her father, she would aid him.

"So her father set him evil tasks, to cut wood that would stick together with a good ax, a well that would dry up for a good bucket, a garden that would grow tougher if you used the spade on it. But Vasilisa told Ian to use the bad ax, draw it up with the bad pail, and use the handle not the blade to spade the garden.

"King Drakos grew desperate and appealed to the circle. As the young couple fled, Boney came with him. When he saw them hiding, Vasilisa having turned herself into a duck, and Ian into a pond, he stabbed the pond, and blood came out. Ian lay there dead. Vasilisa would not leave the body, so they trapped her in her swan form there."

A sigh came, as if the mirror could breathe.

"That was how King Drakos joined their number, but—they were soon, and are still, not pleased with King Drakos. He bends his attention to increasing the wasteland about his home, lest another hero win his way there. They are no more pleased with Mistress Laurenza, who is endlessly involved in teaching her daughters and keeping them home. Indeed, King Drakos has helped her by increasing the wasteland about her home. But that does not stop the rest from grumbling about his want of aid."

For a moment, silence reigned. Biancabella glanced out the window. It had not grown any lighter. She thought that was that the clouds had thickened.

Biancabella swallowed. "You did not mention yourself," she said.

"No," said the mirror. "I fell into your mother's hands, o, years and years after what I have told you of. I know what I have told you because I can see over ages. I have no memories of myself before I found myself in your mother's hands." Its mouth pursed. "She asks me whether she is the most beautiful now and again, but she asks me many other questions, too."

Biancabella nodded gravely.

"Now I will tell you one last tale, one much closer to you, before you set forth on your plan—and may Heaven bless you on it!"

Biancabella sat up straight.

"Once upon a time, a king had three sons. Their names were Ogier, Herbert, and John. The king had a fine orchard, but every year, the finest tree in it was stripped of all its apples the very day they turned ripe, in the dead of the night. The king said to his sons that they should prevent such a robbery.

"Ogier stayed the night first, but fell asleep and saw nothing. He told his father that the apples were stolen away in silence, with no hand touching them. The next year, Herbert did, and said, the same. But the next year, John sat up in the orchard and did not sleep. When the midnight hour came, a brilliant golden bird flew from branch to branch, eating apples. He leapt up and tried to catch it, but only knocked a feather from its tail.

"He brought it to his father the next day. 'Of what use is a feather without a bird?' said his father, and told Herbert and Ogier that whichever of them brought back the bird would have his throne, but since John had uselessly brought only a feather, he would not leave.

"Now Herbert and Ogier set out together, declaring that they would separate when they came to a crossroads. The truth of the matter is—after they had seen and shot at a fox—they came to a town three days' journey out, and there they caroused at the inn and forgot their father."

Biancabella rolled her eyes. They had changed little. She would have known that without their bragging of it.

"After a time, the king grew sick with longing for the bird, and John begged to go, at least to learn of his brothers. Finally, the king yielded.

"John saw the same fox that his brothers had seen and did not shoot at it. The fox said to him, 'Be wiser than your brothers. Do not go into the first inn in the next town.'

"When John came to the first inn, he saw how merry and full of carousers it was. He walked on. The second inn was quiet though well-kept. There, John went early to bed and rose early, and went on with the dawn.

"On the way, the fox appeared to him and said, 'Since you are wiser than your brothers, I will aid you. The golden bird is kept at the castle of the green ogre, up on that hill. Go into the castle at night, and go to the garden. There you will see two cages, an iron one and a gold one, and the golden bird in the tree. Take up the iron cage, and the bird will fly into it, but do not touch the golden cage.'

"John promised to obey, and went into the castle, and into the garden, but the golden cage gleamed so beautiful that he took it, and the golden bird began to shriek and scream, and the ogre rushed out and caught him.

"'What have we here?' said the green ogre, 'but a thief—a thief—and dinner as well.'

"But his ogress wife said, 'We have need of a thief. Does not the red ogre have that magnificent steed that would be so much more worthy as your horse than his?'

"So the green ogre shook John and told him, 'Go and get me the magnificent steed of the red ogre, and I will not eat you.'

"Dejected, John left the castle, and the fox said, 'Better to obey twice than once. But I will aid you still. Follow me.'

"So they went off to the castle of the red ogre. There, the fox sent him into the stables and told him to take the plain bridle, not the decorated one. But the decorated one so dazzled him that he took it up, and the steed whinnied and stamped and roused the house, and the ogre rushed out and caught him.

"'What have we here?' said the red ogre, 'but a thief—a thief—and dinner as well.'

"But his ogress wife said, 'We have need of a thief. Does not the white ogre have that beautiful princess that would be so much more worthy as your captive than his?'

"So the red ogre shook John and told him, 'Go and get me the beautiful princess of the white ogre, and I will not eat you.'

"Dejected, John left the castle, and the fox said, 'Better to obey thrice than once. But I will aid you still. Follow me.'

"And they went off to the castle of the white ogre. The fox sent him into the tower where the princess was prisoner, and told him to use the dingy key, not the golden one.

"And this time he obeyed the fox, and carried off the princess while she slept. For one thing, the princess was more beautiful than the key, with hair as black as a crow, lips as red as blood, and a face as white as snow. When she woke the next morning, she was delighted to be rescued and told them she was named Sophia. Then she heard of the red ogre. She wept and wailed to be given false hope.

"John said to her that he would obey the fox's directions the next time, for the love of her. When they reached the castle, he went to steal the horse as the fox had told him, so they had the magnificent steed. Then they went to the green ogre's castle, and he obeyed the directions again, and so they had the golden bird as well.

"But Ottoline heard of this as they rode back. She found his brothers and gave them directions. Herbert and Ogier killed John and took Sophia, the steed, and the golden bird. Then they waited. The fox appeared with an herb in its mouth, and they killed it as well. Then they went home, and Ogier went first and claimed both Sophia and the throne.

"Herbert was drunk in the inn and did not care. Ottoline found him there, and persuaded him to marry her, and no one came to take this position from her.

"But one winter day, Sophia, sad and subdued as she always was, sat in a window sewing. The needle pricked her finger, drawing blood, and out in the snowy scene, a crow perched on a bough. Sophia sighed and wished for a baby as white as snow, as red as blood, and as black as the crow's wing.

"Nine months later, she had a little girl, whom she named Snow-White, and loved very much.

"As Snow-White grew up and grew beautiful, when she had just turned seven, Ottoline went and told Augusta Gloriana that Sophia was happy. Augusta Gloriana came to me, and I told her that it was true, and that Snow-White was more beautiful than she was.

"Augusta Gloriana raged. She came here, and found it was true, and that Ogier was not happy with his bride, because she was solemn, and did not do any of the royal duties, so he had to do them himself. Augusta Gloriana had her poisoned. Soon after she died, she persuaded Ogier to marry her. Then she took Snow-White and told a huntsman to take her to the woods and murder her, and bring back her heart.

"She was somewhat content as queen, though Ogier passed off all the royal duties on her, and other princes and princesses kept reaching happiness, unless she meddled, and sometimes when she had.

"But what had happened was that the huntsman told Snow-White to run off and brought back the heart of a deer. Snow-White ran off, far and far, and stumbled on some dwarves whom Augusta Gloriana had not blinded from all eyes. They asked her her troubles, and then told her she could stay as long as she did the housework. She had learned it so well that she lived there many years before Augusta Gloriana had time to ask me if she were still the most beautiful, and I had to tell her that Snow-White was.

"The huntsman had wisely fled soon after he gave her the heart, and so Augusta Gloriana turned her wrath on Snow-White. She did not dare face the dwarves, so she dressed herself up as a peddler and set out with a pack containing many goods, one of them an enchanted comb. She found the dwarves' house, and told Snow-White that she should be ashamed of looking so messy. How could they trust her to keep the house clean while she looked so filthy? She had just the thing, a comb that would hold her hair up and neat and out of the way. Before Snow-White quite knew what the peddler was doing, she had her hair swept up, coiled about, and stabbed with the comb. Snow-White fell to the floor, caught in the spell and no longer breathing. With that, Augusta Gloriana ran off, laughing, and returned to me. I assured her that she was the fairest of them all.

"But while I spoke, the dwarves gathered about Snow-White, trying to see what was wrong, and no sooner had I fallen silent than one pulled the comb out. Snow-White's breath came out with the same moment, and they questioned her fiercely. When she told them, they forbade her to talk to any stranger ever again. If they need to buy from a peddler, one of them would do it.

"Now, Augusta Gloriana trusted in her handiwork and asked me many questions about other things, until finally, one day, she asked me about being the fairest of them all. I told her that Snow-White was.

"She was in such a rage that I thought she might break me. But she remembered Anna and asked whether a prince had found her, and on hearing one had not, she enchanted some ribbons. Snow-White went inside at the sight of her as a peddler, and when she called to her, Snow-White put up the shutters. So Augusta Gloriana pulled back and watched the neighbors who talked with her, and heard that a fair was coming.

"She disguised herself as a neighbor and came to Snow-White to tell her that at her age, she had to be properly laced up at the fair, and as a good neighbor, she would show her how to do it. She laced her up with the enchanted ribbons, and they choked the breath out of her. Once more she returned to me, and once more I told her that she was once again fairest of them all.

"The dwarves found Snow-White again and frantically gathered around her. There was nothing in her hair, and they tried everything else to revive her. Finally, one loosed the ribbons, and she began to breathe again. Hearing her story, they forbade her to talk to anyone while they were not there.

"Now several years later—but not so long as the first time—Augusta Gloriana asked whether she was fairest of them all again, and again I told her it was Snow-White. She turned white as salt and stalked off. This time she spent a month cursing an apple, and finally brought it with her. She heard from the other women that the dwarves no longer let Snow-White talk to them when they were not there. So Augusta Gloriana disguised herself as one of the dwarves and brought the apple to Snow-White. No sooner had she taken a bite than she fell down, without breath in her.

"This time, the dwarves could find nothing about her. Finally they made a coffin of crystal for her, because of her great beauty, and there she lies to this day. This time, Augusta Gloriana asked me what had happened to her, and hearing of the coffin, laid an enchantment on her, to blind people from her, so that no one can come to her aid. She asked other questions, as well. When she heard from me that a certain prince might be able to disenchant her, why she had Ottoline turn that prince to a bear, to dissuade him."

After a minute, the mirror spoke more briskly. "But before she turned him, as soon as Snow-White lay in her coffin, she decided to have a daughter, and raise her up as a sorceress. King Drakos and Mistress Laurenza's were showing such promise. But—she was less than pleased with hers."

Biancabella rolled her eyes.

"Heaven grant that she may be less pleased with you after your plan!"

"I will leave," said Biancabella. "My mother set spells on me to let me see through her spells that blind. If I set out, I may find out how to defeat them."

Silence reigned a moment.

"That is dangerous," said the mirror. "Their spells can strike you down. I warned you of the weakness. And your mother will certainly find you."

"She'll ask you, won't she?"

The mirror winced. "Yes. And I will tell her."

"No, she won't." Biancabella flourished the bag. "Everything else I will carry, I packed up and left at the foot of the stairs. I have one more thing to take." In the silence that followed, she pulled blankets out of it, ready to wrap.

For one fearful moment, she dreaded that the mirror would scream for help and ruin all. But silence followed, and she took down the mirror from the wall and began to wrap it up. Then she hesitated. "I can leave you in the woods nearby if it's too hard to be carried like this for long. She won't be able to ask where you are."

"No," said the mirror in the strangest voice that Biancabella had ever heard from anyone. "No. That will be fine."

Chapter 2—The Castle of the Princesses

"Drink, drink, drink!" called the king.

"*Strong* drink!" caroled the prince.

Both men burst out laughing as they, red-faced and rotund, staggered down the corridor.

The maidservant Polly darted aside, into the kitchen. To stand between them and their drink was unwise, however jovial they were. Besides, she might cadge a tart from the cook. Lizzy had made some this morning.

Lizzy, red-faced with heat, looked up from the boiling pot. "Hasn't the queen said anything *yet*?"

Polly hoped that Lizzy paid enough attention to the roasting goose to keep it from burning. But—"No, she has not. Nor has the king."

Lizzy snorted and turned to stir the sauce. "He would never."

Ted, toting in the firewood, grinned. "Not even if the princess told him that she loved him like meat loves salt?"

"Like the king would ever ask," said Lizzy. "And if she did answer like that, he would forget as soon as he sobered up. But the queen—" She shook her head, and her voice turned ominous. "The queen should be wise enough to know that if the princess is stolen from the very castle, we are all in danger. For all we know, she was carried off by a dragon!"

"We'd notice a dragon," said Polly. "They're hard to miss."

"Probably just set out to seek her fortune," said Ted, easily. He dropped the wood by the fire. "Probably slaving under some cook now as a scullery maid."

"Probably not even out of the kingdom," said Polly, sharply.

"She could be," said Lizzy. "If she choose her road with care."
Then she scowled in thought. "Or she could be tomorrow."

#

In the gray morning light, under beams of oak black with age, the
inn's main room held trestle tables large enough for dozens of people apiece. They barely managed to hold the travelers, and that only
because travelers departed as quickly as they could eat.

At the end of table, Biancabella ate her porridge, and her
tongue touched her lips. She had chosen the road more for the
crowd and being the shortest route from the kingdom (only two
day's walk) than for where it would lead her.

Still, just over the border, her legs aching from how far she
had had to walk, the talk was all about the princesses of this kingdom. Twelve of them, no less, and how every night they went to
bed in a locked chamber with no other exit, and how nothing was
heard from within all night, and how the next morning their dancing slippers had nevertheless been worn through from dancing all
night.

"Least of all music," said one lean traveler to the table where he
sat. His eyes large, he leaned forward. "Not a hint of it. Yet they
dance."

"There's no room," said one squarely-built merchant, idly. "All
the servants agree between the beds and wardrobes, they can hardly
tread a measure."

"And," said a boy, avidly, from where he sat beside his father,
"sometimes a man tries to keep watch over them, and *he's never
there the next morning.*"

"Nonsense," said an older boy. "He's there. It's after *three* nights
that he vanishes."

To be sure, other things were spoken of. The rain and how the
roads would be impassably muddy if it continued. The inn-keep-

er's jovial story about how an inn-keeper's daughter had thought to steal a golden feather from a golden goose and ended up stuck to the bird.

"That didn't happen here," said a young woman, sourly. "The inn was by a castle, and the man who owned the goose lead her and a whole string of people past it, and made the princess laugh—it was not somewhere out in the woods."

"Would be better for our princesses," said an old man. "There were *six* brothers, princes, who came and took their turns one by one, and not one of them will return to their father."

An ancient woman laughed. "Better they had all been turned to swans, than that."

"What if they don't have a sister?" said a young girl.

Biancabella finished, her spoon scrapping the bowl bottom, and wondered which one of the circle would do that. Perhaps Boney? She pushed the bowl away. Perhaps it was someone else, whom her mother had not hindered, who had never caused problems for the circle, who yet wanted to cast such a spell.

She stood. But for now, the roads were growing muddy, and the inn stood out in the woods.

A farmer started to idly talk of selling his milch cow.

At the inn door, she stepped from the way, pulled up her hood, and looked about. The inn was here for its being a day's journey from the last inns, either way on the road. Towering firs surrounded it, with only a clearing for vegetables. At least, it was not raining again, yet.

"Be careful with your journey, maid," said the inn-keeper. "Not until noon will you see another house as you go that way."

Biancabella nodded and headed off. The road was narrow, little more than a track. Merchants used mules and seldom carts on it. Shadows from the firs closed about her. The road rose up one hill, down the other side, and up another, and Biancabella stopped, her gaze traveling over the slope. Something had been there, she had seen it.

There, between the trees, a little hut sat under the hillside.

Her tongue touched her lips. As brown and small as the hut was, for all the moss growing on its slate roof, a traveler could see it. Not all of them would take its hollow of a porch for a cave. If the inn-keeper did not know of it—she slowly walked closer. It was time to live up to her bold words to the mirror.

Something moved, off to her right: a little old woman, carrying a great bundle of wood, staggering along. Biancabella rushed over.

"Old mother, can I help you?"

The woman stopped. Eyed her with a bewildered expression. And smiled and chuckled for a moment. "The first traveler who's deigned to notice me in years—and with such nice manners."

Biancabella swallowed. She wished she could ask the mirror.

"Here, with your sturdy young back, you can carry this." She gave Biancabella the wood and hobbled on, to the hut. It was a heavier burden than Biancabella had thought, but she walked on.

At the hut, the woman gestured at a woodpile at the end of long porch. Biancabella lowered the bundle with gladness.

"Nice manners and no complaining, either."

Biancabella straightened. "Isn't it supposed to be the *second* one who complains?"

The woman chortled, but it faded. "Yes. It was." She slumped as if the years weighed on her. "It was."

Biancabella said, slowly, "Old mother, can you tell me something of the princesses of this land?"

The woman cocked an eyebrow. "It's princes he lets try to find out. Or soldiers. Or shepherds turned gardener's boys. Not princesses."

"Have you helped any like that?" said Biancabella, as softly as she could.

"How could I, when they pass me by?" said the woman in anguish.

For a moment, Biancabella closed her eyes. "You are witched."

The woman blinked.

"So that no one can notice you, so that you can not stop the spell." The words stumbled out—and when she had wondered if the circle even had anything to do with it. "The warlock who cursed the princesses to dance has allies who help him by hiding all help from the princes—and others."

"And yet you can see me?" said the woman.

"Oh, yes," said Biancabella. "I'm running away from one, who is my mother. She let me see things. She thought that it would help her."

Moments inched by. Not a deer, not a squirrel, not such much as a breath of breeze stirred in the woods. The woman stood and studied her.

She heard travelers on the road, but none of them noticed the woman, the hut, or her as they gallivanted by.

"And," said Biancabella, "I thought I might learn something against them if I helped the princesses."

"Do you know which one does it?" said the woman.

Biancabella swallowed. It sounded like a test. "I think it's Boney."

"Ah," said the woman. Her eyes closed. "The king won't let you just do it. And he is right. There has to be a man who does it. It's the nature of Boney's warlockry. It has no weakness that you can use."

Biancabella's voice was very thin in her own ears. "I heard—at the inn—that someone has to stay three nights. I don't know what he meant, but he was clear about the three nights."

"Not just anyone," said the woman.

Biancabella let her breath out. The woman did not move. Then, it was not as if she had another task to take up.

Her voice sounded thin in her ears as she spoke. "Perhaps I could help one, then. Even if it might take a while for another to arrive, what with all those who failed."

The old woman reached for the door and pulled it open. Then she ushered Biancabella into a rough hut. The stone fireplace did not even hold ashes, only soot stains on the stones, and the legs of the chairs still had the bark on them. They were comfortable enough to sit on.

The room was large enough that the windows did not illuminate it much, and however rough the walls, they were well-chinked, with no light seeping in. Biancabella sat with her hands in her lap, carefully to keep her gaze intent on the woman where she sat and on the hearth, and to not peer rudely about.

The woman sat with her head slumped, her gaze intent on her hands. She took a minute to speak. "I gave one of them magical laurel plants. A gardener's boy who dreamed of the princesses, and he used them to gain a magical cloak." She shook her head. "Young Michael. He followed them twice with the cloak before he went to the king and offered to stay. But then, the third time, he was offered the cup, and Boney had had Mother Trude bewitch it."

She glanced sharply at Biancabella, who nodded. They did have their powers. She noted to herself that Mother Trude could enchant food. It was not a weakness, but she might need the warning.

"So he drank it. Now he's as baffled and bewitched as the rest. He dances endlessly in a ballroom far underground. All glittering in silver and gold, but surrounded by shadows." She shook her head back and forth. "And since that day, I have never been able to catch one of the young men. Never, ever, ever."

Biancabella let her breath out. Moments inched by, and finally she decided the old woman had said her part. She sat up.

"As if my mother had bewitched you, so they could not see you."

The woman winced.

"Does that mean you can not aid me?"

The woman seemed to age years in the next moment. "No. No, it does not." She did not move, or speak again.

Biancabella leaned forward. "I am Augusta Gloriana's daughter. And I will be the fairest of them all."

The woman slowly turned to look at her.

A black cat with a white blaze down its front walked elegantly out of the shadowed back of the room. Biancabella held out her hand, and the cat sniffed it before leaping into her lap.

"She's a good judge of character," said the woman idly. "If a poor weaver."

Startled, Biancabella said, "Is she Mother Trude's cat?"

Both of them looked at her in silence. It was minutes later when the old woman said, "*Was.*"

"I beg your pardon, my lady cat," said Biancabella. She scratched the cat behind the ears. It purred.

The old woman sighed. Her gaze rolled upward, and she mused, as if Biancabella were not there. "It's not as if I had someone else to hold it for. Not if she has me bewitched."

Biancabella bit her lip to keep from begging. For a moment, she thought of taking out the mirror, but she did not know whether it could speak of anything to persuade this woman, or whether having the sorceress's mirror would turn the woman against her.

The woman shuffled off. The cat rolled over, and Biancabella rubbed its belly and counted out the moments, forcing herself to not stare rudely about.

The woman returned, her hands full. The cat sat up and looked. Biancabella's heart started to beat harder.

The woman shook out her bundle and revealed a cloak, of cloth lighter than the finest veil, but black as night. "I can not give you the laurels, which could give you many things, but—this is a cloak of shadows. It will hide you, and hide you well—not only will you go unseen but it will muffle the sounds you make. With it, you can follow the princesses to their dancing, and return. More or less safely."

She bowed her head over it.

After a minute, she held it out, and said, "Don't dilly-dally on the way. You must make haste to be sure of reaching the next inn tonight."

Biancabella put aside the cat, rose, curtsied, and thanked her as she put away the cloak. "I promise I will not stop to gather flowers on the way." She thought of adding especially not if a wolf asked her, but the jest seemed weak. She hurried out the door, down the way, and toward the next inn.

#

The road wound down into a broad valley, full of orchards, pasture, and field. A river ran through it. Across that, and up the other slope, the royal city stood and gleamed.

Biancabella walked with the other travelers and wondered that Augusta Gloriana had chosen her father and not the king of this land. The city stood like a golden jewelry box, and the castle alone looked large enough to encompass a fair-sized town. It stood in towers and turrets of golden stone with banners in brilliant colors flapping everywhere.

She wondered if she would have to haunt the castle to find the corridors to anywhere, but as she came up toward the great gilded gates, trumpets sounded, and a herald in scarlet and gold announced that a man had come to rescue the princesses.

Biancabella pulled to the roadside with the rest. A drably clad man, not exactly young, walked up the way to the king's hall. A soldier, she guessed. She stepped aside, into an alleyway, and pulled out the woman's cloak. Time was of essence.

The people between her and the gate formed a labyrinth, and she barely made it in before the gates closed—and the soldier and his escort were almost in the hall. She ran after, and only when she, heart hammering and breath coming fast, reached the hall did she wonder whether she had actually had to watch the king and soldier meet.

Wisest to do that, she told herself. It might make a difference.

Within the gleaming hall, adorned with gold and set with massive numbers of mirrors, she glided after them. On his golden throne, the grizzled king wore heavy scarlet robes adorned with emeralds and gold, but he greeted the soldier Robert gravely, as if making welcome the only prince of a great land, and told him all the tale that she had heard at the inn.

That night, he had the soldier at the banquet in the seat of honor, with all the walls hung out with banners. The princesses arrived all arrayed in silk and jewels, and rivaling Augusta Gloriana in beauty, and the feast was served, at the high table, on dishes of gold.

Biancabella could only conclude that her mother had married her father purely out of spite, and without the slightest concern for the wealth. She slipped about the hall between in the servants, in a pattern more intricate than any dancing master had ever taught her, and pilfered pieces of food from dishes here and there for her dinner—as deftly as any peasant lad or lass ever stole from a witch or a giant.

Listening revealed little beyond commonplace chatter of a court.

She purloined a meat pie and stood against the wall to eat it. A mirror across the room showed all the glitter and gleam of the room, but no sign of her. For a moment, the pie felt like ash in her mouth. She was no master thief—she hoped.

She chewed. She should take the cloak and flee. Find a cottage in the forest and grow a garden there. If she could convince her neighbors of the value of her herbs—

She swallowed. Her mother would find some way to find her, she told herself. Cloak or no cloak, mirror or no mirror. Safety lay in using this window of time, not thinking it would last forever.

She eyed the princesses and tried to memorize their names (Lelia and Marjory and Camilla and Rosalie—) and finally, without the names, stole up the stairs after the princesses, the king, and the soldier.

Robert was given a lone candle and ushered to a small chamber off the main room, where the twelve princesses slept in twelve beds. It was large enough for a bedchamber with twelve beds, but truly enough, they could not dance in it. Even their paths as they readied themselves for bed were a crisscross, their shadows by candlelight a hopeless tangle on the wall, and Biancabella stood bolt against the wall to the soldier's chamber in hopes of avoiding them.

Within moments, abruptly, they hastened about to ready themselves for a ball. They donned ballgowns, gold and silver, and intricately worked with patterns—leaves or birds or flowers—far more extravagant than the gowns they had worn to dinner. Their slippered feet were soft as leaf falls on the floor, with the rustle of cloth being only a little louder, and they neither talked nor giggled.

Then the oldest—Rosalie, Biancabella thought—poured out a cup of wine, and put a drop of something in it. One of her sisters spoke to her, and she turned her back on it, as they talked earnestly. The youngest one reminded them that the gardener's boy still danced among the princes without trouble.

Swiftly, Biancabella threw the wine out the window and refilled the cup. Minutes later, Rosalie took up the cup and went to offer it to Robert. Biancabella let her breath out and listened. He drank, and Biancabella could only wonder if the cup had been bewitched, too. Moments later, Rosalie said, "Aren't you going to offer me your arm?"

The candle there was snuffed, and the room darkened. All the more as the other princesses quenched all the candles except one, as if they went to bed. The smell of smoke was briefly sharp.

Robert and Rosalie emerged from the room. Robert looked puzzled, and Biancabella bit her lip and hoped it was enough to pass for the spell. Rosalie walked up to a bed and nodded, as if to signal a servant.

The bed rose from the floor, pivoting from the headboard, its sheets and blankets slanting, an enormous shadow looming on the wall as it moved. The floor gaped beneath, and dark stairs descended into shadow. Biancabella held her breath. Rosalie gracefully walked forward and downward, with Robert a trifle clumsy at her side. Pairing off, the other princesses followed two by two, with the youngest, Marjory, last and alone. At least until Biancabella hastened to stand next to her and walk as swiftly down steps of black stone.

The stairs descended for a long time. The light from behind dimmed swiftly, until Biancabella thought that she found the next stair by guessing from the height, not from seeing it at all.

Then a glitter appeared ahead. It increased as they descended, and resolved into a gleaming, silvery place, and finally into a grove of silvery trees, glittering from no light she could see. The cave arched about it, its black walls dimly lit where the light reached them, and vague shadows elsewhere.

Rosalie did not hesitate on the trail leading through the grove. Not that it would be hard to find the way, there being only one trail and not so much as a glade open within the woods. Biancabella looked surreptitiously around. The towering trees were—trees, not maples, or oaks, or birches, or apples, or pears, or pines. Perhaps she did not know enough about trees to name those leaves, that

form of branches, that smooth bark, but she doubted that a woodsman could have. All were full grown, without a sapling about—or
a bush, or a fern, or moss. The forest floor did not bear any fallen
leaves. Then, it was not earth, but stone. The only mark of the trail
was the wearing away of the rock. She wondered uneasily how often the princesses had walked this way, to wear it like that.

The sound of Robert's boots was louder than the princesses'
feet. Or her own. There was, of course, no breeze—if the leaves here
could rustle.

The trail left the woods between rocky ground rising up to
either hand. Rosalie did not hesitate, though the light slackened
behind them, and their shadows loomed enormous before them.
(Not hers, noted Biancabella with relief.) As the path curved
through the stone, the silver glow dimmed, and another, golden
glow appeared ahead. The stone to either side of the path formed
looming shadows against it, until they emerged and walked along
the path in a golden grove. In this one, also, she could not name
the gleaming trees or see any undergrowth or dead leaves on stony
ground.

None of the princesses hesitated here, either. Biancabella managed only to peer about and see the trees had no fruit hidden about
the leaves.

Again the trail led out of the grove and between rocky masses.
A smooth path, with not so much as a pebble had fallen on the way.

As the golden light faded, another glow appeared ahead.
White—not silvery like the first. Biancabella peered ahead until
she saw it clearly: a forest of diamonds, larger than the other two. In
its heart a lake spread, utterly still, its waters dark. An island bore a
dancing pavilion built of gold, silver, and diamonds. A throng filled
it, dressed in glittering garments. Twelve boats waited at the shore,
with boatmen dressed in garments as brilliant as any of those in the
crowd.

Rosalie got into the first, with Robert. One by one the princesses paired off with the boats, until finally Biancabella carefully stepped in with Marjory. The boatmen started to row out. Low ripples spread from their wake, gleaming for a moment in the light, and sank to nothing quickly. Biancabella told herself not to touch those—waters.

Nothing grew on the island. She timed her step to climb out of the boat as the boatman rose, and stood as one boatman bowed and let the eldest take the Robert's arm, and other eleven princesses took the arms of their boatmen, and all ascended to the pavilion. The crowd—all men—drew apart to let them into an open floor. Robert, awkwardly, joined them, his rough clothing dark and dull, catching the eye in their number.

Biancabella noted no visible musicians, any more than lamps to account for the light. Still, as soon as the princesses and their escorts reached the floor, they formed a circle, and began to dance to an elegant tune, played to perfection. Her dancing master would have pointed out to her how graciously and well they did the steps.

Just outside the pavilion, Biancabella watched. All the other dancers were men, and every time the tune stopped, Robert was chosen by the next princess, and the other princesses choose another partner from among the crowd. Never, she thought, the same partner twice—nor did any princess choose one who had danced with one of her sisters.

When Robert had danced with them all, none of them ever choose him again.

No one broke and ran off at midnight. Or, for that matter, arrived at midnight trailing a gooseherd and a gaggle of geese.

She lost count of the dances, but in due course, the music ended. Without a word, the eldest took Robert's arm, the other eleven took the arm of their last partner, and all proceeded to the boats.

Biancabella timed her step into the boat again, and walked back
with the others.

When climbing the stairs, she realized that, despite the length
of them, she was not breathing hard. Nor was she tired.

All the more marvelous when she walked up the last steps and
realized that the dawn showed outside the windows.

Swiftly, she took up her place against the wall. As soon as the
door opened, she would be gone. To a place where she could think.

#

Biancabella hesitated when the garden came into sight, with blood
red roses visible through the gate's latticework, but the gate stood
open. And was far enough back that she could escape by opening
it, if it came to that.

She just had to remember to not pick any roses.

She walked into the sweetness of the roses and slowly ambled
onward, pausing when butterflies or bees flew by her.

The walls were golden stone, not the darkness of her father's
castle, and the garden was far larger. Often, she could not see the
walls, and the garden itself was lovely, with carefully tended peach
and apple trees, and willows as well. Flower beds bloomed with red
and pink roses and white and yellow lilies, heartsease in purple and
yellow, and more and more flowers. In a happier hour, she would
have asked the gardeners if she might have slips of them, in hopes
of planting them in her own. Broad pools had pink and yellow wa-
ter-lilies bobbing on the ripples. It summoned up such memories of
home.

She sat beneath a willow—the shadows would help her
cloak—and contemplated a pool. Fish as large as her forearm,
ghostly pale and fiery orange in patches, drifted in the waters.

Was Boney behind it? The women were not kept captive as he had kept the other in the mirror's tale. The woman who gave her the cloak might have been wrong.

As for the others—Mother Magda would keep them captive as well, in a tower. She shifted. The chamber was in a tower, to be sure, but Mother Magda would not let them gad about with young men. Mistress Laurenza and King Drakos cared only about their own daughters, and the others were even less probable.

She sat back. The willow leaves formed a pattern of shadows against the sky. She could help break this enchantment even if none of the circle were behind it—as practice, if nothing else.

Therefore, she rose and shifted her place. She still sat in the shade, but she watched the steps that rose into the princesses' chamber, and the servants who went about, and even the princesses when some came out to laugh and embroider and play a lute in the garden.

She watched the gardener's boys with particular intentness. Not one of them wore a cap that completely covered his hair. Certainly not one had a lock of hair that was true gold peeking out from underneath.

Minutes inched by, slowly adding up into hours.

After noon, with peals of laughter, the rest of the princesses came into the garden, with one of the middle ones flourishing a golden ball.

"Watch out, Lelia," called the youngest. "If it lands in a pond, a frog might demand to come with us as the price of bringing it back."

Lelia tossed her head, and her brown curls caught in the breeze. "As if our father would not buy us a hundred more! I could leave a thousand balls in the pool, and never condescend to haggle with a frog!"

"You talk, Marjory," said another, grandly, "as if they were heal-ing wells, and our father needed the water to be cured of illness. Then a frog would be in a position to demand much."

"Or if our stepmother wanted us to bring back the water in a sieve," said a third.

"Now you are *silly*," said the second princess. "You know per-fectly well that you stop up the holes with moss, then. You don't need the frog's advice." She pirouetted. "Just make sure that if some prince lets someone in a pool grab him, he does not get to stay the three nights. Whether it's a nixie or a water goblin."

Ten of them laughed again. Biancabella looked at them all gravely. She wondered whether the princesses minded the magic. Though they did seem to think that a prince might rescue them some day. She sighed. The princes, at least, would be better off. And some of the princesses—Rosalie looked grave, and Marjory wor-ried.

The princesses played catch around the garden. They never let the ball fall into a pool. Biancabella sat in the shade and watched.

And she, thought Biancabella as they chattered, would never master all their names.

#

Descending the next night next to Marjory, Biancabella thought that the walk was not longer than any of the dances had been, but had to add, uneasily, that she did not know whether this strange underground did strange things to time as well as to sleep. She watched the lights, and though the stone was black, it reflected enough of the light that she thought they circled all the way around, spiraling in, so the boats met them where they descended.

Which was of no help at all.

She watched the dancing. Robert had better mastered the art of looking dazed and had need of it. This night, every one of the princesses danced with him, twice. None of the other dancers seemed to begrudge him it.

All her looking about garnered only that there was a goblet on a table, within the dance floor. And nothing to pour from, into it.

No one so much as glanced at it.

But when she returned in the morning, she slipped out the door as soon as she could and fled toward the wine cellar.

At its door, she collected her wits—as if she could carry a barrel of wine anywhere, let alone up the stairs from here to the tower, and then down the stairs and into the boat for the dancing hall—and searched about the castle. It took hours of dodging down corridors of rough stone where guards and servants hurried about tasks or gossiped about their masters, but as the church bells chimed out the noon hour, she found where they kept the stores for journeys. Shelf upon shelf of them, from packs and saddlebags, through tents, to ropes and cords, in a room difficult to search because she could not bring any light, but it included wine-skins.

She stole out of that room in silence. The cloak still ensured that no one looked at her.

Then to the cellar with its vast blocks of dark brown stone, with dew beading on the walls with broad daylight outside. An ax hung on the wall, and she laughed a little. Just as well they were princesses and would never be sent down here to fetch wine or beer. One of them would see the ax, imagine that a child of hers might be born, come down here to get beer, and be killed by the ax falling on him, and never return with the beer.

Which was not, perhaps, just. The princesses, being bewitched, might act more silly than they were by nature.

Biancabella picked a cask of common stuff and filled the wine-skin, taking care that none of the red wine dripped to the floor to betray her, listening every moment to tell if some servant came. Only after she climbed the stairs, as she emerged from the cellar into the day, did she realize that the long hours had barely covered half the day. She still had to wait until sunset.

The castle gates were open, she could go out, buy something to eat, even speak to another person, but she did not know how long it would be until the gates were closed. If she were caught outside, all might be lost.

She closed her eyes.

Even if she stole within at the last minute, and the closing gate only took the heel off her shoe—a heel appearing like that would draw eyes. All very well when a prince was escaping an enchanted kingdom, not so well here.

With a sigh, Biancabella raided the kitchen for bread and butter and went back to watch as she had the day before. She tried, now and again, to ponder her memories of those glittering trees, the circular path, the dark pond and its brilliant island, but she could see no pattern in it.

And she did not dare take out the mirror. The cloak hid only her.

#

That night in the pavilion, Biancabella stole her way through the floor, among the dancers. The music would have been enough to hide her footfalls, the cloak had the aid of how they all stared at the dancers when not dancing themselves, but she feared to touch them. The woman had not spoken of how it could hide that.

She was breathing hard when she found herself at the table. The music was soft and gentle, and she waited. There would be a louder tune later.

Robert danced with Rosalie. Again. The princesses passed him between them, and he never once sat out a dance.

Minutes inched on. Rosalie stopped in the middle of the floor, and no tune started. Biancabella glanced at the cup and cursed herself as a fool. It was full. She had known this night was different, this night Robert would not return, but she had thought it would go as before.

"You have gladdened—"

Biancabella took advantage of her words, however soft-spoken Rosalie was, to pour out the cup behind her. The drink was a shade of purple she had never seen in any drink before, and she doubted that it was wine.

"—our measures with your presence, Master Robert." Rosalie smiled. Biancabella, her shoulders feeling as if a knife was about to driven in, grabbed the wine-skin and poured out the wine despite the silence. The cloak was stronger than she realized; no one turned at the gurgling sound, faint but the only sound in the pavilion. She slid back from the table, carefully stepping over where she had spilled the other drink.

"We would have you gladden them forever." Rosalie nodded to the crowd. They parted, and she came to lift the cup. At least she did not see that the drink had changed. "Here, accept our greeting cup."

Robert bowed his hand, took the cup in hand, and drank. Biancabella bit her lip. He lowered it, and Rosalie took the cup again.

"Will you thus gladden us?"

Robert's voice was slow and awkward. "I think that I will not."

Silence followed. It even took Rosalie a minute to blink. No tide of murmurs flooded the crowd after.

Her voice even more slow and awkward, like the creaking of an ancient water wheel, Rosalie said, "Then we must return with you."

Biancabella slipped through the crowd. Some men started and looked to where she stood, but nothing mattered but that she be at the boats when they arrived.

Except that the waters were sinking away. Her heart hammering and her breath coming fast, she waited, and when the princesses came with Robert, all the other men followed after, and the ground was dry enough for them to walk across. And then through the three groves. Biancabella tried to keep her place in the crowd. They all seemed dazed, and none of them spoke.

The door was a dim light at the top of the stairs when Rosalie started.

"What fools we are! Such gallant men and not once have we chosen one for our bridegrooms!"

Her voice sounded more natural than it had at the pavilion. And her sisters started and turned to face the path, and the men gathered there.

Rosalie took a step in that direction, and then stopped. "No," she said slowly, "I would rather—" Then she blushed. "I would rather choose you than one of them, but you are our rescuer. My sisters should have realized that you should choose whichever of us pleased you—"

Robert smiled. "I am—not young. I would gladly take the oldest." He reached out for her hand.

Biancabella stole up the stairs, unnoticed.

#

Her cloak stowed safely away as soon as she reached an alleyway, Biancabella looked an ordinary traveler and headed for the city gates.

It was not so early as the bulk of the travelers. Robert and Rosalie had found much to talk of, and Marjory when she emerged with the gardener's boy Michael, and they had had much time. Still, the other ten princesses had started up the steps with their chosen lovers, and with the rest of the crowd of men after them, before those outside had started to hammer on the door and ask if the princesses had risen.

She had had to wait through every moment of it, as the sunlight slowly increased and lost its rosy color. She had not, hiding in the corner, even been able to watch the sunrise.

She forced out her breath and told herself to be glad that she had had time to think. She wanted to be far, far away before Boney discovered this. She did not think her mother would protect her from him.

"Candles!" bellowed a vendor. "Fine tallow candles!"

She turned left and into the main road, streaming both to and from the gates. At a booth, a baker called out his tarts, peach and apple and pear. A drove of cattle came down the street. Groans from all about preceded the people pulling to either side.

"Out to prepare the betrothal feast," said an old woman in gray.

"Better one than twelve," said a young man with a tray of peaches. "And one wedding, even a twelve-fold one, instead of twelve. Larger than a single wedding, but not costing twelve times as much."

"And no trouble about the younger being married before the older," said a plump matron in a blue dress. "They'll do them in order."

"At least all but two choose princes," mused the old woman.

A girl shouted with laughter. "Six of them choose six brother-princes! All together, forever!"

"True, true," said the young man. "And the four choose the four princes from the southern border."

The old woman snorted. "And of those from the southern border, Prince Guillaume got left out. He'll probably be glad of that."

"*Why*?" burst out of the girl.

"Why, because his mother and his father would not like any of our silly princesses," said the old woman. "Have you not heard of them?"

The cattle still lowed. Biancabella pulled closer to the old woman.

"Once upon a time, a fool heard that there was an old woman who could give a man wits. He went to her, and found her reading in a great book, and she asked him what sort of brains he wanted—a king's, a scholar's, a soldier's—and he said just ordinary brains. She told him that then she could help, she could give him a pottle of brains, but he had to bring her the heart of the being he loved most and then answer a riddle.

"Well, he said to himself that he loved fat bacon better than anything, and so he went and killed his fat pig, and tore out and brought the heart. The old woman was reading in the great book, and asked him what ran without feet, and he could not guess.

"'You brought me the wrong heart,' said the old woman. 'There will be no brains for you today.'

"He headed home to talk to his mother, but as he was coming, people came running to him to tell him his mother was dying. He hurried home, but she was already past speaking with, and then died.

"He mourned and realized he had loved his mother more than his fat pig, so when they put her body in the coffin, he carted it to the old woman, reading in her great book, and she asked him what was yellow and shone and was not gold, and he could not guess.

"'You brought me the wrong heart,' said the old woman. 'There will be no brains for you today.'

"So he went and buried his mother, and started home, and then thought that neither his mother nor his fat pig were there, and so he sat by the road and wept. A young woman asked him what was the matter, and he told her his story and how he was all alone in the world.

"They talked for a bit, and she told him that she was all alone in the world, too, and she could cook and sew and clean—and she had always heard that fools made good husbands. So they went and married. But the fool still wished he had a pottle of brains. One day his wife said, 'I can see you love me more than anything else in the world. Bring me to the old woman—that will bring my heart—and maybe I can help you with the riddles.'

"So they did, and when the old woman asked him what was the depth of the sea, his wife whispered to him, and he told her it was a stone's throw.

"So the old woman closed her book and told him that he had gotten his pottle of brains already, and they were in his wife's head. They went home and lived happily, and had sons and daughters, and raised them up and married them off. When the children were all settled, they, all of a sudden, had another girl. She was no more than twelve when her mother died, and her father and she grieved over her grave.

"One day, years later, as they worked the farm, the father found a golden pedestal. 'This is much too rich for us,' he said. 'I will give it to the king.'

"Said his daughter, 'If you give it to the king, he will ask where the mortar is. Better to bury it back where you found it.'

"But he did not listen and went to court, and the king asked him where the mortar was and threw him in prison when he could not give it. The man went and lamented and endlessly said, 'If only I had listened to my daughter.' The king heard him and asked him what he meant. So the man explained how his daughter had predicted that he would ask that, and he had not listened. The king sent word to the daughter that if she came to him neither dressed nor naked, neither walking nor riding, neither bearing a gift nor with empty hands, he would let her father go, and marry her to boot."

The old woman spread her hands.

"So she wrapped herself in a fishing net, hitched up the plow to the plow-horse and rode the plow with her foot touching the ground, and held in her hand a bird. When she reached the castle, she held out the bird which flew off as soon as she went to give to the king—

"And he married her," the old woman concluded triumphantly, putting her hands on her hips before she leaned forward. "Does that sound like a mother who would want her son to marry a fool?"

"No, not at all," said the young man.

An old man, leaning on his staff, said, "There'll be many a happy princess who isn't one of ours. Princess Celestine, Princess Rose-Red, Princess Biancabella, Princess Diamond, Princess Jeanette—none of them have had a wooer because every prince has always come to win the dancing princesses. With this all done, there are princes."

"Not Rose-Red," said a lean, travel-stained man, carrying a harp. "She's the daughter of King Wolfskin, and do you think he will be content with a prince noted for *dancing*? After he spent many years as a wolf and only changed back to a man by having his head chopped off?"

Biancabella wondered that the circle had allowed that, and not kept him trapped as a wolf. Then she realized, with the start, that the cows were gone, and the street had been clear to walk on for some time. More prudent travelers had already hastened onward.

She hurried. The father was not the only fool there was.

At least nothing more arose between there and the gate, and then she was out on the road.

At the first crossroad, she turned north. The kingdoms that the mirror had spoken of were to the north, and the princes trapped here had—she rolled her eyes—meant that the circle had little to do to the south. How efficient. She could only hope that the princes moved swiftly enough to marry before the circle stopped them.

She trudged north. Few other travelers went this way, and it grew grassy here and there. Even with her setting out this late, the empty road gave her a chance to get far. A point which had her scowling in thought. Was this to be her life? Endlessly running about kingdoms? She had rescued the princesses, and all the men who wooed them, and she had done it without leaving a sign that Boney could find of her, so she had not alerted the circle, but she had learned nothing of his weaknesses. She could do this in endless fear until she was as old as the woman who had given her the cloak—while the princesses all could marry and live out their lives.

She forced her breath in and out. Had flitting about her father's castle in endless fear been better? And it *was* better than lying in a coffin as poor Snow-White did.

Those thoughts grew colder as she trudged on, and on.

As the sun began to sink, she thought—if only her mother had been like Elinor's stepmother, who wanted her daughters, not herself, to be the fairest—and she jerked her head aside, trying to shake the thought.

Heaven guard and protect her. She trudged on.

When the sky started to show color, her legs ached from walking, but she had already reached the forest at the northern border. She looked about for shelter. Even a cavern would provide it, if she could avoid one that had a bandit band using it as a lair—whether it was enchanted or not.

Or use the cloak against them, she reminded herself. Perhaps she could even tell people of such a band and bring down bloody vengeance on their heads.

Then she picked out a cottage, half-hidden by the tree shadows, and by the underbrush. Even in the dim light, it looked tumble-down. She thought, though she could not be certain, with the thick growth of ferns and moss, that it had had no more than a kitchen garden where peas and cabbages might have been raised, no proper farm. A shed, in the back, might have held a cow.

Then, some kind of woodcutter or huntsman was more likely, here in the woods.

The door did still latch, and it had no sign of a leaking roof, though the hearth was long cold, without so much as a twig of fire-wood by it, all the food gone, and no other sign that anyone had lived there for many a year. Even a robber band would have shown more signs that they inhabited a place.

There were no bodies. She had not seen a grave outside, but might have missed it.

Or, she told herself, the cottage could have been abandoned. She looked about. It was rougher than an inn—it would be dark long before sunset, and with no proper bed, she would be cold and stiff in the morning—but had an advantage over any inn.

Biancabella sat, took out the mirror, and propped it up careful-ly up against the hearth.

"Mirror, what do you think of my adventures under the castle?"

She reached for bread and cheese as the mirror swirled. The shadows meant that she could barely make out the face as it formed, but the voice came clearly enough.

"Carrying me made your journey not quite clear. The warlockry he put on it all to keep it hidden from view still worked." The voice turned drier. "I think being out of the bag would not help. It was only your mother's work that gives you the eyes to see through the beguilements."

Biancabella's nose wrinkled. "The woman seemed to think that the cloak was enough."

"I saw that even less clearly," said the mirror.

Biancabella reached into the bag to pull the cloak out. The cloth seemed thinner than ever in her fingers, and she wondered whether the mirror could see it, when, with a faint whisper, it dissolved to nothing in her fingers.

She opened her mouth, shut it again, told herself that she should have known it was folly to dream of hiding forever using it, and finally said, "I think that the woman had more reasons than one to tell me to hurry."

"So," said the mirror, "do I."

Biancabella sighed and lowered her hand. "Or perhaps she wanted to spare me the risk of my heirs fighting over the treasure when I die. They might end up being tricked and killed by a man out to win his way back to his wife."

"Less likely," said the mirror, wryly. "She did not give you seven-league boots and a sword that would cut off everyone's head as well."

Biancabella ate the last of the bread.

"So. I have rescued twelve princesses and scores of men. I learned nothing useful in preventing the circle from harming me, or stopping their witcheries somewhere else. And I got no credit for it."

"You escaped farther from Augusta Gloriana," said the mirror. "And you did foil one of their workings."

Biancabella looked up. "I wondered—I thought it was Boney, but I could not be certain—"

The mirror smiled with cool serenity. "Be certain, Your Highness."

Biancabella let her breath out. "There is that."

A bird called in the night.

"I wonder that my mother did not choose that kingdom over my father's."

"Your mother did not fare to it. She never heard of a time when she might ruin some princess or prince there. Your father's was the grandest she knew."

Biancabella grimaced. After a minute, she said, "Rumor led me straight to the princesses, almost as soon as I left my father's castle, but I heard only rumors about them and their freedom when I left. Nothing about anywhere else where I might learn something about the circle."

The mirror was silent a minute as well. "When you come to the crossroads, take the path that goes to the north and east."

Biancabella blinked. That would take her angling past her father's kingdom, if it did not put her inside it.

"And keep your eyes open."

#

In the gray morning mist, the crossroad bore no sign to warn her that one path would lead to her suffering hunger and thirst, the second, to her dying and her horse's living, and the third, the one the mirror directed her to, to her living and her horse's dying.

Then, she didn't have a horse. She marked the sun's slant and picked the road by the mirror's directions.

The forest grew ever more thickly there. Towering oaks or maples or beeches blocked out the sky, and ferns and other underbrush grew lushly, often taller than she was. Glades occasionally broke the forest, and were bright with sunshine, and filled with grass that rose as high as her waist, and tangles of white daisies, red poppies, and orange day-lilies, often ill-formed. She tried to look past them, and not notice yellow buttercups and blue chicory as she searched for anything that the mirror might have meant.

It was not as if the commonplace wildflowers of the field could be of aid to her. Perhaps a lone red lily that grew in the forest far from any road might disenchant the spells, but not this.

Her gaze lingered on a perfect, radiant day-lily, as orange as the sunset. She could dress up as a boy and seek a job as a gardener's boy, avoiding the scullery altogether—

She shook her head and hurried along the way, into the next stretch of forest, still doing her best to look about despite all the thickets of bracken. The search kept her way slow, though the most she saw was great misshapen boulders. She thought one might have been a troll, once, in the shadows of an oak and covered with lichen, but walking on showed her that form had just looked like it from that side.

Past that boulder, another glade opened. By the score, butterflies as colorful as a queen's jewelry box flitted from flower to flower or glowed as the air grew warm and held not a breath of breeze.

Biancabella stopped in the shade. She could sit on one of the lower boulders and eat where it was cooler. Though the hour was not quite noon —she eyed the glade. If she ate on the other side, it would be somewhat farther on her way.

Crows cawed, raucously. Her nose wrinkled. It might be nothing, or nothing more than a dead rabbit, but if carrion lay near here, it might be wiser to be gone—and gone at some distance—before some wolf or hungry bear came to savage the body.

A royal blue butterfly danced about her on the still air. She drew a deep breath. She would smell it no doubt, or at least need nothing more than a glimpse of the body in the grass.

The grass rose thick and tall, with daisies and poppies blooming white and red among the blades. She followed the path until she reached the point nearest the crows, cawing in a dead tree next to the road. She pulled up her skirt and stepped around the trunk.

In a hollow below the tree, a young man sprawled, his face as white as salt, unbreathing. Her hand sprang up to her mouth, and her own breath came in and out shallowly. After a minute, she picked out the bloodied rents in his clothing, and she jerked her head away. Then she saw a dead fox, lying with a sprig of a plant in its mouth. She fled, staggering back to the path and dropping to her knees there.

When she finally collected herself, a butterfly perched on a daisy before her, its wings blood-red. She winced. It was well she had not eaten before this.

She forced herself to breathe deeply, in and out, and looked back. None of the crows had descended. Her mouth tightened. She could not stay and ward the crows off forever, and she could not dig the grave alone with only her bare hands. She had no spade, or even a sword, to cut the earth.

Perhaps the man had one.

She winced at the thought of looking. A fugitive thought told her that arranging a dead man's burial might win aid in a quest, not burying him herself—but, she reminded herself, those who gained such aid did not bury the dead in hopes of getting it. She, having hoped, would have to content herself with serving Heaven with such a deed. If she could.

She scowled and closed her eyes, to summon up the memory of the man's clothes. Then she blinked. The rents and blood had distracted her, but the rich clothes had been marked with the golden stag that she had seen so often—on her father's clothes, on her mother's, and uncle's, and aunt's, and on her own—she felt cold—on the livery of servants, on the banners flapping from the castle and over a riding company. But, even if one of the royal family she had known had left the castle to die here, she would have recognized him. Her breath came shallowly. Unless he had died here before she was born.

Slowly her thought inched onward. He bore only a faint resemblance to his brothers, mostly in blond hair.

Her hands shook. Even before the mirror had told her, she had heard the tale, repeated from tavern gossip. She had known, she had known—and now she saw—

Slowly, she opened her eyes and stared at the forest before her. She swallowed. She did not need to look again, she had seen enough: he had not rotted to mere bones while he lay there.

And the fox. The mirror had also spoken of the fox, and why her mother had told her father and uncle to kill it. Her mouth set, she inched back and fought down the nausea as she carefully inspected the withered herb in the fox's mouth. Then she started to cast about the glade. The thickness of the grass made it hard to search, all the more in that the heat of the day bore down on her, until finally, she collected her wits.

A minute later, the mirror lay flat on the ground and assured her that the herb lay nearby. "By a boulder near here, that looks like a troll from the right vantage."

"I saw it!" said Biancabella, hopping up. "Can I leave you here? Safely?"

"Yes," said the mirror.

Biancabella ran off.

The herb grew low and dark green against the dead leaves of the forest floor. Some sprigs had pale, pinkish flowers, though tiny ones. Biancabella picked two sprigs, staining her fingers with sap and rousing a sharp scent, more spiced than floral. With them, she hurried back into the glade. The crows had stopped cawing and merely eyed her, the bodies, and even the mirror.

She drew a deep breath. After a moment, she walked over to the dead fox. Fighting down nausea, she knelt and laid the herb over the wounds.

Her heart beat out the moments. Nothing happened. No one but a fool would have expected anything to happen—

The fox's chest rose, and fell. Its limbs started to tremble, and it shifted, as if uncomfortable. It shook its head, and Biancabella bit her lip. Then it opened its eyes.

It contemplated her for longer than it had taken to rouse. Then it looked about the meadow. Slowly, it opened its mouth.

"Things have gone very wrong, haven't they?"

"How much of it do you want to know?" said Biancabella. "Now, at least? It is a long tale."

The fox looked at the herb in her hand, hopped up, and said, "Save him first." It sprinted over.

Biancabella swallowed, wished she could tell the fox to use the herb itself—but she would be there when he roused, just the same. If he roused. Perhaps there was some difference between them. She stood, more stiffly, and went over to where the fox stood anxiously over her dead uncle. She knelt to lay the herb on the wounds, and there it lay, as if a breeze had knocked it loose and borne it there.

The crows took to the air behind her, their wings beating on the wind, their caws raucous and shaking the air. Biancabella bit her lip. He still looked as pale as bone, and unmoving. The crows swept about the glade and flew over the trees. Their cries slowly faded.

John's chest rose and fell. His hands twitched. Color began to come back into his face.

The crows vanished with distance, bringing silence back.

He took longer to stir than the fox had. And opened his eyes on her. She wondered if she should smile, and then he spoke.

"You are not Sophia."

\#

At the side of the glade, Biancabella sat on a boulder, in the shade, and folded her hands in her lap. The fox sat before the mirror, with the scowling John, as the mirror recounted the tale that it had told

Biancabella of his brothers, and Sophia, and Snow-White, and Augusta Gloriana—and finally Biancabella herself.

When it finished, they still sat. John's face was a frozen mask. Minutes inched by, and Biancabella started to remember that she had intended to eat before this—matter. Her stomach growled at the thought.

John sighed, slowly. He turned his face toward Biancabella. "So," he said, forcing words out. "So you are my niece."

She could not speak, but she nodded.

"And Augusta Gloriana, who killed Sophia, and bewitched Snow-White, is still doing evil, though you do not know what."

She managed to nod, jerkily, again.

The dryness of his eyes frightened her more than if he had wept enough to kill the plants with the salt of his tears.

Chapter 3—The Inn's Secret

The day glowered with the threat of rain. Augusta Gloriana, in the doorway of Biancabella's empty suite, smiled.

The castle had lost a pathetic little ghost haunting it, and without having to let some foolish peasant boy walk off with a ghost's treasure—to give a third to the ghost's family and a third to the poor!—and the princess's hand in marriage. No more glimpsing Biancabella here, there, and everywhere, always flitting about to remind her mother of how she had failed when Mistress Laurenza and King Drakos had not. . . though neither of them, no doubt, could have dealt with so mulish and truculent a daughter.

It had taken her a week to notice her good fortune, Biancabella had crept so secretly. But now, now—it was such a relief—she should have, years ago, taken Biancabella off into the woods and sent her to gather roses. Then she could have whipped up the coach's horses and left her. It would have brought her this relief without suffering Biancabella's presence for all this time. Biancabella would have been eaten—by wolves or bears—then as surely as now—

The mirror, she thought. She had to know for herself—see for herself—that Biancabella had been eaten by wild beasts. It would only take a little wolf to gobble her up, scrawny as she was, but that would be better than Snow-White, with her sneaking about with dwarves when she should have been eaten.

Augusta Gloriana turned so abruptly that her ladies-in-waiting scattered like startled sparrows, and strode off down the corridor. In her own suite, she headed for the room, and even the ladies-in-waiting who had kept up with her pace fell back.

She could profit from experience. Watching Biancabella like a hawk would ensure that no dwarves aided her.

She pulled open the door, and even before stepping into the room, began, "Mirror, mirror, on the wall—"

It took her a minute to realize. She stood staring at the blank wall, with the words trembling on her mouth—"Tell of my daughter, tell me all."

But she would only look a fool, asking the question of a blank wall.

"Who has been in here!" she shrieked. "Question all the servants! Question the guards, and demand who has come the castle!"

She stood with her mouth open a minute. Ottoline, she thought, Ottoline trying to betray her—but no, she had seen the mirror the morning Ottoline departed. She forced her mouth closed, and thought, and then she was glad she had seen it. Ottoline would accuse her at the circle of having neglected so important a matter. She had to get it back before the others learned of its absence, she should, she should—

She grimaced. She could have asked the mirror where anything else was, if it were stolen. But the mirror itself—

Which, she remembered, slowly, she had not seen since before the last time she had seen Princess Biancabella.

"The little sneak," she whispered, "the poisonous little sneak." If Boney had borne her off, she could have gotten her back, but when the brat herself ran away—and when she had feigned such a lack of interest in the sorcery that Augusta Gloriana had taught her—

Her ladies-in-waiting whispered. One talked of a Doctor Know-All who could find things—

Augusta Gloriana whirled.

"Send out the searchers!" she said. "They must search for both the princess and the mirror. The mirror will be able to find her."

If, indeed, they did not find her with the mirror. She thought Biancabella crafty enough to keep it by her.

"And search for the wretched thief who stole them both!"

#

She should have been more discreet.

Augusta Gloriana brooded in the candle-lit antechamber. Ottoline would hear of this, and then the ingrate would gossip with the rest of the circle, and those traitors would turn on her.

As if they had had the wits to gain the mirror in the first place.

Ogier was still swilling ale in the tavern. If he was not sleeping under the table there.

"It's your fault," whispered Augusta Gloriana, staring at the wall as if she could see the tavern through it. Here, she did not need to keep her voice calm and pleasant and regal, and she did not. "After you had returned with a magical bird, and horse, and bride? And let your daughter hear the tale? Biancabella must have let it go to her head. She set out to seek her fortune, like some poor peasant girl." Her eyes narrowed. "She had no other reason. Not a sister with her head turned into a calf's—or a sheep's—not the household drudgery, I have servants do it properly—"

Ogier would shrug and say that he hadn't asked her how much she loved him, or tried to marry her, and so it wasn't *his* fault. And that Augusta Gloriana was not her stepmother, so it wasn't that.

Her breath gushed out. Useless man. If only Biancabella had learned properly, she could have poisoned Ogier years ago, and let Biancabella be crowned. Being the queen mother to a properly wise and prudent queen would be better than being queen consort to a drunken fool.

She stood. She had to be discreet in her search. Ottoline must not find out. That woman, so ungrateful—thinking she should be queen when Augusta Gloriana, not her own efforts, had made her a princess. She should have married her off to a nobleman. It wasn't as if Ottoline could blame a wish for the way Augusta Gloriana was queen and she was not—and Ottoline had not ended up a servant's wife, or an admiral's.

The first thing was to ensure the servants' silence. She swept from the room, the candle flames dancing crazily in her passing.

No sooner than she descended the stairs than she heard the cook laughing as she told some story. She bit down her rage by force. Listen first, she told herself. Listen.

"So this prince, this Victor, he rode off from the castle all moping because—twelve princesses, and not one married him!"

"Lizzy," said the old butler Hal, "there were dozens upon dozens of princes."

Augusta Gloriana blinked. The twelve princesses—but Boney had kept them all in line—

"Wasn't much consolation to him—he went moping off, except that he came to King Wolfskin's castle, and Princess Rose-Red was there."

"So King Wolfskin set him to kill a dragon?"

Lizzy hooted with laughter. "A dragon, Polly? What dragon? No, Rose-Red and Victor fell in love all at once, and Victor was all astounded that he had wasted time on those silly princesses."

"That's the tale," said Hal, sententiously. "All the princes are running off and marrying. You wonder why they bothered with the twelve."

Augusta Gloriana's eyes narrowed. For a moment, she scolded herself: if she had had the mirror, she could have kept those brides and bridegrooms apart. Then she realized that that was folly. Boney had the task of keeping them underground. His was the duty of keeping them there, and if he had needed the mirror's aid, he should have asked for it.

He had failed. She had to find the mirror, and then she could blight all the princesses and princes when the brides gave birth to their firstborn. That would show those fancy little princesses, and Boney, too.

She nodded. That gave her plenty of time. They would deserve it for their insolence, but first of all, Biancabella had to pay for trying to shield them from her just wrath.

She should not let her rage blind her. The silly little thief had refused all attempts to teach her magic. The mirror could not help her there. Yes, it would be a nuisance to track her down, but Biancabella could not stand against her.

#

When her temper cooled to sodden ashes, Augusta Gloriana stalked about the castle with cold, bitter eyes, with servants cringing from sight more quickly than ever before, and ladies-in-waiting envying them. She performed all the royal duties, she gave orders to search for the princess though fewer as no sign of her was discovered, and she stalked about.

Often, thought Jonnet, as she took another stitch and wished the queen had continue to stalk. But this day, she had come to sit with her ladies-in-waiting in the solar. Jonnet scarcely dared look up, but the mood was still clear to her. The gray sky meant barely enough light within to sew by. Yet the ladies-in-waiting did not sing, or propose that someone should read from a book, only sewed with their eyes downcast, without even asking for a candle or two.

Jonnet, in the silence, tried to sew with the rest. She wondered if any of them actually accomplished anything, and tried not to look when Marguerite went to tear out a whole seam as sewn ill. She shuddered whenever the queen's gaze fell on her and pondered whether she could persuade her father to arrange a marriage for her, so she could lament that she had to leave the queen's service.

"One of you talked," said Augusta Gloriana, her voice flat. "The day we learned my daughter had vanished, and that I could not come to her aid with my mirror stolen." Her gaze alighted on them, one by one, and they shrank back. "Talk of a man who knew such things. Who could—find stolen things."

Jonnet's needle froze in mid-air. She had heard of such a man. Who had envied a doctor's wealth and fine dinners, and followed his instructions to buy a book with a rooster on the front and advertise himself as Dr. Know-All. When the local nobleman had demanded of him whether his pregnant wife would have a son or a daughter, he had flipped back and forth in this book, saying son, daughter, son, daughter until the noble's messenger grew weary, left, and told the nobleman that the man must be a fool.

When the noblewoman gave birth to twins, a boy and a girl, the nobleman was more taken with him, and when a ring vanished in his castle, he sent for Dr. Know-All. Who realized the game was up, and just told the noble that it would take him three days, so that at least he and his wife would have three days of noble meals. The first night, as he left the meal, he sighed, and said, "That's one," and a servant he was looking at, one of the three thieves, almost panicked. The next day, he sighed and said, "That's two," when he happened to be looking at the second thief. Finally, he said "That's the last," to the third.

They had panicked and brought him the ring and all their money and begged him to have mercy, so he fed the ring to a duck and told the nobleman to kill the duck and have his ring back.

So the nobleman had decided to try him again, and told him what to guess what was in a box. Dr. Know-All trembled and remembered how once he had merely been poor Master Pinke, and he said, "Alas, poor plucked Pinke!"—and the nobleman had been pleased, for it was indeed not only a flower, but a pink.

Then Dr. Know-All had taken the money the servants and nobleman had given him and went off to another land, with his wife and daughter, to buy a fine house. Jonnet bit off her thread. There, at least, he had known what to do, since either he or the guilty servants had let slip the truth, but only after he was safe.

"Oh," said Linnet, as if she had just realized. "Dr. Know-All? He does not live where he used to." She gleefully talked of how he told that the nobleman that he would have twins, a boy and a girl, and found his ring, and guessed what was in a box.

"But he left with his gold."

Wait, Jonnet told herself, wait. Her gaze went from Linnet to the queen and back, but she could not act now. The queen spoke of searching for him.

That night, Jonnet wrote off a letter to her aunt, telling her to warn Dr. Know-All.

She cringed back when the queen's messengers went off, even before she could send her letter, but after she sent it, she told herself she had done her best, that her messenger went directly.

She went back to sewing in the solar. At least that day, the queen had not come to watch over them.

#

The messengers bowed and cringed, their hats in their hands, and repeated that Dr. Know-All had left before they had reached the town where he had lived.

"Sold his home at a low price—but he'll have gold enough to live in another land."

The queen looked angry enough to turn them all into crows.

Jonnet went on sewing.

"Ho, my queen!" King Ogier in the doorway, waved his hand. He almost looked sober. The queen gave him a poisonous glance. "What is this to-do about?"

"Your daughter vanished," said the queen coldly.

"Off to seek her fortune, no doubt," said the king, merrily. "It's not like you made her do all the housework, so she ran off."

Her voice turned icy. "It's not like she has a golden hood to protect her from wild animals who try to eat her."

"She'll stay to the roads, then. She's clever."

"She's not so clever that she might not end up slaving as a scullery maid."

"Many a princess turned out well after such labors." He tilted his head to one side. "You aren't telling me that she forgot to pack a ballgown?"

Queen Augusta Gloriana went still.

King Ogier turned away. "With that settled, there's no more reason for commotion, my dear! Nothing more to do but wait for the invitation to the wedding."

#

The crescent moon sank toward the horizon, which still showed crimson and violet traces of sunset. But the sky was black overhead, and the stars emerging.

Augusta Gloriana watched the moon.

It was not as if a storm would fit better. They had managed without the mirror before, and the others would claim that one of them should have had it, to keep it better, though none of them had thought of it, and none of them had cast the spells.

She waited out the hours. At shortly before midnight, she descended the stairs with regal dignity—only fools thought a queen needed attendants to be queenly—and went into the gardens. It was not as if she needed to be out before midnight, or a curse would catch her, but then—she smiled—it was not as if she had to hold out until midnight to break a curse.

Arriving early let her arrive with dignity. She nodded as Ottoline emerged from a gate, asked how the herb-gathering went, and listened graciously as Ottoline whined of the problems.

The others came, one by one: the nut-brown Rumpelstiltskin hunched over and peering about; Boney with his hair even more tuft-like that usual; Mistress Laurenza calm in a golden gown (though she had not brought her daughters yet); King Drakos wearing a crown; Mother Trude and Mother Magda muttering gossip to each other, like any two beggar women on the wayside.

"Hail, Queen Augusta Gloriana!" bellowed Boney. "Is all well?"

"All is well," said Augusta Gloriana.

They could not be trusted with the truth. Her eyes narrowed. Least of all Boney. He had nothing to brag of. He had had princesses escape forever. Whatever Biancabella did, she could be caught at.

#

Biancabella timidly offered food. She had enough for all three of them, with the fox eagerly eating cheese, though as she closed up the bag, John watched.

"We'll need more food soon," he said.

Biancabella nodded and stood, and they walked on. Once they left the meadow for the forest on the other side, the forest held no more glades, only a shadowed way among trees.

The fox frisked about the path eagerly enough. Or perhaps warily enough, with how it peered about the trees. John walked with slumped shoulders, and little attention, and Biancabella did not have difficulty keeping herself subdued. The woman who had died before her birth had, for him, been alive just the other day.

She shifted the bag. At least the mirror had told the tale calmly enough. Though, from time to time, some thought whispered to her that John was the rightful heir to the throne, and she had best find a prince on the way, to marry. She shoved the thought away. Before John's restoration, Snow-White had been the rightful heir to the throne, and she needed more safety before she could think of marrying, even for a kingdom.

She let out her breath in a sigh. Or rather, especially for a king-dom. She had the wits to keep her mother from luring her out of the castle to turn her into a duck—Ottoline would help her in that much—but her mother might steal within and turn her into a duck there.

And uncles could be kind to their nieces and thus keep them out of tales.

She shoved the thought away again whenever it rose again.

"There's an inn ahead," said the fox. "Seems quiet enough."

John nodded slowly. Biancabella hoped it was honest enough, though she did not have the cloak to tempt the innkeeper. It was early to stop, but there would probably not be another inn ahead until another day's journey had passed.

She looked about, and gasped. Her heart hammered. She could not be sure—it might not be a bear—she had only a glimpse of dark brown fur—and the trees grew thickly—

John stopped, and his gaze followed hers. Then his hand went to his sword, and he stepped between her and those trees.

"Enough of this," said the fox, sitting upright. "Do not offer trouble when it does not offer itself." It waved a paw. "Besides, the bear is heading off, not toward us."

John's grip loosened. Biancabella nodded and looked back ahead.

The forest still spread as far as the eye could see down the road, and ahead, at a crossroad, stood only an inn, squarely built, half-timbered with dark oak beams and bright whitewash. Its sign hung out front, the paint weathered enough that she could not read it. Hedges of roses surrounded a garden—the roses looking to be the only flowers in it.

Do not steal any lettuce or parsley, she told herself. Or plums, or radishes. Or, for that matter, roses. She looked back at the inn.

A blind man with a shaggy beard and head of hair, both dark but with threads of white, sat mutely at the corner of the inn, with a cup before him. His clothes, down to the rag for his eyes, and face were so weather-beaten that—her tongue touched her lips—she could not be certain how old he was. He had to be younger than he looked.

Or perhaps immensely older. This could be a disguise.

He did not speak, to her surprise. After a moment, she realized that he had fallen asleep there.

She was surprised at how much her heart sank. John closed his eyes and shook his head. The fox padded onward, and John followed. Biancabella fished out a coin for the cup and hurried after. She scolded herself. To expect to find in every beggar a wizard who would feign poverty to put her to the test—and to not think of aiding the beggar for his own sake until after she hoped for the test. It would serve her right if she missed such a test for looking for it so hard.

John walked toward the inn door. No other travelers were coming or going. The windows were made of small diamond-shaped panes, thick and not entirely clear, and she could not see within. She tilted her head to read the sign. The Four Winds. Four puffy things like clouds blowing air into the center of the sign, rather like the "winds" that would appear on the maps Lady Regina had had her study from. Even this close, the blue and gray winds, and the black writing, were none too distinct.

She supposed that no one had to read the sign to recognize the inn, not at this crossroads. Looking down all the roads here showed nothing else of any building stood as far as the roads stretched.

For a moment, as they approached, a beautiful voice came out of the inn, singing, but moments later, a matron appeared in the doorway.

"Welcome to the Four Winds," she called. Her blond hair fell in a thick braid down her back as she smiled on them. Biancabella blinked. What a strikingly lovely woman.

The woman glanced them over. "No horses? Well, we have rooms as well for you—" She glanced at the fox and hesitated.

"Three," said John. "My niece and I, and the fox, will take one room."

Both her eyebrows went up, but she stepped back and waved them into a room set with trestle tables, the walls whitewashed, the roof with enormous oaken beams, the fireplace large enough for an ox, but now empty even of ashes. A maiden bent over a broom, her black hair falling in a braid; she glanced up, and Biancabella guessed her to be a little older than herself—and the matron's daughter.

The matron's voice flowed on. "You are new here, of course, but have you heard of the Four Winds? And the price we charge? Money alone does not suffice. You must tell us tales you have heard on your way."

"We have heard many tales," said the maiden. "Tales of griffins, tales of maidens who can turn into swans, or spoonbills, tales of a prince who was once a snake. But we hear more every year."

Rapunzel nodded. "Tales—" Her voice turned hesitant. "—of wonder." She looked at the fox.

"How many tales?" said the fox, swishing its tail. "That could take quite some time if you want to hear all that I know. And actually, I know more than I can tell."

"You can't just tell them?" said the woman.

"It's more remarkable that I can tell *any*," said the fox.

Biancabella sat on a bench. At least there were no other guests. "Are you looking for any tale in particular?" She slipped out the mirror. John frowned, glanced at the woman, and said nothing. "If you told us so, perhaps we can tell the tale of wonders that you wish to hear."

The woman let her breath out slowly. The maiden straightened. Both of them stared at the mirror. The woman's face was slowly horrible with hope.

"Once upon a time," said the woman softly, "a witch had a garden of marvels. A woman who lived nearby, and was with child, said to her husband that she did not think she could live without some rampion that grew in the garden, though they knew the witch would never, ever sell it. He was an easy-going fellow, and he slipped in to grab some, but the witch caught him and threatened to tear him to pieces. He fell to his knees and begged for his life, telling how his wife craved the rampion. She let him go and even gave him rampion, if he would give her the baby when born. He agreed.

"So she took me. Her name was Mother Magda—perhaps still is."

Biancabella twitched. The inn-keeper seemed not to notice.

"And she named me Rapunzel, which means rampion. I grew up with her for many a year, but when I turned fourteen, she locked me in a tower. To keep me safe. She enchanted my hair— " She laid a hand to the thick braid. "—so that I could let it down when she called to me, and she could climb up it."

The maiden had not moved from where she stood, Biancabella realized. She bit her lip and hoped that no one arrived.

"But one day, I was singing in the tower, and Basil heard me." For a moment, she looked as if dreaming. "He kept watch, and saw Mother Magda arrive and call to me—and then he called to me as well." She smiled. "And I was frightened at the sight of him, because she had told me to let down my hair whenever I heard that call, and then it came to me that she might have disguised herself as a handsome young man. So I told myself that she had not ordered me to make sure she was an evil old witch before doing it. And so I met Basil."

She sighed.

"He visited me often, but he could neither bring me a ladder, nor get a rope—we *should* have thought of curses then, but—"

She spread her hands.

"We married there in secret, and he smuggled me hemp that I could make a ladder from, but one day Mother Magda arrived too soon. Before I could hide him, she flew up with magic and threw him down the tower. I saw him stagger off, I do not know how he lived, and then she threw me out, into a wild wilderness.

"I escaped it and hunted for Basil everywhere, though I was with child and finding it harder by the day. One day, I came to this inn, and the innkeeper, old Walter, let me stay until my twins were born, my Constance and my Florio. Then he offered to let me work and ask all the travelers for news. That would work as well as searching."

She sat, abruptly, and her voice was heavy. "So it did. Neither way worked at all." She swallowed. "Walter had a daughter once, but she vanished. So he left me the inn, that I might continue to ask, but nothing else changed. And now my dear son has been bewitched into the form of a bear—"

Constance hurried over to her mother and gave them a baneful glance. Biancabella slid down on her knees by the mirror and whispered, "Is there anything more than you can tell me?"

"Basil was caught by the thorns at the bottom of the tower," said the mirror. "It blinded him."

Biancabella winced.

"And the two of them are under a curse, to never know each other until he can see her."

Biancabella shuddered. Was there nothing the circle would not do to make misery?

"But there are these weakness—her tears can cure his blindness."

Biancabella tilted her head to one side.

"And they were drawn together, as two such lovers often are."

Biancabella blinked and stood up. She heard voices behind her as she walked out the door. A minute later, she shook the beggar's shoulder.

"You can help the innkeeper who lets you beg here," she said, her voice low.

"I?" he said, his voice ragged as if unaccustomed to speaking. "How can I help anyone?"

"Come with me, and learn," she said. "What harm will it do?"

John appeared beside her and took the beggar's arm. Bewildered, the beggar let them lead him.

Constance glared at her. Rapunzel was blinking her tears away. Speak quickly, Biancabella told herself.

"I have a tale of wonder for you. This blind beggar is under a curse. He will never know his true love again, or she him, until he sees her."

For a moment, Rapunzel stared blankly at him. Then her tears welled up again.

Biancabella braced herself, pulled the bandage off his eyes, and wiped the tears from Rapunzel's face, to smear them over his eyes.

Moment passed, her heart beating one, two, three times. She felt like a fool.

But, as she watched, the beggar blinked. And again. Then his eyes started to focus. Rapunzel's gaze on him slowly took on more intent, as if she saw him for the first time.

Biancabella walked away and picked up the mirror. John urged Constance away, suggesting the kitchen, and followed her in. Biancabella followed, not quickly enough to avoid seeing Rapunzel and Basil embrace and weep.

She pulled the door shut behind her. Constance stared at it. Biancabella looked about, found a table and went to lay the mirror on it. The face looked just a trifle smug.

"I think, princess," said the fox, scratching itself behind one ear, "that it might be pleasant to make a dinner for celebration."

"Is—" Constance's hands moved about, as if trying to grasp something as formless as the air. "Is he really? He sat there—for *years*. I remember him when I was a girl!"

"You were bewitched," said Biancabella. "You and your mother and—your brother. And your father."

Constance sat. And started to cry. Biancabella did not know where to look. Her gaze jerked over the coppery pots, all as bright as mirrors, the fireplace with its banked fire, the food hanging from the rafters—the bear moving outside. And Rapunzel had said—

"Constance," she said sharply. "I think your brother is worried. And your parents can't explain. And—" Her mouth opened and shut. What was she going to say? A red-eyed Constance would only alarm—Florio the more.

John looked as helpless as she felt, and the bear was coming closer.

Her gaze went over to the mirror. No, she would talk about that part later. They had already had surprises enough for this evening. At that, talking about why Florio had been turned into a bear would not help now.

"Pull yourself together, princess," said the fox crisply. "Otherwise your brother might take your weeping as a sign to tear us to pieces, as if we were evil dwarves."

Constance ran a hand across her eyes, and called, "It's all right, Florio. I—" She sobbed. "They'll tell you."

John opened the window. The bear stuck a nose in, and for so furry a face, had a skeptical expression.

"It's good news," said Biancabella. "We told the tale that your mother has been looking for."

The bear snuffled. "And why aren't you packing?" he said, querulously. "Why are you weeping like the princess just pricked her finger on the spindle, and all is lost? What are we waiting for? We should go find him, like the crab—"

Constance managed a bark of laughter in her tears. The bear hesitated.

"You were under a curse," said Biancabella. "All four of you. So that your father could not recognize you, or you him."

The bear snorted.

"He was blind, too. Breaking that broke the curse."

It took him a minute, but then the bear sat, abruptly.

"The fox," said John dryly, "proposed a feast, but then, your parents might not emerge for some time, and I do not know whether—"

"A feast," said a red-eyed Rapunzel, from the doorway, "sounds splendid. To reward the heroes of the hour." She emerged. "Your father wishes to speak to you both, Florio, Constance." Basil followed her in, and he already looked younger and less worn.

John, his face set, went to open the back door. Florio left the window.

Rapunzel said, sadly, "He looked much like you before he was a bear." She glanced sideways at her husband. "What a curse it must have been, to keep us thus blind."

Biancabella looked at her hands.

Basil nodded and went to embrace Florio's shaggy neck.

Biancabella said in a low voice, "I can help with the cooking."

Rapunzel went to the pantry, humming. "We won't be able to have a roast, but there is meat." She began taking down foodstuff, handing it off to Biancabella, and began to sing.

"Over in the meadow in a pond in the sun
Lived an old mother duck and her little duck one."

#

Rapunzel, humming along, stirred another dish. The sunset shone in peach and rosy shades outside.

John, by the doorway, looked down the road. "There—are no other travelers?"

She showed no signs of surprise. "Oh, that happens. Summer has the fairs, and the most travelers come this way going between them. They are at the fairs now."

She picked the spoon up and watched the mix drip slowly before giving it another stir.

"We have to keep watch—you did come, and others might—but it is not surprising that this gracious night lets us celebrate."

#

As the dinner finished cooking, as the stars started to appear, Biancabella introduced them all to the mirror. "It may be able to help Florio as well."

Which, John told himself, was a good thing. Just as helping Basil and Rapunzel had been.

"Certainly," said Basil, "you are a fountain of wonders and marvels."

Biancabella looked at the table, as Constance hung the mirror on the wall.

"Eat first," said the mirror. "The knowledge will keep, and the food will grow cold." It paused. "And this night, you need not fear interruption."

John let out his breath. Many things could be ahead, and all would take some time. He glanced at the bear and reminded himself that Florio might help Snow-White.

Rapunzel indeed made a feast of sausage, and pastries, and more. With cider to drink already. He drank. And looked at his reflection in the mug.

"You could tell us how you came to be here," said Basil, his voice deep.

The fox regaled the table with the tale of his horrible murder, drawing cries of consternation, and Biancabella's heroic rescue of them, drawing looks of admiration to her until she blushed. Quite prettily.

It was hard to remember, now, that he had loved visiting taverns before, because there, the tales were told, and the merry songs were sung. He had torn himself away from the inn that the fox had warned against.

And now—

He drained the cup. Now, he could help Snow-White for her mother's sake. And, he supposed, Biancabella. She was his niece. And helping her would spite her mother.

Until Augusta Gloriana paid for what she had done. He put down the mug.

#

Lack of other travelers certainly made all easier for the meal, with the room glowing golden from the lamps around. Fresh-baked bread with honey and jam—honey alone for Florio, and a plenitude of nuts—and peaches from their orchard, and sausages and cheese and cider in abundance—with the fox munching on cheese, and the mirror smiling benignly over all. Basil, clean and dressed in Florio's clothes, looked almost young as Rapunzel, and she looked far younger than she had.

Biancabella ate. Three times now she had thwarted the circle. Perhaps she had hope.

When John said, "What was the crab that Florio was so worried about?" Rapunzel laughed, her face rosy and bright.

"Oh, we heard many tales here over the years. That was one we heard twice. The first time, a traveler had sailed in from the islands and was heading south again. He told of how he had found an island on which there was a castle. Every night three doves, bright as gold, would fly in and turn into young men, who would drink a toast to a young woman who could not keep silent for another day, but a curse on the woman who burned the crab shell, and then they and all the doors and windows in the castle wept."

"How odd," said Basil.

"But the next year, a man came up from the south. He told how there had been a crab there, who was the son of an old peasant woman, and how he offered to marry the king's daughter. The king said that if he built her a castle of jewels overnight, he could have her. So the crab did. The princess married him, but the king was not pleased. He announced a great tournament, lasting three days, and told his daughter that if any of the knights pleased her better, she could have him instead of the crab. A knight in golden armor won every pass at arms, and both the king and the queen talked of how much more suitable that man was as her bridegroom than a *crab*. And again the second day. And again on the third day, where the daughter broke down and said that the golden knight was her husband the crab.

"At that the queen ran to the castle of jewels. There, she found the crab shell lying there, and she threw it into the fire. The golden knight, at the tourney, cried out and flew off as a golden dove.

"The princess wept and wept and left the castle of jewels to set up an inn, and ask all the travelers their tales—"

She smiled at their staring. "It does work well. Perhaps she had heard of it as Walter had when he suggested it to me. One day the traveler who had come to me, came to her." Her smile broadened. "When she went to the castle, and hid within, the doves came, and made the toast, and wept. But all the doors and windows laughed, and when her husband rebuked them, they laughed all the harder. So they searched the castle and found her, and her husband returned with her and lived with her happily to this day."

She picked up a cup. "I envied her at the time. How I envied her. But I have found my husband again, and without a sea voyage to a far off castle. A toast to the young traveler and the magic mirror she bore."

Biancabella felt her face heat as they drank it. She hoped that the princess and her golden knight were far enough south that the circle did not concern themselves with the two of them.

"There have been other tales," said Florio, his maw covered with honey. "There was the girl whose mother had foolishly said that she did not care if all her seven sons were turned to wild ducks if she only had a daughter. As soon as she gave birth to a daughter, into ducks they turned!"

"She came looking for them," said Constance. "The daughter, that is, looking for her brothers."

"There have been tales since," said Rapunzel. "That she found them and managed to turn them back to young men."

"But she had to go far, far, far north to do it," said Constance. "And not all the tales end—there's Nan."

Rapunzel winced. "She was old Walter's daughter, and she vanished one day. Some time later, a young man—Ned—came through because he needed to speak to a crafty old dragon that was supposed to live in a forest several days from here."

Basil snorted. "No one needs to speak to a dragon."

"Old Walter thought he might. He asked Ned to ask if the dragon knew about what happened to Nan. But Ned never returned."

Silence spread.

"I think," said Florio, "that the easiest one was the tale of the girl who had a star on her forehead. She had been polite to a woman on the wayside and helped her with her child, and got the star on her forehead. So her mother sent her two older sisters after, and they had been so rude that one had gotten a donkey's ears, and the other horns like a bull's. When there was a festival, the mother told the girl with a star that she had to stay home, and put fancy headdresses on the other two. But the girl with a star went anyway, and the king saw her and was taken with her beauty, though she still dressed like a servant girl."

Constance rolled her eyes. "And he said it happened in his great-grandfather's day. It might not even have happened as he said."

Basil said, his voice deep, "Even begging at the corner, I heard these tales. Like the one of how the princess—Snow-White—lived with seven dwarves hiding from her stepmother."

Biancabella's teeth froze in mid-bite. John looked away.

"Have you heard that tale?" said Rapunzel.

"As the fox told, I have—heard—nothing for many a year," said John. "But I heard the tale of Snow-White yesterday."

The fox dropped the bone it gnawed on. "So did I. After Biancabella saved us."

Biancabella pulled away the bread from her mouth. "The mirror helped. And told you."

"And," said the mirror, "perhaps in the morning we might talk of things. An inn where such tales are gathered—perhaps you might help Biancabella as well as she helped you."

Its voice turned grave. "I do not know whether they told you, Your Highness, but the king your father still lives. Unaware that you still live, that you are wed, that you have two children. But—in the morning, we may wish to talk of this more."

Chapter 4—The Circle's Past

Ottoline glared at the castle. Wisps of cloud spread about the moon, like the wild skirt of a dancer who performed in the street for pence, but the moonlight still shone brightly enough to silhouette the towers. In one, a single window glowed, where Augusta Gloriana awaited them all. Like a spy mistress expecting the reports of docile and subordinate spies.

Ottoline, glowering, trudged toward it as if she were indeed a docile and subordinate spy. The dew on the grass heavily wet the hem of her gown. The whole business of a circle—Augusta Gloriana had not *thought* of it before her. Perhaps she could have endured it if only she had remained here while Herbert hunted, but this time—it was insufferable.

She looked over the garden. Perhaps she should insist that Biancabella plant some *useful* flowers. It was not as if Augusta Gloriana had any other use for her. She could set her to scrub in the scullery. It was not as if Biancabella could visit her mother's grave and get help from a tree there. Let alone a red cow could come to her aid from her dead mother. Gardening for her aunt was a mild task.

Then she started. Weeds grew in the garden. Dandelions. Grass in the flowerbeds. Thickets of mushrooms pushing up from the ground so thickly that they uprooted blossoming plants.

Ottoline stopped. Her scowl deepened.

She thought, for a minute, of calling for the servants, but even now it was unwise to make them wonder how she had arrived so near to midnight, though she could beat them all black and blue.

She glanced at the moon. She still had time. She gathered her skirts and darted for a different door and up a different stair.

Moonlight lay cold and white across Biancabella's room. The empty bed did not surprise her. The dust and the cobwebs did. This could not have been a day or two of emptiness, even if roses had yet to engulf Biancabella's tower.

She gathered her skirts and ran with such haste that she reached the tower and Augusta Gloriana before any of the rest. The severe room held a round table with eight chairs, three candles, and arched windows that let in almost as much light as the candles shed. Augusta Gloriana sat there, her head bowed, and looked regal and dignified. She lifted a scornful eyebrow when Ottoline breathed hard.

What a pretense, thought Ottoline. It was Augusta Gloriana who insisted on this dim lighting, as if they were thieves trying to steal the sheets from a bed or impoverished spinners who had to spin at night and could afford no better light. They were a circle of powerful magicians.

She let fall her skirts. "And how is your dear daughter Biancabella?"

Augusta Gloriana paled. "She ran off." She laughed a little. "As if a princess could seek her fortune."

"She could," said Ottoline. "There's many a tale where a princess's mother is wicked, and she manages to wangle herself a prince just the same. It's only keeping watch like a hawk that stops them."

Augusta Gloriana's mouth drew into a thin line.

Ottoline walked into the room and put her hands to the back of her chair. "She could already be married. Have met a prince on the way to a ball and won him over with her beauty and charm."

Augusta Gloriana snorted. "Beauty? She was stiff and wooden. She would win over no one."

"She was already beautiful," said Ottoline, shamelessly. A little exaggeration would give Augusta Gloriana a degree of humility. "I can see that with one eye. And she's going to be more beautiful."

"And," said Mother Magda from the doorway, "she wasn't in rags. You should have kept her in the scullery if you wanted her to be ragged and tattered and filthy on the way." For all her bent back, she walked quite nimbly to her chair. "Run off? They do that. You should have kept her in the tower and not let her gad about like that."

Augusta Gloriana's eyes narrowed.

"Ah, hardly matters," said Rumpelstiltskin, hobbling in.

Ottoline's mouth tightened. As if they could trust him. He had not even told them his true name. He might be more trustworthy than Augusta Gloriana, but that did not say much.

"If she is married, she will have a child. Get the child from her, and that will fix it." Rumpelstiltskin hopped up on his chair. "I will take it on if you wish. If it's too much trouble to lure her husband away and turn her into a duck, hand the whole matter over to me, and that will be the end of that." He smiled. "Best to make preparations now. Find her husband and make him promise. Biancabella might know too much—you were far too trusting of her—but her husband can be tricked."

When Augusta Gloriana only glowered, he shrugged, as the others came in—Mother Trude, Boney, King Drakos, finally Mistress Laurenza—but all of them watched Augusta Gloriana, as if they had heard enough to make the matter clear.

And serve her right, thought Ottoline smugly. So high and mighty as our leader, to fumble so badly.

"She's been eaten up by wolves, most likely," said Augusta Gloriana, straightening to imperious height. "She has never been in the woods before."

Ottoline's eyes narrowed. "Then let us make certain of it. Even if it were not their way to endlessly connive escapes from justice—it will be pleasant to see such an insolent brat attain her much merited fate. What else do you keep the mirror here for?"

Mistress Laurenza nodded, as if they had planned their attack. "It is not like you could teach the mirror the magical arts and have it join our circle, and it is not good at gossip."

Augusta Gloriana was as pale as bone, and Ottoline knew. They should have done—something. Anything. Letting Augusta Gloriana hoard it had been folly.

"It will be a time yet," said Augusta Gloriana.

"She might not have met her prince," said Mother Trude, hunched over like a cat about to pounce. "Yet." Her narrowed eyes moved from face to face. "Cut it off there."

"Or," said Mother Magda, "if she met a witch, perhaps we can help that woman not be a fool, and ensure that she keeps Biancabella bewitched." Then she muttered, "And maybe get her to help us as well, there's so much to do."

"Wise," said King Drakos. "If I had seen that fool Ian coming, he would never have met Vasilisa. Would have taught him not to gamble with his betters."

Gamble and, what was worse, win, thought Ottoline. They needed more in their circle. She could restore a witch's eyesight, perhaps in return for a curse so that the other player would always lose.

"It is clear," said Mistress Laurenza, sounding as if she suffered unending pain and yet would not complain, "that nothing will be done until this matter is dealt with. Unless someone has a matter more urgent than ensuring that Biancabella does not make fools of us all."

Augusta Gloriana did not move.

Boney stood, his knotted muscles shifting. His words ground out. "Show us the mirror, and what it says."

Silence reigned.

An owl hooted.

"You lost it," said Boney, flatly. "You insisted on keeping the magical mirror, and you lost it."

Augusta Gloriana's mouth twitched, though Ottoline thought that the others might have missed the motion. "*You* lost twelve princesses you enchanted without even coming to us to see if we could aid you, and make your spell secure."

"The spell still catches whoever takes the challenge," said Boney. "You!—*you* hogged the mirror so that I could not keep an eye on it. All of us, you keep on as if we were your lackeys, to beg the answers from you."

"How long has it been?" said Mistress Laurenza, her voice full of soft menace. "When did you last have it? You used it to find that prince who could have saved Snow-White—"

"She *says* she used it," said Mother Magda, harshly.

"She broke it," said Mother Trude. "And brought seven years' bad luck on us all."

"As if we could not manage without the mirror at all," said Augusta Gloriana, her face as white as salt, and her words edged with venom. "You admit it when you know I could find that prince without it. To be so helpless and reliant on it but years after I made it—it was wiser of me to keep it here. Who knows what a fool you would be by now if you could consult it whenever you needed?"

"As great a fool as you?" said Mother Trude, and smirked when Augusta Gloriana glared at her.

#

The moon had shifted through the sky, but the eastern horizon showed not even the slightest hint of gray, not even the darkest charcoal. Mother Trude, Mother Magda, and Mistress Laurenza ambled through the garden. Princess Ottoline took off in a great huff.

"She'll be back in time that her husband won't notice she's gone," said Mother Magda, watching her back.

"Would he ever?" said Mother Trude. "With him being so drunk?"

"He'd notice enough that she'd have to scorn him as a drunk," said Mother Magda. "Enough to put her in real danger? Never in her lifetime."

Mother Trude thought a moment, and nodded. Then she snorted. "More trouble than they are worth, these princely bridegrooms."

For a moment, she wondered whether King Drakos had ever considered remarrying, but then, locking all his daughters up in a tower was pointless because they were already swans, and no stepmother could turned them into swans.

After a minute of walking down the path, Mistress Laurenza said, "Believing the mirror was unwise. It was always assuring her that she was the fairest of them all."

"I think," said Mother Trude, picking her words with care, "that the mirror meant within the kingdom."

Mistress Laurenza shrugged. "If the mirror can choose to limit its sphere in that manner, there's no trusting its answers in anything."

"Nothing is perfectly accurate," said Mother Magda, sourly. "But it has been useful. It will be more difficult without it."

"We did manage before," said Mother Trude. She eyed Mistress Laurenza. "On the other hand, you manage only by sticking to your daughters day and night."

Mistress Laurenza sniffed. "I do keep them from running off and making fools of themselves over some paltry prince."

Mother Trude shrugged. "Yet you complain of their—ingratitude."

"Has any maiden or youth ever shown proper gratitude for any gifts showered upon them? Even you, when you tried with that Greta girl—the one that would not let you call her Margarethe."

Mother Trude's face contorted more fiercely than a goblin's. She stamped her foot and flew off into the air.

"What a spiteful thing to say," said Mother Magda. "You have to stick to your daughters day and night."

"And you did not stick to that girl of yours. Who was it? Puddocky, you called her, and you tried to raise her in a village so that your neighbors would warn you if she ran off? And when three princes quarreled over her beauty, you had Ottoline turn her into a frog because you were tired of her?" Mistress Laurenza leaned forward. "I do not tire of the work before me. I still have my three daughters. And even if I turn them into birds on occasion, I do not let them fly off."

Mother Magda glowered at her. "Fly off again."

Mistress Laurenza shrugged and took to the air as a canary.

Mother Magda shook her head and walked onward.

\#

The morning mist spread thin and pale, not veiling the sunrise of cream and gold. Biancabella, coming down the stairs, felt unsurprised to find Constance alone in the kitchen, cooking porridge, and humming over it, and Florio, asleep, curled up by the fireplace.

Constance's voice was little over a whisper. "Are you going to talk about what happened to Florio? With the more you want to talk about in the morning?"

"Yes," said Biancabella, feeling flat. She swallowed. "I can help you ready the inn for guests, if there's things that need doing."

"You're a guest," said Constance.

"I suspect I will ask for rather more than a guest ever asked for before."

Florio snuffled and then slept again.

Speaking more softly, Biancabella said, "I suppose it is traditional for the princess to beg for the position."

Constance snorted. "We're all princes and princesses here."

Biancabella blinked. So they were.

#

Mist burned away, and sunlight made the room glow. She dried the dishes as Constance washed—with an enchanted washcloth that foamed and cleaned.

"It could be better, I suppose," said Constance. "The dishes could leap into the water and cleanse themselves."

"I've only heard of that happening once, when an old enchantress wanted to send the servant girl to the ball," said Biancabella. "She had been polite when getting fire from the enchantress, where the daughters of the house had not."

"I haven't heard of another," said Constance. "And my mother never had to send me to get a coal to light the fire from an old woman's cottage, so I had little chance of that."

"And when she makes you do the chores!" said Biancabella, full of mock horror. She put away a dish. "What will you do when it's time for the ball?"

Constance giggled. "I never heard of an innkeeper's daughter going to the ball."

Biancabella's mouth pursed. She had not, either. Princesses, after they ran away for jobs as scullery maids—noblewomen—peasant's daughters—but not an innkeeper's daughter.

"She could lock me in a tower because someone said I was more beautiful than she was," said Constance, tranquilly.

Biancabella blinked. That bit near home.

"That inn-keeper," said Constance, "always asked her customers if they had seen a woman more beautiful than she was, and they all agreed they had not, and she knocked down their bills, until one said that he had—Valeria, her daughter. So she doubled his bill and locked Valeria up in a tower."

Constance lifted a dish from the soapy water.

"Though it did not work even so well as Mother Trude locking up my mother. Another traveler told her mother that he had seen someone more beautiful, in a tower in the woods, and the mother took her from the tower, and had a huntsman take her out into the woods to kill her—but bandits scared him off, and he fled, thinking they would kill her. They decided to let her be their little sister and keep house for them instead."

"Was that the end of it?"

Constance said, slowly, "No—the bandits did not always stay in the woods, and one day one bandit stayed at the inn and told the mother that he had seen someone more beautiful than she, their little sister who kept house for them. The mother talked with a witch, who took a magical ring and went into the forest, and tricked Valeria into trying it on. Then she fell down dead.

"But after the bandits buried her, one day a prince went hunting. His dogs found the coffin, and he wondered who she was. He thought the ring might tell him, so he took it off, and she woke up again. He took her home and let her stay with his mother, and after a time, he married her."

Biancabella let her breath out and finished the last dish.

"You're all set if a witch turns you into a frog," said Constance. "Outshine the lovely brides of the older brothers with your household skills."

Biancabella put it on the shelf. "You forget, my mother would make the arrow go astray. Or—" She frowned. "Mistress Laurenza would. To make the youngest prince marry one of her daughters instead." She hung up the towel. "At any rate, they would stop the prince from disenchanting me."

"Wise to avoid it then." Constance frowned. "Will you tell of this—Mistress Laurenza?"

Biancabella nodded. "Or rather, the mirror will. It knows more."

"I have to get ready," said Constance. "If we're to sit about hearing the tale, I had best go check the stores now."

Biancabella nodded again. Constance went off. Biancabella sighed, wished for her sewing, and sat to wait. It would not, she told herself, be as long as she had to wait for the evening in the castle of twelve princesses.

Footsteps sounded on the stair. John emerged, yawning.

"There's porridge," said Biancabella.

The fox scampered after John, and Biancabella opened her mouth and shut it again. The bear snuffled and started to stir.

"Porridge," said the bear, sleepily.

"Porridge for me, too," said the fox. Biancabella blinked and went to get bowls. John shoveled porridge into the bear's bowl before he sat to his own. Where he scowled.

"Are we going to get to talk this morning?" said John. "Or afternoon?"

"It might," said Basil, descending the stairs, "be best to do it at once." He smiled. "To get it in the morning."

Rapunzel, following, looked more grave. "Above all else, there is the question of whether we should go to Basil's father. He is old, he is alone, he is grieving for his dead wife and his long-lost son. Only the gravest of reasons would let us leave him to suffer when we could relieve him with a word."

Said the mirror, "The shock of regaining his son would be less than the shock of losing his son again—with his daughter-in-law and grandchildren as well."

Every gaze turned to it. The mirror's expression was serene.

"Already your son fell victim to a curse. Your daughter is ripe for one, and the circle will see no need to be just about such things. And—whenever you have a child, there is danger."

Silence fell. Then Rapunzel blushed and buried her face in her hands. Basil started. Constance squealed with delight, and Florio lifted his furry head to look with interest.

Minutes later, Constance insisted that Rapunzel sit, and Rapunzel looked exasperated.

John sat at the end of the table and said, firmly, "And then it is clear that you are like my niece. Or me."

It seemed to sober them.

"Biancabella fled the castle because she knew of no other way that she might be safe than to put an end to this—circle of theirs. I dare not return for the same reason. You face the same danger if you return to your father's."

He hesitated and glanced at the mirror.

"That would be wisest. You have still left your home," it said serenely. "There is only some safety in recovering from their attempt to kill you forever."

John looked a bit more gray than before.

"How dangerous are they?" said Basil warily. "How long can they imperil us?"

"Long enough," said John. "It is not only that Biancabella is my niece. She had an older half-sister, Snow-White."

He spread his hand.

"You have heard of her. Snow-White grew to womanhood, and was caught by their curses, before Biancabella had even been born. And I was lying dead before *she* was born."

"John," said Basil slowly. His eyes narrowed. "You are—it was the Golden Bird. They said you had—" He shook his head. "They said a lot of folly and nonsense."

"You're Snow-White's uncle?" said Constance.

"One of them," said John.

"It's—been a while," said Rapunzel, sounding dazed.

"Quite some," said Biancabella. "You could tell them what you told me, o mirror. Even John and the fox have not heard that much."

The mirror chuckled. "Tell them—and tell them more. Fear of your mother returning hindered us."

"Tell us all?" said Florio.

"I do not know all. And of what I know, I can not tell all. But I will tell you what I can."

Biancabella shifted in her seat, to see the inn's door. They did not want travelers to see the mirror. Word of it could get back to Augusta Gloriana as word of her daughter had gotten back to that inn-keeper.

She kept half an ear on the talk. Anna, asleep and then threatened with death and devouring. The recapture of the canaries. Ottoline's sad tales, of Leni who went to the ball, and of Anushka and her deer brother—Basil listened to that one scowling the harder by the minute, until finally, as she spoke of Ottoline's being driven out—

"But that was my great-great-grandfather and mother!" said Basil.

"They have done much harm over the years," said the mirror. Basil sank back into silent listening.

It told of Elinor and her death, and how Mother Magda wanted to keep her charges safer—at that part of the story, all four of them, even Florio, stiffened. Rapunzel smiled a little at how Parsley had given even a better reason she had, to bring up her prince.

The mirror went on as if they had sat like stone, and told of how Boney had joined their number, and then Mother Trude.

"Ottoline heard a man curse his seven sons, for playing about when they should have fetched water for their sickly little newborn sister, and so she turned them into crows as he asked. A little while after that, a scrawny little thief came to her because he had been driven out of his village, and she turned him into a wolf that could talk and reason. He was the terror of the forest, until one day he gulped down a little girl whole, and slept after. A woodcutter came by and lopped off his head. That did not please Ottoline."

And then of the three marvelous children, until John spoke mildly at the end.

"Those are my great-grandfather and mother."

Biancabella nodded. She only half-listened as the mirror talked of Rumpelstiltskin, but then the mirror said, "One success went to his head. He wished to have many, many, many children. Mother Trude warned him—told him of a man who wished for that, and found himself eaten out of house and home. He had to go off and steal a dragon's treasure by tricking it into thinking that he was much stronger than it was—he even told it that it had to carry the treasure to his home, because he was ashamed to be seen carrying so little—and then he escaped with his life only because the hungry children descended on him calling for dragon flesh, they were so hungry.

"But that did not dissuade Rumpelstiltskin. He got Ottoline to help. In a city, she turned cats and dogs and pigeons and flies all into rats, which ate the cityfolk out of house and home. Then Rumpelstiltskin offered to lure them away at the price of a copper a tail. He had gotten Mistress Laurenza to make a pipe for that. He lured them all away and came back with no tails. So they tried to cheat him, and he lured away all the children into a mountain—and he outfoxed himself. Many of the children were old enough to get themselves and the others out on the other side, where they settled—and they live there still. But their parents never saw them again."

Basil winced.

"After that, Ottoline decided that she wished to be a queen again. So she trapped a king in the woods and told him that she would help him if he married her.

"He agreed. And he went home and sent his seven sons and one daughter to a tower, to keep them safe and out of her power. But she reproached the king with the cruelty, confining his children like that. As soon as he had them brought back to court, she turned all the boys into swans. Then she accused the sister of bewitching her brothers and drove her off. Whereupon the king died of grief, and his heir exiled her."

For a moment, Biancabella's mouth twitched.

"Did they escape? The princes? The princess?" said Basil, gravely.

"Augusta Gloriana blinded them to each other," said the mirror. "They never saw each other again before they died—the brothers and the sister—and that was the one condition on which the curse would break."

For a moment, silence reigned.

"At least the crow brothers did," said Biancabella.

"Some time after that," said the mirror, "a witch named Zelphine came to Ottoline. She had a son and a daughter, and so thought nothing of marrying a king who already had a son and heir, Sigurd. She would just marry him to her daughter. But Sigurd refused to marry his stepsister. Ottoline turned him into a bear. That did not persuade him to the marriage, and he is still a bear. They could not keep some enchantresses from giving him an enchanted palace there to live, but still he is a bear."

"What will turn him back?" said Constance, looking pale.

Slowly, the mirror sad, "He has to marry a princess, and after that, the curse works out."

Constance raised her head. "I will marry him!" Then she saw all the gazes on her, and faltered. "If he will have me. But—I *am* a princess."

Silence followed.

Basil let out his breath out, slowly. "Better not to say such things, my daughter. Not that you will marry only a king. Or only a man named—" He waved a hand. "—Habogi. Not even to say, humbly, that you will accept whatever husband Heaven sends you, were he a lame dog."

He sat back. The fire crackled. "But said it you have, and bide by it you must, as surely as if you had made the promise when a frog fished your golden ball from a pool."

"And if he will have you," said Rapunzel, tartly, "he must come here to woo you. And marry you before he takes you away."

Biancabella looked at her hands. She gave with one hand and took away with the other, bringing the mirror here.

Constance looked mulish. After a minute, she said, "I *could* have promised to bear him two sons and a daughter with stars on their foreheads and golden chains about their necks. But I didn't."

For a moment, all was silence. Then the laughter rang. Even the mirror smiled.

As it died down, Florio said, "You could have promised a frog to let him sleep in your bed, without so much a promise of marriage," and set them all off again. When Biancabella caught her breath again, she was wondering; it had not been that funny. Constance didn't have sisters to envy her marriage to a king—and she found herself laughing again.

When all was quiet again, the mirror spoke of King Drakos.

"Then Rumpelstiltskin took a notion from them. A king held a ball so that his son could choose a bride, and he helped a poor girl go there—but demanded her firstborn as the prize. When her husband spied to find out the name, Rumpelstiltskin chortled of a false one. Then he had two."

The mirror went on. How Rapunzel's mother had given her up—briefly, but still making Rapunzel pale.

"At another time, two brothers were in the woods. One stole the food of the other, and when the other observed that he was justly called Untrue—he gouged his eyes out and left him. Ottoline saw him—she was looking for beasts that would meet there in midsummer, and talk—and they all laughed heartily at how he fumbled about, when there was a hill on which the dew would cure his blindness so close that he could easily find it, even blind. Ottoline remembered the beasts and had Augusta Gloriana hide them from sight, so the brother never found them, and perished of thirst in the wild."

Then of the Golden Bird—John paled—and how John had died, and his brothers had stolen his reward.

"Rumpelstiltskin took on a new notion. A king went to war, and his wife gave birth in his absence. So Rumpelstiltskin enchanted a pool in the forest, and when the king knelt to drink from it, he caught him by the beard and refused to free him until he promised Rumpelstiltskin what he had and did not know of. And so he had three children in his power."

Then the mirror recounted how Snow-White had been born, and Augusta Gloriana had killed Sophia and become queen, and then had had Snow-White taken to the woods—out of the kingdom, to be safe from discovery—and how the huntsman had spared her, and she had fled far and far, and been found by dwarves. While she lived there, Augusta Gloriana had tried to curse her several times—and Basil had found Rapunzel and they had both been cursed—and finally Snow-White had fallen to a curse that the dwarves could not break.

"Some time after that, a farmer found his field of hay vanished overnight at midsummer. He ordered each of his sons to watch over it. The first year, there was a great rumble and shaking, and the oldest son fled; the second, the same happened to the second; but the third year, the youngest, though everyone thought him a fool and weakling, sat still, and when the noise was over, he found a horse eating the hay. He threw an iron nail over it, and led it off in secret. He did it again, for two more years. The circle realized that something would happen and kept watch.

"A king declared that whoever climbed a glass mountain would win his daughter, who sat at the top with golden apples in her lap. Many tried and failed, but a gallant knight rode up each day. He climbed the first day, a third of the way up, and the second two-thirds, but on the third day, Boney rode up behind him on his haggard but powerful horse, and rode up the mountain, knocked the knight down to his death, and flew off with the princess.

"He found it so pleasant to succeed that he cursed twelve princesses to dance in an underworld dancing floor.

"Soon after that—" The mirror's voice turned dry. "—Augusta Gloriana learned from me of a prince who could save Snow-White from the curse. So she found him, and cursed him into the shape of a bear."

Florio started to nod at that, and then blinked, and blinked again, and stared. Rapunzel and even Basil paled.

The mirror's voice turned still more dry. "It was at an inn called the Four Winds."

Rapunzel covered her face with her hands.

"And so he can't?" said Constance, and her voice broke.

"I did not say that," said the mirror, even more dryly. "She did not ask me whether turning Florio into a bear would work."

"And why would it work?" said Biancabella, her thoughts tumbling over each other. "Anna was freed when Carlos took up the spindle. A bear could do that."

"Valeria had a ring," said Constance, slowly. "That would be harder to take off—but it wasn't that, it was a bit of apple—"

"Which," said the mirror, "needs to be knocked loose. A bear, if anything, could knock it more soundly than even a strong man."

Florio stared out ahead of himself.

"Can he even *find* her?" said Basil, sharply. "Augusta Gloriana would have guarded the place well."

"But not against Biancabella," said the mirror. "She spared Biancabella from such spells in hopes of making an apprentice of her."

Florio slowly stirred, his gaze focusing in the room, and then, abruptly, he swiveled his head and looked at her. Even all the fur could not keep him from looking eager.

"And Florio?" said Biancabella, delicately. "And his curse?"

"It would depend," said the mirror. "If Snow-White would marry him, the curse would break."

Rapunzel let her breath out slowly. "That would be for the best. Perhaps it will help bring us safety by breaking this—circle."

"That would be a start," said Biancabella, sitting up. "But the best place to plan would be—an inn in the woods, at the crossroads, where news of all the world comes."

Rapunzel looked at her.

"And—I think it might be best if I left the mirror here. You can consult it more easily than I can, lugging it about. And it can be hidden in a back corner here."

"That would be wise," said the mirror. "When you and Florio set out."

"No," said Basil, roughly, sitting up. "You have told me of John, but when last you told of him, he was dead—and this fox with him.

And you have told me next to nothing about this Biancabella who lugs you about. We have only the tale of a fox. Is she a young witch out to lure Florio into greater danger? Whom Augusta Gloriana granted powers? You've already admitted that the bear change did not work. It's not like this circle would throw up their hands in defeat at that. The queen would try something else."

With great gravity, the mirror said, "Biancabella is the daughter of Augusta Gloriana, born after she finally managed to curse Snow-White. And she is going to be more beautiful than Augusta Gloriana, and so be fairest of them all."

Biancabella blushed furiously. The copper pots, with their ruddy hue, distorted the color, and the mirror reflected nothing while the face spoke, but she could feel the heat.

"So she set out one day to escape. And prudently took me with her, so I could not tell Augusta Gloriana where she went."

"And she wanders about fighting their curses?" said Basil.

"Why, yes. She had already broken two before she found this inn." The mirror told of the dancing princesses, and of how she had saved John and the fox.

In the silence after, Biancabella thought that though her mother had turned Florio into a bear, it had not been to force him to marry *her*. She said, meekly, "I hope to learn enough to protect myself, and not just run away. So—" She sat up straight. "I will go with Florio."

"It will be a long journey," said the mirror. "Six weeks out, and six weeks back, most likely."

"Speedily a tale is spun," said Florio. "With less speed a deed is done. It does not become a prince to turn back for a mere long journey."

"And," said Biancabella, "we need haste in beginning. Now we can go and return before winter. That will help."

"You are my niece," said John. "And so is Snow-White. It is my duty to protect you twain as best I can."

The fox yawned. "A long journey," it grumbled, "but truly, John, I do not trust dying to have given you more wits."

John blushed a little.

"And—" The fox sat up, and its furry face looked remarkably grave. "—there is no other way. Breaking the curses of the circle, even one by one, is the only way to start whittling down their power."

"There is one other thing," said the mirror. "I can tell you the way to the dwarves such that Biancabella can follow it. But there is a garden and a cottage on the way. Though I can tell you little of it, I think a witch lives there. I can show you—"

For a few minutes, the garden stood before them, with flowers bright and full of bees, and vegetables all about. Fruit trees all but hid the cottage itself.

A charming cottage, thought Biancabella. Then, her mother was beautiful.

A voice rose up front, roughly demanding what kind of service was the Four Winds rendering now.

Rapunzel sprang up, with Constance after. Biancabella went to the wall, took down the mirror, and hid it away in the bag.

"Where will you hang it, out of sight?" she whispered to Florio.

#

The clouds formed a thick blanket of gray, and the air was muggy as they trudged along the forest road. It still formed a path of light, however dim, between two forests of fir, darkness to either hand.

Even after less than a week of doing it, Biancabella felt odd to not be carrying the mirror. She pondered what it had said and sighed.

"Did you notice?" she said. All three of them glanced at her. "The mirror talked about how the rest of the circle does not think that King Drakos and Mistress Laurenza do as much as they should."

"True," said the fox, flatly.

"But not Mother Trude."

John frowned, and said, "No."

"But in all its talk, the mirror did not mention much of what Mother Trude *did*." She spread her hands. "I think that much of what the mirror does not know, or knows but can not say, has something to do with Mother Trude."

John scowled. "How did your mother get the mirror?"

"The mirror's first memory," said Biancabella, "is of being owned by my mother, and it can not see before then, of itself."

The fox sighed. "The last thing we want is for Mother Trude to have the same powers as Augusta Gloriana, to hide things."

"It would explain a great deal, though," said Biancabella.

They fell into silence again. She would have much time to think on this journey, when they had far to go. Florio lumbered on ahead of them. The fox skipped about, chasing an orange butterfly.

John straightened. "I hope that a woodsman does not came with his ax to free us from our companions."

"Oh," said Biancabella, "we don't have a wolf." She glanced sideways at John. "I could sing and see if I attracted one."

His mouth twisted. "Don't trouble yourself on my account."

For some reason, they all laughed and laughed and laughed.

Chapter 5—The Tree In the Garden

"There's the town," said Biancabella. She sounded tired as she looked down into the valley. The road lazily looped about stands of trees, and what looked like marsh, and through farmlands and over a river before reaching the town.

John felt rather tired himself. The time of day could be told only by the length of the shadows, but they had walked for a fortnight already. He wished for the Golden Steed. Though it had borne only Sophia before—

His eyes closed. For a moment, his heartbeat was so hard as to count out the minutes. Always and forever, the thoughts going down the familiar paths, only to remember that that path was cut off, forever.

He opened his eyes again to mark the path. Biancabella, without complaint, walked on. He forced out his breath. His niece. In as much danger from Sophia's murderer as Sophia herself had been. The person seeking out the way to stop Sophia's murderer forever.

The fox looked up at him. He said, "Any reason to be wary of the inns ahead?"

The fox shook his head. "Not that I know of."

John supposed that he would just have to make sure he did not carouse their money away. He slogged on with the rest, though Florio and the fox went ahead. Marshland puddled at the bottom of the hill, with the road muddy and all the footprints, and wheel ruts, filling with water. The iris blooms were long gone, not even the faded rags of petals being left, and the marsh only dreary and green. Except here and there a tree had started to turn vivid yellow or fiery red.

They did have to travel swiftly enough to escape winter, John reminded himself.

Something flew through the air: an arrow, he thought, but not aimed at them. He hurried ahead and came to a small pool with water lilies in pink and gold. He frowned and traced that arc. It should have landed here.

He looked about.

"Biancabella," he called, urgently. She came up behind him, and raised an eyebrow at his anxious tone. "Do you see an arrow lying about?"

"Yes, of course," she said, and pointed.

On a lily pad, a frog sat, as bright as an emerald. It held the arrow in its mouth.

Then her mouth pursed, and she glanced from the frog to him, and back. "Except, you didn't see it—did you?"

"Before?" John shook his head. "Let us wait a bit."

Already, someone came running on the way, and breathing hard. Moments later a peasant lad, pleasant-faced and freckled, though splattered with mud, emerged from the reeds and blinked at them. He carried a bow in his hand.

"I was looking for my arrow—" He looked between them "My mother said we must shoot off our arrows and find a bride that way—"

Biancabella pointed again.

His mouth opened and shut like a fish's. Biancabella pulled back and went on with John. The lad did not glance at them.

Where the road left the marsh, a young man stood at the household of a prosperous merchant, holding the hand of a young woman. All about them, people rejoiced. A young man, John thought, who looked much like the boy in the marsh, and carrying a bow his free hand—as the young woman carried an arrow.

Not much farther on, at a farmer's home, a man, slightly older than the boy and younger than the man at the merchant's, held the hand of another young woman, with his free hand holding a bow, and hers an arrow.

Biancabella sighed. "She can't have cursed those young men, she would not have seen the—*danger* in time. It must have been the frog."

"Let us hope they are more fortunate than the others Augusta Gloriana has cursed," said John.

She smiled at him. "You certainly did your part."

John looked at the dirt and knew it would not hide the heat in his face. It had been little enough, and useless without Biancabella.

She lowered her voice. "John, when you were on your journey, did you spend your money to make sure a corpse was buried? Pay off a debt, or for the gravedigger?"

John glanced sideways at her, and then saw the fox frisking ahead. He opened his mouth, shut it again, and then said, "No, I did not. Whatever he helps me for, it was not that."

Biancabella looked thoughtful for a moment.

"Besides, if the fox were a ghost, why would he have to lie dead until you saved him?"

Biancabella nodded. John let his breath out. He had foiled whatever plan that whatever witch had intended for that frog. He could foil more, perhaps.

It was not as if he had more urgent things to do.

#

By the window, Rapunzel sat, humming, as she sewed new clothes, to fit her husband better than such as he could borrow from his son's wardrobe. Then, she had already sewn a gown of the traditional green, that it might be ready for her daughter.

She did think that the bear might come to claim his bride, thought Constance. She wondered herself. After Florio had left, she had looked at the forest every time she came to the door, or walked by a window, and her heart had pattered with excitement with every glance. She had lost hope as the weeks went by.

"Constance?" said her mother, without looking up. "See if your father is done."

Constance nodded and looked out from the threshold. Her father still chopped wood. Chips flew, and the pile of firewood grew more swiftly than when Florio had done it.

Had done it more than a year ago, before he was a bear. Time was strange. Her gaze passed over the woods. Travelers had gone on, full of tales about how the inn-keeper had married—how fortunate it was that her mother had never told anyone why she asked for tales before Biancabella had asked—and new travelers would not arrive before evening.

But something moved in the trees. She frowned. It was too far off to be clear, but it gleamed golden. A bird? No, it was too large for that. A deer of some kind, perhaps, though the thick trees made it hard to see anything more than its size. She edged out the door, wondering whether the deer would try to lure her father into hunting it.

"Constance!" said her father sharply, but she could not turn away, as it dawned on her that what came ambling through the woods was a bear.

Not Florio. That was clear. This bear's pelt was a rich golden brown. It moved slowly, hesitantly, as if fearful of alarming them, or of the ax kept firmly in her father's hands.

Basil did not lower the ax, but he raised his voice, "You!"

The bear paused.

"Are you Sigurd, who was once a prince and is now the Brown Bear of Norroway?"

"That I am," said the bear, its voice deep, and it bowed its head respectfully. "I have come to woo your lovely daughter Constance."

Then its head swung around to look at the doorway. Constance pulled back and felt her face burn.

#

The bear did not need to warm himself by the fire.

Sigurd, she reminded herself, feeling shy. Sigurd did not need to warm himself by it. Indeed, with the warm day, the cooking had warmed the kitchen past pleasantness for her, as well. They sat in the garden, looking down the western road, where they could just see the sunset in gold and rose, and where her parents could see them from windows.

She sighed, softly, and glanced at Sigurd, and wondered whether he truly wanted to marry a girl so silly than she would promise to marry a stranger on hearing his story. She had just barely heard her mother asking the mirror to be sure of who he was, but after she had heard her father talking to him, and Sigurd gravely saying that he had an enchanted castle in the woods.

"She will have every comfort that befits a princess," he had said, and she had felt her heart pattering the harder.

It pattered harder now. Though, if he was prudent, he would wonder whether she might say that she would accept any child at all, even a pig, or a sprig of myrtle. She looked at her hands. If it happened, she would accept the child Heaven sent, but she would hold her tongue about it, she hoped.

"Do you often get to watch the sunset?" said Sigurd.

"It depends on how much work there is. How many travelers. And I might be working in the garden at the time." She folded her hands about her knees. "I see the dawn more often. It helps that I am wider awake then."

After a minute, the bear sighed. "I wish I could gather you flowers as bright as the sunset." He looked at his paws.

#

The morning was gray, and the travelers had just left, when they wed, almost as quietly as her parents had. Her parents were the only witnesses. Rapunzel fed them a lunch less fancy than the meal they had eaten when the curse on her father had broken—she had less time to cook—but they had not argued when Sigurd had said that he and Constance had to leave after the wedding and the meal.

The air was cool and raw. Constance lay her hand on her husband's furry shoulder as he led the way off. Not down any of the roads, but into the woods.

#

The mirror had spoken of a long journey, and as they walked through pasture and fields, woods and towns, days added up into weeks. She and John talked now and again, and learned at least a little of each other, but at times, Biancabella wished they had bought him black so that he could dress in mourning. At times, she had to remind herself that though Sophia had died before she was born, he had only learned of the death less than a month ago.

As the weeks added up into a month, the road led through forest again. Biancabella looked ahead. They had gone through towns, as the mirror said, but the forest was harder.

With the maples and oaks about, it was a far brighter forest than the one by the Four Winds. Ferns and brush grew thickly under the trees. Streams babbled through it, and pools formed here and there. Sometimes a squirrel scolded them, or a deer bounded across the way, and always the ditches were filled with wildflowers in red and orange and blue.

It held few landmarks. The mirror had not given her any. After the frog, she had tried to look all about whenever she saw anything odd, but never saw more than the first glance revealed. Ducks and their ducklings were only birds, and not even white; trees were only trees; and no hidden cottages held old women who could direct them on their way.

She trudged on. The fox did not frisk about as it had the first day, but Florio and John seemed to still find the way easy.

Wildflowers thickened along the roadside. At first, she thought it formed a clearing like the one where John and the fox had lain, dead. Then she noticed hedges, and past that flowers and plants that did not grow wild. The garden looked so bright.

The fox sniffed the air, but said nothing.

She edged forward. The garden was filled with flowers. She blinked. Entirely too bright. Yellow daffodils and tulips—red, orange, and purple—bloomed in one bed. In another, asters stood violet. Roses were red and pink and white. One apple tree stood in pink flowers and hot pink buds, still furled against the spring; another had bright red apples. Hollyhocks in every shade, and daisies in white and yellow. Crocuses in delicate shades of blue and cream. Sweet rosemary with blue flowers—

It was when she saw the snowdrops in pearly white that she stopped entirely.

"This—" Her mouth shut, opened again, and shut. She sniffed the air, and smelled sweetness that a perfumer would envy.

Then she managed, weakly, "This is a witch's garden. These flowers should not all bloom together. Spring and summer and fall—" She shook her head. At least no plants were dead from winter. Her gaze went over the garden again, and she froze where she stood.

John shifted his weight. "Unwise to linger, perhaps."

"But—I saw, we all saw, this garden in the mirror. Did any of you see that?"

Her finger went out. A rose tree stood behind the cottage. Golden roses opened on every bough.

"If the mirror could not see that rose tree," said Florio, uneasily, "it must be magical."

"Did any of you notice it before I pointed it out?"

Their appalled expressions came before their shaking their heads.

"My mother hides things because they are weaknesses for the circle. Because we could use them."

"It might be true," said the fox, slowly, as if dubious. It eyed the tree, tilting its head to one side.

"It would be best," said John, "to do anything quickly." His voice was grim. "Before the witch notices us. If she hasn't noticed us already."

Biancabella pulled up her skirt to walk over the grass. Even the lawn bloomed with violets both white and blue, and purple gill-over-the ground, and clover both white and pink. The flowers still filled the air with their scent, but as she walked, she smelled something else: pies. She looked. The pastry sat on a window sill as if to cool—seven whole pies—and their scent was alluring.

She looked sharply away. Nothing that allured at a witch's cottage was fit to eat.

She reached the rose tree and looked it over. It looked like the rose trees in the princesses' garden, though even they did not have such rich golden flowers, and its scent was sweeter than any other flower in the garden.

Something glinted. She searched it out among the branches. A chain looped about them, and it bore a lock.

"Who would chain up a rose tree?" she said.

"Someone who wants to master it by magic," said the fox. Its gaze darted about the garden. "It's been done before. I've heard of a spring that was kept back by a chain wrapped around the roots of an oak."

Biancabella, her eyes narrowing, looked about. Something glinted on the back wall: a key hung on a hook. She pointed.

"Isn't that a bit obvious?" said Florio.

She walked over. "Even if my mother did not hide it—and I was the first to notice it—what would the tree do? Uproot itself to get it?" She took the key down. "Besides, if it does not fit, it will be a matter of a moment to discover that."

She reached up toward the lock. After a moment, John stepped over and picked her up, to his shoulder. She leaned forward and tried the key.

The lock slipped open. She pulled it off the chain and into her hand in moments. The links clinked as they fell against the bark. Biancabella held her breath. When a bee buzzed among the roses, she frowned and tugged on the chain. That moved more slowly, the link wreathed round the boughs like a snake, but finally it fell to the ground in a clatter, almost vanishing into the grass.

A note of birdsong sounded. Surprised, Biancabella looked up into the leaves and flowers of the tree. Feathers could just be seen through the leaves—the bird was no larger than a songbird, but it was brilliantly white, so bright it was almost painful to look upon. She could not have mistaken the feathers for the golden flowers.

Hadn't Mother Trude driven off the birds with the cat and dog, when Augusta Gloriana and Ottoline had advised her to?

The bird sang, in glorious and radiant notes.

Her tongue touched her lips. She had set this off. Now, she suspect, it would flow to its ending whatever she did or did not do.

John slowly lowered her, but she did not take her gaze from that bird, still three quarters hidden, as it sang, and it sang, and it sang.

Florio and the fox both looked baffled. John slowly tugged her away from the tree, without looking from the bird.

"Let's go," John said, intensely.

Biancabella started. "This is a spell breaking—"

"All the more reason to leave before it breaks on *us*. What if you broke a spell to keep some monster enchained? You heard the mirror tell of how Boney got loose—I've heard of others. Of a prince who married a golden peahen, but was fool enough to free a dragon, which carried her off." He pulled her about. "You aren't going to save Snow-White if you let a dragon carry you off."

Florio growled a little.

"We need to know more about their magic," said Biancabella. "We can't break the spells in ignorance."

"It's not like the bird will sing us the secrets," said John.

"It's not like we have three magic walnuts," said the fox, "to throw after ourselves if chased. Wisest to not leave our backs open to a danger we do not know. Wisest to watch it through the end, and know."

John opened his mouth and shut it again. His shoulders slumped. Biancabella breathed a sigh of relief and glanced aside. Florio did not look happy, but he did not argue.

Then she heard a clanking noise on the road, and her head jerked around. *Something* was coming.

"Let's not get caught out here," said the fox, and darted toward the orchard. They all hurried after. The trees stood thickly enough, with their boughs low to the ground, to hide them, even Florio. Biancabella tried to catch her breath and looked about. Several trees bore lush, ripe peaches, or pears, or apples. Biancabella looked away, in haste, and saw the others averting their eyes as well. Not quite so obvious as the pies, she thought.

"No windfalls," whispered the fox. She looked down. The grass was indeed free of any fallen fruit.

She picked her way to a tree where the apples were still small and green.

The bird sang on, as if it had not a thought in the world except the song. A cart of tinkers trundled on the road. One drove the cart with its small brown horse, and two walked, because the cart was laden with anvils and heavy hammers, and other tools, and also plowshares and buckets and a hundred other things of metal that clanked as they moved. At least, until the birdsong wound around them, and they stopped to listen.

It sang, and it sang, and then, abruptly, it stopped. Biancabella felt bereft. As for the tinkers, all three burst into tears.

"O little bird," said the driver, "is there anything we can give you for your beautiful song?"

The bird hopped out of the branches, and perched, gleaming white, in the golden roses. "Give me a plowshare," it said, with perfect clarity.

They seemed taken aback at that, but gamely, one went back into the cart and pulled out a plowshare. The songbird fluttered down to the cart and graciously took the plowshare on its neck. Then it flew off, toward the cottage, bearing the plowshare to the roof. The tinkers shuddered and hurried off, their cart making such a clatter that nothing near would have been heard.

The bird settled on the eaves. In the silence after the cart left, there came a grumble from inside.

"Poor old Trude! Poor old Trude!" The face of an old woman peered out the window. Biancabella's breath caught. She had seen that face before, when that old woman visited her mother. She glanced aside, but her companions were intent on the bird and the cottage.

"Do they ever consider me and children? No, it's all that fool Rumpelstiltskin." She shuffled to the door and looked out. "Bet you that Augusta Gloriana blinded them so that the children don't come to me. Makes me and my old bones come to *her*—and she hasn't even got the mirror so we can ask it questions."

Biancabella blinked. Her teeth worried her lower lip. She should have known. Her mother would care more, and learn more quickly, about the mirror's absence.

The bird rattled the plowshare on the eaves, pulling her from her thoughts.

Mother Trude blinked. "Thunder? It didn't look like rain earlier." She inched out onto the porch, scowled at the sky, and then stuck her head out from the porch roof.

The plowshare dropped down on her head, slicing into it and smashing. Mother Trude dropped without a sound, and sprawled on the ground, dead. Blood flowed, slowly, and deeply red, toward a rose bush growing before the cottage.

When the blood struck the root, the bush seemed to swell with growth. The grass grew up, more lushly, and the rose spread out, overgrowing the body, until nothing of it could be seen.

The bird, glowing more brilliantly white, flew down, to the grass strides from where the witch had laid.

Except that as it flew down, its shape grew larger and shifted form, and the brilliance dimmed, and it reached the grass no longer a bird, but a young man. He crouched on the grass, looking at them in the orchard, and stood up: a young man with blond hair like wheat, clothes like any woodcutter, and a square, solid build.

With a look of wonder on his face. He looked down at his own hands, and then back up at them.

Biancabella blinked. A handsome young man, not much older than John—perhaps younger.

Chapter 6—The Witch's Cottage

Golden lamplight glowed in the tower room, and the indirect peach and orange light from the sunset.

"Look," said Esmeralda, flourishing a comb. "Perfectly enchanted! You have only to throw it to the ground, and it will turn into a bramble that will keep anyone from escape!" She grinned. "And, *you*, Aviette, can't even bewitch a candle to light."

Aviette looked away.

"She's *moping*," said Sophronia. "Still wishing we had gotten away when that prince came to pick the oranges when we were enchanted inside them. How ungrateful can you get?"

Esmeralda smirked. "I'd bet she's sure that he would have picked *her* over us. So very sure she's that much more beautiful than we are."

Aviette turned her face away as she felt it grow pink. She headed toward the door, though it offered no more than the orchard and garden outside. Then, Esmeralda and Sophronia had been as eager as she had to escape, but now, it was as if they had forgotten that their mother had held them captive here. And still did.

She reached the gloom and the breezes of evening. Laughter rang from the house, with a cruel edge that made Aviette shudder. Or perhaps their mother no longer held Esmeralda and Sophronia captive, since they wished to stay.

She walked slowly under the orchard trees. Every bough bore both ripe oranges and white blossoms, but she did not look up, at the thick stone walls that encircled the orchard and held not a single door. There was no point, even, to climbing stairs to a tower and looking out. Nothing that she wished to see was closer than thrice ten kingdoms.

What was the point of her mother's enchanting them to see strange and marvelous things if she then never let them see anything outside this stronghold?

Aviette drew in a deep breath, and let it out again. Stop fretting, she told herself. You will only make yourself more miserable. Cultivate patience and hope.

She raised her head. Past the pale orange blossom, the evening star glinted like a gem. For a long moment, she watched it.

Then she started. It was not a scent on the breeze, it was not a change of heat or coldness, it was nothing she could see or hear, but—she leapt to the air, and the canary wings of old returned to her.

Her little heart hammering, she flew up and up. The height of the walls appeared before her, and then below her, and her heart beat as much from fear as from the flight: what if their mother had thought of that, and kept her captive with an enchantment that would catch a bird on the wing?

She flew forward, over the stone. The walls made no more difference than the flagstones of the path. She flew off, over the trees, and wondered if her sisters could hear her still if she sang.

#

Augusta Gloriana sat over her needlework. An intricate pattern of firebirds and gryphons, but a welcome amusement after labor.

"*Now* look what you've done!"

Ottoline stood in the doorway, glaring.

Augusta Gloriana raised an eyebrow.

"As cold as ice you are, but you will be hit as hard as the rest of us." Ottoline leaned forward and spat out the words. "This is all your fault. Mother Trude is *dead*. Utterly dead. Stick stock stone dead. "

Augusta Gloriana did not move. Dead? But that would mean. . .

Ottoline's eyes narrowed. "And all her spellwork is being undone."

"So," said Augusta Gloriana, her voice like ice. "You found the mirror."

Ottoline started.

"You saw how Mother Trude died, and know that somehow I, who have not ventured within three kingdoms of her since the circle met, am to blame."

Ottoline collected herself and stood up straight. The hair fell back from her blind eye. "All her spells are breaking. If you had properly blinded eyes to her cottage, no one would have gotten near enough to harm her."

"I did properly blind them," said Augusta Gloriana. "Did you not hear her complaints that she could not catch children anymore? The spell kept any child away who was too old to be beguiled easily."

"As if you could not bungle them either way!"

"Says the woman who never managed to win herself a king and keep him." Augusta Gloriana lifted her needle. "To leech off my plans and works by seducing Herbert, and then feign you are the equal of me!"

But her thoughts were racing. Dead. She tried to remember whether she had relied on any of Mother Trude's enchantments. She should not have been such a fool. If Mother Trude had been a mother indeed, had had any children, she was just the sort that would let some minx of a girl or pipsqueak of a boy trick her into killing her own children just when she thought she had several plump rascals for her larder. Perhaps she should, indeed, have kept any child at all from seeing the cottage. One of them had no doubt tricked Mother Trude into her own oven or the like. Mother Trude had been a fool not to listen when Augusta Gloriana had warned her of the weakness in the way she blinded people to the cottage.

Now she could only curse herself for her folly, in not seeing that Mother Trude was a weak reed to lean on.

#

The young man looked up, blinked at the sight of them, and took a step. Florio growled a little, and the young man stopped, holding out his hands.

"I—thank you," he said, awkwardly. His gaze moved over them. "Have you—have you seen my sister?"

Biancabella opened her mouth and shut it again.

"She may not be here, she might have escaped with her prince—but they went after her, all those witches—"

"We can search," said Biancabella. "See if we can find her. If she's bewitched—" She spread her hands.

"As I was." He sighed and closed his eyes. His voice was little more than a whisper. "A prince and she ran off. Would that Heaven granted that they escape."

"Who are you?" said the fox. "And who is your sister?" Its tail swished.

"My name is Hansel," he said. Looking at his hands, he added, "Hans, I suppose, now, I was Hansel as a boy." He looked up. "My sister was Greta—we called her Gretel in the day, but she was grown when last I saw her."

Florio lumbered forward. Hans gave the bear a sideways glance, but said nothing.

"Tell us while we search." Florio swung his head about. "Start with the garden."

"Start with the orchard," said Biancabella and started to walk among them. Cherry blossoms, and apple blossoms, and pear and peach blossoms, all fell to the ground from the trees in bloom, and cherries and apples and pears and peaches, from green to overripe, hung from trees. But for all that they ignored the season, they were fruit trees and no more.

A gust sent white petals falling over her. She let out her breath and turned around.

"The truth of the matter," said John, behind her, "is that Biancabella will search, and the rest of us will try to help but know she will have to look again at all we see. It was she who found you as a rose tree, the chain that held you, and the key that unlocked it."

"You never know," said the fox, its hind leg scratching its ear. "Perhaps we can see something."

"How did she—your sister—come to run off?" said John.

Biancabella turned. "That might matter. How did she come to be captive here? At that, how did you come to—" She waved her hand. "—be turned into a rose tree?"

Hans watched her for a moment. Then he let out his breath out. "My sister and I were the children of a woodcutter. One day our mother died. After a time, our father remarried."

Biancabella nodded and moved into the shade of the plum tree nearest to her. She looked up at the fruit, and realized it did not smell half so alluring as it had been before Mother Trude died. How odd. But Hans still told his tale.

"She was not cruel to us, and she did not have a baby that she wanted to inherit our father's cottage, but one day, hunger struck the land. Crops failed, rain made the roads impassable, our father had a hard time selling any wood, even as firewood—there was nothing from the carpenters—and there was little enough to gather in the forest, and peasants came to gather as well.

"One night, I lay awake, I was so hungry—I heard them talking. Our stepmother said that our father had to take us out into the forest and lose us. If they did not have to feed us, they might live, but if they did, we would all perish.

"So I slipped out into the night, and at the brook, I took up the white pebbles it ran over. The next day, when our father cheerfully told us that we were to go with him into the forest, as soon as we were out of sight of the cottage, I started to drop them, one by one.

"Finally, our father told us to stay in a clearing while he cut wood. We could gather flowers and play, he told us. I drew Gretel over to the other side, and told her the truth. Gretel thought that he might regret doing it, so we waited some time, but as it started to grow dark, we followed the pebbles back.

"So that night, our stepmother told him to do it again, and go farther this time. Then she bolted the door. I could not get out to get the pebbles. I tried to use the bread that our father gave up, leaving crumbs, but when the time came to return, the birds had eaten them up. So we were trapped in the night woods."

Biancabella looked at the sunlit trees all about them, remembered the fir forest about the Four Winds, and shuddered. Her gaze went over an apple tree, and she blinked. The red apples seemed to be turning back to green. Then Hans's voice snatched her attention again.

"Gretel shared her bread with me, and we tried to find our way back, or anywhere, in fact. We wandered and wandered, and drank from springs—at least they did not warn us that drinking would turn us into beasts, and it didn't—and saw nothing of anything human until we came to a cottage. That cottage."

Biancabella nodded. Some corner of her mind noticed that petals no longer fell and wondered where all the already fallen petals had gone, but she thrust aside the thought.

She looked toward the gardens, and gasped—loudly enough to startle Hans into silence. Crocuses and snowdrops had vanished, not only the early fading flowers, but the greenery that lingered later in spring. Asters, no longer blooming, bore not even buds. Irises were thick green stands of leaves, with one iris's withered petals barely showing their purple color. A few roses were in full bloom, and some were wilting, but most had passed. Her gaze took in withering and vanishing flowers, but if she had just come here, she would not have noticed anything odd in the flowers that bloomed so seasonably.

Warily, she looked back at the cottage.

"The pies," she said. "They are *gone*."

Hans opened his mouth, and shut it again. "So they are," he said, sounding strange. He shook his head. "They were loaves of bread when we came here. We were so hungry that we just ate, without a thought whose bread they were."

He let his breath out, and looked over a bed of irises.

"I think," said Biancabella, diffidently, "that the pies we saw were enchanted. Perhaps the bread was, too."

Hans nodded, slowly.

"Let us perhaps go a little closer to the road, away from her work," said the fox. "Then Hans can tell us with more safety."

They shifted about. Biancabella saw nothing more about the cottage or the garden changing, and none of the others spoke of such a change. They all turned to Hans, who went on.

"And we heard a voice from within calling, 'Who goes nibbling on my loaves of bread?'

"Gretel called back, 'Heaven's child wandering wild,' and Mother Trude came out and told us to come in and eat soup and cheese and have jam and butter for our bread. She fed us both more food than we would eat in a month at home.

"Then she caught me and put me in a cage. She worked Gretel at chores and fed me up, and told me every day that she would eat me as soon as I was fat.

"Gretel found me a bone, and I held it out every time Mother Trude demanded to test my finger, to see how fat I was, but one day, Mistress Ottoline came. She was going to help a stepmother turn her willful stepson into a bear—but she stopped, and told Mother Trude I was fat, and that they should kill and cook me, so Gretel could not interfere.

"So they did."

He said the words flatly, before a rosebush of blood-red roses. None of them spoke, though John's hand went to his side, where his brothers' swords had struck.

Minutes later, Hans spoke again.

"Gretel wept for me and gathered up my bones, and buried them in the garden. When a rose tree sprang up, Mother Trude put a chain on it, and then put the key on the wall—where I could see it, as you saw—and Gretel never noticed it. She wept under the tree, when she dared, as Mother Trude kept her drudging away, but one day, when Mother Trude was about some business, a handsome prince rode by. He commented on a maiden so brave as to live in the depths of the forest, she told him she had no choice and so merited no such praise, they talked—she warned him that if Mother Trude caught him, she would make him do impossible tasks and then kill him when he failed, there was little she could do to help him, and he was fortunate that he was not bound to come here—he asked how he could leave so lovely a maiden helpless in her power—and finally she and he ran away."

Hans let out his breath. "I was glad—briefly—and it seemed briefer to me—being a tree. But when Mother Trude returned, she called for Mistress Ottoline, and—" He waved his hand. "—others."

"Perhaps we can lay a name to them after," said the fox.

Hans looked intrigued for a moment. Then he said, "They chased after, but they never mentioned in my presence whether they had caught them, or what they had done." He looked at the cottage, and his face showed only sorrow. The words inched out. "I think they did. Mother Trude seemed smug, after. That is why I need to search this place; she might have hidden her."

"And," said John, "you were a rose tree ever since?"

"Yes," said Hans. "It wasn't like being a boy. Time was not the same. I do not know how long it was. Perhaps Gretel and her prince did escape, and marry, and live out their lives, and are long dead, with their great-grandchildren living in his kingdom in peace and content." His voice held no hope at all.

"Did Mother Trude do other things since then?" said Biancabella diffidently.

"Only once that I remember," said Hans. "A girl came here, with a singsong about how they couldn't tell her what to do. Except that as she came in, Mother Trude was working magics. There was a green man, a black man and a red man on the porch, and she crept up—and Mother Trude caught her. And questioned her. She told the girl the black man was a charcoal burner; the green, a huntsman; the red, a butcher—but when she said she saw Mother Trude all afire, Mother Trude said, 'Ah, you've seen me in my true form' and turned the girl into a log of firewood, and threw her onto the fire."

After a moment he added, in the silence, "And admired the sparks."

He looked at the cottage wall. "I don't think we will find my sister."

"Perhaps we will learn something instead," said John. "It will be of aid to us. Particularly my niece." Hans blinked. John waved at Biancabella, Hans's gaze turned on her, and his face grew thoughtful.

"First of all, the garden," said Biancabella. "There were many changes, but it would be like them to cast two or three different spells over it, only one from Mother Trude herself."

The garden itself was flat, and took only a glance. The fence about it took only a brisk walk. The orchard took only a few minutes, for all the trees in it, and she noticed nothing except that now there were windfalls.

She did not pick any of the ripe fruit. Neither did anyone else. When the search was done, they faced the cottage again.

"We can't tell you all my story—let alone all our stories—in the time it takes to search the cottage," said Biancabella, "but we can start." She sighed. And started the tale with the mirror.

Searching the cottage was easier than the garden, and she went on with the tale as they did so. The cupboards were bare of food, to her relief. One held blankets, but shaken out, they revealed nothing more than ordinary blankets, no finer than a peasant might have.

"No moths at least," said Hans.

They came to the cellar door as she started to tell, briefly, of the dancing princesses. She hesitated as John pulled the door open. Then she blinked at the glitter.

"A root cellar without roots," said Florio. Which was true enough. Gold and silver aplenty, though. She turned her face away.

"It's not doing anyone any good there," said John. "What we do not need it to stop the circle, we can give to the poor."

"Silver," said Florio. "It raises fewer questions."

"Mostly silver," said John. "If we need the gold, we will have to have a story for it."

Biancabella went with them to fill her pockets, and turned her attention back to the story. She explained John, and then they came out to the porch again, with the sky ablaze with red and orange over the remnants of garden.

Florio sniffed the air, and then, with a growl, pronounced, "We should stay the night. It is a witch's cottage, but she is dead, and the night is filled with dangers."

"What?" said the fox. "You don't think that money will fall from the stars for us?"

Florio gave him a baneful glance. The fox looked impudently back.

"No," said John. "You would have a little problem giving the clothes on your back to beggars on the way."

The fox snorted and turned to the door. They gathered in the inner room, and no one suggested lighting a fire. John sat down beside Biancabella, and Hans, carefully, sat on the opposite side.

The fox sat up. "Could—did you remember being a boy? when you were a rose tree?"

Hans scowled. After a moment, he said, "I think so. But I thought everything vaguely—even when I knew what the key meant."

After a minute, John went on, "When Biancabella rescued me, we went on."

The night darkened as they, trading off, told him the tales. Hans asked no questions, and only spoke once, when the fox told how the huntsman had saved Jill.

Then, though he was a dark shape in the shadows, he said, "He took her to the same kingdom that I came from. She and he lived in the forest nearby."

The fox hesitated at that. John took up the story. Until finally, their stories arrived at the cottage with them and trailed off into minutes of silence.

"Once upon a time," said the fox, brightly, "a boy gathered wood in the forest, and he found a golden key. He thought where there was a key, there was a lock, and searched for it. He found a silver box, and then he found its lock, and he put the key in it, and he started to turn it." It lay down its head on its tail and declared, "We must wait until he has completely turned it, and we will find what treasures are in that box."

Soft chuckles echoed.

Biancabella leaned back and yawned. They had merely brushed on the mirror's tales, the history of the circle. Silence followed for a long time.

"I would like to go with you," said Hans. "I might be of aid in reaching your sister and niece. And—I might learn of my sister. If you will have me."

"Perhaps," said the fox, no more visible than the rest of the room, "we can trick the knowledge out of them. It's been done before."

"Or perhaps your mirror can tell me, after."

They had already told him how the mirror had seemed not to notice what Mother Trude did, so Biancabella said nothing.

After a minute, she thought that perhaps hearing of him would help the mirror remember things.

Chapter 7—The Dwarves' Cottage

The cave was a bit snug, but that was hardly a fault in a home. Rumpelstiltskin sat back on his chair, carved into the wall, and as elegant as a throne. Good solid walls of clay earth. Tree roots sticking out here and there—things that no one but a fool would mind. Why, his three boys all slept soundly on a bed of dried ferns, with their little wooden toys to hand, not even much resembling the soldiers and horses the boys called them! He could only laugh at his three silly sisters, who did all the work for nothing more than being called Auntie on the wedding day. No lunatic luxury needed, not at home.

One boy, the youngest, stirred in his bed and rubbed his eyes. Rumpelstiltskin raised an eyebrow—how odd—and waited for him to go back to sleep. The boy raised his head instead, looking about. Rumpelstiltskin scowled, and the boy started to wail. The earthen walls dampened the noise, but it did not stop, and the other two stirred. The middle one looked blank, and the oldest started to shriek that he was hungry, hungry, hungry—

How absurd! Mother Trude could never have stayed as one of their number if her spells did not work. Rumpelstiltskin harrumphed and sat back. They had not been hungry like that for years.

The boys did not stop their cries. The middle one started to weep, silently. Rumpelstiltskin felt just a little cold.

#

The morning air was chilly as Constance and Sigurd walked steadily through the forest, almost as dark from the oaks and their thick leaves as the woods near the Four Winds had been from firs. Constance kept one hand on Sigurd's furry shoulder. A squirrel ran through the dead oak leaves. The way was harder when the brush was thick, and she could not even see whether it was a squirrel rather than a deer or a wolf.

Though the forest seemed uncommonly full of beasts and birds.

A scarlet bird flitted across their path. "This is a strange forest," said Constance.

"It's—" Sigurd sounded more reluctant to speak than she had ever heard him. "It's enchanted."

She tilted her head to one side as she considered. "The park attached to the castle?"

After a moment, he shook his head. "The kingdom."

She blinked.

"It was not just the castle that she enchanted. It was all the kingdom."

"Did—what did your father's subjects *think* of that?"

Sigurd sighed. "I do not know. I could tell you that she did not ask me—she did not." His head sank. "But—I hear the tale of Princess Anna, and what happened to her kingdom, and I do not know whether I would have objected if she had asked me."

Constance swallowed.

His voice turned soft. "You can break the curse for them all, Princess Constance."

They walked on, and on, but she had not found her voice again when they came around a bend. A wall stood there. She thought the stone was of a pleasant gray, but rose vines so overgrew it that she could not be certain, and all the rose vines were overladen with red roses.

A gate stood in the middle, of wrought iron, with a gryphon and a unicorn facing each other. The air grew sweeter, as if in a perfumery, and the gate swept open before them, to a blare of trumpets. And she heard—something. Like a cheer. Or perhaps an echo of one.

No one was visible beyond the gate. A green lawn spread out, set with flower beds of roses and lilies and a thousand other flowers. A castle stood beyond. There she could see the stone was gray, though the vines grew over much of it, with snow-white flowers.

She walked slowly down the main path toward the castle door, as if they were watched from every side. Perhaps they were.

The double doors opened as they approached.

Sigurd said, low and fast, "They would be ashamed to offer you dinner while leaving you so travel-stained."

Constance nodded and let the opening door lead her off to a bath larger than some forest pools, but warmer than sunlight and summer could make one. Clothes lay ready when she finished: a gown as brilliant as an amethyst, set with lace, and a perfect fit to her form, making her wonder uneasily as how swiftly enchanted seamstresses could work. Her clothing from the journey had vanished. Perhaps they had used it to judge her measure.

Doors opened again to show her a dining room, far smaller than a great hall, and set for dinner. Her tongue touched her lips. Roast birds and fresh fruit—she had seen no orchard, but they must have one—and white bread with honey and jam and butter. Wine and wine cups.

"They did not stint on dinner," said Sigurd, his voice a deep rumble.

Constance nodded, and they went to eat. For all the hours they spent walking, it was still full day, and they could eat at leisure.

As they finished, she heard music. Her mouth twitched. There would be no masque, and no dancing, for this royal wedding, but they could play music.

As the sky flamed with rose and peach clouds, doors opened again, and she and Sigurd parted. A nightgown in white, and the bedchamber with the hangings pulled back on the vast bed, show-ing the snow-white sheets. She crept in, and the door closed, and for the first time since she set foot in the castle, she thought she was cold.

The door opened again.

Sigurd's voice was light. "This curse, it seems, will break bit by bit."

Her tongue touched her lip. Sigurd's voice, but it could not have come from so high unless he stood—on his hind legs, or just his legs—

She was sitting up without realizing that she had sat.

"No, don't look," said Sigurd, urgently.

She closed her eyes in all haste. Her tongue touched her lips. No candle, no lamp—no rummaging about the room to see if he had left his bearskin there—

"So this," she said, "is not one of those curses where you and all your people will be lions, or bears, by day, and men and women by night?"

"No," he said, sadly. "The enchantment still holds for the rest, and we may not wake and walk about by candlelight. Still—" His voice took on a happier note. "—it has broken in part."

She felt the shifting of the bed from his weight, and then heard him pull the curtain shut, before a hand, rather than a paw, touched her arm.

#

Through the cottage window, the morning was still charcoal gray when the fox snuffled at her face, waking her. Biancabella did not argue, only pulled straight her dress and walked out.

The rose tree had withered overnight. Petals and leaves, both shriveled and brown, lay scattered over the grass. Biancabella shud-dered. The garden had sprouted weeds, as well.

For a moment, she remembered her own garden. She swallowed. Weeds would be growing now. She could only hope that the gardeners worked diligently without her oversight and tell herself that the rankest garden could be reduced to order later, if only she kept free of her mother.

Hans, coming out the door, gave the dying tree a glance. Within moments, they walked down the road from Mother Trude's cottage, into the still thick mist. It did not slacken, and muffled the path ahead, and behind.

Hans looked more easy as they walked farther, and farther. When he glanced back, and the cottage was gone from sight, he smiled. They walked on, into a hollow, and he looked about.

"Do you prefer to walk along in silence?" he said, sounding hesitant.

"As long as you don't mind if you attract a wolf," said the fox, pertly, "you may sing as you please."

"I don't have an ax to drive even you off with," said Hans, gravely. Biancabella smiled, and he began to sing.

"All in a wood there grew a fine tree,
The finest tree that ever you did see,
And the green grass grew around, around, around,
And the green grass grew around."

His song wound on with the road, and Biancabella thought that such a fine voice—it was no wonder that he had sung so sweetly as a bird.

Light slowly increased, the gray lightening into yellow and cream, and the mist thinning to show trees farther and farther off. Hans paused as the sky turned blue.

They climbed a steep hill. The other side descended into farmland, and the road led to a great stone bridge, with mountains beyond the valley. Biancabella's heart hammered. She looked across the valley, taking in little despite its width, to the other side, where distance blurred much, but not that the farms did not continue into the hills.

"I think," she said, delicately, "that that, beyond, is the forest. The mirror's forest."

It looked like little more than darkness about the rising mountains, but the forest where the dwarves lived was already in sight. She drew a deep breath to try to calm herself.

"Is there a village with shops?" said Hans. "We may want to spend some of this silver, or even gold, before we go into the forest again."

"On food, perhaps," said John. "But what else would we need?"

"A magical ship to bear us over land and sea," said Florio.

"Seven league boots," said Biancabella dryly. "Except that I don't think they make them in sizes suitable for bears and foxes."

"Magical beans to make a bean vine that goes up to the sky!" said Florio. "All we need is a cow to trade for them!" He waved a paw. "I do not know what we would find in the sky to get us to Snow-White, but if beans fell into our hands, we could climb to the sky."

"Which would betray us to the circle," said John. "More spectacularly than the others, but then, they would betray us as well. We should not act as if they were blinded to us."

Silence followed. After a minute, a bird, hidden in a tree, sang a few notes.

"Perhaps dying taught you a thing or two," said the fox.

"If they offer something that allows people to see hidden things," said Biancabella, slowly, "we can buy that. If we have gold enough."

"Water," said Hans, firmly. "Water is more important than food, and we can not trust that we will be able to drink from springs. At least, not safely. If Ottoline turns the water so that it will turn us all to deer—no, let us buy bottles for water, and fill them."

"And a sword," said John. "If we can find one."

They all looked at him.

He gestured at his own. "Little help against treachery, but some, and if we find a village all hung in black because a dragon has demanded the princess be sacrificed to it—" He spread his hands. "Even with the help of a bear, two swords are better than one."

"An ax might be better," said Hans.

John opened his mouth and shut it again.

"When my father was young, there was a witch-wolf in the woods. Ate people up, and deer, and cows—but he caught it one day, sleeping off one meal, and he cut its head off with no more than the ax." Hans's mouth twitched. "Indeed, when the wolf had gobbled up the little girl—that was the meal after which it slept—it had eaten so fast that my father was able to chop it open and let her out again. She lived."

Ottoline's, thought Biancabella.

"A battle ax," said John, "is much like a wood ax. But you can't have mastered a wood ax well enough to fight when you were that young. It takes strength. And—I can not teach you how to fight with an ax."

A bird trilled merrily from a tree.

Hans sighed and ran a hand through his hair. "I wonder what they will think of a man dressed like a woodcutter, carrying a sword rather than an ax."

"Why," said Florio, "that you are a prince whose father ordered a forester to take out into the forest and kill—because, after you had gotten him the water of life that would save him, your treacherous brothers had stolen it and replace it with salt water, so he thought you had tried to kill him—but the forester could not bring himself to do it, so you traded clothes and fled for your own safety."

Hans looked at him. "And why am I traveling with another man who not only carries a sword like a prince but dresses like one—though one who dressed for the road?"

"Ah—" said the fox. "He's your loving half-brother who warned you that your evil stepmother was out to kill you, and so you both ran away to seek your fortunes."

"After my father tried to kill me?"

The fox scratched itself behind the ear. "I'm sure it all fits together *somehow*."

"A sword," said Biancabella. "Also a pack, so that you can carry some food, in case that you alone escape bandits. And, at that, a needle and thread, and scissors, and some cloth, for me. I'll pick the cloth. I will need several pieces. Though it should not need gold, only silver at most."

#

When they finally left the city with their goods—finding the merchants had eaten more time than the haggling even—the way ahead seemed farther than the way in, even to just reach the woods. For a moment, Hans cursed himself for not even asking about the distance before pledging to join them.

Then he forced his breath out. What else, after all, could he do with his time?

John straightened, looking ahead, and then point out the inn, The Rooster and the Rose, on the roadside. "We should stay there rather than go on."

Hans glanced back. The city still stood, clearly visible, and the sky was only starting to be touched with yellow and pink. "Despite that time haggling, there's still daylight. Is there no inn ahead?"

"What's the point of haggling over that sword if you don't learn to use it?" said John. "You'll probably outdo me if you work at it, since you are taller and heavier, and we might be attacked by bandits."

"Or a dragon," said Hans, considering the sword. "Though you seem fearless for a man treacherously attacked."

John shrugged. "If I wish to treacherously attack you, I could—tell a king that you had promised to rescue his daughter who had vanished without a trace. Or I could eat up your food in the night."

Hans laughed.

#

Behind the inn, in the sunset, John stood by Hans, showing him the proper grip on the sword.

Biancabella, sitting by the window, looked from the men and at the cloth on her lap. Neither Hans nor John had any clothes but what they wore. They had bought some ready-made, but—she took another stitch—it was a poor princess who could not sew more cheaply, and a better fit, than buying new.

At least, she told herself, she didn't have to start with thistles and ret them, and spin them, and weave them, before sewing, while keeping silent the whole time. For all that they had suffered so much else, Hans and John had not been turned into swans.

She glanced over. Hans stood with the sword in hand, and the sunset gilded him. John started to shift his feet. Florio and the fox came about the inn. They sat to watch, but she looked back at her sewing.

#

Though every night they stopped early for John to teach Hans sword craft, three days' journey brought them to the rising road.

In the gray of the morning, the last innkeeper told them they did not want to go up in the mountains.

"They're miners," he said, as Hans hefted up his pack. "Not smiths. They won't forge you iron shoes to climb over a glass mountain."

"Is there a glass mountain to climb?" said Biancabella, taking up her own pack.

"No," said the innkeeper, "so you really don't need them."

Florio came up beside Biancabella, and snuffled at the dew-heavy air. The innkeeper turned away. Biancabella looked down the road. She could make out the trees, if not very distinctly. Some had turned golden with approaching fall, reminding her to not dilly-dally.

"We shall have just have to make sure that none of us are beaten half to death and thrown into a ditch," she told Florio. "There being no smith to rescue us."

#

The hillsides grew mainly pine. Roots tangled over large stretches of gray stone, and needles, caught in hollows, had turned brilliant amber and filled the air with their scent. The slopes were steep enough that Hans had not tried to sing but spared his breath for climbing.

Streams babbled down the slopes. "Who drinks of me shall be a bear—who drinks me shall be a wolf—who drinks of me shall be a hawk—who drinks of me shall be a panther—"

After the twelfth, Biancabella said, "Shouldn't *one* of them be a deer by now?"

Laughter sounded, briefly.

Hans looked up the slope, and said, "I think there's an actual road up there, not just a track like this."

Biancabella looked up, eagerly, groaned at the sight of the slope, and climbed again where the pines were thickest. The roots spread far and wide enough that only in a place or two did she need John, or Hans, to help her over a steep gap. But, after the hardest climb, it leveled out, into a road with deep ruts from wagons. The mountain climbed steeply again, behind it, but she studied the road.

"Heavily laden wagons," she said, after catching her breath. "Miners have those when they come to pay taxes, or to trade." She looked up the slope. When the fox started up the road, she followed.

The road went up, and up, to windswept heights. Trees to either side grew twisted, where the wind had blown them, but then, as the road curved into the slope, a cottage appeared ahead. Snug, stout, and well-built from wood, with a vegetable garden about it. Biancabella looked it over. Then she hesitated. Seven dwarves, the mirror had said, and they had taken in her half-sister. It would be discourteous to not speak to them.

Besides, they could show her where the coffin lay.

If they were home. They were miners, after all, and it was not late in the day.

John went up to the door and knocked. No one answered.

"Nothing to do but wait, then," he said, turning away. "I do not think we want to fall asleep in their beds."

Biancabella let out a little laugh. "No. Perhaps we can look about a bit, if we do not pry."

Something glinted through the trees. Biancabella frowned. It did not move, like a tool in the hand of a miner returning home, but the trace of a track went through the forest, where feet had beaten the needles into the gray and dusty earth. She walked toward the glint. The trunks often hid it from view, but the track did not break until it led out to a cliff, open to the sky and sun.

On the rocks, a crystal coffin lay. Inside a lovely young woman lay, her eyes closed, her hair as black as ebony, her skin as white as snow, her lips as red as blood.

Beside it stood a little man, as brown and gnarled as the tree roots, glaring at them.

Biancabella curtsied, deeply. The wind tugged at her hair and skirt as she straightened. "Good evening, uncle. My name is Biancabella. I have come in search of my sister Snow-White."

The dwarf froze as if he had been turned to stone. Her voice came back in faint little echoes.

John came up beside her and bowed deeply. "And I am her uncle, John—their uncle, I suppose—and I came in aid of her search for my niece."

He gave the coffin a sideways glance. Biancabella wondered how much Snow-White looked like her mother.

Before the echoes died away—"A likely story," said the dwarf, his voice sounding creaky, his gaze fixing on Florio.

Florio reared up on his hind legs and did something like a bow. "And I am Florio—a prince, cursed to this form by her wicked stepmother, who thought it would keep me from rescuing Snow-White." He sank back to all fours and lowered his voice. "It won't, and that is all I seek. I have no intention of accusing you of coveting my treasure."

The dwarf's mouth twitched so faintly that Biancabella thought she might have dreamed it. But the dwarf said, "My brothers will have my head if I just let you do as you please."

"Then," said Florio, sitting back on his haunches, "we will wait. After the length of our journey here, to wait until sundown is no great time—and still less next to the time she lay here."

The dwarf pointed to a spread of stone, paces away.

"Wait there," he said.

Biancabella nodded and obeyed. To her relief, it offered shelter from the wind, and a place to sit.

"A pleasant rest!" said the fox.

#

The sunset, gleaming orange and crimson, cast long shadows. The dwarves came, slowly, through the woods, and the shadows distorted their appearance still further.

Still, when they, all gnarled and bearded, stumped out onto stone and the clear light, Biancabella knew she could never have taken them for humans. Some were darker or lighter, and others more ruddy, and all of them looked more earthy than any human being could be.

They conferred together in low voices that did not echo at all. When they glanced over, Biancabella swallowed.

Finally, one growled that they could come into the cottage, where they could speak, and decide what they would do in the morning. She rose with the others, but as they returned by the track, she could not help noticing they carried their picks and their shovels with them.

Behind them, Snow-White's coffin gleamed like a jewel in the sunset.

#

The cabin roof was—barely—high enough to let John and Hans stand, and both sat on the floor as soon as they could. The room glowed golden from the polished wood, and the lamps set all about. The dwarves served them bread and honey and cheese, and mugs of cider, and their gnarled bodies and faces looked all the less human for the way they sat on chairs like any human at home.

Biancabella sat with her arms wrapped about her legs as Florio spoke of how he heard of Snow-White, and how he learned that the curse on him was to prevent his rescuing her—and how the mirror had revealed that the curse would not do that.

"Huh," said one dwarf. Biancabella thought he was not the one who had kept guard. "A likely story."

"When," said the fox, looking up from bread without honey, "is the story of how a curse is to be broken *likely*? They do not *like* likely ways. It breaks too easily that way. They even spread false tales. Like kissing frogs when what the frog needs is to be thrown against the wall."

"Or have its skin burnt," said the dwarf. "Except that may kill it."

The fox nodded. "But that's more commonly princesses. Princes turned to pigs, that's when burning their skin may help."

The dwarf snorted.

Another one spoke—not the guard, his beard was too reddish. "If she can be saved here, there is no need to ask. We can watch by the dawn."

#

With the bright dawn, over the pine-covered mountains, thin clouds and the sky were touched with pinks and creams and shades of delicate orange. A breeze came up from the valley, and the air was icy chill. Biancabella pulled her mantle closer. She would not have dreamed it could be this cold in the summer.

Hans shifted to stand between her and the breeze. She smiled at him.

Florio, his fur gilded by the sunlight, stood with the dwarves, grumbling and skeptical, who kept eyeing him. He ambled about the coffin, standing between it and the cliff edge. He barely fit there, looming over the crystal, and with the sunlight behind him, he was a dark shadow, glowing about the edge where the sunlight passed through his fur.

Biancabella bit her lip. The mirror had been her mother's, it had told her mother over and over again where Snow-White was, without it Snow-White would never have lain in this enchanted sleep, and they had no reason to believe that she could be woken, and by this way, except that the mirror had said so—

Florio's heavy paw swept out and pushed the coffin off the rocks. It fell off the rock and hit the ground, cracking. Snow-White's body shifted forward, falling.

Biancabella's breath caught.

Snow-White's arm shifted. After a moment, she coughed—and coughed again. Her breath came slow and ragged, and a minute later, she opened her eyes and looked about in a daze, and then, as she sat up, in wonder.

Biancabella blinked. Her gray eyes—Snow-White's eyes were as gray as her own.

Snow-White's gaze settled on Florio, and she did not move.

"Much has happened," said the red-bearded dwarf, stepping forward. "Come inside to hear the tale."

"Who—who are they?" said Snow-White, looking from Florio to the rest of them.

John bowed. "I am your uncle, John. This is your sister Biancabella." Snow-White blinked and eyed Biancabella uneasily. "As for the rest of us—the dwarves are wise. It is too long a tale to tell on a cliff, in the cold."

#

Snow-White sat on the other side of the hearth from Biancabella, and her gaze flickered anxiously from John to Biancabella and back. Florio sat by the door with remarkable calm. From the back wall, Hans watched. The fox lay before the fire in apparent perfect contentment.

Biancabella folded her hands in her lap, as if she recited a lesson for Lady Regina.

"It began with old Meg," she said. "She fussed over me and told me that I would be more beautiful than Queen Augusta Gloriana."

Snow-White shifted. "Meg? There was a nursery maid of that name at the castle."

"Oh, yes," said Biancabella looked at her hands in her lap. "She didn't talk of you much. Except when I got too grubby in the garden, and she said that you didn't get into the dirt so much."

Snow-White giggled, and then looked startled.

Biancabella plowed on, with consulting the mirror and setting out, finding the inn and learning about Florio.

Snow-White's head turned. Her gaze settled on Florio and did not stir as Biancabella told how they had come here and disenchanted Hans on the way.

Biancabella finished the tale, and minutes inched by. She fought down the impulse to say something—anything—in the silence.

"There's much that you are not telling me," said Snow-White.

"Much," said Biancabella. "I could tell you much more of what they did, to many people, and how they joined forces with others—and how Mother Trude turned a little girl to a log of wood and burned her on the fireplace."

Snow-White flinched.

"But I thought it best to save those hours for later, and tell you of Florio and yourself, and myself and John." She leaned forward, resting her head on her folded arms and so on her knees. "And Hans, since he is here, even though his tale only brushes on yours."

Snow-White let her breath out slowly.

"And the fox, of course."

The fox rolled over.

Snow-White's gaze moved from one of them to the next, until finally her gaze settled back on Biancabella.

"What do you think, o most gracious Clear And Pure White As Dazzling Snow?" said one dwarf.

Snow-White paled but sat upright, folding her hands in her lap. "I think that I will go to speak with this mirror. I am certain that this princely bear and his companions will consent to protect me on the way." Her gaze flickered over Florio. "And then—we shall see."

"So we shall," said Florio.

She looked at her hands and sounded a little breathless. "It's a pity that it could not be a kiss."

"More likely it would be your having to cut off my head with an ax—though these good dwarves could give you an ax to accomplish that," said Florio.

John shifted his weight. "Then," he said, "we had best make all haste in the morning. The journey will not be easy."

"Not as they stand now," said a dwarf, back in the shadows. Firelight flickered, and lit up his gnarled face in parts. "They have to be ready to defend Snow-White. Their swords might suffice, but might not. We will arm both Hans and John."

A crack sounded from a log in the fire, and a plume of sparks shot up the chimney.

"You do indeed to go with them," he said to Hans, "so that you may defend her and her sister?"

"Where better can I go?" said Hans. "If I do not overhear them or someone who knows their secrets in their woods, I may yet trick them into revealing the truth. I can hardly find my sister more easily by running off."

The dwarf nodded.

"And one for Florio as well," said another dwarf, sitting at the table. "She may need defense after he is no longer a bear." He sat back, looking pensive. "Nothing too grand, they won't cut through iron, but they will be better than you can get from ordinary smiths. Sharper."

"Even good enough to kill giants," said a third.

Snow-White smiled. Biancabella let her breath out and told herself to be glad of the rest.

A dwarf sitting by the fire nodded, and said, "Take the road all the way down. The track is hard enough climbing—it's harder going down."

Another one said, "And we will tell you another road back to the Four Winds."

"One," said a third, grandly, "that does not go by that cottage, even with the witch dead."

Biancabella winced. One witch was dead. They might well meet more if they went by it again.

#

When she woke the next morning, Biancabella found that Snow-White had risen earlier yet.

Morning was, again, colder here than in the valley. The hearth was cold, the cupboards were closed, she did not even know where the bowls were kept.

The dwarves all snored away in their beds; the men and the fox all slept on the floor. But—not Florio. There was no more sign of him than of Snow-White.

Perhaps Snow-White had gone for water, she thought, and crept to the door.

The air outside felt as chilly as autumn. She pulled her mantle close and still shivered. By the corner of the house, in the sunlight,

Snow-White stood with a bucket at her feet, deep in conversation with Florio.

She opened her mouth, shut it again, and edged back. Then Florio looked at her. Moments later, Snow-White, pink-cheeked, snatched up the pail, ignoring how the water spilled, even on her skirt.

"I hope you slept well," she said brightly. "I was going to prepare breakfast."

"I could help—if you need it," said Biancabella, diffidently.

After a moment, Snow-White started walking and said, "The kitchen is not that large. We would get in each other's way." Then she smiled. It looked only a little forced. "You have no choice but to force the poor stepsister into the kitchen to do the work. And I shall be glad that I do not have to wait for the ball."

"Then," said Biancabella, "I shall sit and sew." She stepped out of the doorway, and Snow-White came in. "And be glad that you can not put out the light, since it's from the sun, and then send me off to get fire from the witch in the woods."

Snow-White laughed. "You are the younger, after all. But wouldn't—Augusta Gloriana keep you from reaching the witch?"

"Why, that's your reason for sending me, because I can see her."

Snow-White's smile was radiant. "The dwarves won't let the fire go out like that."

"Ah, well," said Biancabella.

"We shall just have to be like Kate and Anne." Snow-White poured the water into a pot already three quarters full and glanced at Biancabella. "Did Lady Regina tell you of them?"

Biancabella shook her head.

"You may want to get your sewing first." Snow-White turned to the firewood. The fire had not been banked the night before, to Biancabella's surprise, but she said nothing.

By the time Biancabella returned with the cloth, Snow-White had the fire half-set up. A minute later, when Biancabella had the linen spread out in her lap, Snow-White brought out a bit of flint and steel.

Sparks flew at the first strike, the tinder caught at once, the flames licked first at the kindling, and then, strengthening at the logs, until it burned.

At the first try. Biancabella no longer felt surprised that they did not bank the fire.

Snow-White put the water by the fire and leaned against the wall, carefully not watching the pot. "Once upon a time, a king had a daughter named Anne and a queen had a daughter named Kate. Because the king and queen were both widowed, they married each other. Kate and Anne loved each other very much, but the queen was jealous, because Anne was more beautiful than Kate. So she consulted with a hen-wife, who told her to send Anne to her first thing in the morning, making sure she ate nothing before it.

"So the next day, the queen sent her. Anne went on the way, and went through the kitchen, where she took a crust and ate it. When she came to the hen-wife's house, the hen-wife had her take the lid off a pot. Nothing happened, so the hen-wife told her to tell the queen to keep a better lock on her larder.

"The next day, the queen showed Anne to the door, but as she went along the road, she met some peasants working at a farm, who gave her some roasted grain, so she ate it. When she came to the hen-wife's house, the hen-wife had her take the lid off a pot. Nothing happened, so the hen-wife told her to tell the queen that a pot won't boil without fire."

She glanced down. The pot showed no trace of steam yet.

"The third day, the queen walked with Anne to the hen-wife, and when Anne lifted the lid, a sheep's head leapt out and fastened itself over Anne's pretty head. The hen-wife and the queen laughed, and Anne ran off, weeping, to the castle, where Kate found her. So Kate took a fine linen cloth, wrapped it around Anne's head, took her by the hand, and set out with her to seek their fortunes.

"They walked, and they walked, and they walked—and Kate picked nuts on the way. So many that she and Anne could eat their fill and still she could fill her pockets with them—and finally they came to a castle where there were two princes. One was sick, never left his bed, and slept all day. Whoever sat up with him at night vanished, and was never seen again. Kate said she would sit up with him if they took her and her sick sister in.

"So that night she sat with him, and at midnight he stood up, looking witched, and walked out of the castle. She chased after, and he mounted a horse, and she hopped up behind him, but he was so witched that he did not notice. His hound came chasing after.

"He rode off and was hailed by an owl sentry. It demanded who came, and he said, the prince with his horse and his hound—and Kate said, quickly, and his lady fair, and the owl let them by. The horse bore them into a hill, where dancers were all a-glitter with enchanted garments, and the prince dismounted and went to dance. They made him dance every dance. When he collapsed from weariness, they fanned him until his wits came back, and they made him dance again."

Biancabella bit her lip. The twelve princesses were luckier than they knew; they had not been so weary after their dances. She wondered if Boney had been behind this one.

Steam started to rise from the pot.

"Hours later they let him stagger back to his horse, and Kate rode back with him. Everyone was astounded to see her the next day, but she only said that she would stay with him for a second night but only if they paid her in gold. They agreed. The prince slept all the day, and the next night, he rode off again. Kate slipped in the same way, but when they made the prince dance, she knew what they would do, so she went off and searched the castle instead. She came upon a baby playing with a wand, and a lady there said to another that, back at the castle, there was a princess with a sheep's head, but if she were touched with that wand, she would be as beautiful as ever she had been.

"So Kate took the nuts in her pocket and rolled them toward the baby, who dropped the wand and took the nuts, and Kate took the wand from the floor and brought it back. The next day she searched out Anne as soon as she roused with the rest of the castle, and touched her with the wand, and she was as beautiful as ever she had been.

"That day, Kate told them she would stay for a third night only if she could marry the prince. They agreed at once, and when she went to the dance, she searched the castle again. This time the baby played with an apple. A lady said that one bite from that apple would break the spell on the prince, and he would never have to come to the dancing again. So Kate rolled the nuts toward the baby again, and snatched up the apple as soon as the baby lay it down.

"As soon as she was back at the prince's bedside, she roasted the apple on the hearth. The prince started to rouse and said that he thought he could eat some of that. She gave him it, and he ate it, and when the people came to see whether Kate was still there, why they found him and her, cracking nuts and talking by the fire.

"So they went down to the rest of the household, and by the great hall's fireplace, they found Anne and his brother talking, for his brother had fallen in love with Anne as soon as he saw her lovely face. So the sick prince married the hale princess, and the hale prince married the sick princess, and both of them lived happily ever after."

Snow-White went to pour the oats into the seething water.

As she stirred the pot, Biancabella said, "Which of us would get the sheep's head?"

"You are, after all, the queen's daughter," said Snow-White, slowly.

"I've already been to one enchanted ball three times," said Biancabella. "You can have that, I will take the sheep's head."

"When you already know you can survive and even triumph at them?" Snow-White scowled fiercely, and then waved her spoon like a specter. "I know! We will stay out of her power, and no one will get a sheep's head."

Biancabella smiled, briefly, and sighed. "I hope so."

"You've not failed yet," said Snow-White. "Not in anything you've set out to do against her. Or any of them."

"I saved the princesses," said Biancabella, slowly. "Basil and Rapunzel. Perhaps that frog. Hans." She spread her hands. "But I have learned *nothing* that will let me defeat her."

"Mother Trude is dead," said Snow-White. "Perhaps the spells breaking here and there will kill them each in turn."

Biancabella managed only a brief smile. To say—perhaps not, would only be to whine. She looked at her sewing.

If she ended up wandering about the lands as she had about the castle, a silent little ghost—at least on the road, she freed other people from curses. They could be happy, though she could not.

She could no longer remind herself that unlike Snow-White, she was not lying in a coffin. She would lie in one herself if it would bring her as much happiness in the end—which was folly. Snow-White could not get a prince to rescue her, as she had gotten one to rescue Snow-White.

"We must live in hope," said the fox, brightly, at her elbow. "One day we can bring down this circle and break all its curses."

Chapter 8— The Return Journey

The garden already faded. Flowers withered, leaves yellowing, stalks slumped to the ground.

Say what you would about Biancabella's work in the garden, thought Augusta Gloriana, at least it lasted for more than a week. She glared at the cankered roses.

"A bungled job," she breathed. "The roses on Anna lasted a century. They're still growing, at that."

A rose tree's withering was far past what the rest of the garden showed. Leaves and petals lay scattered over the ground, leaving the branches bare. Moss and mushroom already grew on the wood.

Augusta Gloriana frowned and came closer. A chain lay sprawled over the ground, wasting its enchantment, its lock lying open. An enchantment *she* had made. She hunted about a bit, and her fingers found the key that she had given Mother Trude. "A bungled job indeed."

"A bungled job indeed!" roared Rumpelstiltskin, coming out on the porch. "The little brats were *hungry* this morning. They wailed and caterwauled and shrieked until I had to go to fetch them bread! And all because you could not keep your brat obedient!"

Augusta Gloriana straightened with majestic dignity. "You don't accuse Mistress Laurenza of that when all three of her daughters got away."

"She caught them again!"

"Not without help," said Augusta Gloriana coldly.

"But before they killed any of us!" He shook his fist at her. "You haven't asked for help—have you even *looked* for her *yourself*? Did you throw up your hands in despair when the mirror was gone?"

"I have consulted other sources," she said, grandly.

"What? A talking salmon? A talking dog?" Rumpelstiltskin leaned forward. "The Sun?"

Augusta Gloriana glared at him. "It's not like she's the only thing that could do harm. You and Ottoline—that time when she made so many rats in the city, and you lured off the rats and got them to try to cheat you, and lured off all their children into the mountain—you failed. Every one of them escaped out the other side."

Rumpelstiltskin glared at her. "Got their parents."

"You got them so you could get the children. And you lost every one of them."

"Biancabella wasn't born then," said Rumpelstiltskin. "She was born for this—and wandering around to do it."

"Boney lost all those princesses—all twelve of them married already—after she was born, and no one saw a sign of Biancabella there."

Rumpelstiltskin's lip curled. "But she did *this*."

"It ruined *your* work, too," said Ottoline, sullenly. "She got that woodcutter's son, after he killed my wolf."

"You got the woodcutter *and* his wife," said Augusta Gloriana. "The children were superfluity after those two were driven out into the woods for killing them, and starved there. And—she didn't get the daughter."

Ottoline's lips pulled back from her teeth. "*He killed my wolf!* And you—you helped with the woods, and you helped with the chain—"

"*And* with the key!" Augusta Gloriana produced it with a flourish. "What is it doing here? Was she really such a fool that she didn't hide it inside an egg, inside a duck, inside a fish, inside a dog? Oh, it is so fun in your eyes to taunt them with escape—and then they escape, and you complain! As if it were *my* fault that *you* waste *my* work!"

Ottoline took a step back. "It was an enchanted *tree*. How on earth could hanging the key on the wall do any harm? Do you think his branches reached out to take it, and then unlocked the chain?"

"That harm?" Augusta Gloriana pointed at the grave. "If that's not harm, why do you complain so of Biancabella?"

Silence reigned for a moment.

"Not good enough," growled Boney. "The key was well hidden until *she* came along."

Said Augusta Gloriana, loftily, "Says the wizard who was flooded out of house and home by his own apprentice because the boy learned *half* a spell from him."

Boney's eyes narrowed. "Fool boy."

"Not such a fool that he didn't learn that half spell!" She leaned forward. "And—he got away. Back to his father and all set to use the magics *Ottoline* taught him, for cheap charlatanry, and nothing more."

Boney spat out the words. "What's a week or two of freedom? He did a few tricks in that time, changing himself to a beast and having his father sell him—and then, he needed his father to take the halter." He snorted in contempt. "Easy enough to trick his halter out of his father, and ride him back to home. All I had to do was keep from tormenting the horse on the way—his only hope was someone else to free him out of pity—and I had him back in the stable to suffer for his disloyalty. To suffer long."

He leaned forward. "*You* will never get Biancabella back, to have to worry about how to keep her from escaping on the way. And *she* is never going to content herself with tricking country bumpkins."

"If only," murmured Ottoline, "because she never learned to change shape," and, as Augusta Gloriana glared at her, smirked.

Augusta Gloriana, her face twisted with disgust, looked away. Ungrateful, Ottoline was—and foolish—as bad as Boney. "You didn't torment him enough. You got another boy in your service, and your horse not only got away with him, but made his fortune and got back his own form."

"That time," said Boney, with dreadful sweetness, "I did not ask you for aid. What was the point of that if things are not done better for your aid?"

"Let me know when you have another boy," said Augusta Gloriana, "and I'll show you how to keep him captive."

Rumpelstiltskin said, grimly, "That won't suffice for an answer. We must stop her."

From the way Ottoline glared at her, Augusta Gloriana thought she would have to arrange something for her to just get her help with the finding.

#

The road wound on, but the inn stood by it, in the midst of the pastures. Charcoal clouds lowered over it, and though it would be an hour to sunset, Biancabella could barely read the sign that said The Queen's Rose.

Though she thought the weathered painting had something to do with the difficulty recognizing a rose.

Hans glanced at the yard before the stables, and at John. Thunder growled. John shook his head, and they all went into the inn.

The fire gave some light to the room. Only a few travelers drank ale in the corners. Snow-White shook her head.

"Let us see what sewing we can do, in this light," she whispered to Biancabella.

"At least," whispered back Biancabella, "we do not have to sew seven shirts, after we spin and weave the cloth, and not speak a word the whole time."

"Or even spin it from nettles." Snow-White smiled. They took the fire-side seats, and Snow-White spread out the cloth that Biancabella had fetched from the pack. It looked yellow by the fire-light—then, if it did, it would do no harm. Coarser than the cloth she was used to, but by that very fact, less likely to raise questions.

"Though," said Snow-White, shifting the cloth, "it would be pleasant to have an enchanted spindle, shuttle, and needle."

"Wouldn't the needle suffice?"

"Ah, not to win the prince." For a moment, Snow-White looked grave in thought. Then she took up a needle to thread it, and glanced aside at Biancabella before gathering the cloth in her lap.

"You might find the knowledge useful. A peasant girl was left all alone after her grandmother died, and made her living by spinning, and weaving, and sewing."

Biancabella nodded, taking up some cloth and her own needle.

"But, in that kingdom, the prince wanted to marry a girl who was both the richest in a place and the poorest."

"Was he under the curse?"

Snow-White hesitated. "Not that I heard of. Though—it would be a crueler one than to have to marry Snow-White-Fire-Red—for her, the only question was whether she lived, not whether she could exist—except—" She glanced at Biancabella again. "—he came to her village and saw she was the poorest girl there. And she watched him from the window for long after he had ridden off.

"When she sat to spin, she sang an old verse she had learned from her grandmother, 'Spindle, o spindle, haste you away, and bring to the house a wooer today.'

"The spindle leapt out of her hand and spun off over the road. She looked after it, but when it vanished with distance, she went to weave. She remembered another verse, 'Shuttle, o shuttle haste you away, and guide to the house a wooer today.'

"It leapt from her hand and started to weave a carpet to the house, and never was a carpet so fine, with figures of roses and lilies and birds in flight.

"When the shuttle, still weaving, passed from sight, she took up her needle and sang another verse: 'Needle, o needle, so sharp and so fine, ready for a wooer this house of mine.'

"It leapt from her fingers and embroidered her little cottage into a splendid house.

"When the prince rode back, following the spindle, walking on the carpet from the shuttle, and seeing the house the needle had made, he declared that she was certainly both the richest and the poorest girl in this village, and he married her. And they lived happily after."

Snow-White smiled again and looked at her sewing.

Biancabella looked at hers. Snow-White would have a far better chance of earning her living at sewing. Her stitches were so much faster, and so much finer. If *she* were tested against other brides for her sewing, she would be fortunate if the king declared that he would wear her clothing when he had no need for finery; if he received a shirt fit for a wedding feast, Snow-White had sewn it.

Biancabella bent her head over the cloth. Hans and John needed clothes for when they had no need for finery. It would have been wise to buy more cloth even if Snow-White had proven slower than she was.

#

The sky showed pink and cream, and the fox pointed out the inn ahead. Another Black Bull. John nodded and barely let them take a room before he had Hans out in back, to practice. For over an hour.

At least, he was improving, thought Hans, in a lull between the thrust and parry of the bouts. Though if they had to fight a dragon, or even a nine-headed troll, it would be John who had to fight.

From the intensity that John pushed himself, John knew that as well.

The fox watched them, its dark eyes sharp, and Hans wondered if it, too, could comment his swordplay.

"That'll do for tonight," said John.

Hans hoped he kept his relief from being too obvious. He put up his sword. Snow-White, Florio, and Biancabella sat to one side—over her sewing, Snow-White had sometimes talked with Biancabella, and sometimes with Florio, such as now—and Biancabella, looking up from her sewing, watched the two of them as they came back, the fox frisking alongside them.

Hans wondered, for a moment, which of the sisters the mirror would say was fairest of them all. He was no judge of the matter. Every time he looked at Biancabella, he could only remember her, glowing in the sunlight in the middle of the garden, as the curse on him shattered.

Biancabella looked down, took a few more stitches, and shook out the shirt. "Done. One less shirt we need to buy ready-made."

"But we must buy more cloth," said Snow-White. "If we can—Florio talked of how different this route is."

"There should be cloth merchants," said Biancabella. "There are towns and cities on the way, no doubt."

Snow-White shook her head and stuck her needle into the cloth. "How did I do it? I was only nine! How did I walk so far in the woods? I should have stumbled out into settled lands somehow."

"I—would have to ask the mirror," said the fox. "But I think that Augusta Gloriana might have bewitched the forest so you could not see any way out."

Snow-White flinched.

"Perhaps," said Biancabella, slowly, "she sent you to—strange beings in the wood, and thought it would mean ogres, or giants."

"Or dragons," said the fox.

Hans shook his head. "I think—the same spells might have caught me and my sister. If I have the directions right, she and I wandered very far when we should have escaped the woods sooner."

For a moment, they stayed in silence.

Then the fox shook himself. "Dinner. Deep thought and empty stomachs make a poor mix."

#

The sky was still gray. Then, the day would be gray. Biancabella sighed. Her skirts were covered with dust, but if those clouds fulfilled their promise, they would be splattered with mud before this day was done.

She walked into the dew-laden meadow, where flowers bloomed. The height of summer had brought loosestrife blooming purple by the river, and clover red and yellow, and dainty bell-flowers a lovely blue. One pair of flowers, both deep heart's-blood red, drew her eye. She had never seen such a blossom before.

A peasant woman came running over the field, her black hair and red skirts flying behind her. Her nut-brown face came clear, and the terror on it. Biancabella opened her mouth, trying to marshal the words to see if she could help—perhaps she should scream for Hans and John, perhaps swords were needed—and then the woman reached the pair of flowers and pulled up, as her body began to shift and shape.

Biancabella stood with her mouth open. A third flower stood with the first two. The same shape, the same shade of red—

A man rushed across the field—dressed like the woman, as prosperous peasant— and looked about, frantically. His gaze went over the three flowers as if he did not see them.

"Are you looking for something, good man?" said Biancabella.

He gawked at her. Then he said, hoarsely, "It's my wife." He swallowed. "A witch turned her and her two sisters into flowers. Then she gave her a chance—let her become a woman again, and come to me tonight, and get turned back in the morning—now!" He wrung his hands. "If I can pick her from her sisters, they will change back, and if not, they will all die."

Silently, Biancabella pointed. He started. "How could I have missed that?" he muttered.

Biancabella opened her mouth to tell him which one, and he darted forward. "The one without dew!"

Moments later the flower was in his hand. Then, it was not, as the flowers started to turn. Biancabella pulled up her skirt and hurried back to the inn. Another curse, gone. She smiled sadly. For someone else.

#

That day, she watched along the way, but saw nothing uncommon. Not a frog with an arrow, not a strange enchanted garden, not a flower that looked uncommon, or a merchant looking everywhere for a common flower oddly missing when his daughter had asked him to buy it for her.

Now they walked along the same road, winding through the valley toward the marsh that they had seen before. Any curses that were there, she had walked by the first time. The dwarves' directions had only taken them by a route that would avoid the cottage.

In the marsh where the frog had found the arrow, the trees were already turning scarlet and gold with fall.

Biancabella sighed and reminded herself that they returned to the mirror at Four Winds. Perhaps it could tell her another path to go on, another curse she might break, another way she might foil her mother and her circle. Rumpelstiltskin, she thought. If she could rescued those children he took—

The fox, scampering ahead, stopped in its tracks. Then, it scampered back. "The way's blocked," he said, and scratched its ear with its hind leg. "Wedding party."

"Are we in the way?" said Hans.

The fox shook his head, and Biancabella peered ahead. At a crossroad, the wedding party appeared, bedecked with flowers in gold and purple, and dressed in colors as bright as the herbs could make them. She glanced over them, and blinked. Three brides and three bridegrooms.

"Two of those brides look familiar," murmured John.

"And all of the bridegrooms," said Biancabella, but her gaze fixed on the bride that she had not seen before, a radiant maiden with rosy cheeks and nut-brown hair. Not looking the least like a frog.

With the procession past, it was only another hour to the inn, and the inn-keeper, when Snow-White mildly asked, shook his head, and said, "Wasn't that a tale and a half?" He served out the cider, and bowls of fish stew. "Old Widow Smith said that her sons were to shoot off arrows, and whichever damsel took his arrow up was to be the son's bride. One was taken up by a merchant's daughter, one by a rich farmer's daughter, and one—well, her son Jannik came out of the marsh with his arrow and looking grim.

"So she gave her sons linen thread and said that whichever bride wove and sewed it the best would be her favorite. The merchant's daughter made a rough shirt that the widow said was fit only for a dog to sleep on. The farmer's daughter made a clumsy shirt that the widow said she might wear to keep finer clothes clean. Jannik went into the marsh and came out with a splendid shirt that the widow pronounced fit enough for a festival." He leaned forward. "She's wearing it now, for the wedding."

Snow-White nodded.

"The next day, she gave her sons flour and told them that whichever bride baked the best cake would be her favorite. The merchant's daughter made a cake fit only to be fed to dogs. The farmer's daughter made a cake fit for eating before harvest, when stores were scarce. Jannik went into the marsh and came out with a cake fit for the finest of festivities.

"So the widow said that her sons should bring their brides to the wedding feast and dance before them all, and whichever bride danced the best would be her favorite. Jannik wept and wept while his brothers went to fetch their brides, but his mother chased him out of the house and told him to never return without her.

"Hours later, a fine carriage came out of the marsh, and in it a beautiful damsel with nut-brown hair and rosy cheeks, and everyone said she was as beautiful as both the other brides put together. When she danced at the wedding, she was more graceful than a swan, where the merchant's daughter blundered—" He hesitated and glanced at Florio, who blandly looked back. "—blundered about like a sheep in the marsh, and the farmer's daughter like a calf."

"So," said John, "the widow will not face having three different favorites."

The innkeeper smiled.

"And has she told any story about this?" said the fox. "This—bride who came from the marsh?"

"She *said* that she was held captive by this witch, a Mother Magda, in the middle of a town. All the neighbors would spy on her to make sure she spoke to no one—right neighborly, to help Mother Magda so—but then three princes rode by, and saw her, and quarreled over her beauty—so loud Mother Magda turned *her* into a frog."

"Not even locking her up in a tower first?" said Biancabella. "Straight to being a frog?" The inn-keeper nodded. She wondered if the knowledge would ever prove of the least use to her.

Once they shut the door in their room, Hans said, "I wonder if it was Ottoline who turned her into a frog."

Biancabella tilted her head to one side, thinking.

"Or perhaps Ottoline had given her the spell," said Snow-White, "and she wanted to test it."

"At least it's broken," said Biancabella.

#

The early morning sky showed rose and peach colors, wildflowers in stands of purple bloomed along the road, and next to a bush with red berries—with birds flitting about to eat them—Snow-White and Florio waited on the road, knowing the others would not take long.

Though long, thought Snow-White, grew shorter by every day on this journey. Her heart beat harder with excitement. A clear day, on which they could make good progress. "Only a day," she murmured.

"If all goes well," said Florio.

"We live in hope," said Snow-White, letting her hand rest on his shoulder. "Mother Magda does not always manage to give her charges pig-snouts, or bewitch them to forget." She swallowed, and tried to force some cheer into her voice. "I will not ask you to dance at the wedding."

Florio's laughter was a deep rumble.

Biancabella emerged from the inn, talking in a low voice to Hans. Snow-White stilled, watching them. A pretty picture. She might think that Biancabella was more beautiful than Augusta Gloriana—if only she did not look so anxious.

But John emerged behind them, and the fox bounded ahead. Journey first, thought Snow-White. Perhaps completing it would ease Biancabella's fears.

#

In the thick gloom of firs and encroaching evening, Biancabella looked ahead. That had, indeed, been the last turn, and she could see the Four Winds clearly. Her breath gushed out.

Snow-White seemed to slow. After a moment, her hand went out to seize Biancabella's. Her voice was low and fast. "Is that it? Where the mirror is? And Florio's parents and sister?"

Biancabella nodded. Then she realized that her sister was not looking at her. "Yes, that is it. The Four Winds."

Florio came up beside them, and even as a bear, he looked imploring. After a moment, Snow-White started, and looked at him.

"Please," she whispered, "make me known to your parents and sister."

Biancabella fell back. The others joined her as Florio and Snow-White walked ahead. The fox sighed dreamily.

Rapunzel walked out of the Four Winds. She looked rather—subdued. But she smiled at the sight of Florio, turned to call into the inn, and walked forward.

Basil emerged within moments, and they spoke. Biancabella bit her lip, waiting.

A few words drifted out toward them, and Biancabella heard, clearly, only one: "Married."

Biancabella blinked. They might be talking of the wedding, and then, with a rush, the memory of Constance's promise came back to her. Rapunzel waved them to come in, and she was not too surprised to hear, in the welcome, that Constance had married and left with her husband.

"I wonder," said the fox, its head tilted to one side, "how many travelers will take Snow-White for Constance."

"Too many," said Basil. "I have already been taken for Florio scores of times. I do not think I have corrected a tenth of them."

#

In the kitchen, by the banked fire, they ate first and heard, to no surprise, that no traveler had brought any news that could help them. So, as evening colored the sky, Rapunzel put aside the dishes, and said, "There is plenty of time to consult the mirror with the travelers all abed."

Snow-White blinked, considered, glanced at Florio, and started to blush. "I—I think I will wish to consult the mirror. Later. If it can tell whether Augusta Gloriana misled me in the forest. But—I have no great questions to ask it. Let Hans ask first, since his sister is still lost."

Biancabella rose to her feet. "It's in the same room?" she asked Rapunzel. John and Hans both stood, but she led the way up the stairs, until the fox leapt up before her, running toward the mirror.

The face appeared within moments, and Hans stood before it. John leaned against the wall by the window, and the fox by him.

Biancabella awkwardly sat with her arms about her knees, on a chest, and reminded herself that the first concern was to keep the mirror hidden. She looked at the face, cool and severe.

"Your father and stepmother are dead," said the mirror.

Hans swallowed, but showed no other sign.

"Ottoline stirred up the village against them, asking what had happened to you and your sister, and they gave no very clear answer. They were exiled into the forest. And unlike you and your sister—they starved."

His face set like stone, and Biancabella winced. They had not even been eaten by beasts.

The voice went on. "It is true that I told you little of Mother Trude. I can not tell all that I know, and I do not know all that might be known. Even now, I can not tell you where your sister is. I only know that the Bird of Truth might help."

Biancabella blinked. "I hope it's not your sister," she said. "The bird."

The mirror's voice turned dry. "No, I am not sending you on to my sister because I can not help. And just as well. She would just have to send you on to the third."

"Then off to the four winds," said Hans, "if things go badly. The four winds in truth, and not here—until the North Wind knows the way." He frowned.

"I fear," said the mirror, "that I can not even tell you where to find the winds."

Biancabella sat up. "But what I meant was—is the bird Gretel?"

"No," said the mirror. "It is the same bird that Jean and Pierre sought, and Isobel returned with. Long before your time."

Hans nodded. He turned to Biancabella. "My sister has no connection to your quest."

"It—" Biancabella paused and marshaled her thoughts. "She was Mother Trude's prisoner for many a year. Who knows what she might have overheard? Even only considering how to defeat this circle of theirs and not how her freedom would thwart them, finding her would be a wise thing for me to do, if I can."

Hans sat still.

"First you have to find the Bird of Truth," said the mirror. "Or else another way to find out where she is. I do not know whether there is another way, one I do not know of."

"Isn't it—you told me about the garden," said Biancabella. "That was where Isobel found it, and her brothers too, even if they failed to gain it."

"When Isobel claimed the bird, she did not reconcile her mother and her father," said the mirror, "but she did free the bird from the garden. The problem is no longer that it is kept caged far away and surrounded by perils, as the Golden Bird was."

John twitched.

The mirror went on. "It is that it flits about freely. Since the days when it told the king the truth, no one has ever caught it again."

"Always dangerous, telling the king the truth," said the fox philosophically. "Why, there have been kings who let a foolish peasant marry their daughters rather than let him tell a truth." Its right leg came up to scratch its ear.

"Was that the peasant who herded his hares?" said Snow-White, from the doorway.

"Oh yes," said the fox.

"You have heard many tales?" said the mirror.

"What else was there to do when snow engulfed the cottage?" said Snow-White. "Even I told such stories as my mother told me. And a few from Meg—she spent as much time rapt and listening to my mother as I did."

She took a step forward, and hesitated, looking toward Biancabella. "Are you going to stay for the wedding?" She looked more anxious than Biancabella had ever seen her before.

Biancabella opened her mouth, shut it, and said meekly, "Yes, yes, I will."

Hans turned. "Do you have a question for the mirror?"

Snow-White stood for a moment, looking blank. Then she blushed, and managed to choke out, "I wondered how I managed to reach the dwarves safely. I was only seven."

"Augusta Gloriana had the paths lead you that way," said the mirror gravely. "She was sloppy. She had too much confidence from having led Hansel and Gretel to Mother Trude—and she did not particularly want you to go somewhere except—nowhere with humans."

Snow-White bit her lip. "I could have ended up with bears, offending a family by breaking into their home and causing havoc."

"Bears?" said Biancabella. "Ottoline might have cursed then, but she would not have enchanted them so they could have a home. Sigurd does have a home because of another enchantress."

"How true," said the mirror. "And, Hans, it might be wiser for you to wait for Biancabella. The way will hold perils that only she can see."

For a moment, an emotion flashed over his face, but Biancabella could not read it. Then he gravely bowed his head. "If they will let me stay at the Four Winds."

"Of course!" said Snow-White, smiling radiantly. "And we are hard at work on my wedding gown to hasten the day." She hesitated. "I have to go help Rapunzel."

"Of course," said Biancabella, and Snow-White rushed off.

"Florio wooed well, for a bear," said Hans.

"Very well," said Biancabella. She looked at her hands. "The mirror—said—" Then she managed to force the words to rush out. "That weddings were times of great peril because it makes the circle's magic stronger, such a time."

"That is true," said the mirror, calmly.

Biancabella looked up. "Staying might reveal a way to fight them." After a moment, she added, "Force them to reveal what happened to your sister."

The fox said, "How true. Even beyond your sight—" It gave a half bow to Biancabella. "—it would be wiser to wait until the wedding is done."

"Perhaps there will be a traveler," said John, "who is looking for the ogre's three golden hairs, and we can ask him if he can learn where your sister is."

"Perhaps we could ask the Bird of Truth about more things," said Biancabella. "Not only his sister, but how she, and we, can all be kept safe from the circle." She stood. "We should use the time to think what questions to ask—and ask what travelers may know of the Bird of Truth!"

#

John watched the others go. Biancabella glanced sideways as if realizing that he was not moving, but went on.

Feeling like a fool, he still waited until they were gone before he turned to the mirror, and asked, "What happened to the Golden Bird? And to the magnificent steed?"

"The steed, your brothers handed over to the stables," said the mirror. "They bred from it—and it died in due course, as it aged like any horse. They have many magnificent horses from it. As for the Golden Bird, Augusta Gloriana keeps it captive still."

John let out his breath. Perhaps he could rescue the bird at least.

#

Asters and goldenrod filled the ditches with purple and gold. The shelter of the inn made a corner, facing south and west, warm enough for Rapunzel and Snow-White to sit and sew the wedding gown (and for Florio to sit about, watching the road).

A third woman would only add to confusion. Besides, thought Biancabella, both women could sew much more finely, and with greater speed, than she could.

She had seen Rapunzel laying aside much smaller garments to take up this one instead, but Rapunzel had time for that.

Just as Hans chopped the wood at a good clip—and not after he had foolishly chosen the sound ax, which had caused the wood

to join together again, and had the ogre's beautiful daughter remind him of her advice to use the broken ax. She smiled. He used a
sound ax—but she was quite certain that in need, Hans would heed
the ogre's beautiful daughter's advice at once. Then and when they
tried to escape—her smile wavered a little.

She walked toward the garden, where John and Basil worked.
Basil dug the sort of holes she had always gotten the gardeners to
do, but John was hard at work picking peas.

"Can I help?"

Basil raised an eyebrow but pointed her at rows of carrots and
a basket she could use. She went to pull them. She had never, at the
castle, ventured into the kitchen gardens. Pulling up the first carrot
did not cause a black cloud to come and swirl her away, nor did a
voice command her to stop and account for what she was doing. It
did not even pull free for the hole to open to the underworld.

Then, of course, this was neither flowers nor a turnip. Biancabella industriously set about stacking carrots in the basket.

"Peas and beans, and carrots and turnips," said the fox, idly. It
rolled over on its back. "Did you ever have trouble with bears who
wanted to make bargains?"

Rapunzel laughed. "Not in my day. I was still in the tower when
a bear came by and demanded half the harvest—when it was still
spring."

Said Snow-White, "What happened?"

"Why, old Walter—but he wasn't old then, he was still
young—told it that he agreed, and the bear could have the top half,
and he would the bottom. So Walter planted turnips and radishes and carrots, and the bear got all the leaves when Walter got the
vegetables. The next year, the bear told him, he got the top, and the
bear got the bottom. Walter agreed, and that year he planted beans
and peas and lettuce. " Rapunzel smiled. "The bear was so angry
that he burst."

The rest laughed. Biancabella went on pulling carrots. After it settled down, she said, "I wonder what Ottoline thought of that."

"Not every talking bear came from Ottoline's handiwork," said the fox. It rolled back over to lie right-side up on the grass. "And if it did—it might have come from one of her streams left running, and she never knew about it."

Biancabella nodded and rose to carry the full basket inside.

Snow-White eyed the basket and said, "Fond of gardens?"

"Oh, very much so." Biancabella looked at her grubby fingers and smiled. "I took charge of the garden at the castle. The gardeners still had work to do, but I weeded and did much of the planting. Heartsease and roses and asters—" She looked down at the basket.

"You're lucky that you did not ask your father for a rose," said Rapunzel.

I would never ask him for anything, she thought. Not even if I could curse him to be unable to sail his ship backward or forward if he did not remember to bring it back to me.

She said, "Perhaps I should have. Then I would have a bridegroom whose home had a magnificent garden."

Snow-White laughed. "Is that what you have dreamed of? A garden, not the bridegroom who owns it?"

Her thoughts fled, and for a blank moment, Biancabella stared at nothing. She had dreamed—"Of nothing," she said with care. "My mother would have raged if I wished to marry. It was safer to not think of it, so I would not say anything."

For a moment, the only sound was the rustle of leaves. Hans lowered the ax and looked at her.

She straightened and twisted her neck a little from the stiffness. "But yes, I think my bridegroom would be best if he came with a magnificent garden. He would shortly find that he no longer had the charge of it, so he had best also leave it to the gardeners under my authority." She spread her free hand. "Or else, like Princess Marjory, I could just marry a gardener. I would not even insist that he rescue me from dancing every night."

Snow-White smiled.

"Once I learn how to put an end to the circle. And their danger."

"What?" said Snow-White. "You will not dream of marrying until then? No matter how long it takes?" She lowered her needle. "Every princess in the world has married with the knowledge that evil wizards and sorceresses and ogres and witches were out there, hating her happiness. She might get turned into a white duck if she allowed a witch to lure her into the garden. Her mother-in-law might get a false letter ordering her death and pack her off to foreign lands for her own safety—so securely safe that when the secret is out, and the letter known to be false, her husband the king will have a hard time finding her. Her child might be born a sprig of myrtle if she said something unwise." A gust of wind blew through the tree branches and made the flowers nod. "Destroying the circle will not bring you safety. You will have to take some risk."

Biancabella shrugged. "Perhaps I will meet a prince—or a gardener—who needs to marry me to be disenchanted."

Snow-White's face worked for a moment.

Florio looked over. "Though I was a bear, and we met a dwarf while you and your sister were together—I fear I have no brother to marry you."

Laughter rang about the garden.

"And, Mother, I expect you to pay careful attention: if you get a letter from me ordering you to put Snow-White to death, ignore it. Don't hide her away."

"I'll hide her somewhere I can find her again," said Rapunzel.

Chapter 9—The Plot Against

In the woodland clearing, the others had gathered already. Dim shadows with distance, but Augusta Gloriana knew they watched her reproachfully. As if she had forced them to gather here, in the dark and dew, rather than in the castle's finely furnished room. They had not even cast the spells to ensure there would be no spies. When it was a matter of doing work, they trusted her.

Augusta Gloriana swept on, her head held high, down the road. Her daughter had done no worse than Mother Magda's, or King Drakos's, or Mistress Laurenza's, and it was refined madness to gather in a clearing like beasts.

If only that fool Doctor Know-All had not known to flee the kingdom! She might still have managed, if one of those silly dancing princesses had only chosen to marry Prince Martin. But, no, the fools—all twelve of them!—had to marry this prince or that, and six of them had even thought it wonderful to marry six brothers. So Prince Martin had ridden home without a bride and found the doctor's beautiful daughter, and married her. With the daughter, the doctor, and the doctor's wife under Prince Martin's protection, getting the answer out of him would take far too much effort for so uncertain a result.

She had to do it the hard way.

An owl hooted as she reached the clearing. At least it was not filled with songbirds and butterflies, and the wildflowers were colorless by moonlight.

She did not flinch as she moved to her place. The hard way would not be that hard. Biancabella knew not a scrap of magic. If they thought that she could confound one of them, let alone all of them, they had learned nothing over the years.

The dim moonlight—when they could have sat by brilliant, golden candlelight!—left them colorless and gray. The air was already cold, and the dew heavy enough to wet the hem of her gown. Perhaps that would encourage them to waste no time.

"Biancabella has been found," said Augusta Gloriana.

"Took long enough," growled Boney.

"Perhaps you should have lent us your horse," said Augusta Gloriana, "and then we would have caught up more quickly."

"I have work of my own," snarled Boney.

"We did ours. We know where she is."

"Because she broke another spell," said Ottoline, with almost as much of a growl as Boney's own.

"One devised at the time," said Augusta Gloriana, shaking her head sadly at such short-sightedness. "We have to do such things to find her."

Ottoline's mouth tightened, but she did not say that Augusta Gloriana had suggested they do it as a way to stymie a couple's happiness. Prudent of her.

And, of course, Ottoline would not tell that it was happenstance that it revealed Biancabella, because Augusta Gloriana had not told her. Looking smug had kept that secret.

"I have work of my own to deal with," said Ottoline, "and I not only do not need your help, I can help you while I do it."

"You have not trapped Sigurd into marriage yet," said Augusta Gloriana. "Before you talked of bringing Zelphine into the circle—and now you talk no more."

Ottoline took a step back, and her tongue touched her lip. "I—it was a test."

Augusta Gloriana snorted. "A test indeed. Of her or of me? It was quite an intricate spell you had me work for her. It is not for nothing that I usually hide one thing from others, not to make one person see so little."

"You did not seem to find it hard."

Such heady flattery. Augusta Gloriana's voice turned sweet. "And I received nothing in return except Zelphine's complaints that it would not work properly at night."

"It was a test," said Ottoline mulishly. "To see whether she could help with our work before risking her being a waste. That would require her to work with our spells."

"Our spells? That was *my* spell."

The cold wind blew by them. Ottoline straightened. "As if you enchanted him into a bear. It was a test."

"Yet you thought she had passed it," said Augusta Gloriana. "Enough that you talked with confidence."

Ottoline's face twitched.

"Enough," growled Rumpelstiltskin. His teeth glinted by moonlight. "Finding her is no matter. Enchant her. Bewitch her. Curse her. Kill her. Burn her bones. Keep her from being dangerous. Unless *you* are the next one she is to kill."

"Even if," said Mother Magda, her eyes narrowed. "If you let her kill you, we shall have to stop her—and stop her despite all your spells breaking."

"Then—" King Drakos frowned. "—then she won't be able to see the hidden things—"

"She won't have to!" said Mother Magda. "They won't be hidden! Everyone will see them! If you haven't watched any spells that Mother Trude laid disband on you, the rest of us have!" She turned to Mistress Laurenza. "Haven't you?"

Mistress Laurenza said, slowly, drawing out the word, "Yes."

"Something has happened with your daughters," said Augusta Gloriana, pouncing. "You let Mother Trude's spell hold them! And made no other provisions!"

Mistress Laurenza straightened sharply. "Esmeralda and Sophronia are hard at work at their studies! They will come to the circle within years!"

Silence lasted for a time. Another owl hooted.

"And," said Boney, with dreadful slowness, "Aviette?"

"She did not kill Mother Trude," said Mistress Laurenza, with all speed. "Biancabella first. I was not so foolish as to give my daughter freedom from my spellcraft before she proved herself worthy of it—Aviette is not the danger!"

"False!" said Rumpelstiltskin. "Both are dangers. If one is greater, we should still have the power to bring them both to heel at once. What are two insolent girls before the power we gather here?"

"I have already tracked Biancabella," said Augusta Gloriana, keeping her voice smooth. "I lay plans as we speak. I have already begun to limit those who can help her—which is always a danger. But I will not rush the matter and risk bungling it. That has always been a danger."

Her gaze flickered to Mistress Laurenza. Who had failed. And first had deceived her, telling her that daughters could be curbed if rebellious, and taught proper ways. She would never have risked having Biancabella if Mistress Laurenza had not misled her, and hidden her failure with Aviette.

"Perhaps you can tell us what plans you have put into effect in order to secure Aviette again."

"And soon," said Rumpelstiltskin. "You were as fool as Augusta Gloriana. You also gave your daughters the power to look through when Augusta Gloriana hides things from eyes. How else could Biancabella have found Mother Trude's cottage? But your Aviette will be as much of a menace."

"Ottoline can help," said Mistress Laurenza. "She helped you—"

"Ottoline," said Ottoline, "has work of her own to do! All the more in that you are too busy to help *her*!"

#

Through forests ablaze with scarlet and orange, the company rode through the hills, all twelve of them, all laughing, and singing, and making. All six of the brides wore crowns of woven goldenrod, and all six of the bridegrooms, ones of purple asters.

Boney watched them. If they had not insisted in marrying with great pomp and circumstance, such that it had taken months to ready the wedding feast, all twelve of them would have come much sooner. He might have failed to catch them, and he certainly would have had to rush to do it. But now—

He strode onto the road. "How dare you intrude on my lands!" he bellowed and glared at them all. They gaped at him, and within moments, they gaped forever, granite statues of horses and princes and princesses and flowers. Gray and dreary, down to the flowers, among the vivid gold leaves of autumn.

"Heh." Boney nodded. Let Her Ever-So-Royal Majesty Queen Augusta Gloriana match *that*.

He turned back to the hill. His stony house was—just—visible if you looked at exactly the place where the branches parted enough to see the slate roof. Smoke rose from the chimney.

He harrumphed and walked up the hill. The princess had better have his dinner ready, and he might just heckle her about the place smelling of human flesh. She'd give him a story about a raven dropping a human bone down the chimney.

Kari, he remembered suddenly. Her name was Kari. Odd to remember that after so many maidens.

He snorted. Kari had better remember to bake a good meal. Turning people to stone always made him hungry.

He came to the door and was surprised to see Mother Magda sitting at the hearth. Kari, her hair falling down her back in a single gold braid, was stirring the soup and, at the same time, trying to keep from turning her back on Mother Magda. It had made her clumsy enough to spill flour and bits of vegetable about the pot.

"Humph," said Boney. "And what are you doing here? Trying to steal my cook away to your tower? I should keep a better eye on her—she'll think the work will be easier."

Kari stiffened.

"You fool," said Mother Magda. "Just because Queen Augusta Gloriana and Mistress Laurenza are off pothering over their fool daughters doesn't mean the work stops. It means those two rascals can't be called on to do their share of it. And they spend every hour of our meetings on their folly, so we do not have time to talk."

Boney snorted.

"There was a queen, who was dying, and had only a single daughter," said Mother Magda. "I got the queen to make the king promise to never marry again except to a woman as beautiful as she was, and one who could wear her ring."

Boney snorted. "And now that his daughter's the only one who is, and can, he needs to be pushed to marry her?"

"Oh, no," said Mother Magda. "That went smoothly enough. He didn't manage to marry her, because she chopped off her hands, and then she could not wear the ring. But he chased her off into the forest because of that."

"Forest? That goes bad," said Boney.

"There it is. A king found and married her, and even had cunning silver hands made to replace hers." Mother Magda rocked back in her chair. "I had hopes of the mother-in-law, there."

"And?" said Boney.

"Suggested that she could steal her baby, smear blood on her mother's mouth, and claim she had killed and eaten the child. Or she could arrange for her son to go away, and then write to him telling him that his bride had given birth to an animal." She shook her head. "At least, I tried to suggest it. No sooner than I had started than she was giving orders to have me thrown out. And she had objected to the marriage! She truly let me down. But I will not let that stop me."

Boney snorted. "You may have to."

Mother Magda's eyes narrowed. "I thought of getting King Maximus to attack the kingdom. He's already returned from another war, and he did well there." She rocked back and forth. "And since we can not rely on Augusta Gloriana, I've worked some on spells to hide my workings from idle eyes. It will be a test."

#

In the morning mist, Snow-White stitched along on—a shirt, John noted. She nodded to him.

"Wedding gown done?" he said.

"Oh, quite," said Snow-White. She held up the shirt. "And Florio will manage with his own clothes for a time, even though he and Basil will both wear them. But you and Hans will set out as soon as the wedding is over." She smiled, lowering the cloth. "Biancabella brought herself some extra clothes, but it befits me to aid my benefactors."

John looked down at the cloth. So little, so late, to only save her daughter after so much suffering.

Snow-White sighed. "And you are as bent as Biancabella on doing nothing until you deal with the circle?"

"Having been murdered once by them—" He spread his hands.

Slowly, she nodded. "And—what will you do after?"

For a moment, his thoughts froze. The sooner that hour came, the happier he would be, but years beyond it were blank to his imagination.

"Perhaps," he said carefully, "I will write a chronicle of the circle. Prudence has helped many a prince and princess over the years. I might have escaped the circle if I studied more industriously."

Snow-White looked pensive as she studied him. Then, soft-voiced, she proposed seeing that the shirt fit.

#

The castle door swept open before her. Constance pulled her mantle more tightly about her. The bitter wind still tugged at her hair and made the dead leaves rattle as they skittered over the path.

Constance sighed. For all that the castle servants were as unseen as the wind, the garden was not that enchanted. Leaves turned yellow and fell, roses had long faded, and soon she would have to take her walk within the castle. It held galleries where she could do that, with no paintings but with windows that would look out on the bare branches of the garden, and the snow.

At least, she had not found a chamber with many dead maidens, or a gate into Hell.

She stopped in the lee of the wall, by the gate. She would go back in and take the rest of her walk on a gallery, she decided.

"Fair lady, sweet lady—" called a crooning voice, shaking a little.

Constance felt colder than the wind. She turned to face—an old woman, bent over her staff, with hair as white as snow. And with only a single eye.

The woman tried to bow more deeply. "All honor to our prince's bride! I have come to do you service. I have come to tell you that you must burn your husband's bear pelt, or he will ever be a bear, and his kingdom will ever be bound."

Constance swallowed and licked her lips.

"You have heard of the prince who was born a pig? How his bride saved him thus? And many a bridegroom saved his frog bride from her fate that way."

Sometimes that killed the frog, Constance thought, and sometimes it betrayed her beauty to the king.

The old woman lowered her voice. "Some brides have to cut off the heads of their bridegrooms. A frog is not that hard, but a lion?" She shook her head. "A bear would be as bad as a lion. So much easier, burning the skin."

Constance forced herself to incline her head, and said, "I thank you. You have made clear to me what to do."

#

Which was even true, she noted as she sat on a chair of red velvet in the private chamber off the bedchamber and told Sigurd the story as her husband sat before the fire.

"Sometimes burning it frees the man, but never when a mysterious woman like that urges it. So, we wait. And I do not burn your fur. And we can hope that means the curse can be broken without your vanishing and my having to chase after you."

"How sagacious my wife is." Sigurd shifted. "Did she pretend to be a beggar?"

Constance shook her head. "Ottoline must have known it would look even more suspicious in this land. Just as she knew not to try to trick my mother into asking me to do it."

Sigurd nodded and let his head rest on his paws. Then he sighed. "I might have thought it a sign the curse was breaking, like a snowdrop toward winter's end."

"Perhaps it is. Perhaps she tried because she is desperate. Usually the cursed prince tells his bride that if only she had waited a little while longer, the curse would have broken."

#

Moonlight lay in cold rectangles over the floor. Sigurd lay asleep, and she did not wish to move to wake him. Her gaze drifted over toward the fireplace, and she smiled a little at the dull red that was the only sign left of the banked fire.

A shadow surged past it. Her dazed thoughts took a moment to realize it was human in shape, and that she had screamed. Then she jumped from the bed toward the figure. Her hands struck thin arms, as hard as iron, and the figure roughly shoved her back, but Sigurd reached out to grab—her.

The moonlight fell on her face, and Constance gasped at the one-eyed woman at the gate. She held the bearskin as well.

"Insolent child! Can you not even do that?" the woman screamed. "I curse you to this: you shall go to your brother's wedding, and if you are kissed while you are there, your husband shall be borne off from you, and you shall search for him for a year and a day in the wildest of wilds!"

Then Sigurd's hands in the moonlight held only the bearskin. He lowered it back into the gloom and pulled back toward the bed. Constance swallowed.

Minutes later, Sigurd said, "At least we know your brother is hale." His voice was rather hollow.

#

A gust of wind sent a flood of golden leaves past the window.

Rapunzel looked critically over the green gown. Snow-White's hair tumbled down her back over it, and Biancabella, by the window, ate an apple and thought that between the cut and the silver embroidering of stars and leaves, it could hardly be finer.

Just as well. Her fingers were sore from the sewing. She had not done a third of what either of the other women had, but her fingers still objected.

She leaned back. Something moved outside, and she turned to look. Then she hopped up.

"Constance is coming," she said.

Rapunzel blinked. "What?" she said, as if the words made no sense. Snow-White paled a little—Biancabella had not realized she could grow paler—and started to say that she had to get out of the gown to greet her.

"I will go greet her and tell her that you will come as soon as the gown is safe from dirt," said Biancabella.

Hurrying down the stair, she found Florio and Basil deep in conversation over the stores and told them the news before flitting out the door.

Constance moved with a slowness that surprised her, and her bent head matched her grave expression. She looked up on seeing Biancabella and said, "No one must kiss me!"

"Ah," said Biancabella. "I'll help ward them off." She turned to the door as Basil emerged, and said, "Don't kiss her!"

Before she knew it, they were all warned, and Constance had received cautious embraces from all her kin, and met Snow-White and Hans as well, and they gathered round a table to hear stories. Constance explained the curse before all else.

"And so—we will have the wedding tomorrow," said Rapunzel. "Her dress is done, we have food enough for a feast, and we can hardly invite any guests or find any entertainer to make it grander if we waited for a year and day—with the autumn making the travelers fewer, we will have less custom—and if they know, the sooner we are done, the sooner we will be safer."

Silence fell for a minute, in which no one said that the wedding's being done would not make them much safer. But then, thought Biancabella, waiting would not do so at all.

She looked at her cider. Perhaps she could set out to search for more. John might help her, and perhaps Hans.

A log, with a sigh, settled deeper into the ashes in the fireplace.

"I wonder," said John, "whether Ottoline wants him to marry this Zelphine's daughter still."

"Who else?" said Biancabella.

"Perhaps she means to marry him herself."

Biancabella sat up in a start. "She's married already! She's my aunt!" After a moment, she added, "And Snow-White's too! And—" She pointed at him. "Your sister!"

John blinked at the last and winced, but said, "Sigurd's married."

Constance, her hands folded in her lap, grimaced.

"So," said Snow-White, "the wedding is tomorrow."

#

Biancabella talked gravely with Rapunzel as the morning porridge pot bubbled on the fire.

Snow-White, at the table, sighed a little and looked away. Both Florio and John looked at her. Constance raised her eyebrows.

She forced herself to speak, her voice carefully low. "When we talked about her marrying, I almost made a fool of myself—I started to tell her that her parents would want her to be happy."

Florio snorted.

"Perhaps," said John, delicately, "Ogier would not actively want her to be miserable—I doubt he would have wished that for you, even."

"He did not," said Snow-White. "He paid me little heed over the years."

"You can assure her that her uncle wants her to be happy," said Florio. "And her sister as well."

"Tell her," said the fox, looking up from scraps of chicken, "that nothing would make Augusta Gloriana more miserable."

In spite of themselves, they laughed.

#

A dog yapped, down the road. Biancabella looked up from slicing carrots for the feast. Rapunzel looked out the door. "So, we shall have a guest for the night."

A boyish traveling minstrel with a brightly colored tunic of red and green, boots covered with dust, and a lute slung on his back, trudged up to the door. A little, bright-eyed dog bounded beside him, with vigor surprising this late in the day given the distance they must have traveled.

Rapunzel went out to greet him, and Biancabella went on chopping. A minute later, on her return, Rapunzel smiled.

"We shall have a lute playing for the dancing," she said. The dog yipped and jumped. Rapunzel's smile deepened. "And some dancing from the dog as well."

"Humph," said the fox from the hearth. The dog stared, and then growled. "Yes, you insolent little puppy, I was talking of *you*." The dog looked startled, and the minstrel hauled it back.

#

Outside the window, the first stars gleamed like diamonds against the deep blue of the sky. The horizon was deep red and orange and darkening by the moment. Soon he would shed his bearskin. And wait, as he had waited all day as a bear.

Sigurd sat on his haunches, looking over the garden. Fallen leaves spread over the beds and the lawn in golds and red, and asters bloomed violet among the snapdragons still colorful in pinks and reds and oranges. If he had been asked before, he would have said of course he would be glad to take on a man's form, however briefly, though his beloved bride were far away.

And he did not care. He almost wished he would not. To lie down, alone, in the great bed only reminded him that Constance would not take her place there. This was worse than waiting to learn how they might finish breaking the spell.

He sighed. "If only I had a magical mirror."

Nothing could answer. Not even a breeze stirred.

"Not a mirror such as Biancabella found. That would be more than my humble needs. Only one where I could look from afar and see how my beloved, my bride, my Constance, fared."

Stars appeared over the sunset turning pure violet.

"Or a magical pool." He shifted his weight. "With a magical salmon that would tell me how Constance fared. Better than betraying a bride to her evil mother."

A wind rustled by him. He felt suddenly, as if from nowhere, stiff. The fur seemed to tighten around him, and not let go.

For a moment, he could not breathe, while his heart drummed in his chest. He had felt like this before. Once. As the spell had first taken hold, turning him into a bear while Zelphine had gloated before him.

Now he felt what he had not then: a pressure on him, irresistible, to walk off from the house. Into the woods. He could not feel the destination, but he knew—he knew—he was being borne off to the castle where Zelphine and her daughter waited for him, to force him to marry her.

He trudged along the halls and out the door. The sky had darkened, and stars had increased. How? How could this happen? Constance would never have betrayed him. Her family would never have committed any folly. The spell could not be changed at a whim.

Constance could not have betrayed him, his heart wailed.

No thought of his slowed his pace, through the garden and into the woods. The moon rose soon after, before the last of the sunset vanished, and shed some light on the way. At times, he moodily thought that he would fall over a cliff and at least be free of Zelphine's threatened marriage, but his paws always found sure footing.

He trudged on as the moon rose and began to sank. Exhaustion did not slow him, even when moon set with the sky already lightening. Or make his steps less sure.

What curse would allow so simple an escape?

#

The clear day was cooler than the days before, with leaves heaping up in odd corners like a fleeting dragon's hoard. Basil courteously saw the minstrel off. Biancabella, humming under her breath, swept and happily remembered the wedding: Snow-White, dressed in green, radiant with delight, and Florio, his fur neatly combed, looking as pleased as his bear face could manage.

They had danced to the lute's tunes, they had watched the dog dance and laughed as it leapt to lick their faces, and they had eaten the meal of chicken and pastry and fresh-baked bread and what seemed like half the garden cooked up.

A gust of wind sent red leaves flying about. She smiled. How angry Augusta Gloriana would be to see all this.

A sound came down the stairs. She glanced at the shadows and concluded it was indeed rather late in the morning. Rapunzel looked up with a bone-white face, and Biancabella bit her lip. Curses did not always break at once. Even if she ignored all that her governess had taught her, they had the story of Constance before them.

Sometimes you tried to break the curse, and the cursed person died in agony.

Footsteps followed. Biancabella's fingers tightened on the broom, and told herself that Snow-White would be wise and not burn Florio's bearskin. Even were she a fool—fool enough to imagine disasters for her children before she had married—she had listened to Constance.

A dark-haired young man came down the stairs with Snow-White. Even with Basil sitting at the table, Biancabella still blinked at the sight of him.

Constance leapt to her feet. "Florio!"

He, laughing, threw up one hand. "Don't kiss me, sister!"

Biancabella let out her breath slowly as Florio's radiant family gathered about him and his bride. She looked away. She had done that, she told herself, and should be proud of herself. Then she realized that Hans, grave-faced, stood in the doorway before her.

Hans smiled. It made him look sadder than before. "How lovely happy endings are."

"So they are," said Biancabella, and resolved to wait only until Constance took her leave before she spoke with the mirror. She could leave the next day if she laid her plans at once. Winter was coming, but giving her mother more time to plot was unwise.

#

Constance, unkissed, walked off into the woods. Scarlet leaves cascaded on her in a breeze.

Rapunzel smiled a little, but then sighed. Constance had, after all, grown wistful as she had watched her brother, so easily disenchanted. "Perhaps she will return to Sigurd to find he's as shed of his bearskin as you are."

"Heaven grant that he is," said Florio. "We shall hear soon enough. Every traveler will exclaim over how the kingdom is disenchanted."

Basil frowned. "Perhaps—perhaps we should send word to my father. After all, I also am disenchanted, and I have a wife and two children he should know of."

In the silence after, Biancabella said, "I wish to speak to the mirror. I wish to leave on the morrow, and I hope to learn some way that I can travel that would benefit me."

John nodded. After a moment, Hans did as well.

"I will come with you," said Rapunzel, standing. "You will need supplies for the way. Best to know what your path will be."

Moments later, Biancabella stood before the mirror as the face slowly came into view, as serene as ever. Rapunzel sat, her hands folded into her lap, and Hans and John lurked by the door.

The fox leapt up on a box and looked attentively.

"I have come to find out what I may," said Biancabella. "Before I leave. Constance left—"

"She will find that the castle is bare," said the mirror. The words tolled out like a church bell for the dead. "It holds no servants, no food, no clothes, no lights. Sigurd travels from it as far and as fast as his feet can bear him. Against his will."

Biancabella's mouth fell open. Then she pulled it shut to swallow. After all they did, after how careful Constance was—she felt John's hand on her arm, pulling her back to sit.

"She can't!" wailed Rapunzel, looking pale and aged. "She—no one kissed her!"

"There was a dog," said the mirror.

Moments inched by.

"The dog?" said Biancabella, her thoughts moving sluggishly. The dog that had—licked her face? "Was it one of them in disguise? Or did Ottoline transform someone to do it?"

"Neither of those," said the mirror. "Nor was the minstrel one of them. She—" Biancabella blinked. "—was just offered a suggestion that she might come with her dog this way, to better hide the direction of her journey, and to win a few coins that would aid it."

"Offered by?" said Basil, coldly.

"Offered by Ottoline."

John all but snarled. "And she did not come within so much as eyesight of us, to hide herself." His hand formed a fist. "If she had come closer—"

"She's not an entire fool," said Biancabella, quietly. They should have had Constance come up here before she left. Now, even if they chased after her, who could catch her? "We should have wondered. We did not even notice that the minstrel had disguised herself as a boy."

"She used magic," said the mirror.

The wind rattled the window panes.

"Is he—does Sigurd have to marry this Zelphine's daughter?" said Biancabella.

"No," said the mirror, "no. Zelphine had a daughter, yes, but she also had a son. She was content, for a time, to let the curse work on Sigurd, to bring him to obedience, but her son wanted to marry, so he built a house—a fine house in a hillside. Then he found a peasant woman. She had three daughters—Leocadia, Anthia, and Rhode—and they were so poor that she scarcely managed to feed them all. He offered to hire one as a maidservant. She did not like the look of him, but Leocadia said she had to help the family, they were so poor she could not sit about, and so she went with him, giving them the first wages that he gave her.

"She realized he was a sorcerer soon enough, but kept her mouth shut and cleaned and swept and dusted and cooked. He was pleased enough, but one day, he put her to the test: gave her the keys to the house, and an egg that she was to carry everywhere, and told her not to open a door while he was gone on a journey.

"She lasted for a time, but after a while, she persuaded herself that the room needed to be cleaned like all the rest, and opened the door. Then she dropped the egg, because the room was filled with bodies that had been all torn to pieces.

"That day, the sorcerer returned, asked for the egg, saw it covered with blood, and tore her to pieces.

"Then he went back to the peasant woman and told her that Leocadia was finding it hard to do all the work, Anthia was needed too, and gave her a pile of gold as Leocadia's wages. Anthia said that if Leocadia could do the family that much good, she ought to go, too.

"She found the place strange, because she never saw Leocadia, and the sorcerer's excuses were weak, but she kept it clean, and the sorcerer put her to the same test. She waited only until he was gone to go to the door, because she thought it might tell her what happened to Leocadia—which it did indeed—and the sorcerer was back in minutes, and she was torn to pieces as well.

"Finally, he went back for Rhode, and she went to find out what happened to her sisters—and when she did not find them in the house, she asked no questions. The sorcerer was pleased with that, thinking she did not concern herself, but in time, he put her to the same test.

"The first thing she did was put down the egg somewhere safe, and the second thing she did was open the door and see her sisters. She tried to put their bodies back in order, and found that they joined up again, and her sisters came to life.

"She hid them. When, weeks later, the sorcerer returned, he checked the egg and was well-pleased with her. He told her that she was so good and faithful a housekeeper that he had decided to marry her. He would send for his mother and sister at once.

"She told him that as his betrothed wife, she wanted to send gifts from the household to her mother, since there would be no more wages. She would make up a bundle for him to carry, and she would prepare for the wedding while he brought it. Thus, he would show he would be as good and faithful a husband as she would be a wife by carrying it to her mother without looking. She would watch from the window as she worked, and so know it.

"She took gold and silver, and her two sisters, and bundled them up, and put food on top, and told him to give it all to her mother. He took it up and trudged off. It was very heavy, and he thought to look inside. He put it down, and then he heard a voice shrilly scolding him, 'I can see you! I can see you!'

"It was Leocadia, but he thought it was Rhode, so he lifted it up again, and walked on. Much later, in a forest, he thought the trees would hide him, and he lowered it again, and a voice shrilly scolded him, 'I can see you! I can see you!'

"It was Anthia, but he still thought it was Rhode, so he carried the bundle to their mother and turned about.

"Meanwhile, Rhode had dressed up a dummy in fine wedding clothes and stood it by the window, looking out. Then she covered herself in honey and rolled in feathers, and walked off down the way. She met Zelphine and her daughter, who thought she was some strange creature, and asked her the way.

"'I am Fitcher's Bird,' she said, 'Fitcher's Bird I am—and I walk backwards the way you wish to go on.'

"So they hurried off, and her son hurried to join them, and they looked about. Zelphine told him that his bride sat about at the window and had done nothing.

"'What a layabout!' said the son. 'She sat there to watch me, and did nothing of what she had said she would—she only acted a good housekeeper to win me!' They went up to chastise her, and found it was only a dummy—but by then, Leocadia, Rhode, and Anthia had told all the people about how an evil sorcerer lived in the hill. A whole crowd of them went up to burn the house out. Zelphine died there, and her daughter and son as well."

"And serves them right," said John.

"Perhaps it does," said the mirror, "but it left the castle where Zelphine lived with her daughter empty. That is where the curse will draw Sigurd."

"And," said Biancabella gloomily, "Constance will be unable to find it because Augusta Gloriana will stop—"

"Ah—" said the mirror, shaking its face back and forth. "No. If Augusta Gloriana made it impossible for Constance to reach the castle, that would also make it impossible for Sigurd to reach it."

"If Zelphine can't marry him to her daughter," said Hans, "why would that matter? Did they just forget?"

"No," said the mirror. "Mark who told your minstrel."

Biancabella's thoughts moved slowly. "She is not happy—Otto-line—that she is married to Herbert."

"So," said John flatly, "she wants to marry Sigurd. And is using the spell."

"Yes," said the mirror.

Biancabella bit her lip and collected herself. "Is there anything we can do to help Constance?"

For a moment, all was silent.

"Not now. Perhaps not to come, either."

"The dog," said John, fiercely. "Was that a creature that should not be trusted?"

"It was a dog," said the mirror, mildly. "Once upon a time, a sorceress turned a maiden into a living doll, no larger than the maiden's hand had been. She lived in the grass.

"But one day, a peasant woman sent out her twelve sons to find brides, and bring back a shirt that the bride had spun and woven and sewed. The eleven oldest refused to let the youngest go with them, and stole his horse.

"So he stood in the grass, and the doll came out to ask why he stood there. He told her how he could not travel to find his bride and could not return home without one. So the doll told him to bring her some flax, and she would do the deed for him. Within a day, he returned home with the finest shirt his mother had ever seen. When, many weeks later, his brothers returned, they had shirts, but some were such that a man might wear while cleaning tools, and others were fit only for rags.

"Then the mother gave them each of a puppy and told them to have the bride train the dog. The eleven brothers rode off, and the youngest went to the grass, and there the doll trained the dog so well that it could keep watch, and herd sheep, and hunt deer, and dance and do tricks as well. He brought it back, and the mother was charmed. But the brothers returned with their dogs. Some did not bite.

"Then the mother told them to bring their brides, and she would ready the wedding feast for the day. The youngest went to bring the doll, and she set out in a silver spoon, drawn by a mouse. And they came to a bridge, and she fell in. He jumped in to rescue her, but when he did, she had turned into a full-sized woman, and she was radiantly lovely. His mother was much taken with her, more than the ugly brides of her other sons, and so she named the youngest her heir.

"But—the king of their country was attacked, and summoned up all the peasants, and was still defeated so that all his men lie in prison. The bride who had been a doll got up, disguised herself as a boy, and took her lute and her dog and went to see if she could charm the king who triumphed. King Maximus, he is. But first she went to cast about the kingdom, so that she would come from the other way and not make him suspect."

Silence lasted a minute, broken only by the gusting of the wind.

"Well," said Rapunzel flatly, her hands folded in her lap, "may Heaven bless her path. It would profit us nothing if she fails."

Biancabella frowned. "Why would they just use her like that, and not even care that she escaped their spells? She might even win back her husband."

The mirror chuckled. Biancabella blinked. Nothing they had done had ever struck her as funny.

"None of them cursed her," said the mirror. "In fact, the witch who cursed her was the same witch who cursed the prince to have to marry Snow-White-Fire-Red, and who gave the horse to the prince—the one that had crushed Boney's skull."

Biancabella let her breath out.

Hans snorted. "So they don't mind her." He hooked his hand on his belt. "You told me that the Bird of Truth might help me."

"It might. I would advise you, like that minstrel, to cast around that kingdom, because King Maximus is a tyrant. You are luckier than she, because you can avoid him entirely. He did not invade that kingdom she came from for any good reason, but because he thought he could gain from it—the kingdom has been unfortunate in its kings ever since the king refused to heed the Bird of Truth."

It hesitated. "I know of nothing along the way, except that there is a kingdom troubled by the want of a king, but that means little."

John shifted, but his voice was crisp when he spoke. "I have pondered King Drakos. Can something be done to help his daughter and the prince?"

"In order to reach his lands," said the mirror, "crossing burning deserts, a traveler would need more than ordinary water. He would need the very Water of Life. And that alone can save Ian, as well."

John leaned forward, intent.

"And, on King Drakos's request, Augusta Gloriana cast a spell to hide the land where that water is from all who were alive, or yet to be born, when she cast it."

The mirror paused a moment. Biancabella scowled. That was specific. She wondered if she were included in that.

"That, Prince John, was while you lay dead."

John swallowed. His gaze went to Hans, and then back to the mirror. Biancabella looked at her hands. After a minute, her thoughts managed to come clear: if John could see the way there, she should help Hans, who had no such aid.

"The circle has not been idle," said the mirror. "While you worked, they worked. The six princesses who choose to marry six princes who were brothers—they rode too close to where Boney lives. He turned them to stone. Augusta Gloriana has blinded the way, so that their youngest brother can not find them."

John groaned. "There is no choice. Let Hans go to find the Bird of Truth, let me go to find this Water of Life. Perhaps there is a chance that they will not have laid seven more curses by the time we've broken one."

Biancabella said, quietly, "It would be best if I went with Hans, since you can see the way to the Water of Life."

John's face twisted.

"Since I seek only to find a way to stop them, which is like going to I-Know-Not-Where to bring back I-Know-Not-What—possible only if—" She waved her hand in the air. "—an enchantress who can turn into a bird tells me how."

"Perhaps Vasilisa can tell you how," murmured the mirror, "if the water of life lets John rescue her."

"Until then," said Biancabella, "undoing their work may let me stumble on the way." She smiled, and hoped it did not look too strained. "That is how we put an end to Mother Trude and all her evil spells."

John's grave gaze was steady on her face.

"I will be—grateful for her aid," said Hans.

"I can go with her," said the fox, brightly. "Since she is your niece. And protect her." It scratched its ear with its hind leg.

#

They had much to do that day. Heed the mirror's directions, and pack what they could carry. Rapunzel spoke to a low voice to Basil soon after they came down, as they went about packing.

Shortly after, Basil came to them bearing food. "I think that I will not, after all, go to speak with my father."

He looked rather gray.

"Is there something we can ask the Bird of Truth for you?" said Biancabella.

He shook his head. "No more than you were going to ask already. How to stop them."

#

"Now you see," said Augusta Gloriana, spreading her hand in the chilly moonlight. "Already Constance, who had thought herself more wise than us, chases her bridegroom through the wild. Ottoline has her wholly trapped. It is just a matter of outsmarting them."

She would persuade the circle to return to the castle, and its comforts, before the night was done, she told herself. The cold and the damp and the dark would do her work for her.

Glances colder than the air looked back.

"As if *Constance* were a danger," said King Drakos. "She can not win her way to my kingdom. Your daughter—"

"My daughter?" snapped Augusta Gloriana. "As if she had the water of life in her back pocket." She swept her hand toward Mistress Laurenza. "Ask her! Her silly Aviette could *fly* there." She looked over. "Have you even found her?"

"Are you saying," said Mistress Laurenza, "that your spells will not keep Aviette from seeing Vasilisa and Ian?"

Augusta Gloriana's eyes narrowed. Well. There was no point in pressing her for an answer—all the more in that she had clearly given one. What did she form this circle for, if they expected her to serve as the maid of all work?

"You speak as if a spell were as easily wrought as speaking," she said. "But I am ready for that. Already I have incited King Maximus to cut off roads, so that no one can pass, and now—now we must stir up winter storms, so they can pass by no roads."

"A thousand pities," said Mother Magda, dryly, "that you can't get her on shipboard. A shipwreck would do her good." She put a finger to her mouth "Or perhaps we could get someone to throw her overboard."

"She can do no more than see through spells," said Augusta Gloriana. "Prudence can manage with that. She can not travel by magic, taking on wings and flying over all difficulties. Far more dangerous—far unwiser to give that power before the girl can be trusted."

Rumpelstiltskin harrumphed. "If we had the mirror still, we could find Aviette and Biancabella easily—and the mirror, too, at that."

Boney laughed, a bone-deep sound. "Set your house in order with what you have. Rumpelstiltskin and I *keep* ours."

Said Augusta Gloriana, "You came to me swiftly enough when you turned those princes and princesses to stone and wanted them hidden from prying eyes."

#

They left the Four Winds at dawn, as if they were any other travelers, and at the crossroads, they took another way, which she had not walked down before—and none of the others had, either. It went on through the woods, where tree after tree bore no leaves, or only a ragged scattering of red and gold. Here and there an oak still showed green, but even there red and orange and dark coppery brown covered most of the boughs.

It was the grass on the road that Biancabella most noted.

With inns every night—and without the fox ever telling them to favor one inn over another—they walked for three days, meeting few travelers either on the way or at the inns.

On the third day, in the morning mist, the innkeeper sent them off with the warning, "There's a crossroads—make sure you do not take the northern routes. Takes you out of the kingdom—you go through forest instead."

Biancabella nodded solemnly, adjusting her pack.

"All the more in that it's the winter," said the innkeeper, as if he were telling her more to delay her departure than give her knowledge. "The ways are hard, and you should be not be caught on them. You want to make it to King Maximus's lands. He puts down robbers like they ought to be—other lands, you get their chief coming out to talk some maid into promising to marry him, so he can lure her off, and the band *feast* on her—or they tear apart a family in the road—or they go and change messages you carry—"

Or they open an inn and seize you in the night, thought Biancabella.

"No, stick to King Maximus's kingdom," said the inn-keeper.

"Biancabella," said Hans, cheerfully. "We have to be off."

The inn-keeper turned on him. "You have to be careful—"

"To leave on time, so we are not caught by night," said Hans, and she all but ran to join him. The fox frisked on the way, chasing copper-colored leaves.

#

The oak forest had boughs laden with leaves of every shade of brown and a forest floor littered with dead leaves. Hans sang merrily along.

"And on this tree there grew a fine bough,

The finest bough that ever you did see,

And the bough on the tree, and the tree in the wood,

And the green leaves flourished thereon, thereon, thereon,

And the green leaves flourished thereon.

"And on this bough there a fine twig,

The finest twig that ever you did see,

And the twig on the bough, and the bough on the tree,
and the tree in the wood,

And the green leaves flourished thereon, thereon, thereon,

And the green leaves flourished thereon."

Biancabella smiled, looking about. Months and months before
they saw another green leaf. Though not three years, three months,
three weeks, and three days—

They came to a stream, and after a few paces, it splashed over
a waterfall—a low one, no higher than Biancabella—and into a
broad pool. The road circled about it, and no nixie rose from the
waters, to try to seize either man.

Behind the pool, a bridge took the road over the stream, and
beyond it stood the crossroads the mirror had warned of.

With a signpost that marked the ways. Not that they had to rely on it. Biancabella let her breath out. Herself and Hans and the
fox, to the north and east—John to the north and west. And swiftly, so as to use the remaining day to travel as far as they could.

At least the signpost indicated directions, and not that whoever went one way would suffer hunger and thirst, and the other,
would die though his horse would live, and the third, would live
but his horse would die.

"Heaven protect and prosper your journey," said John.

"Heaven protect and prosper yours," said Biancabella.

The fox headed off down their road, and glanced back over its
shoulder.

Chapter 10—The Winter's Journey

"You're going straight through the old town?" said the inn-keeper's daughter, pouring cider into their mugs again.

"Oh, yes," said Hans.

She shook her head. "I suppose it's not dangerous. Or not too dangerous."

The gray-haired inn-keeper, in the back of the room, snorted. "Anyone who would go through the town would—would go up to a ruined castle covered with roses—and get himself torn to bits."

"Or pick a rose?" said Biancabella. How often they got so much advice, she thought. "From a rose bush that is obviously in a garden?"

"Or even one from two rose trees before the house of a widow with two daughters," said Hans dryly. "That would be rude. We shall keep our hands to ourselves, then."

A loud snort came from the kitchen. The cook looked out, shaking a ladle at them. "Nothing so fancy about them. They just moved out when the king died without an heir. Never mind any plant you see."

"That would call for not picking the roses, either," said Biancabella.

Hans winced.

If they found any blooming roses at this season, they would both keep their hands far away.

The cook snorted again. "Wise of you. It's not an easy day. 'Twill take you all day to reach Kingston. Without stopping to pick flowers, like some fools do."

Thinking of the danger, Biancabella opened her mouth. Then she glanced at Hans and shut it again. She wondered if the rose tree had grown only after Mother Trude had—finished. Then she reminded herself that the tree had grown from his buried bones. It would have to have been after.

Still—she did not think he would find it witty to talk about it.

"Princesses were stolen away by magic," said the inn-keeper's daughter, wide-eyed. "Because they gathered flowers."

#

Noon was near, but at least, the buildings of the old town rose before them.

Biancabella swallowed. They had seen no one since halfway through the morning, but even so, the town's emptiness seemed unnerving. Roofs had lost tiles, or fallen in, or been overgrown with ivy. That, at least, was flourishing green. Biancabella wondered if there would be holly on the way.

They walked quickly through it. The fox all but trotted in its haste. Then they came about a corner, and in the middle of a circle scorched into the earth, a rose bush grew. Biancabella's mouth went dry. A single, flourishing rose bush with a single rose in perfect bloom, delicately colored, like the dawn, in pinks and creamy yellows.

She stood and stared.

"What is it?" said the fox, snappish. "It's one of the harder days, the inn-keeper said. We need to make good time to reach the inn by sunset."

Mutely, Biancabella pointed.

With a grunt of surprise, Hans stopped. Far outside the scorch marks. The fox scowled.

"Did—did you see where the fire burned?" said Biancabella. "Before I pointed it out?"

Hans sighed. "I think I did." He ran his hand through his hair. "I think we found a place that the mirror spoke of. The place where they burned Elinor at the stake." Then he looked at Biancabella. "Is there a chain or something of the kind holding the rose bush?"

"I can not see one," said Biancabella, faintly.

"I've heard the tales," he said grimly. "You have to take up the plant and then keep it safe in a pot or the like. If you do not see anything to help her—we could kill her if we erred."

Biancabella looked away. She had, indeed, been fortunate in saving Hans.

"Pity the mirror didn't tell us," said the fox, brightly, its tail swishing the air. "Let us go on. Perhaps the Bird of Truth can tell us."

Now, that was a cheerful thought. Biancabella walked more briskly, only partly to leave the rose in distance. Before they left the town, the royal castle was visible in the distance. The town below was not visible, but there, she knew, they would find the next inn.

#

Kingston hove into view steadily as the evening approached, and Biancabella forced herself to not slow. Hans and the fox were sober and silent, viewing it. The castle was hung with banners in black and deep violet, and the town below was subdued, all the crowds going about their business in drab colors, gray and brown and dull blues and greens, and many a soul wearing black. She bit her lip. Some town buildings were also hung with black banners.

"We'd have heard if there were a dragon," whispered Biancabella.

"And," said the fox, "there's no princess." It trotted up the next rise and stood there, watching, as they caught up. "There's a prince," it said idly, "but the story was that he was to marry, and then something went wrong." It paused, and said, less idly, "Death, perhaps."

"Which would explain the array at least," said Hans. "Mourning."

Biancabella glanced sideways at him. She would not put slaying a dragon past him. And then—he could marry a princess whose mother was very different from her own.

But not here, she thought, and felt oddly pleased.

#

"We'll be glad when the mourning's over," said the inn-keeper of the Laughing Rose. He shook his head as his wife dished up the bowls of fish stew. "A full year of this, for a princess who never even once set foot in the kingdom."

"Well, you're a hardhearted fellow," said his wife, pushing the bowls in front of them. "It's a sad tale."

Biancabella took her bowl. The room was filled, with a few travelers tucking into the stew, but mostly townsfolk drinking ale.

"We have not heard the tale fully," said Hans. "And we know how rumors spread. I've heard of tales that said an ogre lived in a castle, which actually had an enchanted princess."

The fox looked up, inquisitively.

"Here, we have the sort of tale that makes you wish for a dragon instead," said the wife. "A hero could slay it, then. But our king, King Niels, arranged for a marriage to a princess from another land."

Biancabella nodded.

"While she was coming here with her maid, they came to a bridge, and the maid went to push her over. The princess begged for her life and promised to never tell man or woman or child what the maid had done, but the maid jeered at her and said she would tell a horse or a stove or *something*, and drowned her."

Biancabella, icy cold, wondered whether her mother had suggested that to the maid, or whether she had worked it out on her own.

"Then she donned the princess's clothing and came with a sad tale of her attendants being lost in the river. Our prince, Prince Thomas, was less than taken with her, but the arrangements had been made.

"But one day, a peasant lad saw a reed growing from the river, and made a pipe from it. Such a pipe! He could play such a tune that everyone would weep, or dance, or fall asleep by it. So word was sent that he had to come to the castle and play for the wedding. He came, but as soon as he was here, the pipe began to play a new tune, denouncing the maid as her murderer.

"Prince Thomas went to the river where the reed had grown, and had them dig. Sure enough, the princess's body had been buried there. He sent word to her parents, who sent back word that the maid had sworn to care for the princess, and that if she failed in that duty, she should be thrown into a barrel set with nails, and have it dragged by horses until she died. She suffered the sentence, but—the princess was dead. The prince went and had the pipe put in her dead mouth, but even that did not revive her."

"Wasn't much chance of that," said the inn-keeper as he poked the fire.

"Tales have been told where it did," said his wife. "Pipe never played so marvelously again, either. So Prince Thomas had her buried, and declared a year of mourning."

"Nearly over," said one drinker, a grizzled old man. "Only reasonable, for a princess, no wonder King Niels agreed, but it will be over soon."

"Then the prince will need a new bride," said a tiny black-haired woman over her ale. "Not going to be easy. The king is not so much as trying, and no ambassador has so much as suggested a new bride."

"It's not like it's wise for him to sit around and see if someone kills some giants," said a nut-brown woman, back in corner.

"Princess Katrina happened on her husband in the day—but she had to hold an inn and let everyone stay there the night, and winkle the tale out of them, before she finally found it was a peasant boy named Niels who did the deed."

"A good king," said the grizzled man, "and they didn't name our king after him for nothing, but not a wise way to find a bride. Few are the brides who can kill giants."

"There was one who killed a whole army," said a ruddy woman of middle years, but no one seemed to think of a response to it, and silence fell.

Biancabella ate.

A young man stared at his cider.

"Perhaps he should hold a ball," said Hans. "And hope for a more fortunate ending."

The inn-keeper snorted. "You don't believe that story about how the girl was a witch?" Nods and murmurs of agreement all about—Biancabella's tongue touched her lips.

"That," she said, "would make it even more unfortunate. We came through the old town. The place of the burning is still charred."

"There's tales," said the young man without looking up from the cider, "that there's stronger magic about that."

"I—saw something that looked odd," she confessed.

He slapped down his mug. "I'll see for myself."

She opened her mouth to speak, and then shut it again. Offering to go with him would only raise questions of why she had such powers. Where they had once burned a woman as a witch, they could it again.

#

The last few days, inns had stood along the way, sometimes with a bit of village clumping about, but sometimes as lonely as the Four Winds.

This evening, as they came over a hill, the inn perched at a crossroads was another solitary one. It held no other travelers this night. The inn-keeper, bent over the garden fence and hammering away, looked up with surprise and hastened over, leaving tools strewn about, to bow and welcome them to the Golden Stag.

Minutes later, they sat by the fire as the innkeeper's wife said, "Rabbit stew, with carrots," and the innkeeper vanished outside. The sound of the hammer came soon after.

"Not many people on the road to Kingston, this late in the year," said the innkeeper's wife, putting down the bowls on the table.

"We're not," said Hans. "We're going over the river."

Soup slopped from the bowl.

Moments later, with the bowl new filled, and her rag mopping the table, she said, "It's been months since a traveler went that way. Because of the trouble, what with the king."

"We heard," said Biancabella cautiously, "that there was trouble along the way, because of a kingdom without a king, but if that were enough to make a way utterly unsafe, no one could travel at all."

"Other lands may suffer from bandits and the like for the want of a king," said the woman firmly, "but when the land had just lost a king, it is unsettled past measure."

Biancabella looked at her soup. Her reflected face looked back, blankly. The Bird of Truth, she reminded herself. The king would not return and make the way safe in time for them to speak with the bird.

She ate.

"Even if you travel without trouble," said the innkeeper's wife, "you will have a hard journey to reach the next inn before sundown."

#

The forest to either hand was thick with still green pines. Here and there, a stand of leafless birches stood, white and ghost-like. Their yellow leaves had scattered over the forest floor and faded to a wan beige. The pines' dead needles were still amber-red and scented the air. Biancabella was not certain whether the day was actually warmer than the day before, or the shelter from the wind merely made it seem so.

Not so much as a peasant seeking firewood ventured through the trees.

Which, she reminded herself as they hurried, was better than facing bandits or wolves. It was not as if she had escaped a tower she was imprisoned in only to find her father's kingdom lain waste by war. Kingdoms did hold lands where few people lived.

A bird sang in the trees. The fox frisked ahead, a brighter orange against the dead needles.

"I wonder if he'll find anything," said Hans.

Biancabella glanced at him.

"That man back in the Laughing Rose—I was wondering what he would find. Besides charred earth."

Biancabella let her breath out. "I hope so." She had told Hans and the fox of it, and they had seen it—but they had seen where she looked, too.

The fox abruptly stopped on a hillock. Biancabella hurried up.

A doe looked at them. Biancabella's breath gushed out. Its hide was not pale brown—or gold, or white—but a gleaming gray like lead. Its eyes were great and mild, and after a moment, it ambled onward.

Biancabella took a few steps after it.

"It could lead us to a witch who would turn us to stone," said Hans.

"Or a wise man who will tell me that a peasant boy will grow up to marry my daughter," said Biancabella. "So that I will go try to kill the boy, and as a consequence, he will end up marrying her, and I will end up endlessly ferrying people across a river, magically bound to the ferry." She glanced sideways at Hans. "Or he'll tell you."

"Don't be foolish," said the fox. "Obviously, the wise man will tell *me* that." He circled around. "And I will admire his judgment."

A childish and gleeful laugh came out of the woods, and Biancabella started. The doe had not needed to lead them anywhere.

Moments later, a woman ran after a small child, with the doe lingering behind her, at the edge of the woods. The child roared with merriment as the woman swept him up and to her shoulder.

Sunlight glinted, and Biancabella's tongue froze in her mouth. The woman's hair was blond, and the child's as well, but what gleamed was her hands. Made of metal—it had to be silver—and yet they moved as easily as any woman's hands ever did.

Then the woman froze in place. The child fussed, without drawing her attention. She whispered, barely loud enough for them to hear, "You can see me."

Biancabella, slowly, nodded. It was at least an indication that this woman might not turn on them as Mother Trude had on Hans and his sister, if she were hidden by the same spells.

The woman shifted her child in her arms and rose to her full height. Her voice, clear and melodic, rose. "I give you good day. May Heaven protect you, when your path has brought you this way." Her gaze went among them, and her eyebrow went up, a little, at the sight of the fox. The child looked at them, and then turned shyly away. "If you came this way by chance, I would bid you return and choose a more fortunate way. If you came this way to find the bridge across the river, I would bid you return and choose another way to another bridge."

"It was a good stout bridge," said the fox, uneasily.

"It was," said the woman sadly. The wind pulled on her hair, making strands as bright as wheat float on the air. "But King Maximus thinks nothing of such things when he wages war. Even less of whether the land he conquers will make him prosper if he destroys such things."

Biancabella's heart beat harder, like a drum in her ears. This could not be the war where the lute-player's husband had been taken, but the same king might attack twice.

"Madame," said Hans, "you seem to know much of what chances here."

She raised her head. "My name is Genoveva. This, my son, is Edward. I was the queen of this land, and he, its prince. Now I and my son enjoy the hospitality of this doe in the wild forest. If you do not scorn to share it, perhaps I can tell you some things that you may need knowledge of."

#

Genoveva led the way uphill. A stream babbled beside them, through rough rocks. The pines grew twisted by the wind, and finally, they reached a grassy sward, with rough outcroppings behind it. Pines grew over it, but below a cave mouth gaped.

The cave was set with heaps of dried fern, and seemed warmer than any cave should be in this weather, even before a fire sprang up on logs. The smoke rose and did not cloud the cave, Biancabella did not see how, and the doe settled between them and the forest.

Genoveva went to lay Edward on the ferns.

Biancabella sat on another heap of ferns and felt colder than she had on the days of wind and frost. At her sideways glance, the doe only looked back at her with great mild eyes, but for all she knew, it was an enchantress bound into that shape by Ottoline's spellcraft.

The child slept under a little blanket, and firelight glided them all. Hans sat still and watchful. The fox sat bolt upright, all ears. Biancabella folded her hands in her lap.

The woman sat. "I—am a princess by birth, the daughter of King Ogier, and his wife, the late Queen Doralise. She—died when I was seven, and before she died, he pledged to her that he would never marry a woman except one who could wear her ring." She looked down at her hands and whispered, "Why do they always ask for that?"

"They don't," said Biancabella, almost as softly. "Sometimes, they promise never to refuse their daughters anything, and then your wicked stepmother just has to persuade you to ask him to marry her."

Genoveva sighed and looked up. "I wished that he had, and that I had—a wicked stepmother is better than a father who decides that as the only woman who can wear your mother's ring, you have to marry him. And he locked me in a tower to keep me safe until the wedding. But—" She lifted her hands. "—I managed to stop being able to wear her ring. So he chased me out into the forest."

Hans winced, and looked caught between sympathy and haunting memory.

"There King Hendrik found me and wooed me, and brought me back to his kingdom, where he made me his queen and had these hands made for me. It is, after all, a kingdom famed for the wonders of its automata.

"But—King Maximus had attacked the lands to the south and east, only, having conquered them, he turned and came to the west. His forces caught King Hendrik with only a few men about him and killed them all." Her breath caught. "When—when the news came back, an old woman claimed that I had done it, through witchcraft. And that my child had been born a dragon, and not a human child at all. It had been smuggled out of the castle and would return to demand a bride—and my actual son was smuggled in to replace him, or was at most the younger of twins."

She twisted her hands.

"She roused up the crowds so thoroughly that the queen mother had me smuggled out of the castle to the forest—for safety."

Hans turned his face away, staring into the fire.

"In the forest, this doe found us. We have lived here this last three months, under its protection."

The fire snapped. A plume of sparks rose.

"King Maximus has not attacked again, I do not know why, but I do not dare venture out for fear of it." Her mouth pursed, for a moment. "And where would I go? Even were the bridge up."

She turned to look at them. "You may have to cast about far to find your way around. I do not think they would suspect wayfarers of witchcraft to harm the king, but they might."

The fox nodded sharply. "Where does your husband's body lie, Your Majesty?"

Genoveva gawked. Biancabella blinked. Hans slowly turned to look at the fox.

"It seems to me to be the quickest way through the kingdom, if something can be done." The fox stood. "All the more in that there is no need to wait for morning."

#

The herb was evergreen, there was that advantage. It was good to have one advantage.

The fox picked its way over the frozen ground, where hoof and foot print in mud had frozen into ridges and dips as hard as rock, and the moonlight turned them into a maze of shadows.

"The fox went out on a chilly night," it sang, "It prayed to the Moon to give it light, for it'd many a mile to go that night."

Then a hand lay sprawled on the mud, emerging from shadow. Moonlight leached all color from it, but its nose confirmed the dead man lying in the tree's shadow, and the others about. Half a dozen—it lifted its head and sniffed for something else. He might have given Genoveva false hope. The herb could not travel far; if John's brothers had not struck where they did, John would still lie dead, and if the herb did not grow near here—

The scent struck its nose. More like spice than most greenery—but enough to have the fox leaping through the brush toward it.

#

The dawn was pale and rosy, and the company looked even more dazed as the time wound on, and the wintry scene became clear. Except for King Hendrik. He looked only fiercely intent on their path.

A man's voice rose out of the cave as they approached.

"And on this twig there stood a fine nest,

The finest nest that ever you did see,

And the nest on the twig, and the twig on the bough, and the bough on the tree, and the tree in the wood,

And the green leaves flourished thereon, thereon, thereon,

And the green leaves flourished thereon."

The child laughed with glee.

King Hendrik's shadow fell over the entrance. The faces within looked up, pale in the gloom, and then Queen Genoveva ran out of the cave to throw her arms about his neck.

#

Biancabella watched the snow fall outside the cave. Flake after flake. In the back of the cave, the deer lay, awake, with the sleeping boy, and King Hendrik spoke with his men. One urged again that he should come with them.

"After all that's happened already?" said King Hendrik. "They will curse me to forget Queen Genoveva as soon as someone kisses me, and do you think my mother could restrain herself after seeing me alive? Nothing could restrain her. Not even the prospect of telling me that she sent Genoveva away to be so safe that she will not be able to find her again." He shook his head.

Biancabella looked away, thinking of poor Constance.

"And," said Hendrik, "it would not be safe to bring little Edward before the castle is secure."

Edward stirred and started to rise. Genoveva hurried to him.

Hendrik smiled. "It would be as foolish as the queen's not naming my son until I return, and having you all call him Nix-Naught-Nothing until then."

The men nodded, and then separated their numbers according to his command. Three quarters of the men rode ahead, and the rest took up their guard about the cave. Hendrik came back in, and Genoveva smiled quietly.

He nodded to Hans, Biancabella, and the fox. "I fear that the queen's news to you did not convey the disaster that you face. No roads to the north lead to where you wish to go. There were three bridges, and King Maximus destroyed them all."

Hans's mouth tightened.

"The only route is to go into King Maximus's lands, or to fall back, and circle about the mountains. It will be a hard journey by winter, but the mountains will be impassable. I can not recommend King Maximus's land, though I may overstate the peril to you three."

Biancabella nodded, slowly. "So—we would go back the way we came, and then circle to the south."

Hendrik nodded.

Hans stood. "It would be best to leave at once. It was a hard journey to make it this far in a day."

Hendrik blinked. "We would be glad to make welcome and feast those heroes who saved myself, my queen, and my realm."

"Your Majesty," said Biancabella, "if we had lingered as long as you would wish us to, among those who wished us to linger before, we might never have come to your aid. There are others whom we wish to aid."

Hendrik's gaze flickered over them, lingered on the fox, and darted back to where the doe sat in serenity.

Let him think that we are enchanter and enchantress, thought Biancabella, as long as he speeds us on our way.

"Certainly," said Genoveva, "you will—any of you will—be welcome whenever you wish to come." She stood, smiling. "We will be certain to arrange a marvel and a wonder for you to see if you so return. And for now, may Heaven bless your journey with an ending as happy as ours."

King Hendrik nodded. "And a way somewhat easier."

Biancabella tried to smile, remembering John, lying dead.

Outside, the snow still fell.

#

John looked at the slope before him. Crags and cliffs, and the road little more than a path half-hidden by dead, yellow grass. The way was nearly as steep as the crags. Clouds billowed behind in charcoal gray and towered higher than giants—he could only hope that Biancabella did not face so rough a path.

He stamped his feet.

And that he could find a place to camp, and that before it began to snow. No more inns stood on this way. The inn-keeper at the Golden Blackbird had laughed when he told his route, and said that he could not hide that he went on the way to the mountains.

His eyes narrowed. Augusta Gloriana did not put the key to defeat her where it could be found easily. She did not wish her evil plans to be upset. If he failed here, as he had failed Sophia, one day no doubt Biancabella would risk her life here because he had failed her as well.

He watched the roadside warily, looking for a cave, or a hollow, with some shelter against weather.

He came around a bend, and in the middle of the road, a dwarf bore a staff twice his height, which he held flat and blocking the way. He came no higher than John's waist, his iron-gray beard flowed down his face to his feet, and his figure was wiry and strong. The dwarf eyed him sharply. John's eyes narrowed. With a slope of stone below and a tangle of brambles above, making it impossible to walk by him.

"Huh. What brings a traveler to these parts?" said the dwarf.

"Going about my business," said John, sharply. "In a hurry."

"Huh," said the dwarf, eyeing him.

John looked back, and the thought struck him that the dwarf had to have some place to live here. He drew a deep breath, and said, "Please forgive my rudeness, grandfather. I am deeply troubled at heart."

"Huh," said the dwarf again. He looked up John up and down. His eyes narrowed. "There are wiser places to seek shelter from the storm."

"Not if you seek the water of life," said John. "I—it is the only way that an evil curse can be broken. And I do not wish to fail in my quest, so that others will come after me and face the same perils."

The dwarf's voice was half a growl, but he said, "That is a more courteous answer." He turned the staff and thumped the end on the ground. "If you come with me and do not scorn my hospitality, I will give you shelter from the storm, and tell you more of what you seek."

John thanked him. The dwarf stumped off along the road, up the slope and farther up still, as the day darkened beneath the clouds, until John wondered if he was being lured to the summit, to face the storm's full rage.

The cloudy sky started to be visible through the trees ahead—they were near the top. The dwarf looked pleased and trudged onward, but moments later, he turned aside, into a cave, with a fringe of roots from the trees that overgrew it.

John had to duck his head to get inside, but within a stride, the roof rose, and the dwarf opened a door to a room where even the rafters were high enough for John to get by. An enormous fireplace blazed with fire, and about stood wooden furniture—chairs, tables, chests, and enormous cabinets where an open door on one revealed a bed behind—and all brightly painted with stars and hearts, flowers and leaves. Several chairs, one table, and one of the cabinet beds were large enough for him.

With the door shut, it was warm enough that John pulled off his hat and undid his coat.

"A poor thing but my own." The dwarf bowed.

John bowed back. "What can be finer than hospitality to the stranger?"

#

The morning burned brightly. Sunlight glared from the snow. The road could be told only by the absence of trees, and John found himself contemplating whether the snow would break his fall if he missed the way and walked off a cliff.

"Wise of you to come no later," said the dwarf. "You would have to bide until spring and go then. As it is, you will have to stay the winter at the castle there." He handed John a loaf of bread. "Now, go straight down the road and do not stop, because you must reach the end by midnight. It will be dark already by the time you reach the gates of the castle. There you must throw half of this loaf to each of the lions there, so you will not have to stop for them. Go on. And on. To the innermost chamber. There you can ask the princess for the Water of Life."

John nodded solemnly and was glad that the night would have moonlight.

#

That the road had leveled before noon was of some aid, but the footing was not steady even on the level.

John trudged along in the snow, with night gathering around and the moon casting more shadows than light. He thought it was just enough light that he could keep going. Barely. For all the trees to either hand—grim dark sentinels in the whiteness—gusts of wind blew snow on him. It stung his face, and then snow wriggled through every gap in his clothes to melt there. He bent his head against it and told himself that a castle would have shelter.

He peered ahead and saw only darkness. His mouth set. A dark castle would at least give shelter from the wind. He bent his head again and trudged on. His boot slipped so deep in snow that when he pulled it up again, snow slipped down inside it. And melted.

John let out his breath slowly and took a few more steps before he realized that the shadows looming ahead of him were too block-ish in shape to be more trees. Even a cliff might afford shelter.

The shape slowly came clear in the harsh whiteness. A fortress with few windows, a single wrought-iron gate, with lions to either hand. Wind had swept away the snow before the gate, and the stone slabs there showed clearly. Moonlight left the lions colorless and gray like statues, and they sat, but they shifted and looked about with dark eyes, enough for him to know they were living.

His heart hammered. John swallowed, trying to slow it, and re-minded himself that dropping the bread in the snow would ruin all his chances. He inched closer and closer, until he stood on the stone slabs. There, carefully, he pulled off his gloves, ignored how the cold bit at his fingers, and reached for the bag with the bread.

One lion growled, deep in its throat.

He forced his breath out, and in again. Then he drew out the loaf, tore it in two, and looked up at them. The lions looked back. Their faces were imperial, indifferent. He took the bread in each hand and walked forward. When a lion started to rise, he threw the halves.

The lions pounced, catching them, and started to eat. They did not even glance aside as he pushed open the icy iron of the gate and slipped inside.

The courtyard felt warmer already, with the air calm and still. The great doors stood across from him, and he crossed the flag-stones to pull it open.

Torches blazed, burning such warm shades of orange and gold that his breath gusted out in relief. He pulled the door shut behind him, and was shedding his hat and opening his coat before he real-ized that the flames of the torches did not stir. They stood without flickering. And, he remembered, they had not flickered when the door stood open, letting cold air and hot flow about.

He grimaced, and forced himself to speak. "That is exactly what Augusta Gloriana would do."

The words, aloud, did not hearten him. Or, for that matter, rouse anyone in the castle. He walked down the room, letting his footsteps ring. The door at the opposite end stood open a little, letting him see the great banqueting hall, ablaze with candles, the table all set with fine dishes—roasts and heaped up ripe plums and peaches, great loaves of white bread with honey and butter beside them, golden goblets filled with red wine—and all the banqueters about, all along the table, though not at the high seat. Not one of them turned to see him. Not one of them so much as blinked as he inched down the hall.

A door stood at the back, behind the high seat. When he reached it, no one in the hall moved, but the door opened easily to his touch. The air that puffed out was cool, but nowhere near so cold as the outside. Behind stood a silent room, not quite so broad as the hall but with a roof that was much higher. A pale floor spread to octagonal walls of white marble, and vast pillars of sky blue marble, and the vaulted roof was painted with dark blue and hundreds of stars, which glowed and lit the room dimly. Halfway into the room, a pale stair began and rose up to a door almost invisible in the wall. John set his shoulders and climbed.

The door, though as white as the wall and like marble to touch as well, opened easily. The corridor behind was narrow, no more than one man could walk through, and warmer than the room behind. It turned at once.

John started down the way, lit to either hand by lanterns that hung every few paces, and endless turns. The walls to either hand were covered by dazzling tapestries showing marvelous beasts—dragons menacing princesses, unicorns charging toward men who stood before trees, firebirds in fields where they ate scattered grain—all worked in brilliant colors and with the finest of stitchery, so perfectly that once, when he came around a corner, for a moment he blinked and thought a golden horse stood before him.

John walked on and on down the labyrinth. No one stirred in the way, and he was starting to think he might walk here for days when the corridor ended in a small, round chamber, nothing but rough gray stone except that a lantern hung to his right hand, a door led out the opposite side, and a tall clock stood to his left hand.

Its face was set with the sun, the moon, and the stars, it bore fields of tiny ripe wheat, hills of green, and a sea where a ship fought against the wind, and its hands showed the hour was eleven. One hand ticked onward, marking the seconds, and John felt the color seep from his face. He had walked for hours, and he had only one hour left.

He ran for the door. It pulled open, and a lion silently roared behind—the wind from the door had pulled the tapestry into motion, and a merchant cowered before the beast. John squared his shoulders and fled down the way, ignoring firebirds who flapped their wings over an enormous horse, and dragons whose fires flickered as they loomed over soldiers. The thought that these tapestries were finer than the earlier ones had to be dismissed as a distraction, and he ran to make up time.

Once, his heart hammering, he stopped to draw a deep breath, and wished the clock had chimed the hour of eleven: it would have told midnight as well, let him know he had failed and had no more need to strive. He shook his head and ran onward, though a gryphon turned its sharp beak to face him, as if considering whether to eat him up.

Another door appeared ahead of him, and his heart sank. Perhaps he would be as still as the banqueters within a minute. He went forward and opened the door.

It opened to a room so cluttered that at first it looked small. It took a moment to take in that all the bookcases and tables with stacks of paper and books, and inkwells with pens stuck in them, filled a fairly large room, lit by—he thought—a lamp, though a bookcase hid it from him. He walked within.

The lamp on the table came clear, and an hourglass with sand in the upper part, but not sifting through, and some papers and an inkwell. He inched onward. A woman stood beside the table. Her back was to the door, and her long black hair fell down it, over her plain gray robe. Her hand, with a feather pen in it, hung in midair.

Except that as he watched, her hand lowered, slowly. Her head tilted, to look at the hourglass. His breath gushed out. The sand trickled.

Then her hand went down swiftly, dropping the pen, as she turned toward the door. Her rosy-brown features looked very different from Sophia—but very lovely. At the sight of him, weary and travel-stained, her face lit up brighter than the lamp.

"O! You have saved us all!" She leapt forward to kiss his cheek, and he felt his face heating.

She laughed. "You did not come to save us, I can tell—you came for the water of life. Come!"

She took him by the hand and tugged him back through the room. The stones of the wall roughened, until they looked like a natural cliff-face, and they came around a bend to see water flowing from the rock, into a hollow carved in the rock.

Over the gurgle of the water, a clock chimed twelve. The woman laughed.

"We will gladly give you as much as you can bear or desire, for rescuing us all."

#

With the halls coming to life again, the servants outnumbered the courtiers, and the woman—the Princess Belsante—sent them running about to ready things. It took him a few minutes to realize from the talk that this must be a principality—no one spoke of a king or queen.

A warm bath, a warm meal, and then a bed for him—the princess held off the curious courtiers with sharp reminders that he had traveled far—and when John woke, the servants had laid out clothes for him in blues and greens.

"Her Highness wishes you to come to the garden gallery when you are dressed, if you please," said one maid.

Probably prudent, thought John. He rose and dressed before the fire, and a maid scurried before him down the corridors. Courtiers in their finery bowed and curtsied at his passing, but none of them were in the gallery. The long walk, sheltered by glass windows, showed a slope beyond. Leafless trees stood here and there, but only their branches were visible over the snow.

And, John suspected, not all of the branches. It was not snowing, but the sky was still leaden gray, and the wind sent puffs of snow flying here and there.

Belsante, lovely in violet, looked out one window.

She sighed and turned to him. "I hope you enjoy our welcome, Prince John. I know you must think you require the water of life, for you to come at this season, but—" She sighed again. "It will sustain life, and far longer than other water. It will not bring to life except in such conditions as—if a princess must have a spindle pulled from her head to break a spell, so too some magical spell is keeping someone dead—"

John nodded. "I was told of the water because of a magical sword that slew a prince. I—well know that only some times do such magics work."

She brightened, though her tone remained solemn. "Even so—these tasks you would do, you will not reach them if you leave at this time. Nor, I fear, for many a month to come."

John bowed. "As long as you do not make me dance to exhaustion every night, or take offense if I should pick a rose."

Belsante laughed. "Still less will I ask you to watch over the horses by day before the dancing begins, and threaten to cut your head off if they escape. Come, give me your arm, and I shall show you the castle where we are bound for the winter."

John offered his arm. As Belsante took it, he wavered for a moment, thinking of songs and dancing and games to while away the long winter.

He collected himself. "I would be particularly grateful if you showed me the library, Your Highness."

She arched an eyebrow. but said, "Nothing is too good for our rescuer!"

#

The clock tolled out the hours. John blinked. For all the flying snow outside, he could see that the day had darkened, now that he looked. He looked down at the book. He had learned nothing. Again. Several days of reading, broken only with practicing his swordplay, spent to learn nothing but that certain books held nothing of use for him.

He sat back and arched his sore neck. He did not read for amusement, and on many of the days he spent trudging on the road, he had accomplished nothing except to pass through lands where he could accomplish nothing. He sighed.

"Good evening," said Belsante from the doorway. Light poured around her, making her a shadow against it. "You should light a lamp when it gets this dark—but then, if you read too long, you will not learn so well and may miss exactly what you need to know."

John sat back, trying to marshal words, but the very difficulty convinced him that he was tired.

The hall's light lit up her smile. "Come, eat dinner, join our evening sports, sleep the night—you will study better in the morning for it. And you have many mornings to study."

#

Biancabella pulled her cloak more tightly about herself.

Evening was dove gray, the clouds not threatening snow, but blotting out the sunset. A few peasants shifted about their cottages, bearing firewood, or tending the beasts.

The road was ruts in the snow, and drifts engulfed the harvested fields, with only here and there a dead plant holding dried leaves or seeds over the sweep of white, but Kingston stood beyond.

Biancabella let her breath out in a long gust. It formed a cloud on the air. The journey away had been easier than the journey to, but they were there, and before sunset.

They trudged along, the fox sometimes giving great leaps to get over the snow, and Hans still sang.

"And in this nest there sat a fine bird,

The finest bird, that ever you did see,

And the bird on the nest, the nest on the twig, and the twig on the bough, and the bough on the tree, and the tree in the wood,

And the green leaves flourished thereon, thereon, thereon,

And the green leaves flourished thereon."

The three of them plodded into the streets, but she was not so weary that she did not notice that people gave them all sidelong glances. At the Laughing Rose, the innkeeper shortly confirmed that they had come out of mourning, but seemed even less cheerful than before. His wife hurried off as soon as they had their dishes.

Biancabella looked at the bread and stew and started to eat. The sky darkened toward night. As she pushed the bowl away, the door opened abruptly, and a young man walked in. Biancabella licked her lips. The young man who had been drinking cider, the last time they had been here. He walked directly toward them, hesitated, and said to the inn-keeper, "Is there a private room?"

Biancabella stood. She knew from her own kingdom that royalty would sometimes go drinking in common taverns. At least this one had not drunk himself under the table. His face set, Hans also stood, and the fox. The young man did not blink. Even when the inn-keeper called him "Your Highness" while escorting him to the room.

He had barely shut the door before he said, "What did you know about that rose?"

So she had told him enough. It was hard to feel relief, with this agitation on his part.

"Nothing more than what we told you," said Hans, firmly, folding his arms. "Tell us what you know."

Prince Thomas let his breath out. "I went to the old town, I saw the rose there, I had it dug up and brought to the castle—and now, every night, when I go to sleep, things happen. Thing are straightened up, some are cleansed, any tears in my clothing are mended—and I see nothing." He shook his head. "Sometimes, during the day, when I am away, but never, no matter how late I stay up, do I see something."

He looked about at them, desperately. "After—after Petronil-la—she was so beautiful—and so innocent—and I do not know whether anything—" He shook his head.

"Feign sleep," said the fox brightly, sitting up. "Feign sleep and watch."

"Perhaps," said Biancabella, though her heart thundered, "you will see dainty little elves, all naked, going about doing the chores, and if you make them clothes, they will run off and never be seen again."

The prince gave her a sidelong glance.

She spread her hands. "And perhaps not. There is danger in everything. Always. But if you do not, you may never know."

His face worked.

She drew a deep breath. "And if not, let me instruct you in the care of roses. If the ladies of your court discover the reason for your conduct—I have heard of times where they descended on such a flower and tore it to shreds."

He winced.

"You can still save such bushes, if you act with enough swift-ness, and care, but you will need to know how—"

He looked away from her.

"That is, if they do not come back. Them. Those who instigated Petronilla's drowning, and had Elinor burnt at the stake, might re-turn to make certain that she dies. Then, my counsel will be useless."

He reached for the door. "Then I will take care not to need it."

#

The voices from below were loud and cheerful, as if some merry drunks were already deep in their cups—Biancabella opened her eyes a crack and peeped at the window—even though the dawn was no more than charcoal. Hans, in the other bed, and the fox, curled up on hers, were both sound asleep still.

She supposed that clouds could keep it dark. She pushed back the covers with care, trying to not disturb the fox, and it rolled over on its back, and yawned.

"Did a wicked witch get burned in the city square?" it grumbled. "They're rejoicing as if—" Then it blinked and hopped up.

Biancabella went to straighten her clothes and her hair, as swiftly as she could, but before she was done, the fox was back, and bright-eyed.

"O, you should come, come at once—" It frisked on the floor. "Come and see!"

Hans threw his arm over his eyes against the light. "See what?"

"Come and see!" said the fox, and darted out the door. They went down the stairs after it, to a room already full of revelers.

"You're almost too late!" called the innkeeper's wife, beaming and rosy-cheeked. "Prince Thomas is wasting no time!"

Indeed, when they left the inn to join the rest of the teeming crowds, the bustle bore them off toward the castle—the snow was soon trampled down by all the feet—and though the morning light was still pale, they could see clearly as, beneath King Niels's approving eye, Prince Thomas led out his bride, the lovely Elinor.

"A wonder and a marvel," said the innkeeper's wife, warmly.

Biancabella nodded slowly and forced herself to smile. Envy was unworthy. Were Prince Thomas and Elinor miserable to the end of their days, it would not make her days one jot better.

#

The day was warm enough to melt the snow, some. Water dripped from the branches—for a moment catching the sunlight and flashing like diamonds—and puddled on the way, and even formed mud enough to splash on them. It did not make the journey easier.

And, thought Hans, it would only grow worse as the day went on. Snow slipping into boots to melt was unpleasant enough; putting a foot wrong in this might flood the boot it wore.

"I wonder," said Biancabella, as pensive as if walking down a garden path. "The rose could turn back into Elinor, but the reed could not revive Petronilla. I wonder—" She shook her head.

"Likely," said the fox, daintily leaping a mud puddle, "they've gotten better at doing this."

Biancabella looked at the fox.

"Anna escaped with no more aid than her prince could give—Snow-White did not, not without the aid of a magical princess who could see through magical lies, and knew that a prince could save her even if he was a bear."

Biancabella looked away, but not quickly enough to hide the pink in her cheeks.

She had not thought it through, thought Hans. "John and King Hendrik could be saved just the same. Both of them were after the circle learned the tricks of their—trade for many more years."

"That," said the fox more slowly, "turns on where they died. They can not die too far from the herb, or it won't work." After a thoughtful silence, it added, "Also, neither one died —well, none of the four died at the hands of anyone in the circle. But perhaps one of them made sure that maidservant did it right, so Petronilla would stay dead."

"That," said Biancabella, "sounds unpleasantly likely."

She looked ahead. A stand of birches stood as white as the snow, and the road descended to a bridge. A standing bridge, King Maximus had not gotten this far, but the descent looked slippery. She sighed and headed to the side, where the trees were. Ready to grab—

"Let me go first," said Hans.

#

Biancabella supposed it was a swamp. The road had been raised above the level, and still was sodden snow, and heavy walking. About them, the snow smoothed out the hollows and hillocks. Here and there, willows' thick trunks bore only hanging bare boughs. The only break was the river, a thin ribbon of black water between two rims of ice, and winding all about as if it were, in truth, a ribbon dropped carelessly to the floor.

The road curved in many places to avoid the waters, and the ground between had such puddles that she did not even think of leaving the way, as they trudged on. And on.

They could not stop, Biancabella reminded herself. These were the lands where Boney lived. If they did not get free of it before nightfall, she feared for their fate.

A voice came down the way—singing, almost dirge-like. "Willow, o willow."

Hans and Biancabella glanced at each other. The fox already leapt forward, standing on a hillock and looking ahead.

A young man stood there, dressed in drab greens and browns, his head covered with a cap as he looked over the river. After a moment, he blinked, looked over at them, and blushed.

"I beg your pardon. I thought I was alone with my sorrows. Forgive me my discourtesy."

Hans shrugged, wandering forward. "You are not alone on this road with sorrows. Perhaps if we shared our stories, we might find our ways eased."

The stranger laughed—a short bark.

"No news. Indeed, that is my news. My father wished me and my six brothers to wed, and sent them off to find brides—and one for me as well. For many a month, we heard nothing, and then we heard that they had been trapped by the curse on the dancing princesses, but were now free, and had wed six of them."

He looked over the road. "When we did not hear from them again, finally, I could not bear it. The news had reached us, my brothers could have as well, and though my father said he could not bear to lose me as well, he yielded in the end."

Wind blew among the branches. Wet clumps of snow splattered the ground.

"He should have stood fast. I am lost and have no way to find my brothers."

My mother's fault, thought Biancabella. The mirror told me.

Snow fell in melting clumps from the nearest tree. The prince looked at the fox. The fox looked back with bright eyes, and the prince swallowed and lowered his voice.

"There were these beasts. I helped—a hawk trapped in a thicket, a salmon that had landed on a riverbank, and a greyhound caught by its collar—and they each promised to help me. I thought I had hope, but now I have none."

Biancabella wondered. Perhaps her mother thought those beasts harmless because they could not help without winning to Boney. She licked her lips. "I have—heard—of a place near here. Where travelers might get trapped."

He scowled at her.

She forced a smile. "It is not far, and it is not wise to linger here in the cold and damp, all the more with night coming. The walk will help warm you."

Hans looked at her with narrowed eyes.

"And it is on our way. I fear we are on urgent enough journey that we could not help you without that lucky chance."

Hans looked away. They *would* go on if this turned up nothing, Biancabella resolved. It was all very well for John to go to rescue Ian and Vasilisa, but Hans would be baffled whenever her mother laid any spells about. And Gretel might suffer as grievously as Hans had.

The young man looked full of hope as they headed out. Biancabella glanced over him, and said, "Or perhaps you should return to your father. He is not a weakling, this wizard who turned your brothers and their brides to stone. And he is protected by magic."

"What manner of magic could protect him from a good sword blow?" said the prince.

"He has no heart in his body," said Biancabella. "As long as that is true, and you do not find his heart, you can not slay him."

That seemed to sober him, but only a little.

The road rose soon after. The sparse willows among the puddles and river gave way to a forest, until the trees were as thick as a thicket about them. Snow had slipped from any perch on any tree, leaving them stark against the sky.

Between the leafless branches, Biancabella began to pick out the gray of the castle against the paler clouds of the sky. She glanced at it now and again, when the branches allowed. Smoke rose from its chimney. When they were as close as the road would bring them, so she could be as sure as she could—

They came around a bend. Twelve statues of riders stood before them, in gray granite: six men and six women, dressed merrily, but with horror on their faces.

The fox's eyes narrowed, and its head shifted from side to side as it peered about.

"What is—" The prince blinked and saw what stood before him. He paled, and even swayed a little. Hans reached out to steady him with a hand on his arm. The prince nodded gravely and looked about.

Biancabella, cursing herself for a fool, looked about as well. The castle loomed, though the branches hid half of it. "Is that a path there? I think it leads up to the castle."

His face lit up. Moments later, he walked up the path without so much as a glance back. The thickets hid him from view, and after a minute, Biancabella sighed.

"I hope Boney is not home," she said.

Hans laughed, deep in his throat. She glanced sideways at him; that prince could end up as stone as his brothers had, and as Hans had ended up a tree.

"He did not even ask whether he might do anything that might aid us," said Hans, "and you are concerned that he might fall into misadventure."

"Telling him about my mother would hardly do anything but expose him to danger," she said, and then she felt her face heat. She looked away and said, quickly, "You—your plight was worse than his—and we couldn't help you so easily—"

Hans laughed again. "Perhaps my having killed Mother Trude helped you think I might be in less danger?"

She managed a smile. "And, of course, you did offer to help us."

"A prudent judgment on your part, Master Hans," said the fox. "I made sure I looked everywhere, and I know I looked where the path was before our fair princess pointed it out. It was not there." It capered about the road. "We have no choice but to take her as our guide on our journey."

#

"A little earlier," said the rosy-faced woodcutter, "and you could have made it. But not now."

Biancabella could not argue against that. She looked at the gorge filled with rushing water, and the bridge that barely could be seen beneath the flood. She could not even ask why they had not built the bridge higher up. The gap grew so much wider that a bridge would have been impossible.

Hans's face was set and sober. "How long before it goes down?"

The wood-cutter shrugged. "A day, two—probably at least three—but if there's another storm or two, a month or more is possible."

Hans's shoulders slumped.

"All the worse after what King Maximus did," murmured Biancabella.

"Huh?"

"Cast down the bridges in King Hendrik's kingdom," she said. "Good solid bridges, travelers used them. It will not be easy to build them up again."

"Get a wizard to do it," caroled the woodcutter. "One who will do it for your giving him whoever is first to cross it. Then you chase a rooster across, and whatever damage he does in his anger because he wanted a human, you can patch up. The bridge will last."

He tromped off into the woods, and the fox shook its head. "That sort of rogue would try to chase *me* over the bridge."

"And what would you do then?" said Biancabella, turning toward the inn.

"Why, leap about until he stumbled across in his attempt to catch me! Then the wizard would take him off and turn him into a horse, and serve him right." The fox peered ahead at the inn. "Such a simpleton wouldn't pick up the knowledge how to turn himself into a horse that way—or even how his rescuer could perform impossible tasks and so win a princess."

"You never know," said Hans gravely. "I learned things just by listening."

The fox tilted its head to one side.

"Once, a boy feigned he could not read," said Biancabella. "Learned from his master in secret."

"A horse," said the fox, "won't get a chance to read books." And then it looked up and read the sign of the Giant's Rest.

"Good evening," said the inn-keeper, coming out. "Shelter for the night! Have you any precious object to commit to my care: a table that springs up with food, a donkey that sneezes gold, a stick that will beat me black and blue? No? Just as well, then. Come in, come in—I'll fetch you dinner—"

The common room was less full than the inns had been during the summer, but had far more than any other inn not in a village—and every one of them talking of the flood.

"Here's to hoping it's not a mill grinding out water," said one thin man, over his ale, and when greeted with scorn, added, "Haven't you heard that's why the sea is salt? There was a mill that would grind out all manner of food, and one day a sea captain stole it to grind out salt, except he hadn't listened well enough to how to *stop* it. It sank his ship, with all the burden of the salt, and the mill's still down in the sea, grinding out salt to this day." He drained his cup.

"They always remember in time," said one tall, brown woman. "Like the women and her daughter who had to eat their way back home through sweet porridge—there's nothing like losing your life to focus your mind."

"Perhaps the waters will stop for that, then," said Hans. "Someone will know how to stop it."

"As long," said the fox, "as it washes away any ogre that takes up residence down there."

Which drew all gazes and turned the talk to murmurs. Hans picked out a table, and they sat, with the fox hopping on the table-top.

The inn-keeper slid bowls of soup before them.

She eyed the watery stuff—a sad thing, of vegetables and little meat—and picked up her spoon. Princesses had finer meals than this, if they did not run away. Those who ran away and found themselves jobs as scullery maids had worse. She ate.

"At least it's not raw thistle," she said, her voice low.

Hans smiled briefly, and then said, his voice as low, "I think that our prince, if he succeeds, will have to come with his brothers and their brides this way."

The fox lifted its muzzle from lapping up the soup, and tilted its head to one side. "Why, yes, I think they will. The river runs long. The other bridges aren't near."

"And no ferrymen?" said Biancabella.

"Never have been," said the fox. "Just as well. Who would want to risk having the ferryman push the tiller under your hand? Then you get to be the ferryman."

"They don't all do that," said Biancabella, demurely. "Some of them demand your hand, or your foot, or your head, as toll."

Hans snorted. "Best to wait for the bridge, then."

#

The clouds covering the sky were a silver gray like a pale dove. They rose and sank like hills, offering neither rain nor snow, but Biancabella had not left the inn to look up—only down.

The water, she thought in despair, had risen higher overnight. The shadows in the water might have been the bridge, but she wondered whether she imagined it, from knowing where it had been.

"Now," said the innkeeper, "this is the sort of weather where a rich merchant should throw an infant into the river."

Biancabella eyed him.

"When he's heard the tale about how the poor man's son will marry his daughter. He always persuades the poor man to give him the boy to raise, and then goes and throws him in the river in the silliest of manners, so the boy floats down the stream until a miller fishes him out."

"This sort of flood," said Biancabella, "would wash him out to sea. Then he would wash up on the shore for some poor widow to find, or some fisherman would find him in his nets—better than a wishing fish—or even a golden crab that offered to be his son."

The inn-keeper roared with laughter. "Truly there is no way to escape having your daughter marry such a son."

Biancabella smiled a little. "Sometimes it's a poor girl who is fated to marry a rich man's son."

"Eh, not so bad," said the inn-keeper. "He could meet her at a ball or something."

"Dangerous when a poor boy marries a princess," said a tall woman. She came up from behind, eyed the river, and rolled her eyes. "So often they are just thieves."

"Oh, yes," said a wiry man. "The king goes and orders a thief to carry out impossible thefts, and next thing he knows, the man's stolen the princess—and not from some ogre who carried her off."

"Ah, well, it turns out all right," said the inn-keeper. "There was one, a shifty lad, whose mother said he would end up hanging from a bridge—not this one—it was in a city. But he set out. His mother offered him more bread and her curse or less bread and her blessing, and he choose more bread and left with her cursing him every step. He won a princess, but one day, as they went over the bridge, he told her about what his mother had said, and as jest, she held out a magical handkerchief, and he hung from it—only a tower fell over, and such was the noise and clatter that she started, and let go, and he fell to his death."

Biancabella's tongue touched her lips. After a moment, she concluded that her mother probably had had nothing to do with it. A thief's happiness would not matter so much to her. And the rest would do nothing. Even Mother Magda, as long as the thief had not stolen the princess from her tower.

It might even have happened before their time.

A gust of wind made the trees shake, and the innkeeper and most of the guests went in.

Not quite resigned to more hours inside the rooms, with nothing else to do —she should have brought more to sew—Biancabella walked along the road a bit, eyeing the river. Not much higher, she told herself. Perhaps it would drain.

The fox leapt up on a boulder, and eyed it itself. Its tail lashed the air. "Speedily a tale is told, with less speed a deed is done—they tend to leave these parts of the histories."

Biancabella smiled a little.

"If it goes for much longer," said Biancabella, "I may just hunt in the woods for some old wise woman who can give me a chicken to eat, and warns me to save all the bones, and then I will build a bridge out of them across the river."

"And if you break one, you have to cut off a finger to use in its place," said Hans. "No. It would be better to meet an old man who can summon all the birds in the world, and get an eagle to carry you over—at this distance, to carry all three of us would not be so long that we would have to worry about keeping it fed."

Biancabella nodded, solemnly. Then she laughed, and laughed, and for all Hans and the fox stared, still laughed.

Finally, she mastered herself and said, "We would not need the eagle. The old man could summon the Bird of Truth as well. Then there would be no need to cross."

Hans snorted. After a minute, he said, with great gravity, "There might be. The Bird of Truth might say that Gretel was on the other side."

"There is that." Biancabella smiled. Then she sighed. "I wonder if the mirror could direct us to where Gretel is, if we knew where it was."

In their silence, the river roared. She bit her lip, and then shook her head. "I thought that perhaps it could not speak of what the circle already knew and therefore did not need the mirror for, but—my mother certainly knew where Snow-White was and had no need for the mirror to tell her."

There was a sound, far off, and indistinct, but loud enough to be heard over the river. She tried to peer over the hills—it could not have been close—but could see nothing.

Then, with that sound having died away, a few fat snowflakes drifted down. Biancabella winced, and the way they melted did not raise her spirits. Either harder going on the road, or a greater flood—

"Here's to hoping," said Hans, "that Heaven guarded John's steps. Higher in the mountains, farther north—it would have been far heavier snow for him."

#

Sunlight shone in the western windows, and John stretched and sighed. He had, of course, found nothing, as he had in all the days where duty had driven him to this wearisome reading. He was stiff from sitting over the books, and—he marked his place and stood—soon Belsante would come to discover whether he had vanished into a book in truth—or so she would profess.

In spite of himself, he smiled. The evening would be song and stories in the winter hall, without windows but with a roaring fire and bright colors of red and green on tapestries.

But as he walked toward the winter hall, the servants seemed subdued, and the courtiers whispered in the corners. He almost wished that someone would stop him, but he reached it without challenge.

Belsante, looking strained, still nodded to him and beckoned him to come over. A man and a woman stood before her, the man a nobleman who had joined the winter revels more than once, but—if he remembered correctly—had returned to his lands. The exquisitely lovely woman beside him had never joined them. She wore a fine gown, green embroidered with scarlet, and a mantle of blue lined with black fur, but her hands, just visible outside her sleeves, were red and worn from labor.

John looked between them. Perhaps the nobleman had had a ball at his castle, but a bride who came from the scullery—even if she were, like Biancabella, a run-away princess—did not explain Belsante's anxious face, or why she looked at him.

Perhaps a stepmother was intent on destroying the bride. Or perhaps Augusta Gloriana was behind it, or one of her cohorts. He doubted it would be Mother Magda, but Ottoline could be as spiteful as Augusta Gloriana.

Calmly, Belsante told them that they were Lord Nicholas and his bride Tatiana.

Nicholas bowed. Tatiana curtsied.

"Tell him how you found her, Lord Nicholas."

He bowed again. "Your Highness. I rode my sledge along the road when I came upon the river, where this unfortunate maid was breaking open the ice with an ax, and washing yarn dyed black, and other yarn dyed white, in it. She told me that her mother had ordered her to never return until she had washed the black yarn white, and the white yarn black.

"Such was the cold that I had to take her up and to the castle, or she would have perished—but after a time—" He smiled, and Tatiana looked down bashfully. "—we went back to her home to collect her dowry, and she had a great sledge with chests and boxes, all carved with snowflakes. Her mother had had her father store them all in a shed out back."

John nodded slowly. He had heard tales like this one.

"So, Tatiana," said Belsante, "tell me how you came by such a sledge."

Her cheeks colored as if she stood in frost. Tatiana said, softly, "My mother ordered my father to abandon me out in the forest, she said we did not have enough to eat. Father Frost came to me and chilled me to the bone, and I kept telling him when he asked that I was warm enough."

John winced. Belsante nodded grimly.

"It felt like hours, but it could not have been, because I survived, and he gave me warm clothes and a sledge filled with a marvelous dowry." Tatiana smiled wanly. "If you believe a woman who would tell such lies."

"And while you were there —there was your mother and your father and perhaps your older sister?"

Tatiana blinked. "My sister Dania—"

"She was still there when you left?"

Tatiana nodded, and her voice was faint. "She was."

Belsante nodded again and turned to John. "Now I wish to speak with you on matters of state.

Both Nicholas and Tatiana looked startled, but bowed and curtsied. John nodded as gravely as he could muster, as the two withdrew.

"Do you know everyone in this—circle that you spoke of?" she said, her voice intense. "Everyone at all who belongs to it—even if you do not know them by sight?"

"Yes." After a moment, John added, "All of those who came to the castle to confer together. I do not think they would have let anyone stay away—and not once or twice, but all times, such that Biancabella would not see the other person, ever."

Belsante scowled. It did not become her, and she pushed back her hair.

"An ogre lives in this land. He roams the winter, and can make it colder still, but if he catches you alone, he can sometimes be appeased by flattering him past reason."

"Then he showers the flatterer with rewards?"

"As he did Tatiana."

"I do not think they would let him in the circle," said John. "Why, Lord Nicholas and she may be happy together because of him, not in his despite. That is unlike anyone in the circle." After a moment, he added, "The spell that hid you away in here may have kept them from noticing his deeds."

Belsante looked grave and sighed. "You have already done more for me and mine that we can ever hope to repay. Still, it would be a kindness in you to come with me when I go to Tatiana's village, even though we leave within an hour. And will probably be too late."

#

In a hollow in the woods, with snow mounded all about, the cottages stood half buried, with smoke rising from their chimneys. John turned his head despite the wind lashing at his face, to look at Belsante. She looked grimly at one cottage, where sounds of wailing came.

"Too late," she said, and urged her horse forward.

An old man and woman wailed over a young woman's frozen corpse, and neither of them noticed the arrival. Some neighbors came forward, bowing or curtsying. It took Belsante only a moment to establish that the dead woman was Dania.

"What was she like?" said John. "Dania? Did she not have a sister named Tatiana?"

"And they were different as night and day," said an old woman. "Tatiana was always bright and cheerful and grateful for everything, though they worked her to the bone—and Dania, they gave everything to, though she was lazy and greedy, and cruel to Tatiana."

Some peasants winced, but when John pressed, they admitted the truth of it.

He spoke in a low voice to Belsante. "This Father Frost sounds quite unlike the circle. They would aid the cruel and lazy, just as they would harm the grateful and industrious. I told you how Elinor's sister married the prince."

Belsante, slowly, nodded. John looked at the dead woman and winced. To think that her killer was too good for the circle's taste.

The old woman laid a hand to his wrist and spoke in a low voice. "Good prince, when you empty out a bottle—fill it up again as soon as you can."

She swept about, her shawl hiding her face, and vanished among the villagers before he could question, or thank, her.

#

The flood had sunk by the second day, and on the third, the argument was whether crossing it by noon was safe—not for fear of the floodwaters, but the question of whether they could reach another inn before nightfall.

"Never wise to be caught in the night," said one traveler, his gaze darting about as he huddled into his cloak. "Never. You take a light for friendly lodgings, and the next thing you know you have landed among robbers, and if you have not just happened to find a magical blue belt lying around in the forest—why, that's the end of you."

The inn-keeper laughed. "Well, the end of you, perhaps. This lovely young lady—they would adopt her as their sister!"

Biancabella managed a smile but only a little one. That would go ill for Hans—and she could not imagine what would happen to the fox. Her gaze went down. Also, the snow had given way, most places, to the dingy landscape of dead plants, and mud. Travel would not be easy.

The inn-keeper's son ran toward the crowd. "Papa, Papa! There's a *crowd* of travelers coming! All *grand*!"

The crowd of guests murmured. Some pressed forward. Biancabella pulled back with Hans and the fox. A company of fourteen, all on horseback and laughing merrily, heedless of the way the mud splattered their fine horses and their legs. Seven men and seven women—Biancabella let out her breath—she had seen all but one of the women before. Most recently, twelve of them as stone.

"It seems," murmured the fox, "that our lost prince did not need his brothers to find him a bride."

Biancabella drew in her breath deeply and let it out again, slowly. Or, for that matter, more than to be pointed at Boney's stronghold to disenchant them. Not like her, who after months of journey was no closer to safety than at the beginning.

Safety for herself, at least. She had secured it for *others*—she forced her breath out. She would not be safer if these princes and princesses were still stone, or wandering the wilderness, or slaving in Boney's kitchen.

"Your Highnesses!" said the inn-keeper. He bowed deeply, and the guests about aped him, while he talked on. "You gladden our inn again. You have been gone for so long, and we heard tales about dancing princesses, but that was months ago."

Laughter resounded from them.

"An evil sorcerer turned us to statues on the way," said one princesses. "We rode along the road, to reach their father's kingdom, and this—horrible man appeared!" She shuddered.

"Making wild accusations," said another, "and he turned us to stone!"

"But," said the oldest prince, with relish, "he reckoned without my brother—he had thought he had gotten us all."

That prince blushed.

"And without Princess Kari," said a third princes. "Imagine—he carried her off from her mountain of glass and just put her in the kitchen as if she could do nothing!"

The seventh woman colored a little, but kept her face calm. "There was little enough to do. It was not until Prince Pierre came to me with the knowledge that Boney kept his heart outside his body that I could do anything."

Prince Pierre looked fondly at her. "Then she did everything: hid me when he returned in the evening, and told him she feared for her protection if he were to perish. So he told her that she was safe because his heart was not in his body, and she told him that could hardly reassure her. He told her it was in the hearth, and as soon he left we went to dig it up and found nothing. But she knew what to do. She festooned the hearth all over with flowers and said, when he returned in the evening, that it was to honor the place that guarded his heart, but she could not feel quite safe, knowing it could be dug up.

"He laughed and said it was in the well. So we tried to dredge it up to no success—and she festooned the well with flowers. He laughed that evening, as well, and pointed out seven hills to her, and told her there was a lake on the seventh, and by that lake lived a hare, and inside that hair there was a dove, and inside that dove there was an egg. And inside that egg, there was his heart. So she kissed him and told him now she knew she was safe.

"The next morning, I set out and reached the lake. The hare started up, and I called on a greyhound that had promised me its aid, and the greyhound caught it, but the dove burst out of it and flew off. I called on a hawk that had promised me its aid, and it snatched the dove out the air, but the egg burst out of it, and fell into the lake. I called on a salmon that had promised me its aid, and it brought me the egg, and though the heart burst out of it, I could still stab it through, and that evil sorcerer died with a howl you could hear seven hills away."

"It was louder at his house," said Kari, with a smile, looking fondly at Pierre.

"All of us became flesh and bone again," said the oldest prince. "The only trouble we face is how we may most swiftly let both our own father, and Princess Kari's parents, know that we are all safe and well."

"You may find trouble," said the inn-keeper, his forehead creasing as if in thought, "if you take this road. The bridge can serve, but it is a day's journey to the next. Travelers who have faced so evil a danger know that it is best to find shelter at night—and not the shelter of a robbers' den!"

"Perhaps that would be wisest," said the oldest prince.

Pierre blinked. His gaze turned on the fox, and after a moment, he dismounted, exclaiming, "You are those who told me of the heart!"

All fourteen looked at them with rapt fascination.

Hans winced.

#

As the firelight glided their faces with fiery gold, the princes and princesses all nodded sagely.

"We shall go by the northerly route, then," said the oldest, Prince Bertrand. "We shall send messages by these travelers, but travel as far as we can along the same route that you three go by."

Chapter 11—The Mother Acts

"It will be an early spring," said Princess Gina, lightly. "With this sort of melting—why, I expect to see snowdrops any day!"

Her horse looked to have brown legs from the mud, only lending weight to her opinion, and her sisters prattled of birdsong and leafing trees. Kari smiled softly, and perhaps reflected that she and Pierre would be heirs to her father's kingdom, leaving his father's to whichever of the other brothers his father choose.

"It's rather a late fall," said Pierre. "Expect asters."

Biancabella trudged along. The princes could not have bought them horses if they wished for them, for there were none to be bought, and when they had dithered over it, Hans had urged having horses would only bring robbers on them, and that the three of them had trouble enough without having to flee into the forest.

She glanced over woods. For a moment—she blinked and looked again. She did not see violet again.

Then, though her mother could not use magic to hide from her, what she had seen had been in a thicket of brush and boulders. A jester in motley could hide with ease and without a bit of magic. Spring flowers could do so more easily.

Hans's voice rose ahead, talking of King Hendrik and how the war had ended.

Prince Bertrand said, "May Heaven grant that that will put an end to King Maximus's wars. If he continues to press onward, he would reach even our father's lands before long."

"He still has to take King Hendrik's," said the fox.

"And," said Hans, "the danger is all the more reason for us three to make haste." He bowed. "I thank you for your escort thus far, but the bridge ahead is where we part."

"Oh no," said Gina, though without much heat. Exclamations, of wishing them well and that Heaven would shield them on their journey, did not slow the parting long. No sooner than they had walked onto the bridge than the company headed off, more briskly than before. They had not walked far on their road when the sound of the horses faded behind them.

Hans looked over his shoulder. 'Boney. Dead," he said, grimly. "The circle will be furious." He shook his head. "It's a good thing, but—*furious.*"

"Very much so," said Biancabella. She swallowed. "I—I think I saw my mother in the woods."

The fox started and turned to look at her.

"Or—I may have."

#

Mistress Laurenza picked her way over the snow, and the re-frozen ice where puddles had formed by day. The forest grove was dark as well as cold, but—they could hardly go to Augusta Gloriana's castle for this. Even more so than after her latest failure.

"Where's Ottoline?" said Rumpelstiltskin, surly. The shadow of the firs left his face a dark void, unreadable.

"She—could not catch the hints," said Mistress Laurenza. "I could not lure her far enough from Augusta Gloriana—not and ensure that Aviette *stays* in her bird form. *She* will make no trouble." For a moment she remembered that ungrateful daughter, cheeping forlornly on a leafless bough, but that brief satisfaction gave way at the first thought of the problems before her. She shook her head.

"Until some prince gives her a drink," muttered King Drakos, but so softly that she could feign she had not heard him.

"Why have her anyway?" Mother Magda glared at him. "She'll just blab. Thick as thieves, those two. Why would Ottoline settle for a mere prince except that marrying him let her be at Augusta Gloriana's beck and call? Then—once the great Augusta Gloriana learns that we meet to curb her, her rage will be great." Her lip curled. "As if founding the circle made us her servants."

"What sort of fool cares?" King Drakos's voice was crisp. "First Mother Trude, then Boney, and both times, it was *her* spells that failed. I can only rejoice that I depended on neither of them. And that my daughters are obedient—or bound, and that before I had the threat of their moving against me."

Useless fool, thought Mistress Laurenza, her eyes narrowed. What had he ever done for her? But she sweetened her voice.

"The matter is," she said, "that Augusta Gloriana makes plans to—break her daughter's heart."

Mother Magda looked at her warily. "She did come to me for help with some spellcraft."

Mistress Laurenza's lip curled. "You should have told her to, rather, break her head. There will be a thousand princesses whose hearts can be broken for being so annoying in their—delicacy. One more doesn't matter. Forgo the chance and instead put an end to her."

Mother Magda snorted and gave a decisive nod.

She had their attention, Mistress Laurenza judged. "And I have a way. There is King Maximus. He is not married."

They all looked thoughtful.

#

Ice spread everywhere, and Biancabella glared. First the water melted, then it froze—she almost envied John, in the mountains it would stay snow—and she picked her way up the slope after the fox. Footstep after careful footstep—and for all her care, her foot slid out, and she crashed into the earth. Her hand flew up, catching her, and she breathed hard, but—for a moment, she thought she had suffered nothing more than scraps to her hand.

Then she moved her leg, and her ankle stabbed. She cried out in pain. The fox scrambled back, but could do nothing.

Hans hurried up behind her, nearly slipping, and she called, "Be careful!"

He went on one knee beside her and tested the ankle. After a minute, he said, "I don't think it's broken, but you shouldn't put weight on it."

"There was a castle in the next valley," said the fox.

Biancabella nodded. They had seen its turrets.

Hans turned to her. "You can't stay here, but I will get help—and there's a woodcutter's hut ahead, until I return." He glanced sideways and down. "The fox can stay with you."

"Of course," it said, and loped on ahead. Four legs had to help, thought Biancabella.

With ease, Hans scooped her up and walked after the fox, with great care, toward the hut. Biancabella frowned. No smoke rose from its chimney, though wood lay heaped in the shed beside it. The fox poked its nose into the door. It must have been unlatched. It slid open, and the fox vanished within.

"Ah," said Hans. "Not a woodcutter's at all. A huntsman's. Probably used only when he's looking for quarry for the king." He shouldered open the door. The room behind had benches, a hearth swept entirely bare of ash, and a bed without a scrap of blanket on it.

The fox looked up from a perch on one bench. "The huntsmen have not been here for some time."

"As long as there are not twelve of them, all looking alike," said Biancabella mildly.

"That would be better," said Hans, lowering her beside the fox. "You could point them to the king, despite your mother, and then when the one of them who is the princess he promised to marry *does* marry him, they will be grateful. They could hasten us on our way."

She smiled. "Then, I suppose, I should not turn into a rock to await your return."

"Of course not," said the fox. "And still less a flower so that you will perish when you despair of his return." It curled up, its tail coming around toward its nose.

"And," said Hans, "I promise not to chase after any white deer that will lead me to the grave of a murdered man, where his ghost flies about like a bird and reveals how his widow disguised herself as a man and works as a servant."

"Of course not," said Biancabella. "That would be the king, anyway. Go. Heaven watch your path."

"If robbers come here in the dead of night," said the fox, "we will convince them we are a pair of demons and scare them off."

#

Sunlight slanted through the windows when the fox woke again. It yawned and blinked. "He has to be back by now!"

Biancabella, wrapped in her cloak, stirred a little and realized how cold and stiff she was. She spoke, and her voice was a croak. "No. He could have fallen on the ice." Or—she tried to not remember that glimpse of Augusta Gloriana. She could have turned him into a bear.

"I will track him down." The fox hopped down and looked inquisitively at her. She nodded, and it ran off into the woods.

She leaned back and told herself that she was no worse off than when she had left her father's castle. She had saved the dancing princesses and all their dancing partners, and John and the fox, without anyone lifting a finger to help her. An ankle was a passing trouble.

At least, she had not escaped from Mother Magda only for Hans to be cursed to forget her as soon as anyone else kissed him.

For a moment, she could not breathe.

Then she forced the air out, and in. Her mother used her spells to aid others in the circle. She would certainly demand that they use theirs to aid her. After Mother Trude and Boney both, Augusta Gloriana would be bent on using anything they could against her.

Mother Magda could well have cursed him.

She wrapped her arms about herself, against the chill.

Minutes inched by. The sky turned quite pink and peach. Finally, the fox reappeared. It held an enormously long stick in its mouth, dragging it rather than carrying it as it brought it to her. She took the stick and realized it would serve for a crutch.

"There's a royal court down there," said the fox, its tail lashing. "Hans is gadding about as if you did not sit here."

"He's cursed," said Biancabella, fumbling with the crutch. "He's under a curse to forget me. I realized it almost as soon as you left. We have to rescue him."

The fox's eyes narrowed.

She stood, steadying herself on the crutch. "Or I have to rescue him, and you can come to protect me."

The fox snorted but trotted toward the door.

#

The path down had been easier than the path up, but still left her wondering whether they would been wiser to wait out the night, as the sky darkened with every step. When they came within an arrow's shoot of the gates with some clouds still scarlet, Biancabella let her breath out with relief. People were looking at her.

"What sort of beggar," said one lady, indignantly, "comes to impose rags and dirt in the middle of a royal feast?"

"Come, Gertrude," said the man who had her arm, and Biancabella froze at Hans's voice. She barely heard him go on, saying the king and his queen were generous with the unfortunate.

Her gaze went across the company, wondering whether anyone there would indeed have pity on her as she looked upon face after face. She stopped on reaching the king and queen. The king merely watched as the queen spoke in a low voice to the princess next to her, a tiny slip of a girl, who nodded eagerly and took the coin the queen gave her.

Then the princess crossed the distance between them to offer Biancabella the coin and tell her, in a sweet high voice, that she could find shelter against the cold in the stable, and the queen would send the court physician to see to her. Biancabella bowed her head and thanked her—telling herself that having learned as a princess to be grateful, she should be as able as a beggar.

Then she hobbled toward the stables. She could talk to the fox then, to plot and plan, and at least be out of the wind.

It took her by the kitchen, where she heard the cook telling the scullery maid that she had to bring the food to the beggar girl.

"I, for one, won't be carrying anything to some filthy wandering beggar."

"The princess did," said the scullery maid in a thin and girlish voice.

"The princess did!" The cook threw her hands in the air. "The princess! The beggar's brat! Her mother served here as you are serving, and begged for the place! No wonder her daughter gets along with another beggar!"

"She's the queen," said the scullery maid, even more timidly.

"She's the queen." The cook pointed at her with a ladle. "But everyone still calls her Catskin."

#

The doctor's lantern cast a pool of light as he firmly bandaged up the ankle. The fox sat in the shadows, but its eyes glittered in the light.

"It is not that bad," the doctor said. "You will need the crutch, but it should heal without laming you if you are not foolish."

Biancabella nodded and leaned back on the straw.

The doctor smiled. "Sleep, yes, that is wise." He headed for the door. A moment later, he said, firmly though his voice was low, "She is sleeping now. Let her rest. I will tell you that she is doing well and should be able to walk well within a week or two."

"She's not lame?" said the king.

The doctor shook his head. "She must have fallen in the last day or so, the bruising has just begun."

"We shall see her in the morning, then," said the queen. Footsteps sounded, going away. Only one pair, Biancabella thought. The fox's gaze turned, with the stray light picking out its eyes in the gloom.

"William," said the queen, urgently, "the cook is spreading rumors again."

The king sighed.

"And I can not bear it that she is saying it about Katherine—William, my father was a nobleman."

She surprised a grunt from him.

"Not in your kingdom, up in the hills. And he didn't want a daughter, he wanted a son, he told his servants that the first wooer to come for me could have me—I tried to put him off with the demands for the gowns, and then for the catskin cloak—but if I had not run away, they would have made me marry him."

"And you preferred being a scullery maid," said William.

"Yes. I did not want him ever to find me. But—if you find my father—"

Biancabella looked over. She thought that Catskin wrung her hands, and kept quiet. They walked away, and she let loose a sigh.

"Fortunate Catskin, to have found her bridegroom without the circle meddling," she said, softly.

"She didn't use magic," said the fox.

Biancabella glanced over, saw nothing, and said, "She didn't?"

"I looked about." The fox shifted on the straw. "They talked, telling all the new servants what the cook said. She wore marvelous gowns she had brought with her, but they were finery such as a nobleman's daughter could wear, not sewn by magic. She went to the ball, she ran away and changed out of them—but not quickly enough the last time, she threw her rags over her gown, and William pulled them off again."

"Ah." After a minute, Biancabella said, "May Heaven bless finding her father. Perhaps he will have grown more gracious."

"They know the story of Elinor, burned at the stake, here," said the fox.

"And?" said Biancabella in exasperation.

"Some courtiers tried to accuse Queen Catskin of bewitching King William. He sent them packing. I—think—we will only gain mistrust by saying that Gertrude bewitched Hans."

"Ah," said Biancabella, feeling flat. She had nothing to say to that. She waited, listening, but the fox, which had done such work in saving John from his troubles, said nothing more.

Minutes later, she shifted again. "I—I can only remember the time my mother tried to teach me how to enchant birds to speak. She was trying to convince me to learn magic, and she thought I would find that the most fascinating of her spells."

The fox tilted its head to one side as it listened.

"She told me at the time that many spells of forgetfulness could be broken that way."

The fox's breath came out in a sigh. "I've heard of that."

"Who hasn't? Two enchanted doves tell the story of their suffering, and the next thing the bride knows, the bridegroom has thrown off the spell and fled back to his first love. I could not have learned her magic even for that, it would have been madness, but if there were only—" Her breath hissed out, and she sat up, not heeding the ankle.

Her words fell over each other in getting out. "Genoveva. And Hendrik. They did seem grateful. And their kingdom is *famed* for its automata. Surely the artisans there can make birds that talk. Clockwork birds."

"Ah ha!" said the fox. "And do you know what else I learned?"

Biancabella rolled her eyes. "What did you learn?"

"There's a bridge. A new bridge, built by an automaton. You could get there in a week or two. Err—later, when you can walk."

#

Mud, thought Biancabella. The fox had reckoned without mud. Though the day was filled with pale sunlight, mud was everywhere.

At least the fox trudged along the road without complaint, though it looked more brown than red itself. Then, they had had no choice. Here and there, the river had threatened the road with flooding. At this place, while its banks were high enough, the river itself was filled with such a frothing flood that even a magical ferry with the ferryman bound to row people across would not try to cross.

The bridge ahead glittered like silver.

"It looks like something conjured up by the impoverished wooer to convince the king," said Biancabella, "to let him marry the princess."

The fox leapt up on a roadside boulder. "If he could conjure that—he would be wise to make the king promise first, and only conjure after. Otherwise the king might take him for an evil sorcerer and demand more and more from him."

"That," said Biancabella, "is the sort of thing that ends with his demanding that all the wolves in the kingdom be rounded up at his court, and his discovery that many fierce beasts are not something you want at your court."

"It's unnecessarily unpleasant on the way," said the fox. "It's all very well when the king ends up trapped as a ferryman, but who wants to have to visit the dragon first?"

"Much better to visit the king and queen," said Biancabella.

#

The royal city had walls of stone, not metal, but the gate had automata, lions of gold and wolves of silver, to enforce the guards' words. Biancabella glanced through the gates and saw the distance to the castle. She bit her lip. She might be best off as a beggar here, as well.

Trumpets sounded—high, light, and clear. People grumbled, moving aside, and some children talked in excitement about seeing the king or the queen—

"Or *both*!" said one girl with relish.

"Move back," said a guard to Biancabella, his tone tired but efficient. "Their Majesties won't want to see you in their way."

"They might," said Biancabella. "They will be able to say so, then."

The guard scowled at her.

"Dear me, good sir," said the fox, "there are many considerations here."

The guard eyed it warily, pulling back.

"Who would wish to tempt fate by an evil deed to a stranger who appears poor and unfortunate?"

Riders appeared in the gate. Biancabella's gaze flew over, and she opened her mouth before she wondered what to call, but King Hendrik already noticed their standing in the road, and frowned. Queen Genoveva looked over, and cried out.

"Biancabella!"

Minutes later, guards were firmly detached from the ride to escort her safely to the castle, that she might rest, and eat, and wash before they spoke.

#

The gown was pale dove-gray, and the folds fell around her ankles softly, with none of the stiffness and dirt of the last days. Before the fire's warmth, Biancabella leaned back against the seat. It was a plain room, the seats unadorned, a chest and a desk of plain dark wood, but the windows, with their lead-lined panes, freely let in the wan winter sunlight.

The fox still stretched out before the fire, though it must have been dry from its bath. Then it shifted and looked toward the door.

Biancabella rose and then curtsied.

Genoveva stepped forward and took her hands. "What a shock it was to see you there—and so much more to see you only with the fox! I would have sworn that Hans would have seen you to safety even if he found his sister."

Hendrik stood in the doorway, looking grave.

"He's not looking for his sister, either," said Biancabella, making both of them start. She shortly told the story. Genoveva exclaimed over it, and Hendrik's face grew more and more set, like flint.

"So I thought of something my mother had tried to teach me, how to enchant birds to speak, and how that can sometimes break these spells—since merely seeing me did not." She drew a deep breath. "And what should I think of but your kingdom, where such fine automata are made?"

Hendrik blinked, and his face turned utterly calm as if transformed. "And you think," he said mildly, "that they can make you birds that can fly in this court and tell the story of how you and he traveled together?"

"Certainly if it can not be done here, I will find it nowhere else," said Biancabella. "I will have to wander the woods in hopes of finding a little old woman in a hut who can tell me how. I can not appeal to my mother for mercy."

"We can not have that," said Hendrik. "Though I fear you may have to stay the rest of the winter here."

The fox rolled over on its back. "Alas. We shall have to suffer the hardship of warmth, shelter, food, and ease. Somehow."

#

The royal nursery was brilliant with color, its walls hung with tapestry of green with blue and purple flowers, and all manner of beasts from dragons to pigs. The floor was covered with blue carpet, and the fireplace blazed. Before it, little Prince Edward, dressed in red, chortled as he played with the fox, as brightly red. Biancabella smiled.

Genoveva appeared at the door. "No time like the present. The sooner the birds are commissioned, the sooner they can be done, and you can return to the rescue. Therefore even on so cold a day, our business is urgent enough to leave the castle."

Biancabella stood. Minutes later, maidservants swathed them both in mantles of vivid violet, both thickly lined with fur. Then they were out the door, and into the winter.

"As the days begin to lengthen," said Genoveva, "the cold begins to strengthen."

The wind tore at them, pulling on the hems of their skirts and mantles. Genoveva pulled her mantle more closely about herself. At broad noon, with the skies a cloudless sapphire blue, the streets held only those about their business. Genoveva must have meant her declaration that the business was urgent. Biancabella wondered how long making the birds could take.

A flamboyant weather-vane, a rooster in scarlet and green and yellow enamel, whirled about into the new wind. It was not clock-work.

Much of what she saw was not, Biancabella reminded herself, though it could be hard to tell in this city. Houses were still built of wood or of stone, but fences were built of black wrought iron, shaped into climbing rose vines and sharp thorns, and gates were silvery dragons, and wells had pumps shaped like ever-filled jugs—though, as some kept filling up the buckets as long as they were offered, some pumps might be automata.

Then Genoveva picked out a shop with windows guarded by golden bars shaped like lilies. She walked briskly toward it. The shop sign was silver and gold, with cogs and gears forming some-thing like a mouse on it.

She followed Genoveva into the warmth. Apprentices and journeymen, with their heavy leather aprons laden with tools, turned from their work in gears to bow, and one ran off, calling for Master Frederico.

He emerged, a plump, short, and balding man, with only a thin fringe of pale brown hair, but he smiled radiantly. He wore the same oil-stained and tool-laden apron as his apprentices and bowed even more deeply than they had.

"Your Majesty! Such a delight to see you! It is always for a com-mission for a marvel and wonder, and such are always a better field for my skills than commonplace work." His smile broadened. "As long as you do not ask me to make a golden lion that you, or the king, or this fair companion of yours can fit in. This time I wish a challenge!"

"This modest fellow is Master Frederico," said Genoveva dryly. "If anyone can do what you wish, Biancabella, it will be him."

"If, if?" said Master Frederico. "Do you not know that money can do anything? Such as buy whatever automata you desire?"

Genoveva laughed and shook her head. "Even at the time, even as he let him marry Princess Pearl, King Domenic pointed out to Gian that money does not suffice. Without his wits, he would never have succeeded."

Master Frederico spread his arms. "Put my wits to the test!" Biancabella told him.

He turned grave before she was half-done. At the end, he muttered a bit and then decreed, "You must tell me *exactly* what these birds are to say. I must build it in. Something that was set to say what you will—" He shook his head. "Too much chance of error when you introduce the words. You must decide beforehand so I can build in the words. Everything must be flawless!"

"Will that speed the matter?" said Genoveva.

"Oh, it should certainly take no more than two months," said Master Frederico, idly.

#

Genoveva led Biancabella back by the same route but once inside, after they had shed the mantles and stamped snow off their boots, she led the way down another corridor, and at one window, stopped and pointed.

Over the door of the house opposite was written the motto, "Money can do everything."

Biancabella's mouth formed an O.

"Built by a rich young man, Gian, when he came to the city."

The wind rattled the window pane, and they stepped back.

"For putting that up over his doorway," said Genoveva, "King Domenic said that Gian had to figure out where Princess Pearl was hidden away, that was something that might be done. Gian did it by having a lion automaton made, and hiding in it, and it was so marvelous that the king borrowed it for three days to show the princess."

"Which," said Biancabella, "was why he needed wits as well." She shook her head. "Wiser to make the king a great loan when he is in dire need of money. Even if you look like such a fright because of the conditions on your wealth that only the youngest princess will consent to marry you."

Genoveva laughed. "Though it does have the peril that the youngest princess may refuse to believe you are the frightfully ugly man she promised, because you fulfilled the bargain and cleaned yourself up." Then she turned sober. "And the older sisters are so bitter and resentful that they passed up this rich and handsome young man that they kill themselves. No, being gibed at by your father-in-law is better."

Snowflakes drifted down from gray skies to the streets.

#

Constance looked at the path before her. At least, she hoped it was a path. The gray sky had started to sift down more flakes on it.

Her hand went to her waist. She would not be the first to give birth while hunting for her husband. Once, three princesses had read the forbidden book in their father's library, and learned that the older two were to marry kings, and the third a pig. After she had foolishly taken a witch's advice to disenchant her husband, the third princess had had to chase after him, and given birth in the house of the Moon.

Constance's eyes closed. Not that knowing better than to listen to the witch had helped her much. She felt as if her toes had been replaced with chips of ice, her toes were so cold. She would be glad of anything from a peasant's hut to the house of the Moon. She feared that soon she would be glad to find a cave in the hillside.

She forced her breath out. Soon she would find herself wishing for a cottage even if the householder was a hedgehog, or sprig of myrtle, or one of the other foolish wishes she had avoided for her child.

She plodded on.

Past a stand of pines, there stood a snug little house with smoke rising from the chimney. For a moment, she blinked. What an odd place to find it—she stood a stumbling step toward it.

The door flew open, revealing a gap of warm golden glow, and a dark shadow moved out of it, toward her. Constance found herself bundled over the threshold and sitting by the blazing fire wrapped in a red blanket, with the door shut against the snow, and the fire swiftly burning away the cold air that had followed her.

An orange marmalade cat sat on the mantle and blinked at her.

A woman of middle years, her hair and gown both amber-gold, bustled about the room, and Constance held out her hands to the fire. Courtesy, she reminded herself. Always be courteous. Or you might end up having toads fall from your mouth and dying a miserable death—

And scorning hospitality as simple was discourteous. Even when you did not have a choice between a festive inn and a quiet one—she smiled. She had known which was the prudent choice before she heard John's tale, but she had yet to face it.

The woman pothered around behind her. She did not turn to stare.

This woman might yet ask her to work as a maid. She swallowed. If she needed to, she needed to. Winning her way to Sigurd might need her to earn something along the way. Iron shoes that she could wear out, or with hooks so she could climb a glass mountain.

"And so Sigurd's bride arrives!" The woman arrived with a bowl of soup in her hands. "I trust that he told you of me and my sisters. And how we enchanted the kingdom."

Constance blinked and looked over. Her mouth, she realized distantly, was hanging open, but she could not pull it shut. Enchantresses had helped Sigurd with the castle, and perhaps the kingdom would be better off this way—and their names were—

"My name is Theodosia," said the woman kindly.

Constance pulled her mouth shut and managed to agree that he had. "The mirror did, too." Her eyes prickled. "But Florio told me how you asked him to—plant flowers in the garden."

Theodosia laughed. "Golden lilies, and silver lilies, and little star-white flowers, but perhaps I could have watched what he had planted."

"He had the gardeners plant all sorts of flowers. He told them that if a maiden, or a merchant, picked any of them, they were to catch the thief. Golden lilies would not have been picked out in that planting."

Theodosia laughed again, a deep chuckle. Constance sighed, looking away.

"It was a beautiful garden," she said, longing for those golden hours when they had walked, and sat, in it. Almost she could wish that Sigurd would stay forever a bear if the price of freedom was so high—she pulled her thoughts back. Unwise to make wishes.

"And you did not linger there?" said Theodosia. "Sometimes the captive comes back, to the king's castle after she's been stolen away by a witch in a stone boat, or to the king's hen house because that is where his wife took refuge."

"The castle—I could not stay there."

Theodosia frowned.

The words stumbled out. "All the spells were failing."

Theodosia scowled. Constance's tongue felt like lead in her mouth.

"Dear me," said Theodosia, slowly. "I knew that Ottoline made much trouble, twisting the spell like that, but I did not know that she ruined the castle." She shook her head.

"It would be like her to, if only she found a way."

Theodosia looked thoughtful, and as if she were staring past the walls. Then she nodded and looked at ease.

Constance plowed on. "I have to find Sigurd. And soon, before she forces him to marry her."

The baby kicked. She closed her eyes. Before the baby was born was best.

"You have time," said Theodosia. The fire crackled. "The twisting of the spell means that Sigurd will be a long time reaching her—Augusta Gloriana's hiding, not quite perfect, will mean he will spend months traveling—but it will still keep you from finding him before then."

Constance opened her eyes. "Is he all right? Is he well? Has he shelter from these storms?"

Theodosia, grave, looked at her. "Yes. That she would not touch, for she wants him to arrive sound and hale. And Heaven willing, you shall follow him." She managed a smile. "I, and my sisters, can help."

#

The hearth blazed, lighting up the room, and all the courtiers wore red and green and blue. Hans, in his borrowed finery, felt awkward, all the more in that he could not remember a tale to amuse the company.

Gertrude stood before them all, in violet. She leaned forward, avid for praise.

"Once upon a time, a man had two sons. He summoned them to his deathbed and told them that all he could leave them was his cottage with a pear tree that bore fruit both summer and winter, and with it, his curse, and his cat, with his blessing. One son, who was named Pietro, asked for his blessing, and the other, Fortunato, for the pear tree, and so the man died, and Fortunato turned Pietro out, and the cat with him, and lived on the pears from the tree.

"After a time, during the winter, he realized that pears were vanishing in the night, and so he stayed up and caught a fox stealing them.

"'You miserable wretch!' he shouted. 'I will kill you and put an end to your thieving ways!'

"'Spare me, great one, spare me,' said the fox, 'and I will make you a great nobleman and win you a princess for your bride.'

"'That I will believe when I see it,' said Fortunato, but when the fox asked him for a basket of pears, he gave it.

"So the fox took the basket and ran off to the king. There he said, 'My master humbly begs you to accept this small offering.'

"Everyone at court exclaimed over such a thing: pears in the middle of winter! The Princess Nanelia, who particularly loved pears, was particularly taken with it, and spoke of how gracious his master must be, and offered him golden coins as a gift in return.

"So the fox took another basket the next week, and a third the week after that. For a time, Fortunato abided, but as spring approached, he said, 'You foolish fox! No one will wonder at the pears in the summer!'

"'Just as ordinary people must wait for ordinary pears,' said the fox, 'you must wait for an extraordinary marriage.' Which overawed Fortunato. One day in the spring, the fox said to Fortunato, 'Go down to the river, take off your clothes, and bathe.' Fortunato did so, and the fox hid his clothes. Then it waited for the king to ride by.

"'Help, help!' it called. 'Most gracious king! My master, who gave you so many pears this winter, has been attacked by robbers! They stole his clothes, slaughtered his retainers, and threw him into the river to drown! He has been swept down here, and I can not save him!'

"The king sent his guards at once, and they drew Fortunato out of the river and dressed him like a noble. He rode along in the carriage with the king and Princess Nanelia, but the fox ran ahead.

"It came to a field where cows grazed, and it called out to the cowherds, 'You are all in danger of your lives! The king is coming with a great band of soldiers to destroy your lord! Your only hope for safety is to tell the king that all these cows belong to Master Fortunato Pear.'

"Then it did the same when it came to a field filled with sheep and a field filled with goats. The king was quite pleased with such wealth.

"Finally, the fox came to the castle that ruled over the land, and told the guards that they must say the same to protect themselves, and urged the master to hide himself in the oven for protection. Then the fox stirred up the fire, so the master burned to death, and Fortunato was installed as the new master, and the king married Princess Nanelia to him.

"The fox still went back to the pear tree to feed Princess Nanelia the pears during winter, but one day, it asked Master Fortunato, 'If it happened I died, what would you do for me?'

"'After all you have done for me?' said Master Fortunato. 'I would bury you in a coffin of gold.'

"The next week, the fox lay down in the garden as if dead, and the gardeners asked what to do.

"'Throw the body in the dung heap,' said Master Fortunato. And the fox leapt up, snarling, and proclaimed that after all it had done for him—and when it knew that he was just the owner of a pear tree. At that, Master Fortunato threw a roof tile at it, and killed it. The body was thrown on the dung heap, and Master Fortunato lived prosperously after that."

Hans winced and looked away. Neither King William nor Queen Catskin looked much pleased, but laughter came all about from less heedful courtiers, and exclamations about how the fox should have known better than to threaten his master.

"We've had one, let us have another." A woman turned to Hans. "Master Hans, tell us a story!" She was roundly seconded all about, for all that he tried to beg off, and then he remembered a story.

He leaned forward. "It was a dark and stormy night." He ignored the scowls at the odd opening. "The bandits gathered round the hearth in their lair, where the fire blazed. The chief said, 'Antonio, tell us a story!'

"Antonio said, 'It was a dark and stormy night. The bandits gathered round the hearth in their lair, where the fire blazed. The chief said, "Antonio, tell us a story!"

"'Antonio said, "It was a dark and stormy night. The bandits gathered round the hearth in their lair, where the fire blazed. The chief said, 'Antonio, tell us a story!' —"

King William roared with laughter. Queen Catskin smiled beside him and said, "Admit it, Lady Gertrude, Master Hans has outdone you!"

Many courtiers laughed and smiled, but others looked sullen.

Gertrude looked like she had bitten down on a bitter fruit.

#

John sighed, looking at the page. It was dark outside, but then, it still grew dark early, these days. Belsante would roust him from the room soon enough. They had danced the last three nights.

In this room, he learned nothing of use. He had read plenty of useless tales. He leaned back, stretching. Tales of a foolish boy who had bought a bean, and it had grown into a beanstalk that grew up to the sky, and found a cloud with a giant's castle on it—easily robbed. Of a princess imprisoned in a tower, and a prince who had turned into a canary to visit her. Of a man who married brides and forbade them to enter a chamber, and murdered them when they did—and how the last one was saved by sending off a white dove. Of a man who had inherited a pear tree that always bore pears, and a fox who stole from it—

He grimaced, lowering his arms. That one he might, in due course, find useful. The man had killed the fox and lived for many a year in prosperity, when he had heard that his newborn daughter would marry a poor boy, also a newborn. So he had found out where the boy was, persuaded his family to hand him over, and thrown him into a river to drown, but then the boy had swept downstream and been found by a miller. The fox could have warned him that it would not work. Indeed, every time he tried to kill the boy, it failed, and not only did the boy marry his daughter, the man had ended up trapped in an enchantment forcing him to ferry everyone over a river. Fortunato indeed.

He looked about the room. He hoped he would never so much as tempt the fox to ask what sort of funeral he would give it, let alone to put him to the test. He snorted a little. The fox could not threaten to reveal the dread secrets of his past to his bride.

His smile smoothed out. In the back corner of his mind, he knew that Belsante already knew them.

He sighed, marked his place, and closed the book. Sophia would never hear them, but he had not thought about that.

"I admire your zeal, still," said Belsante, from the doorway.

John turned slowly to face the silhouette of her. From her sweet voice, she must be smiling. "Shall we dance again tonight?"

"We do not have the enchantment of Boney to dance all of every night, we would end up like that prince who spent all of every day asleep in exhaustion because the enchantment forced him—tonight we tell tales."

John sat up, and every inch of him complained. At the least, he had move before he froze in place as if he had spoken to the Bird of Truth. He stood and bowed. "As long as I do not have to ransom the lives of my companions by telling of how I had been in greater peril than they were."

Belsante laughed. "You were prudent to bring no companions—and to not set out to steal a horse with bells. Though my not owning such a horse must have made your restraint easier."

"No doubt it was my great prudence that led me to steal the Water of Life and not the Horse of Bells. It might let me reach King Drakos, but the bells would warn him, too."

She laughed again. John offered her his arm, and they walked down the corridor. The great hall, with its gathering crowd, was a glowing doorway ahead of them, and not far of a walk.

"In fact," she said slowly, "since you have told me your story, I shall tell a tale of my ancestors."

"Oh, will you?" called a girlish voice. She stood in the doorway peering down.

Belsante laughed. "Sit, sweet Zoe. Yes, it is time for the tale to be told while you are here."

Servants had already put another seat near the high one.

"Once upon a time," said Belsante, "the prince in this land was lazy and gluttonous, and so fat that he could not walk about, and his subjects called him Prince Tubby. He had a son, just grown to marriageable age, who was gracious and handsome, and named Desiderio, and all the maidens sighed for him, and he never so much glanced at any of them.

"One day, Prince Tubby called Desiderio to him, and said, 'My son, you have all that can make a man happy, except a bride and a son. Marry well, father an heir, and you shall have everything to let yourself grow fat and content.'

"'My father,' said Desiderio, 'I have no desire to marry a woman of our kingdom. They are all pink and white, and their roses and lilies do not appeal to me. But I have dreamed of a lovely lady, rosy-brown and with hair like a raven's wing, and she stood in a radiant garden filled with flowers and fruit trees. The fruits were such that I have never seen them—but I wish to marry her.'

"'Ha,' said Prince Tubby. 'What prince can marry a dream? Do you not know your duty? When you are already too skinny, thin as a bone, and will waste away to a shadow if you sigh after this maiden?' When this did not move Desiderio, and a peddler came by with fine fruits from far away, Prince Tubby bought them—strange orange fruit—and asked his son to dinner to tempt him with them and remind him of such earthly pleasure.

"But no sooner had Desiderio seen the fruit than he swore those were the garden's fruits. He summoned the peddler and questioned him, and so learned of the far-off land of the sun where such fruit grew. He set out to find his bride there, rising up in the dawn and riding off with great haste. His father—hours later, when he rose—sent riders after him, to bring him back, but it was so many hours later that they could not find him.

"Desiderio, after a few days, rode more steadily and with less speed, for weeks and weeks, and every week the sun grew brighter and the weather hotter, and the flowers and fruits stranger.

"Far, far, far to the south, he came to a house where an old man lived and offered him hospitality for the night if he would tell him why he traveled. Desiderio said, 'I do not know if you will think me a fool, but I have dreamed of a garden with fruit like golden apples—they are called oranges—where there is a beautiful princess inside one, and I wish to make her my bride.'

"'To rescue a princess from evil is never folly,' said the old man. In the morning, when Desiderio rose, early though it was, the old man was up before him. He pointed to a hill and said, 'Behind that you will find a walled orchard with a house in the center. The gates are all rusted shut. Leave your horse there, and do not force them, but use this oil can to oil them, and they will open easily. A dog will come barking fiercely at you, but throw it this cake, and it will let you by. A woman will be cleaning out an oven with her hair, and you must make sure to give her this brush. Finally, there will be a well, and you must take out its rope and stretch it in the sunlight.

"'Then you must not go into the house, but around to its back. There you will find the orchard you have dreamed of. Pick an orange, whichever pleases you best, return to your horse, and leave at once. But whatever you do, do not open the orange until you reach a well or a spring or a stream or some other water, and once you have your bride, stay by her side and do not leave her for an hour until you have brought her safely to your father's house. Remember the evil that strikes is the one you least look for.'

"Desiderio thanked him, promised faithfully to do all that he had said, took what he offered, and rode onward. At the gate, he dismounted and went to oil the hinges, and the gate openly easily. The dog fell silent at the cake, and the woman accepted the brush. Once he had stretched out the rope, he reached the orchard, which had both white flowers and golden fruit, but he kept his wits about him and picked the finest orange and left at once.

"A great voice rose from the house, 'Rope, rope, leap up and strangle him!'

"The rope said, 'All these years and you have left me to rot in the well, but he laid me out in the sun. Let him pass.'

"Then it called, 'Baker, baker, throw him into the oven and bake him.'

"The woman said, 'All these years and you have given me nothing to clean this oven but my own hair, but he gave me a brush. Let him pass.'

"Then it called, 'Dog, dog, jump up and bite him and eat him up.'

"The dog said, 'All these years and you have never given me so much as a crust, but he gave me a whole cake. Let him pass.'

"Then it called, 'Gates, gates, close on him and crush him.'

"The gates said, 'All these years and you have left me to rust, but he oiled me. Let him pass.'

"And Desiderio passed through the gates, mounted his horse, and rode off.

"He saw no sign of the old man's house, and the land about seemed strange, and he could not see any sign of water. Once he remembered his father's table and how sweet the juice of those oranges had been, but he remembered the old man's words and rode on. Finally he came to a spring, watered his horse, drank himself, and went to open the orange. A little canary, as bright as the day, flew out, and called, 'I perish from thirst! Give me water!"

"Desiderio took up the spring water in his hands and held it out to the bird. No sooner had it sipped that it was a lovely woman with hair as dark as night and with rosy-brown face, standing by the stream, and she was exactly what he had dreamed of.

"'You have saved me,' she said, and kissed him, and told him her name was Zizi.

"He told her his name, and of the old man's warning, and they headed north—more slowly, since the horse could not bear them both, and they talked all the way. They had some cold harbor of nights, where inn-keepers took them for a pair of wandering entertainers and bade them sleep in the stable, but they went on. When they came to his father's lands, and saw his father's castle, Desiderio said, 'I have stayed with you both night and day until we came to this place—but if we come to the door like this, as dusty from the road, my father will hold you in contempt. I will go and get fine clothes and a carriage, and you will arrive in splendor, and he will regard you in the highest esteem.'

"Zizi said that the old man's warning would be wiser to take as meaning arriving at the castle, and they could slip in a back door and have her change there, but Desiderio was obstinate, and finally she consented to hide in a tree over a spring and wait for him.

"But while she was there, an ugly and foolish girl, the oldest of three daughters, came to the spring. She looked down, saw Zizi's reflection, and thought to herself that she was too beautiful to fetch water for her family. So she threw down the bucket and went off.

"Soon after, her mother sent her second daughter, who was a little less foolish, but uglier still, to find out what took her so long. The daughter picked up the bucket where her sister had tossed it, and saw the reflection. For a moment, she told herself that she couldn't be that beauty, but then she told herself there was no one else, and she threw down the bucket because she was too beautiful to fetch water.

"Finally, their mother sent her third daughter, who was the most ugly of all, and not quite the fool. This daughter looked down, saw the reflection, and realized it was not her. She looked around until she saw Zizi, and said to her, 'How unpleasant it must be, sitting in the tree like that! You have no robbers to fear in this land, or dragons either. You can come safely down.'

"And Zizi let herself be lured down, and the third daughter stuck a pin in her hair, and she turned back into a bird.

"And the third daughter plopped herself down by the spring, and when Prince Desiderio appeared, she lamented to him that a wicked witch had found her and cursed her. Prince Desiderio cursed himself and his folly, but he could not be fickle, so he dressed her in the fine clothes and brought her back to his father, who jeered at him for rejecting the brides of his own land.

"But as the cook was cooking their feast, the bird appeared in the window, and said to him, 'Good evening, cook.'

""Good evening, bird,' said the cook.

"'Sleep now, that the meats may burn, and the false bride may not eat them.'

"The cook fell asleep at once, as if the entire castle had been cursed, and when he woke, the meats had burned.

"At once he sent for new meats and started to cook them, but the bird appeared again and again sent him to sleep.

"When he had set new meats, and the bird appeared again, he went to wring its neck, but Prince Tubby had come to see what delayed his meal. When the cook told him it was the bird's fault, he said, 'Such a pretty bird! How could it do anything evil?' He stroked its head, and found the pin, and pulled it out again, and Zizi stood before him.

"Much wondering, he brought her into the hall, where Desiderio rose and proclaimed her his true bride, and the false bride derided Zizi and claimed she was the witch who had bewitched her, and the pin was nothing. She struck her own head with it, turned into a monstrously ugly bird, the color of mud, and barely escaped the hall with her life.

"So Zizi and Desiderio married, and reigned after his father died, as—" She smiled a little sadly. "—as I reign after my father died."

"And they reigned long and well," said an old knight heartily. "And happily."

The talk in the room broke up a little, and John frowned.

"What sad thought troubles you, Your Highness?" said Belsante, her voice low.

"Only thoughts," said John. "I wonder if your witch was Mistress Laurenza."

Belsante's tongue touched her lips. "Only if she were very old. It was years and years ago."

John shrugged. "Perhaps the spells were passed from witch to witch. I could ask the mirror in time, but—it would not matter."

"I suppose it would not." Belsante glanced sideways. "Perhaps the tale will profit you, in being careful what you leave behind."

John sighed. "With what lies before me, I think I will remain wary about ever promising anyone to return. The witch who plagued Zizi did not follow her back to this land, but I can not promise that the circle will not follow after me."

#

The cat looked at her with unblinking eyes, and Constance smiled radiantly back at it. In the cradle, the baby snuffled a little, and went back to sleep.

"Be off with you," said Mistress Theodosia, sweeping the cat off. It ambled away.

"So, you're going to name the baby?"

"What else?" said Constance. "I could say we will just call him Nix Nought Nothing until we could ask his father what to name him, but—" She spread her free hand. "Sigurd is wise and would know that someone who makes a riddling request of him is asking for his child, but why make it easy?"

"All the more in that you know that Rumpelstiltskin is one of that circle."

Mistress Theodosia said it pleasantly enough, but Constance still winced.

"I will name him Dag. His—father and I talked of names, and it is a royal one, from his house."

Mistress Theodosia laughed a little. "Shall you call his sister Aurora when she comes?"

"Perhaps," said Constance, not knowing whether to smile or to weep. She closed her eyes. "I suppose they would ask him for a day, and I will have to trust he will remember that they ask in a riddle who dare not ask outright."

"At least we didn't give him his first sip from the skull of a raven," said Mistress Theodosia.

"Ew," said Constance.

Mistress Theodosia chuckled. "The problem is that such a drink means that the boy grows up knowing the language of birds."

Constance raised an eyebrow.

"So when ravens gather about and chatter about how, one day, his father will bow down before him, he will listen, and when his father demands that he translate, and beats him if he disobeys—he will still throw him from the household at the news."

"At least he had the ability to speak with birds," said Constance.

"True enough. He came to a village where the peasants wailed of how their well had gone dry, and the sparrows of how it had gone dry because a snake was drinking it up—and he killed the snake and saved them all. The king heard of that and had him come to the castle to find why it was plagued with great flocks of birds. So the son told him that the birds were angry because woodcutters cut all the trees on a certain hillside, where they lived. The king ordered it to cease, and the birds flew off. The king was so pleased that he married his daughter to the son, and sent them off the journey about the realm. They came to his father's house, and his father bowed before them, and his son drew him up, saying that now he had to believe it was not insolence that had put the words in his mouth."

#

Smothered in snow, the royal garden was only rises and dips of whiteness. Here and there a tree managed to poke its branches over the surface. Even sitting by the window was a chilly business.

Biancabella's fingers tightened on the sewing in her hands. She could not travel in this weather, even if she had the birds to hand, and the news from Master Frederico, a week ago, had been that three more weeks were needed. Queen Genoveva and King Hendrik has been pleased at the news. It must have been swift work, however slow it felt.

She looked away. She had lived through many a winter in her father's castle, unable to work in the garden. Perhaps she did not have lessons to attend to, but she had sewed in those winters. It would not catch the eye of the king, and it certainly would not inspire that king to dispose of the husband that she did not have, so that she could marry the king instead.

She fingered the needle. Then, she could sew for seven years while keeping silent, and it would not disenchant her seven brothers whom their wicked stepmother changed into swans.

She laid aside the cloth and stood. Fortunate for those brothers that they did not exist—she lacked the patience.

She walked down the castle corridors and peered out the windows. Two months and three weeks, and if tales told true, four days. It was not as if she had to serve a blacksmith for seven years to get the iron shoes to climb a glassy hill.

And if she did rescue Hans—what then? She could hardly marry him as Snow-White had married Florio, not with the peril of her mother's rage hanging over them.

She scowled. Her mother would not turn him into a bear as she had Florio. She would not kill him as she had killed John. She would—she would persuade some troll-witch to carry him off and have her troll brother take his shape and pass himself off to her as Hans.

She looked out the window. Snow had muffled all the houses, and she sighed. Or turn Hans to stone, knowing his sister could not come to save him. Or kill him, after learning where the fox could not save him with that herb.

Wind gusted against the window, bringing a sparkling spray of snow. She sighed again.

At that, perhaps she would rescue him, and Hans would need to marry a princess to disenchant her. She had, after all, said that she would marry a prince to disenchant *him*.

Maybe—maybe she still would. She drifted on from the window. She supposed it depended on the prince. She scowled. If she found one asleep, so that she would have to stay by his bed for three years, three months, three weeks, three days, and three hours, until he sneezed, and she greeted him, she would fail. She managed poorly this one winter.

Voices sounded down the hallway, and laughter followed.

"Biancabella!" called Genoveva. "Come! We are telling stories, and it's no worse than watching the snow—it will not slow the handiwork!"

Biancabella sighed. Then she walked into the room, small and with a fire burning fiercely in the hearth.

One lady-in-waiting leaned forward, with her sewing unheeded in her lap. "Your father's kingdom—does it border the sea?"

Biancabella shook her head. "Two or three more kingdoms, depending on how you go."

"That would be good," said the lady, leaning back with a little smile. "For all the stories about being lost in the forest, I think it would be better than being set adrift on the deep blue sea."

"Come, Fenella," said Genoveva. "Have you really a tale about being set adrift?"

"Oh, yes," said Fenella. "Once there was a lad, quite simple, but he had the power of making things true with a wish. He still labored to get firewood to support himself—he was *simple*—and one day, the princess looked out the window and laughed at how he wrestled with his load. She said that he should have a boy—to help him, she meant—and he said that she should have one.

"Soon after, she felt sick. The king and the queen were worried and brought in all sorts of doctors who hemmed and hawed and finally told them that the princess had a sickness that would resolve itself in nine months. The king was furious and locked her in a tower, but nine months after the lad's wish, she had a beautiful baby boy.

"The king was more furious than ever. He spoke with his wise men. As soon as the boy could walk, he had all the men of the kingdom rounded up, and gave the boy an apple—whoever the boy gave the apple to was his father. The boy walked past all the nobles and knights and rich farmers and merchants and poor farmers and artisans and down to the rough workers and beggars, where the lad was, and gave the apple to the lad.

"The king was most furious of all. He ordered the princess and the lad married at once, and then he threw them both, and their son, in a boat and had it set adrift. The princess was in despair, but the lad was too simple to realize their danger and, after a few hours, wished for some grapes, and grapes appeared in the boat with them.

"'Why do you not wish us ashore?' said the princess.

"'Feed me on grapes,' said the lad, 'and I will.' So she did, and he wished them ashore, and the boat came up on a sandy shoal.

"'Why do you not wish that this shoal was a fair and prosperous land where you and I are king and queen?' said the princess.

"'Feed me on grapes,' said the lad, 'and I will.' So she did, and he wished that the shoal was a fair and prosperous kingdom where they were king and queen, and the shoal spread before them into a land with broad farmlands, lush pasture, and green forest, with ports for many ships, and a glorious castle of white stone, right before them.

"'Why do you not wish yourself to be a wise, handsome, and virtuous man, fit to be king of such a splendid kingdom?' said the princess.

"'Feed me on grapes,' said the lad, 'and I will.' So she did, and he wished himself so. Then they went into the castle with their son, and because now he was wise, he did not make more wishes, they had caused trouble enough."

Laughter and agreement sounded all about her.

"Once upon a time, when wishing still did some good," said Genoveva. "And some evil."

"But," said Fenella, "one day her father took to the sea in a ship, and the lad wished a storm to bring the ship to the island—safely, but unable to leave. So he went down and made the father welcome, and brought him to the castle, where his son was playing with a golden ball.

"Then he wished the ball into the father's pocket. His son wailed about the loss, and the lad found it on the king, and the king was distressed and flustered and unable to explain that though he looked like a thief, he had not stolen it.

"So he told the princess's father that she had gotten with child by the same way as the ball had appeared in his pocket, and brought her out to be reconciled with her father—and gave his son back the golden ball."

More mirth spread about, and Biancabella smiled, briefly. She wondered whether she would use a wish to reconcile with her father.

Her breath came out. She wondered whether he had noticed that she had left. She supposed she might reconcile with him, if he wished it.

Heaven grant that he might never wish it, came a fugitive thought, and she winced.

#

Moonlight gleamed over the snowy scene. Snow-White could not even tell where the garden had grown.

"Good thing that the midwife got here hours ago," said Florio, his voice much calmer than his face.

"Yes," said Snow-White, "and this is not, after all, your mother's first childbed."

Florio grimaced.

Snow-White looked back at where the road lay hidden, without travelers on it. A good thing. Rapunzel and Basil would expect them to run the inn, but she felt as if she might manage to cook a meal for their eating, if they would content themselves with plain food.

Florio came up behind her, and his arm looped about her waist, his hand resting easily below her belt. Snow-White sighed. Yes, there was that, too—

"Was that?" said Florio, sharply, pulling away, and Snow-White blinked and listened. The cry of a tiny little newborn—

Within minutes, a smiling Basil came down the stairs. "You have a little sister."

#

Snowmelt dripped from roofs. When it fell into the shadow of houses, long icicles formed, to glint like diamonds when the sunlight shifted. But the streets were passable, and those who had urgent business moved about.

And, thought Biancabella, it was warmer than when she and Genoveva had gone to order the doves. She still pulled her mantle more closely about her.

At the shop, their entrance did not draw eyes. Master Frederico's voice rose, in haranguing tones, telling them not to bungle the case.

"The finest work this workshop has done yet, and for a princess no less. You ham-handed oafs should be wise enough to take care for *that.*"

Genoveva swept forward. The doves sat on the table, and even lit only by lamplight, they gleamed in gold and silver. Biancabella thought she would have no difficulty getting them to Hans. The courtiers would be agog to see such a wonder.

Master Frederico looked over, and his smile spread broadly across his face. His finger touched the head of one dove.

"Coo, coo," it said, shifting about. "Don't you remember?"

The second one cooed, and said, "No, no, I do not remember."

Biancabella swallowed. "Show me how to do that." It sounded like a croak in her ears, but Master Frederico nodded.

#

The grass still spread, dingy yellow, about the castle, with no spring growth. Snow clumped in corners. Almost all the trees, farther off, were leafless yet, and the few showed leaves tiny and still all but yellow.

Biancabella straightened the red scarf on her head. Genoveva had insisted that she could not look like the beggar woman who had come the same day that Hans had—and that leaving the fox in the woods was not enough to disguise her. Otherwise, that Gertrude who had enchanted Hans might know Biancabella.

Now that she faced the castle, she thought that Hans might not recognize her in her strange feathers, which was mad. He had not recognized her before. She tramped up to the doors.

"I have a wonderful wonder," she told the guards. "A marvelous marvel."

One guard snorted. The other said, "To show King William when he's off in the hills? Or to show Queen Catskin when she refuses to poke her nose from her chambers except for actual business?"

"Why, to show the courtiers, then." Biancabella glanced inside the gates where men practiced with swords. One, she realized, was Hans. Courtiers gathered around, rapt. "It must mean dull days when they can attend neither the king nor the queen."

"Like they would buy such a marvel off you," said the first guard, with a sneer. "When it would look like rivaling the king."

"They could tell him what a wonderful wonder and a marvelous marvel it is when the king returns. Look!" She plopped the box on the ground, opened it, and pressed the back of the birds' necks. Gleaming in gold and silver, they leapt out and perched on the gate. One woman in the company inside poked her neighbor and pointed. More gazes turned toward her, and two swordsmen—not including Hans—lowered their blades to look.

"Madwoman!" shouted the guard, and drew every gaze in the courtyard. Some hurried over—a maiden with her golden hair and green skirts flying behind, a youth with fox-red hair—and all the swordplay ceased. The guards scowled.

"Oh, let us see it," said the maiden in green, and agreement followed her.

"Coo, coo," said the first dove. "Don't you remember?"

"Coo," said the second, sadly. "No, no, I do not remember."

All within shifted toward the gate. Guards gave Biancabella frustrated looks but did not seem ready to lay hands on her. She thought she saw Gertrude in the crowd but could not be certain. Hans—Hans looked only as amazed as the rest.

"Coo, don't you remember the witch's cottage, where you were turned into a tree?"

"No, no, I do not remember."

"Don't you remember how Biancabella unchained you and set you free?"

"Coo, coo, no, no, I do not remember."

"Coo, coo, don't you remember how you turned into a bird, and dropped a plowshare on the witch's head?"

"No, no, I do not remember."

Master Frederico had shown her that the birds said exactly what she had called for them to say. Biancabella turned her face toward the crowd. Such eager, bright faces, shifting about, hiding Hans from her. She stepped closer, peering at them.

Gertrude's face appeared for a moment, set in a mask of fury. Biancabella gulped and looked on, inspecting face after face.

Then she saw Hans. How puzzled he looked as the dove sang of how they had waited for the flood to subside so they could cross a bridge, and then his gaze fell on her.

The confusion vanished. A moment later, his face was a mask of calm as he turned and walked away. Biancabella bit her lip. The doves finished their cries, and grew still as metal. Courtiers exclaimed over this wonderful wonder, this marvelous marvel, and Hans edged around the wall of the castle.

"I will bring them back when the king or the queen may consider them." She seized the birds from the gate and stuffed them away. "You may tell them what a wonderful wonder and marvelous marvel it was."

She picked up the box and fled the castle, despite the protests that followed. The road turned, so that a stand of holly hid her from the castle. Hans stepped out and took the box from her, and they started to run down the road.

Minutes later, panting for breath, they stopped in the forest.

Hans said, "I suppose I could have asked them a riddling question about whether my old key or my new one is better—but running away seems simplest."

"Especially," said Biancabella, "since I did not have to climb a glassy hill on iron shoes or let the North Wind carry me east of the sun, west of the moon."

The fox appeared at the top of the hill. "And you haven't run that far to get away. The castle might still send someone after you."

Hans rolled his eyes, but they walked on.

#

In the stillroom's dim light, Ottoline glared at the herbs. Dried up, desiccated, and nearly useless. Then she glared about the room, small, windowless, with walls of unadorned stone. Were she queen in her own right, with her own king and her own castle with its own garden, she could arrange things more fitly, but Augusta Gloriana did not care that she did not have as much authority over the garden as some peasant wife. Even Mother Magda had more authority, but—as if Ottoline were not her oldest friend—Augusta Gloriana had arranged for her to marry a mere prince.

So as to keep her on hand, no doubt. Her lips curled. Thinking that a woman with one eye had to be grateful for what she could get—

She pushed aside the herbs and glared at the wall.

And the rest of the circle mistrusted her, because of that. As if they blamed her for Mother Trude's death. Why she had poured all that time and effort into those two spells for Mother Trude, to ensure they would work after her own death—she did that so seldom!

Even for herself! When Mother Trude had been a mere witch, not even married into the nobility, let alone royalty!

She forced her breath out. And Augusta Gloriana had made it harder for her to marry a king by saddling her with a prince. She raised her head. No matter. She would be patient a while longer, and have a king instead of a prince. That was a proper reward for all her hard work, and the others would not sneak about behind her back.

A knock sounded on the door.

Her eyes narrowed. The servants would not be so bold.

She strode over and opened the door to glare out. Augusta Gloriana met her gaze and blinked.

Good, thought Ottoline. Let her learn that I grow angry.

"Good morning. The circle has need of your skills."

Ottoline spoke flatly, and harshly. "Oh."

"Biancabella travels alone, and with no one to aid her. I found a bitter, harsh, resentful man, always unlucky in love." Augusta Gloriana smiled a little and lowered her voice to a whisper. "If it's not past your power to make him a *dragon*, we have her already."

"You expect me to do better than Boney?"

Augusta Gloriana laughed, a glorious pealing sound. "Better than Boney? Who does not take it for granted that you will outdo him? He was never your match."

#

The forest trees were still all but leafless. Many bore red or green buds on the tips of their branches, but formed only a thin veil. All the greenery grew thickly across the forest floor, among the dead leaves, where pools of snow melt spread about with edges of mud.

Hans's voice rose among the trees.

"And on this bird there grew a fine feather,

The finest feather, that ever you did see,

And the feather on the bird, the bird on the nest, the nest on the twig, and the twig on the bough, and the bough on the tree, and the tree in the wood,

And the green leaves flourished thereon, thereon, thereon,

And the green leaves flourished thereon."

Biancabella smiled.

The next town came into view, and her smile deepened, thinking of the inn and the beds in it, when the smile faded.

"Is that town really hung in black?" she said.

Hans scowled. "Yes." He glanced at her. "It could be mourning for royalty. As we have seen already."

Biancabella nodded, slowly. "And—I have not seen my mother again."

Still, they walked up slowly. When Biancabella heard the anxious voices, about how they had to sacrifice the princess to a dragon to keep it from destroying the city, her heart sank.

"Red Ritter will save her!" said a snub-nosed boy, fiercely. "He promised, and he's a mighty knight! He will save Princess Silverhair—and marry her!"

"Pshaw!" said a woman with nut-brown hair, loudly. "He is *all talk*! Hunting bears and wolves is nothing next to facing the dragon. He will flee like a coward. And the dragon will gobble up Princess Silverhair."

"And," said a red-haired little girl, scornfully, "King Igor won't *let* him marry Princess Silverhair. Not for just killing a dragon."

Biancabella let her breath out. She could hope for the princess's sake that Red Ritter was more as the boy saw him and less like the woman's view. She glanced sideways. Hans's face was stern and im-placable.

The streets, with mud tracked over them, were subdued, for all the crowds of people going about necessary business, and others gossiping in the softest tones.

She and Hans—and the fox—also had business of their own. Biancabella walked on. The fox did not frisk about, but stayed close by their feet, watching the crowds, until they reached the square where the inn—the Golden Firebird—was, standing opposite to the castle.

The square was filled. The crowd was uncommonly quiet as they stood, facing the castle.

King Igor and his queen stood on the steps. A princess with long, flowing silver hair and a face red and ugly with weeping wrung her hands. With them, a huntsman in red stood, glaring into the shadows of the door, where she could just make out two figures. One, she thought, wore a dress of violet.

Her mouth went utterly dry. She could only stare as Augusta Gloriana swept out in violet. Ottoline followed her, ungracefully. She wore cloth of gold, but with her hair in that impossibly ugly arrangement to try to hide her missing eye, and her every move-ment calculated to prevent her hair's disarray.

Biancabella's heart hammered in her chest.

"Have no fear, good princess." Augusta Gloriana pointed across the square at Biancabella. "That woman there is a princess just as much as you are. And an undutiful, ungrateful, insolent princess at that. Her blood is as good as yours, but that alone about her is good. Driven out for her ill conduct—not even for such petty mat-ters as comparing her father to such commonplace things as salt—"

Biancabella tried to rally her voice. "You tell such lies—"

But even as she spoke, snakes and toads formed in the air before her. Ottoline smirked as they fell to the ground, and she gawked.

"See? That was her reward for insolence to an enchantress." Augusta Gloriana shook her head sadly.

Biancabella looked wildly about. Every gaze look on her without friendliness. She swallowed, feeling no monstrous creature in her mouth. Her thoughts slowly pulled together to realize she saw no sign either of Hans or of the fox. She told herself to be glad, they were her only hope.

Her heart still hammered like a drum.

#

Hans stood as unmoving as when he had been a tree. Biancabella did not, futilely, fight against the armed men who drew her off—one holding her by each arm—and he did no more than he had when Mother Trude had maltreated Gretel.

His gaze went up to the castle. Augusta Gloriana had vanished.

"Wise of you," said the fox, its voice low. "That Red Ritter would not come even to Princess Silverhair's aid. He will not come to Biancabella's."

"How did you know?"

"I didn't. I guessed. If I had guessed wrongly, well, it would be a matter of a moment to rejoin her." The fox watched Biancabella vanish into the castle.

Hans winced.

Then he said, "Was that really Augusta Gloriana with them?"

After a moment, the fox nodded. A carter shouted at them, and they slid from the way.

"Fairest of them all? She looked so ugly that half the women in the land are fairer than she is. Snow-White outshines her—but Biancabella doesn't have to grow more beautiful. She was all but a fiend."

"Ah." After a minute, the fox said, "That was the hatred. The anger." Then its voice sharpened. "Look. Now."

Her purple gown sweeping around her, and a little smile on her face, Augusta Gloriana descended the stairs. All the crowd pulled aside to give her the way.

Regal, thought Hans. Queenly. He let out a breath. Smug, he noted, but despite that, he had to concede, beautiful. And—more beautiful than Biancabella. Still, he thought with sudden fierceness, Biancabella was worth twenty of her.

#

The tower room was so cold that she wondered whether the dragon would take her corpse if she froze to death.

She paced back and forth. She was not locked up her for protesting how her father had imposed impossible tasks on a hapless youth, forcing him to summon all the wolves in the kingdom, and so the wolves would not eat up the court, letting the youth free her. Or because the king had taken a fancy to her after her wedding and sent her husband off on an impossible quest, and tried to marry her himself, and so her husband would not return with magic that could free her. Or because a witch—her mouth tightened—because Mother Magda had locked her up for safety, and entered and left by her long hair, and so no prince could climb her hair to rescue her.

In all of these tales, the princess had time. She did not face being sacrificed to a dragon the next day.

#

The street was lit by light from the houses about, and moonlight where they did not reach. The air grew very cold.

"No," said the fox. "They imprisoned her in a tower." It shook its head. "There is no way you can get up to her safely, let alone escape with her. Unlike Rapunzel, she can not cast down her hair."

Hans closed his eyes. "We can not go to the inn. Those two women might recognize me, and they would certainly notice a talking fox." He squared his shoulders and opened his eyes. "Or any fox. And at that, I do not want to avoid your counsel."

The fox shrugged. Hans could hardly blame it for not thinking it could offer him much better advice than he could think up on his own.

His thoughts stumbled on. "It would be best to be as near as possible to where they intend to offer her, so as to reach it most quickly in the morning." If he could do something besides die in her defense.

The fox shifted its head. "There are farms out there. A beggar might seek shelter."

Hans stood still for a moment. Then, he was a beggar. Begging for shelter, even if the farmer did not know it was also to save Biancabella.

With a young, hale man, the farmer would not think he was a wizard putting him to the test. Which, Hans reminded himself, was only the truth.

#

The moon rose higher, but still cast long shadows: crisscrossing where the branches wove their webs, and lines from the trunks, thin for saplings, broad for the patriarchs of the forest. It leached color from the scene. Even the fox looked gray.

Hans stamped his feet as he looked about. The hillside where she would go was plain enough, it loomed high enough that he had seen it back in the town, but ice and shadow made the footing treacherous. He needed, indeed, to be as close as possible in the morning.

Only one farmhouse stood near. He supposed he could hope for a cave if the farmer turned his dogs on him. He could hardly abandon his sword in the wet when he needed it in the morning, but the farmer would likely take him for a robber rather than a beggar.

The fox, he realized, looked back, toward the crossroads. Down the roads came three men, moving with slow deliberateness, as if greatly aged. They turned at the crossroads and came toward him. The moonlight on their faces showed how lined they were.

Hans bowed. "Heaven prosper your path, grandfathers."

The first of them smiled. "Heaven prosper your path, grandson. We look for the farm of Marko the Stingy, in hopes of shelter for the night."

"I also," said Hans, "am in need of shelter."

The second said, "You can wear a robe of ours. It will make you look more like a beggar."

"And I," said the fox, "will take your sword. And bring it to you when you have shelter."

Moments later, the fox trotted off into the woods with the sheathed sword in its mouth, and Han pulled the offered robe over his clothes. They headed off as soon he was done, and he followed meekly, bowing his head as much as he was able. He still loomed over them.

Dogs barked almost at once, loudly and fiercely. They pulled against their leashes into the moonlight. Their teeth were sharp, and their bodies both large and muscular.

"Peace on this house," called the first man, over the barking.

"Heaven's blessing on all who dwell within," called the second.

"Be off with you!" The firelight within lit the man from behind as he shook a heavy staff at them. "With the dragon ready to eat up my fat cows, do you think I have room here for some useless mouths?"

The old men bowed. Hans, hastily, did as well. The dogs snarled and roamed in the reach of their leashes, glancing now and again at their master.

"Shelter from the night would be generosity to poor travelers, too far from shelter," said the third.

"Like I build my sheds for sheltering you," snarled the man. "Dragons could come and burn them up."

"Please, Father," said a little voice. A girl came up beside the man. "Let them stay in the hayloft. It won't do any harm."

"Huh," said the man. "You see that big lunk they have with them. He could do labor enough to keep them from begging, if he would only work."

Hans stared at the ground, keeping his mouth firmly shut.

"One must be kind to the simple," said the first old man, and Hans's mouth fought to open. He tightened it. If Biancabella made herself a beggar, he could pass as a simpleton.

"We assure you that he does not have the power to grant wishes, which he would use foolishly in his folly," said the second.

"I'd beat you all black and blue if he did," snarled the man, but the little girl pulled on his sleeve, and he ordered them off to the hayloft.

They bowed.

"May Heaven grant all good things to all your household for your generosity," said the third man, somehow managing to sound sincere. They walked off, and Hans followed them, obediently. The dogs barked behind them, and the man growled at them to be silent, but Hans did not look back. Only at the door did he stop and hold it open a minute. The fox slid within, the sword in its mouth. Hans took it.

The fox laughed. "Well done and ill paid." It glanced up at him. "I didn't help those dogs avoid being killed by their master, so their

barking is not ungrateful—but the fool farmer thought they were
barking after *you*." It shook its head.

It leapt ahead of him, and up in the hay, curled up in a ball.
Hans laid down the sword and lay down beside it. The old men
gathered across the hay, but, he told himself firmly, gratitude alone
should keep him from prying. He closed his eyes.

When he opened them again, he tried to judge from the stray
light how far the moon had moved. Then he realized that the light,
though whiter than snow, was not the moonlight. His eyes open
only a crack, he shifted his head.

The three old men sat together, gleaming, dressed in robes of
silver and gold.

"What shall we do on this day?" said the first old man.

"We shall punish the evil," said the second old man. "Let this
farmer lose his lands and his wealth, and drudge for years. Let us
give his wealth to the poor peasant boy Vasily, who lives by the mill
up the river."

"We shall reward the good," said the third old man. "Let his
daughter marry Vasily and live long and happily with him, and let
our companion wake in the morning at a time when he may go to
do as he wishes."

The door below creaked. Hans turned and saw Marko the
Stingy glaring up at them. His shoulders set. Marko must have
heard. Having heard, no doubt he would act against the boy, and
thus bring about his losses, and the marriage.

The thought of that did not assuage him. Marko the Stingy
would indeed throw a child in the river. The spring floods could indeed bear Vasily far off.

Then Hans yawned and could not keep his eyes open. Moments later, he opened them again. The morning was paling from
black into gray, watery sunlight slipped through the cracks of the

barns with the icy morning air, the three old men had vanished, and the dragon still threatened, whatever he had dreamed.

They had said he would wake in time. They had not said that he could not waste that time by lollygagging. He stood. The fox bounded off before him.

#

The forest had so little snow left on the ground that the pine needles and fallen leaves still peeked through half of it. It gathered only where sheltered from the wind. Hans and the fox trudged on. They came out on the hillside, and the wind had so blown over it that dead grass showed more than snow.

The footing was still treacherously slick, and the place where the chains waited was stark against the grass.

"Over here," said the fox. "It'll be safe."

For all the time walking, the morning was still charcoal gray, and Hans crept along the slope. So bitterly cold it was here, and he had to stay still to ensure that no one noticed him. They would let Red Ritter defend their Princess Silverhair, but for him to defend Biancabella—they would think the dragon would return in a rage at being cheated, no doubt.

The fox's breath hissed out. "Hurry!"

Hans looked over his shoulder. A procession, easily marked by its lanterns, approached. He scrambled to the outcropping the fox had found. The shelter from the wind was little enough.

It let him see enough to note the red-clad man among the guards.

"You're being a fool, Red Ritter," said one guard—the captain, Hans guessed. "Let the dragon eat this foreign princess."

"Don't be absurd," said Red Ritter, grandly. "It will just return to demand the true princess. It must be slain!"

Hans let out his breath slowly. Perhaps, perhaps—the fox snorted and glanced sideways at him—but then Biancabella came into view, bound. Pale as she usually was, she was paler this morning, like the snow around her, and their only mercy was that they had left her her own clothes, warm enough that she would not freeze while she waited.

The guards chained her to the rock, and Red Ritter, his hand resting on his sword's hilt, stood on the rock over her, looking over the scene like a sentinel, but he did not turn toward the two of them, if he even saw them behind the outcropping.

The guards stepped back from the chains and hastened down the slope. Hans let his breath out slowly. It formed white puffs on the frosty air, but the sky was turning from gray toward cream and pink—having lightened while his attention was wholly on the guards.

The fox leapt up and flitted off. Hans blinked, but he wanted to draw attention only at need. He looked down the road. The guards had vanished with distance. Wind blew over the ground, and snow hissed over the grass.

"That will do," said Red Ritter. He hopped down from the rock. "If some adventure saves you—why, I will be right here to claim credit."

Biancabella looked at him with narrowed eyes. "And you'll kill me if I do not promise to say you did it? Even though I am a foreign princess, that I suffered sword wounds from a dragon will betray you!" She shook her head. "You should have learned what happened to Red Henry when he tried your trick."

Red Ritter's face contorted. "You petty little—"

Hans rose from the outcropping. Neither one noticed as Red Ritter stepped toward Biancabella, looming over her, until Hans came up behind him.

For a moment, Red Ritter gaped. Hans grabbed the man's sword and threw it down the hillside, away from the town. Red Ritter stared after it, glanced at Hans, took a step forward toward the sword, and then turned and ran the other way.

Biancabella laughed, but it sounded thin and thready. Hans looked at the chains. If he had a magical dog that could bite through iron as if it were meat—or a sword that could cut through—but the fox could not even help him if the dragon set the hill ablaze.

The wind blew on, from the city, past them, and down into the valley where the dragon would come.

"Are you cold?" he said.

She shook her head and pulled her mantle closer. "Keep watch," she said. "If the dragon surprises you—"

Hans turned to look down the slope. "It would be too much to hope for that it would be a dragon no larger than a man."

She laughed again. "You could lure it into a coffin if you offended it enough—but that would require that it be so offended with you that it would care whether you were dead."

"Perhaps it would carry you off to marry you," said Hans, gloomily, and Biancabella glanced sideways at him, smiling. He felt like ice. Did she think he jested because he felt certain that he could win? He had not learned that much swordplay from John, or even practicing with the other men at King William's court.

A hiss sounded from the valley, and all other thoughts ceased. Victory was one thing, but fleeing like Red Ritter, or cowering like the other men of the city, was another.

The scales were red—a muddy red, and touched with other colors, but bright enough and distinct enough against the last snows and the dead grass of dingy yellow.

The dragon inched onward, its belly flat against the ground, and it hissed again. "I'll show 'em, I'll show 'em—she promised, she did—and she—" It lifted its head for a moment, sniffing the air, and hissed again. "I'll eat her up if she lied, so she wouldn't be such a fool. Turning me to a dragon that could eat her up if she lied—she didn't lie, she didn't, she would never—"

Biancabella frowned. Hans could only agree. Was the dragon trying to persuade itself of something?

Biancabella leaned forward and looked at him imploringly. He inched over. She whispered in his ear, "Ottoline."

Ottoline? She changed the shape of men and beasts—she could have turned a man into the monster. Hans nodded. If she had turned this dragon to its form—his eyes narrowed—the dragon perhaps had less practice in fighting than he did.

Its head inched up the slope. Practice or none, the dragon could swallow both him and Biancabella whole, and it knew to keep its belly to the ground.

He had the sword the dwarves had made, he reminded himself. And its eyes were vulnerable. He watched its head shift, and the wind hit them with a fierce gust.

"Be careful how you talk," said Hans, in an ordinary voice, somewhat louder than usual. "If it breathes fire on the hillside, the smoke could blind us, and we don't want it to realize that."

Biancabella's eyes narrowed, but down in the valley, the dragon lifted its head and breathed out a gust of flame, engulfing the hill. The grass lit up, and its smoke blew into the dragon's face. Behind the smoky veil, the dragon gave a grunt of startled displeasure.

Hans, sword in hand, strode down the slope toward it and watched every moment for any sign of that shape moving in the smoke.

"I'll show you—" The dragon reared up, looking over the smoke. Hans leapt to the attack, and the dwarves' sword sliced through its belly. The blood fountained, and Hans leapt aside, away from the blood, away from where the dragon would land, falling. If it fell at once—

Its eyes still burning and alert, its head came down by him. Its mouth started to gape, and its breath was already burning hot. Hans leapt to the attack again, at those dark eyes. The sword sank deeply in the one, and the thrashing coils made him leap back out of range. His heart hammered. It might survive, as it survived the first blow—if it opened its mouth, he had little shelter—

Smoke billowed out, but no fire. Moments inched by as his heart pounded. He coughed, but the wind bore the smoke away, slowly clearing the air. The thrashing slowed, the coils sagged, its good eye picked him out and glared balefully, and after a moment, the dragon opened its mouth and failed to breath smoke. Blood formed a pool under it. Hans inched back, and back, and the dragon sighed and perished.

His foot hit something that clanked. Biancabella's hand came down on his arm. "My hero," she whispered, her eyes bright, and kissed his cheek.

Hans blushed. She smiled so radiantly on him—she did not need to grow more lovely than Augusta Gloriana, she was fairer than her and Snow-White both.

"If I could cut you free—I would have, and left that city to its conniving with Augusta Gloriana and Ottoline."

Biancabella let her breath out slowly. Then she said, "Isn't that the fox?"

So it had returned, thought Hans, and looked down the slope, to see the fox bounding along—with something glinting in its mouth.

It was not long after when the fox arrived, grinning about a key ring.

As Hans unchained Biancabella, the fox said, "Took longer than expected—but I see our stalwart Hans has proven his valor as

Red Ritter did not. Let us wisely depart before Red Ritter, like so many a villain, decides to claim the credit by slaying the hero."

Biancabella laughed a little, and rubbed her wrists. "He's not so near that Hans can't cut out the tongue of the dragon first, as proof of his claim."

Hans lowered his hands, with the key. "You can't mean me to marry that Princess Silverhair!"

"You can't mean to allow Princess Silverhair, with all her flaws, to marry whatever knave comes along to take the dragon's head. All the more in that I expect it to be Red Ritter. Throw the dragon's tongue in the first river we come to, to be rid of it."

#

The night was bitterly cold, with ice forming on the puddles as they approached the inn. Every breeze was a chilling blast.

Though, Biancabella had to concede, they had traveled long and hard to get here, and it was late.

The Rose and the Stag—she passed under the sign with the others, and Hans went to get their room. Biancabella pushed back her hood. No one paid their arrival any heed. All eyes had turned on the plump traveler with rumpled brown hair in the middle of the room. His nose was still red from the cold, but he held an ale cup in hand, and was in the middle of his tale.

"So Red Ritter came to the king and said that the treacherous little princess had used magic to run away—an evil fox had stolen the key to let her escape the chains so the dragon would eat up the city—and Princess Silverhair, too!"

"A likely story," said a thin woman, sitting back in the shadows, her voice sour.

"Oh, very likely," the man said. "He had the dragon's head and said the princess should marry him because he has saved her. Except—" He looked about as if daring them to guess. "Except that someone pried open its mouth, and its tongue was gone!"

Laughter resounded all about, and exclamations about how Red Ritter should have not fallen for that old trick.

"So the real dragon-slayer is out there and can prove his case," said a young man.

"Bet he'll be back in a year and a day to claim Princess Silverhair," said a young woman, bright-eyed.

The traveler told how he had ridden his horse at full speed as soon as he learned that the way would be free of the dragon, after its danger had hindered his journey, and Hans touched Biancabella's shoulder.

They stole off to the room, leaving the chatter behind, and once inside, Biancabella sat on the bed and laughed and laughed.

"It will serve Princess Silverhair right," said Hans, "when I do not return in a year and a day."

Perhaps Ottoline would blame Red Ritter for the dragon's death, Biancabella thought, which ended her laughter.

Chapter 12—The Compass

The bear lumbered through the woods and the melting snow.

Big, clumsy, foolish thing, thought Rumpelstiltskin. There, it would find that pool within the next valley—he scampered over the snow to slip within, and look up. Easier even then the usual king, who was at least human—

The bear trudged up to the waters and looked down. Rumpelstiltskin reached up and grabbed its ears. It roared and tossed its head, but his grip was strong.

"And all this for nothing," said Rumpelstiltskin. "As if I would keep you captive forever, to show you off to the king! No, I will let you go and for nothing more than a dawn and a day—"

The bear roared, shaking the trees, and brought its maw down on the arms holding it. It bit once, and Rumpelstiltskin screamed.

The bear shook off that arm and turned to the other. Rumpelstiltskin let go and sank before the bear could tear it to bits. It trundled on, and Rumpelstiltskin glared at it. That knave Ottoline, making the bear so powerful it could fight off *him*—he would show her, he would show them all.

#

John put another book back on the shelf and looked at the tomes lined up beside it. How tedious the hours had been, searching, and how profitless. He would leave here with no more knowledge than he had come with.

At least, useful knowledge. If anyone asked him whether witches ever turned boys into ducks, he had learned that they did.

He turned his face away. He had the water of life, and saving Belsante and her kingdom was not a little thing.

Out the window, the snow was sinking and vanishing, opening up his path. The sunset still gleamed pink and gold. He did not have much time, this late in the turn to spring, to ready himself.

#

The ballroom gleamed from the tapers, and the figures moved in stately measures. Belsante's face was grave and composed as they moved together.

"It is a pity I must leave," said John, "but so many people are in danger while Augusta Gloriana and the others are at work. You and your kingdom are not safe."

Belsante nodded, gravely. They twirled about in the measures. In their new positions, she said, "Neither are you."

John swallowed.

Her hands tightened, just a little, on his. "I will give you a compass, a treasure of the land, that will let you mark your path with more certainty." They twirled about another measure. "And, if, with that, you do not return within a year and a day, I will take my army and come looking for you, to come to your aid." She smiled. "After you have broken a spell on my entire kingdom, I can hardly leave you to suffer under some bewitchment, if you are caught."

"You do me great honor." A fugitive thought said that Sophia would not have been so brave, whatever his peril. He felt guilty and disloyal, but could not shake the thought.

"And since you are leaving me, I shall expect you to partner me for all the dances this night."

"Of course, Your Majesty," said John, and felt his face heating.

#

The treasure room glittered around them. Belsante ignored them all to take down a bronze compass. It bore no jewels, but its sides had scroll-work, and sigils were delicately engraved about its edge. Its arrow shifted about in a manner that could not mean it would find the north.

"It is little used," said Belsante. "The chronicles speak little of it. But it can certainly find things." She lifted her hand. "Point to the kingdom where John came from." The arrow settled at once.

"How much must you tell it?"

She cocked an eyebrow.

"If—"

She handed him the compass.

"Point to the place where I can find what we need to defeat Augusta Gloriana."

The compass whirled about, in circle after circle, faster and faster.

"Stop!"

It stopped. He drew a deep breath. "Point to where Biancabella is."

Obediently, it pointed—somewhat more to the west than before. He tried King Drakos's lands—it shifted about—and then Ian's body, where it pointed directly.

"I shall have to master its secrets," said John, "but even this much will certainly be of use."

Belsante smiled radiantly. "We have bottles here—I will give you one that you may use. They are enchanted to hold as much as you put in them in the span of three hours. It may make a difference."

#

Where the stream banks had stood, torrents of foaming water rushed and flooded the trees about. The calm air held more than a bit of chill. John strode along, his pack filled with food, and picked out the flowers on the forest floor. Some white, some blue, all familiar, but only vaguely. Biancabella could tell all the names, no doubt, but for him, he knew only that these were signs of spring.

The compass hung from his belt, tucked away in a pouch that kept it from sight, and not from mind. If Biancabella had learned more, perhaps she could use it more than he could. If he found her. If he could turn that far from his path, if she were not to the west still—

With there being only one road, he had no need for it yet. If the compass pointed over the forest or, worse, the flood, he would be a fool to leave the way.

Footsteps sounded in the forest. John stopped, near a towering oak. Not everyone could remain on the way, and not all those who had to leave it were bandits, but only a fool would trust his safety to that.

A man walked among the trees, haggard and way-worn—his nut-brown hair and beard had grown long. He carried a bow, though unstrung, and his gaze swept over the trees. John did not know what betrayed him, but the man shook his head.

"Ho, traveler, be wise," he called. "These woods here are witched. And they have witched me. Wiser of you to leave before you are caught."

John came from behind the tree. "And how have they witched you? And do you know the witch's name?"

The man stared at him.

"A witch wronged me, and I would aid you in any way I can against one." When the man still did not move, he said, "My name is John, and I once loved a woman named Sophia, who died because of a witch."

"She—she might have been turned to a bird," said the man. "Your Sophia. Even a duck. You might yet rescue her."

"You are kind to try to hearten me," said John, "but I know beyond doubt that she is dead. Nor can she be roused by a kiss. I would gladly aid you against another, lest you join my plight. All the more if the witch is one of those who wronged me."

His heart beat harder in the silence. The bottle of water weighed on him, but —Vasilisa and Ian he might still help, as they had rescued Snow-White after Hans. And their foul plans should be foiled whenever he could.

After a moment, the man shuddered. "My name is Karl. I am an archer, a huntsman, and one day I went hunting in the woods. I saw a beautiful bird, small, but like fiery gold. I shot at it, and wounded it, and it said, 'Do not hurt me, good huntsman, take me home and I will show you a wonder of wonders, a marvel of marvels.' So I took it home, and when midnight came, she shed her feathers and was a maiden of radiant loveliness. 'Marry me and make me your wife,' she said. 'I must flee my wicked mother.'"

Karl let out his breath. "And for a time, we were happy. Her name was Aviette—"

John twitched, but Karl went on without hesitation.

"—and she insisted on hiding as a bird when people came by, she would perch on a tree and not even sing, but people noticed how my clothes were all mended, better than ever before, though I did not go to seamstresses. So King Maximus came to my cottage and insisted on seeing my bride.

"Aviette took to wing, and then a dark fog enclosed her, and she was gone."

Karl let out his breath. "King Maximus forbade me to ever set foot in his realm again without her, but I—would have sought her out anyway. Except—I have searched for months, and though I thought myself a woodsman, I keep being turned back. I think it is witchcraft." He shook his head. "I don't know whether to hope that it is."

John's eyes narrowed. How like them. "Her mother must have told the king. To flush her out."

Karl looked at him, sharply.

"Was her mother named Mistress Laurenza?"

Karl took a step backward, and spoke fiercely. "*How* do you know that?"

"She was not the one who killed my Sophia, but she was party to it." John walked toward him. "To thwart her is a noble deed." Karl flinched, and John went to his belt, to pull out the compass. "If this can work against her magic, we can find your bride yet."

He held it out. "Show us the way to Aviette."

The compass pointed directly toward a torrent. John nearly groaned, but Karl's eyes were fixed on the compass, and he moved it about to reveal that she was far enough distant that the compass did not budge. Karl's expression was caught in hope and doubt.

"I can show you—show me the way to Karl," he said. It swiveled around, and the needle moved as he moved his hand about.

Karl let his breath out in a deep sigh of relief. "Aviette told me of her mother. I may be able to win her back, if only I can find her."

John nodded. "They have their weaknesses." He swallowed down his complaint that Sophia had not escaped by one. Despondency would do them no good.

It certainly would not get them past that torrent.

"There was a tree felled over the stream a bit farther down," said Karl. "Where the stream was narrower."

#

Beneath the dark clouds, the forest trees showed no signs of buds. From the tips of the branches to the roots, the dampness turned their bark black. The dark leaves underfoot moldered into the earth, and no flower grew. Broad puddles were dark with mud, leaving their depth unknown. The brush of the undergrowth had no leaves any more than the trees, but often bore thorns.

Though, thought John, at least once they had managed to pass the torrent by the road, they had not had to cross more such streams.

Karl looked hopefully ahead. John felt nothing but weariness. They had trudged on and on, with Karl shifting between elation and abject despair, and John could see the point of both. Perhaps Aviette was east of the sun and west of the moon, and they should have sought out the four winds instead, so that the North Wind could bear Karl to that tower. The circle had not triumphed so often by letting their curses be easily dispelled.

"Look!" called Karl.

John hurried to join him. Down in a valley, a castle stood, built of warmly orange stone, with towers about, and a wall encompassing an orchard, though the highest branches reached over the wall.

Karl lowered his voice. "Look at those birds," he whispered, and his face was alight with joy.

John gave him a sidelong glance. The birds were so small that only their brightness let them be seen at this distance, and he knew that Karl could not be certain which one was Aviette—if any.

Still, the tower was clearly magical.

They walked down the slope. As they came within hailing distance of its door, the birds within twittered frantically and descended toward the trees, out of sight. Silence followed, with not so much as a breath of breeze. They walked on, and John noticed that the castle had poles about it, with skulls stuck on them, and one still bare.

John forced himself to look down from the poles to his footing. Sometimes the witches succeeded. Most times, perhaps.

Karl seemed to have not noticed the poles. He walked up to the door and knocked. The sound echoed less than it would have on a door for a cottage, let alone a stone house like this one. Karl did not move, not to leave, not to knock again. Many minutes later, the door inched open. Karl straightened to his full height.

A woman looked at Karl with narrowed eyes. Even in the shadows of the doorway, she all but glowed, her hair fiery gold, her queenly gown pure gold, her delicate face like ivory.

Perhaps she did glow—he could not be certain. He did wonder whether, with her witchery, Mistress Laurenza was really less fair than Augusta Gloriana.

Her gaze was so intent on Karl that John thought he passed unnoticed.

"I am here for my wife," said Karl.

Mistress Laurenza watched him with narrowed eyes. He neither spoke again nor stirred from where he stood.

"Do you think she's to be had for the asking?" said Mistress Laurenza, spitting out the words.

Karl did not flinch.

Her face worked. "You can have her only if you know her. I'll have no knave coming her and abducting my daughter on the pretense she's his wife."

"I will know her," said Karl.

The woman's lips twisted in a sneer, and very unlovely she looked. "If you fail in this, there will be no more of you—I will cut your head off and stick it on a pole, and have my full set." Her hair swept the air toward the empty pole.

"I will know her."

"I might even give the skull to some peasant girl to light the fire at her stepmother's house, and you will burn it all down, with her stepmother and her stepsisters and her fool self as well."

"I will know her."

Her face contorted with fury, and she pointed to the ground. Three canaries flew, as fast as falcons, and struck the earth to stand up as beautiful young women, with fiery copper hair, pale faces like ivory, and white gowns. Each one looked as much like others as if one woman stood by two mirrors.

"Give me your hand," said Karl to the first. She held it out, and he took it, for a moment. Then he turned to the second and did the same. Then again, with the third. John could see no difference between her and the two before her in her motion or hand, but Karl pulled her closer. "This is my true bride and true wife."

For a moment, Mistress Laurenza's face contorted with fear and rage. Aviette looked up at Karl in an agony of hope, clinging to his hand. The other girls pulled back, and their faces shifted subtly, and their hair changed in shade, one more golden and one more brown. Then their faces contorted in rage.

Mistress Laurenza's snarl was barely intelligible. "You'll have no joy of her." Her hands flew up, and she and the other two maidens flitted inside as canaries, too swiftly to be seen. Mist engulfed them. John could not see the two of them, let alone the castle wall, and the forest was far past reaching.

"She—we can not escape." Aviette's voice was tremulous. "The mist is like the forest, it will not let you find the path."

"I can not find the path," said Karl, "and yet here I am."

"Do not move." John raised the compass. "Show me where Karl and Aviette stand." The arrow did not quite point where their words had come, and he raised an eyebrow, but he followed it, and could see them when he came within a stride of them.

Karl's smile was strained. "I did not find seven men, who could look so sharply as to break a thing to pieces by their glance, or shoot a fly off a horse a league off, but—John has a compass that can show us the way from here."

Aviette still looked anxious, her gaze on the compass.

"He found me the way in here," said Karl.

A bit of a smile appeared on her face. "Then let us flee."

"Put your hand on my shoulder, Karl," said John. "And put yours on his, Aviette." He closed his eyes and took a deep breath. "Point to the safest way from this castle."

The compass moved slowly, but definitely. John led them off and did not dwell on how their path could be the safest without actually being safe. They went on and on, and trees appeared ahead. It had felt much longer than it was, John realized. He trudged on.

A scream came from the castle, and the mist vanished more quickly than a blown-out candle flame. Aviette glanced over her shoulder and said, "Run!"

They ran. The forest engulfed them. John kept glancing at the compass—to run about in circles would deliver them into Mistress Laurenza's hands—and then a vast wall of thorns reared up before them.

"Give me your hands," called Aviette. John obeyed, and moments later, he found himself a boulder beside two more.

Canaries flew up, shrieking in fury. "She must—the wall must not be strong enough—she got through! Follow her! She must not escape!" They threw themselves forward, onto the thorns. Moments later, the shrieks changed to pain. "There's a way, there must be a way, she could not fly over—"

One loud cry pierced the air. John felt the stone shape holding him, preventing his flinch. The thorns dissolved into air. Mistress Laurenza lay face down on the ground, blood pooling dark red about her. The other two—their hair less red than Aviette's, now—sprawled, staring about, their gown stained with still scarlet blood.

"She—keep looking, Sophronia," said one. "She can't have escaped!"

Sophronia's breath came out in a cough. "Don't—don't be a fool, Esmeralda. She's escaped." Then she slumped forward.

"I'll get her!" shouted Esmeralda, surging up. "I'll get her for this, for killing them—" Then she coughed up blood.

Minutes later, he felt the stone, without shifting an inch, turn to flesh. He glanced aside, where the other two stood again. Aviette, white as salt, stared at the blood and the bodies.

"My sisters—they weren't always so evil—if they had escaped earlier—"

She turned to her husband and hid her face in his shirt. Karl put his arms about her and whispered soothing words.

For a moment, John looked grimly at the bodies: lovely women, in horrible death. Then he looked away. If they had not been party to Sophia's death, that had only been because Augusta Gloriana did not need their aid for it. They would have joined in killing Snow-White and Biancabella as readily—and Hans as well, as if his killing Mother Trude was an injury.

"How—" Aviette shook her head. "I would have slipped out and told you how to know me if you had waited, but I have never heard of a man who could, without some trick, find one woman when the enchantress makes them all look alike."

"Your fingers," said Karl, his voice low and rumbling. "You sewed. You sewed so many things that the marks where you pricked yourself with your needle marked you out."

John turned his back on them, and then he looked at his compass and went up the slope. It let him look through the trees to the sky. Then he shouted. "Storm!"

Karl looked up.

"It may not be a snowstorm, but if we get no shelter, they may yet be the death of you both yet."

John looked down at his compass. Shelter nearby—he asked it.

"I don't want to turn us to stone again," said Aviette as she and Karl came up the slope.

"You don't have to—there's shelter there—" He pointed. It was not visible among the trees, and he started to run.

Moments later, he heard footsteps after him, and when he came to the cave, he peered within, establishing it held neither bears nor robbers. Karl came up beside him, with Aviette slung over his shoulders.

"No time to gather wood," said Karl, grimly. The clouds loomed over them, the shade of charcoal, and hazy about the edges where rain or snow already fell.

John walked in as Karl lowered Aviette. Bare stone, and the roof was barely high enough for Aviette to walk without stooping. He could stand where it was the highest, and Karl could not stand straight at all.

"We shall have to hope it does not grow too cold." John sighed. "It may not even be snow. Only rain.'

He thought of the torrents and winced. The waterways would be floods indeed.

At least the cave floor bore great rocks. Karl sat on one. Aviette's gaze flitted from him to John and back.

"Now that we have shelter from the storm," she said, timidly, "you might tell me how you came to find this man, and why he aided you."

Karl looked over. "You did not tell me all of that. We had too much of the path on our minds."

Thunder boomed. For long moments, it rolled on and on, prohibiting all speech. John let his breath out. He had not seen the lightning, but this would be an unpleasantly long storm. He would have time to tell his story, and that of the circle.

Aviette and Karl—he could barely see them, but the circle would be as pleased with them as they were with Hans. They needed to know what danger they were in.

"Your mother," he said slowly. "She was not alone. There were others she worked with on her enchantments."

"Of course," said Aviette. "There was Ottoline. She came to my mother's house and offered us spells."

Rain began to drum on the earth. The ground before the cave mouth was marked with great splotches of wetness where the raindrops fell.

Aviette's hands tightened on her skirt, and she raised her voice over the rain. "I—my sisters scorned her, but that was the spell I used to protect us."

John wondered for a moment whether Vasilisa had learned that spell from Ottoline. Of no import—

"Ottoline is married to my brother, and my other brother is married to Augusta Gloriana."

He told how that came about, raising his voice when the rain pelted, and pausing when the clouds thundered, telling the story to his death. They paled and stared. Then he told them the story of Biancabella, and returned to his own tale after.

"She—you're going to King Maximus's lands," said Aviette. "I can't—we can't—" She buried her face in her hands.

Karl's voice was low. "Hard it will be to find a place in another land, but we can not return to his power. We may not be so fortunate as you were, with the fox and your niece."

Perhaps he would end up casting about the land to reach King Drakos's, thought John. Rain drummed over the ground outside. But they would not want to and—he had a sudden thought—would not need to.

"Princess Belsante might find a place for you, if you go by the way I came."

Karl shifted as the thought sank in.

Aviette's eyes closed. "Yes. Yes."

"I can not promise that you will be safe there," said John. "There are still the others of the circle."

Aviette laughed. "After what you have done already? What is there to fear?"

"This thunderstorm," said Karl, and Aviette calmed some. John turned his face away for fear lightning would show what somber thoughts that brought.

#

Trees barely showed any buds, the early willow had leaves still brightly yellow, but the pastures were thick with sprightly green grass. The road was still muddy with snow melt and rain. To the side, the ditch still held yesteryear's dried plants, their seed pods torn about by birds, but now were sodden in a flood.

Biancabella looked ahead. More trees stood there. Birds, chorusing, perched on every branch. Continually, birds rose and flew about, black before the bright sky, before settling again. They looked like a cloud about the trees. She sighed. None of them were the Bird of Truth, or the last inn would have had the tale. They had had so little else to talk of.

With the road this muddy, the next inn would be a hard enough journey without her maundering on. She plugged on. Hans, mud-splattered, trudged beside her without lifting his head. He had not sung at all today. The fox barely looked red as it slunk along the way, now and again hopping to cross puddles.

She was past trying to avoid the puddles herself. If only because the mud all about them was hardly better; her boots still squished.

A crossroad stood ahead, and a traveler walked down one of the ways—not the one they wanted, she thought—

The fox lifted its head. It swerved aside, looked at the ditch, and pelted down the way. The traveler blinked, as if seeing the red had woken him, and looked about.

"Hallo!" He waved.

Biancabella blinked for a moment before she ran down the
road to meet John at the crossroads. The fox already frisked about
his feet. She threw her arms about his neck.

A minute later, Hans, grinning, strode up. "Did all go well?"

"I'm still headed toward King Drakos's lands," said John, "but
things went well if slowly. Though—" His tongue touched his lip.
"—I have news for you."

#

The Grinning Gryphon—the sign swung by the door. It was the
only trace of motion about the inn.

"Ho! Innkeeper!" Hans went into the inn, shouting. Minutes
later, the innkeeper came grumbling that he had expected no travelers, he had no others, they were three kinds of fools to travel in
this weather. He did let them in, to bide by the fire while he and his
went about their work. The orange light warmed the space nearest,
and left all the rest of the room in chilly shadow.

The best of all arrangements, thought Biancabella. She hung
her boots as close she as dared put them by the fire, to slowly
dry out, and the dress and mantle she had worn, a little farther
away—and she could watch, and yet listen and talk—and they all
would huddle near, and so could speak softly as they traded their
tales.

John scowled at the dragon and agreed with her that Ottoline
had had her hand in that. But his account of the death of Mistress
Laurenza silenced them all.

"Three," said the fox, its voice flat. "Mother Trude. Boney. Mistress Laurenza." It sighed. "Inevitable. The only way is to pick them
off. But the others shall grow more angry and more desperate with
every death."

Its dark eye reflected the fire. One log shifted, with a cracking noise, and a plume of sparks, brilliant in the smoke, shot up the chimney.

Hans shifted his weight. "Are you going straight to King Drakos's lands?"

"That would take me through King Maximus's lands. I think it might be wise to go about. Neither our minstrel who brought Constance so much grief nor Karl inspire hope in my safety there." He sat back, his face hidden in shadow. "I can only be glad that Belsante is safe, and hope that Karl and Aviette are, as well."

"The compass can lead us to the Bird of Truth," said Biancabella, "and the Bird of Truth can tell you the wisest route to go to King Drakos's lands."

"We hope," said John. "The books at Belsante's castle said that the bird never answered questions. That you went to it, and hoped the truths it deems timely are good for you. It might tell me the wisest route. It might not."

Hans slumped against the fireplace, closed his eyes, and did not speak. Much later, the log in the fire, with a great crack, sent sparks that filled the smoke. His face, lit up by it, was grim.

"Did—" Biancabella swallowed. "Did the books tell you anywhere else where we might learn answers to questions?"

Hans opened his eyes. "Or even have answers themselves?" After a moment, he said, "This Princess Belsante—would she make welcome travelers if we came from you?"

"It was not a large library," said John. "I had many weeks, and read it through. No. It told nothing of any use to us."

"We—we don't have Mother Magda jeering at us when we listen to what the bird has to say," said Biancabella. "And—" She managed to put some strength in her voice. "We wouldn't listen anyway. To *her*."

Hans look at her.

"I went in hope that, Heaven willing, the bird would say *something* of use."

Hans sighed. "You went because you had no other way to fight your mother."

Biancabella folded her hands in her lap and said nothing. She still had no other way.

"We shall go on. John's compass will do the trick." Hans's voice was dull but certain.

John frowned in thought. "Perhaps that is what I should have been asking the compass. For the *wisest* route." He pulled it out, and the metal glinted in the firelight. "The wisest route to the Bird of Truth."

The needle began to twirl.

"The *safest* route to the Bird of Truth."

It settled to pointing north and east.

"So," said John, pocketing it again, "it knows safety and not wisdom."

"You live, and you learn, and thus you grow wise," said the fox, brightly, and yawned.

#

The next day was bright with sun, and warm for the season. In patches, the road was even dry. Here and there spring flowers pushed through dead leaves, crocuses in shades of cream or violet or brilliant yellow, star-like scilly more blue than the sky, and oddly enough, small irises in violet. She had never seen irises this early, or that small.

But every time she looked up, sunlight glittered on the spread of water over the fields—glaring in brightness, and featureless. From time to time, she wondered whether the circle would go after Aviette and Karl, Kari and Pierre, as they had come after her. Then she would chide herself as a fool. The circle would go after them, but it would not spare her.

Toward evening, across the still sodden fields, a crossroad came into view, and a troop of soldiers riding toward it. Biancabella's nose wrinkled. She could still hope that they took another route.

When they rode down their path, she sighed.

"Here's to hoping they don't push us into the ditch," muttered Hans, going aside.

"At least we're close enough to the inn to dry out before we freeze," said John, as they gathered on the roadside, where the ground was driest.

The soldiers rode up but slowed as they approached. Biancabella sighed. So they were going to take the occasion to push them into the ditch.

The soldiers drew up before them, spears leveled. Their captain came forward. Biancabella's mouth went dry. Out of the corner of her eye, she saw the fox dart off, and she astounded herself by managing to not look, and draw attention to it.

And she had feared the ditch.

Chapter 13—The Royal Castle

The city rose up on the hillside, built of pale stone and gleaming in the dawn. The muddy road wound on through fields and over a river before it would reach it. Biancabella trudged on. Hans and John both walked in silence, as they had since the soldiers arrested them. John looked remote and despairing, though at least, Biancabella reminded herself, the soldiers had not stolen the water.

As if it would do any good in its bottles.

She sighed. At least they had seen nothing more of the fox. But then, that meant the fox had not stolen the keys and freed them in the night—and there had been several nights.

More people came gawk as they drew nearer the city, but as it had been along the way, so was it here: sidelong glances and pulling back, as if they feared the king's rage even where his prisoners were concerned. Even nobles, wearing fine clothes and riding fine horses, did not overtly stare or approach.

Or perhaps they saw nothing unusual in three prisoners. Biancabella twitched at the thought. She had to admit that they looked like three commonplace travelers.

At noon, when they passed through the city gates, half-timbered buildings lined the street. Half-leaved trees sometimes marked a block, and several buildings had window boxes—now bare of flowers.

Crowds on the street parted so swiftly that she could not judge their numbers, and they continued up the streets. It still took an hour until the soldiers marched them through the castle gates.

The guards spoke to the soldiers in low voices. Biancabella stared at the towers and wondered how long they would molder in prison before the king deigned to see them.

A page boy ran up. "Now."

The guard nodded and stepped back. The soldiers headed toward two great doors. The shadows inside did not hide the crowd of courtiers, and Biancabella swallowed. That had to be the great hall, where the king himself sat to give judgment.

In the back, on his throne, the king sat there, wearing his crown. He had awaited them, he had thought them important enough for his entire court to await them—she felt like ice.

Biancabella did not know how she walked up the stairs without falling flat on her face. This escort was not to honor them.

A murmur rose among the courtiers. She could not make out the tone. Perhaps it was disapproving—of the way-stained travelers, no doubt, not the king.

The king was blond and bearded, and his robes were gold, to make him all the more leonine. His deep voice resounded.

"How wan and pale the lovely maiden grows, forced to travel with sorcerers on hard journeys."

"I—" Biancabella stared at him, and words froze on her lips. What could she say that would matter at all? Between the tales of Genoveva and Aviette—and the poor minstrel lass seeking her husband—she knew what manner of man he was.

"Show her to safety," he said, inflecting his voice a little more gently. "They will not be able to harm her in the tower." Then he scowled. "As for these sorcerers—it is a thousand shames that you are so negligent that their fox escaped, but to the dungeons with them! Fox or no fox, they will work no witchery there!"

#

The worst of it was, thought Biancabella, sitting on the bed in her tower room, that she had seen no sign of any of them. Not her mother, not Ottoline, not—Mistress Laurenza, Mother Trude, and Boney explained themselves, but Mother Magda or Rumpelstiltskin might still come. Even King Drakos might have found the three of them dangerous enough to move.

But to all appearances, they had not needed to.

She looked about. Plain blue carpets and plain blue tapestry, a bed with a blue coverlet—not all the same shade of blue. Windows with diamond-shaped panes of glass—

Her thoughts caught up to her eyesight, and she leapt from the bed to try the window's latch. A moment's attempt cured her. Perhaps she might have dropped from the window to the roof to begin her escape, if she did not injure or kill herself since she could not fly like Aviette, but King Maximus had sealed the windows shut.

She collapsed on the bed. Heaven help her, the room had nothing more to survey. It seemed bent on making her consent to marry him from sheer tedium.

If—if she had learned magic from her mother, perhaps she could have learned how to become a bird like Aviette—

What a fool you are, she scolded herself. Her mother would have taught her many other things first, and insisted on her helping with evil plans, and—what if she had? Mistress Laurenza had kept Aviette captive for many a year after she could become a bird.

But it was all words, she could not feel it.

#

Torches flared, here and there, in sconces on the walls, but the guards escorting them carried their own; the spreads of shadow were too large to get through by the wall torches alone. Even by the orange light, John's fixed face looked pale. Hans wondered if he looked the same color.

Wan prisoners—men who had seen nothing of the sun for months if not years—peered out through barred doors, and the guards jeered.

"No other minstrel pleased the king with his playing, and how his dog danced!"

"And if there were, there wouldn't be another fool one who asked for a companion for the road!"

"New prisoners—and these ones are *sorcerers*!"

With that, the captive soldiers melted back from doors. Hans fought down a sigh. King Maximus would keep prisoners from joining forces.

The guards went on. And on. Far past the cells of the soldiers, into deep corridors.

"I don't envy the man who has to bring them their meals," said a guard.

Another snorted. "Don't bother. Sorcerers like this can feed on air. King doesn't have waste food on—"

A heavy hand pushed at Hans's back. "None of that! Get on with you!"

Hans, quite certain he had not slowed, staggered on. Minutes later, they reached a cell with straw for beds, and a heavy oaken door. A tiny window showed a gleam of sunlight.

A guard frowned. "They might turn themselves to birds and fly out. We haven't got a sorcerer of our own to chase after."

The others laughed. "If they could do that, they would have fled the court."

They slammed the door shut, and Hans collapsed on the nearest straw, staring at the window. He had done nothing to rescue Gretel, and now he had imperiled Biancabella—his eyes closed, and he could still see Biancabella moving, pale and silent and regal, between guards.

John scrambled across the room. Hans blinked, and looked over. The sunlight silhouetted John against the window, but even so—he had something in his hands, which he was taking down.

"Straight from the king's kitchen, and piping hot," said the fox, and Hans scrambled up as John sat to open the basket.

"You won't need to drink the water of life to stay alive," said the fox in satisfaction.

"Biancabella," said Hans, his voice hoarse in his own ears. "Have you seen her?"

The fox was only a shadow in the sunlight, but he could see that it shook its head. "They talked, they said she was in a tower—"

John looked up. "She is. At least, the king said she was to be taken there. Guards escorted her off."

"Ah," said the fox. "As when they wanted to sacrifice her to the dragon." Hans winced. It sat. "I could try to reach there. I could also try to find keys, which would be of more help, but I could do both at once."

"Don't get caught," said John. "We need you to feed us."

"Perhaps not for long," said the fox, and scratched at its ears. "I heard courtiers talking. They egged on the king to set you impossible tasks and execute you if you fail."

"And how," said Hans, "can he set us an *impossible* task if we are sorcerers?"

"My father would not, on those grounds," said John, "but I have no doubt that my brothers would not be troubled by it." His voice sounded uncommonly deep. "If we do not perish for the want of food while he keeps us here, I have no doubt that he will use that as proof enough of sorcery."

Silence followed. King Maximus would burn them at stake as readily as they had burned Elinor. If he did not think of it on his own, Augusta Gloriana or one of the others would suggest it.

"Impossible tasks have a way of biting back," said the fox, but without much strength.

Hans let his breath out. The king, perhaps, was not the great peril. "Did you see them? Augusta Gloriana? Ottoline? Mother Magda?"

"Wouldn't be Boney," said John, "but Rumpelstiltskin might make her an offer."

"To go to a ball at King Maximus's court and astound them with her beauty?" said Hans. "It's more likely that she wants an escape from it, and to make them overlook her as ugly. Dress her in a coat of catskin, or of all kinds of furs, or even turn her into a bear."

King Maximus hoped, Hans realized, and bit his lip. He had heard the tales. Of a prince who ceased to be a frog because the princess had thrown him against the wall in a fit of pique—and he had married her. Of a princess working as a scullery maid who amazed the prince when she appeared in lovely attire at the ball and so disgusted him in her grubby working clothes that he threw things at her—and still she married him when she revealed herself. Or, at that, a prince who was robbed of a princess of three magical treasures, and only won them back by trickery and turning her into a donkey—and still he married her.

Biancabella wouldn't do that, he told himself. The lad who had won back his treasures only by giving the princess a nose six feet long had wisely returned to a miller's daughter that he had met on his journey, to become a miller instead of a prince, and he had been a simpleton. Biancabella was a wise and prudent princess—

Who wanted to stop her mother more than anything else. She had even said that she would marry a prince to break a spell.

He started to pace. King Maximus was under no spell. Her mother and the others would be more likely to egg him on than bewitch him, but perhaps she would think she could gain power from the marriage to stop her mother.

"I hope you're thinking of something useful," said John. "And come to a useful conclusion before you trample me underfoot. Or the food, either."

Hans stopped, blushing, and hoping the shadow hid the heat in his face. It was not as if he were free to throw all away and marry himself.

"Biancabella might have ideas," he said, gruffly. "If you could win to her."

"Perhaps," said John. "But—in case you were not listening—no, the fox has not seen any sign of anyone in the circle, or heard rumors of their presence here."

"When rumors are plentiful," said the fox. "All about how King Maximus tried to hunt a gold wolf and injured it, but it got away. He was in a rage—I think they would talk of the circle if any of them had come here."

"How they must love King Maximus, so ready to do their handiwork," said Hans. "If he only masters magic, I think they would make him one of their number."

#

Folly to worry about the compass, when all three of them were prisoners, and the king ready to execute them on a whim.

The king would judge based on the reports of this, thought the fox, watching the royal messenger stride through the woods. Soon the man would reach a crossroads, pull out the compass, and ask again. And the fox worried.

"Ho!" A deep booming voice echoed from the hills, and a shadow fell over the messenger—and the fox, it was so large. The messenger did not move an inch, or shout, but grew pale. A great hand reached down to rest on the messenger's shoulders. Another came down to slip the compass from his hands. The messenger grew paler still, and slumped to the ground.

"What's this?" The giant's voice boomed as the enormous fingers took up the compass.

"What's what?" Another giant looked over. "Oh, it's too small for you. You should give me it. Being smaller, it suits me better."

"Your hands are too small," said the first. "You'll drop it."

As their voices boomed on, the messenger regained his wits, if not his color. He took one glance at the giants, and scurried away—from the giants', from King Maximus's court.

For a moment, the fox thought of offering to settle the dispute. But they were not disputing over a sword that could cut off their heads, it could not wield such a sword if they had, and they would not trust a fox. Not even a giant was such a fool as to trust a fox to settle a dispute.

#

Ladies, giggling, came down the tower stair. Remembering how its red showed, the fox crouched carefully in the shadows, but they seemed so rapt in their chatter that it could have done anything except sprawl on the steps, and still gone unnoticed.

And possibly that.

"Imagine having to consider whether to marry King Maximus!"

"She's as silly as—"

Their giggles stopped, and the other three looked at the fourth, who blushed.

"—as that king who fought King Maximus. After he already had all those soldiers captive. That shows how great a king he is!"

"Master of seven kingdoms," said another. "Against a king so petty he married a bride without hands!"

None of them, as they hastened out the door, mentioned that King Maximus had not actually conquered King Hendrik's kingdom.

The fox bolted up the stairs and tried to jump up as high as it could, putting its forelegs on the door. "Biancabella, Biancabella!"

#

From the window, she could just see the garden. Most of the trees were still utterly leafless; some had a haze of red on their boughs. She sighed. She could delude herself into thinking she could see green sprouts, but not early flowers.

If she had been a boy, she could have fled her father's castle and sought a job here as a gardener's boy and worked in the garden forever.

Her gardens—the gardens at her father's castle—would have crocuses in delicate blues and creams and violets, and the scilly in vivid blue.

If her mother had left them alone.

And why would she not? She was busy with stopping *her*, not spitefully tearing up her handiwork.

Biancabella sighed. That was, if Augusta Gloriana did not find this captivity sufficient. If she did—if she thought King Maximus enough to hold her captive—she was no doubt roaming the land, looking for other lives to ruin. There was only so much Biancabella could to distract herself from that knowledge, and from her helplessness.

There was a scratching sound on the door.

She gave an exasperated sigh. The next bevy of courtiers, all of them sighing over her folly in rejecting King Maximus and speaking of their envy at her having caught his eye. How she envied Aviette, being able to fly off.

"Biancabella, Biancabella."

She froze. She knew that voice. What—

"Do you know what danger you are in?" she said through the grill, her knuckles already white from her grip before she realized she had crossed the floor.

The fox, its black nose within inches of her, shrugged. "If I wanted safety, I would have run off into the forest as soon as you revived me. Better yet, I would never have helped your uncle. Or—"

She heard the sounds on the stairs.

"Jump," she said, holding out her hands. "We haven't much time, especially since you've got to wriggle through the bars."

Holding the fox while it squirmed into the room—with laughter and footsteps echoing up the stairs, and her heart hammering, all the while—garnered her a few strikes of its claws, but it leapt down and darted under the bed, leaving her with sleeves twisted about her arm. She tried to pull them straight and wondered what would happen if King Maximus decided that she was a sorceress as well.

It would probably involve a beating and a bath of milk. The sort of thing they did when a princess went away of nights to dance with evil sorcerers of her own will. Since she doubted that he would be one of those heroes who broke the dancing enchantment and then rejected the princess as untrustworthy.

"If you left the tower," said a lady from the doorway, "you would have a maid to make sure you were all neat and tidy. You wouldn't have to act as your own."

She turned her face away.

"A maid? She'd have a score! Leaping to obey her for fear she would turn them off! And ladies-in-waiting, too." The other lady sighed. "How lovely it would be, escorting you about the court—and you could insist on balls, and going riding in the springtime, and—" She sighed again. "—letting all the lords and ladies woo."

Biancabella's eyes rolled.

#

Moonlight inched across the floor. Quenching the lamp did seem to convince courtiers that she had gone to sleep.

The fox, sitting on the bed, was a dark shadow except where its eyes glittered by moonlight.

"An impossible task," said Biancabella, almost in a whisper, and nearly groaned. "Here's an impossible task: devise a task that you could carry out, that would aid our escape, and that King Maximus would actually try to force one of them to do."

"That last might be the easiest," said the fox. "He sent Karl, remember?"

"It was not as if he could get Aviette just by sending Karl away to die," said Biancabella. "Perhaps he thought Karl was such a simpleton that he would bring Aviette back."

"It would be easy enough for you to get him to do it," said the fox.

Biancabella's head whipped around.

The fox's eyes glittered. "You could say that he was not protecting you from them, because they are no sorcerers—one of them bragged to you that he could do something, and never did it—and that he should prove him to be a liar."

Biancabella drew a deep breath. "There are many things I could claim that would not free us. Or even any of us."

"Also what John or Hans could do. John got the waters, yes, and Hans killed the dragon, but there are still things they can not do."

Biancabella sighed and leaned against the wall. "Ottoline will not turn anyone into a dragon to menace the land. Not when the last failed, and certainly not when I am already prisoner here, and John and Hans as well."

The fox's eyes narrowed. "We would need—" Its voice trailed off. Then it muttered, and she heard only, "—other rumors—"

Abruptly it leapt off the bed and scrambled for the door. There, it looked up as if suddenly remembering it needed help.

Biancabella laughed a little and rose to help. At least the fox would find gadding about by starlight easier than she did.

#

Biancabella sat with her hands in her lap. Her gaze was fixed on the doorway, and the bars in the window.

Every disaster in John's journey had sprung from a time when he had disobeyed the fox, she reminded herself. As for her father and her Uncle Herbert—they had ignored what the fox had said from the beginning, and so never had a chance.

Her tongue touched her lips.

The fox had talked to Hans and John before it had told her what to say. They knew what she would say, and they needed her to say it, for their own safety.

The sounds of giggles rose up the stairs, and her eyes closed.

"My lady, my lady—"

"Have you come to lie to me again?" At least keeping her voice frosty was not that difficult.

For once the ladies said nothing.

"Claim that the king is protecting me from evil sorcerers when there is no such need."

She managed to stand. That, at least, was a whole truth.

"What would you say of a man who claimed to be able to summon all the wolves in the kingdom but never did?" The ladies at the door pulled back as she approved. "Surely a lying braggart whom the king should prove to be a liar."

The women scuttled off. Biancabella leaned against the door. She remembered servants who claimed, out of jealousy, that another servant could sew an immense amount of flax in a single night, or go down into the underworld to save the princess captive to trolls, or steal things from a witch.

At least Hans and John consented to her misleading the court about them.

The church bells rang.

#

The courtiers murmured as the guards dragged him in. Hans heard just enough to know that they expected him to be a starveling by now.

King Maximus looked him over with narrowed eyes, but said nothing about his health. "You stand accused of claiming you can summon together all the wolves in the lands. We will have no such charlatans in our lands. You will do so or die."

Hans nodded. "I will go into the forest to do so."

"No, you can not claim such a thing—"

"You charlatan," said Hans, and the court was silent. Noises he had not realized were there—went silent. "You speak as if I asked for a ship with a deck full of grain, a deck full of dead beasts, and a deck full of honey—or merely to scatter a field with grain—but the kings who were asked for such things granted them, because they knew that wonders were not for the asking."

His heart beat so loudly in his chest that he felt surprised that King Maximus did not hear it. He hoped that the king did not remember that when it began with a field scattered with grain, to catch the firebird, it ended with Princess Vasilisa, won from a far off land by the same servant, tricking the king to his death, marrying the servant, and making him king of the land in the place of his old master.

As King Maximus scowled at him, he had less hope by the moment. They had had no choice, he reminded himself. To linger in their cells until they perished was folly worse than this, and he had known when first the fox proposed it that it might fail ignominiously.

"So," said King Maximus, "like the insolent peasant girl, who is asked to raise chicks to hens in a day, you have not the shame to admit you can not do it. She asked for grain that had been raised in a day to feed them—you ask to be taken to the forest."

Hans shrugged. "I did not realize that taking me to the forest was as difficult as raising a crop of grain in a single day."

King Maximus's lip curled. "Take him out to the forest. And as for you, sorcerer, know that your fellow sorcerer stands hostage for your honesty."

#

The forest floor was still sodden from snow melt, but the day was uncommonly warm. Hans walked along in the sunlight, carefully picking the highest ground. Green sprouts grew here and there. He wondered if the fox could have pulled off this plan any earlier in the year.

A flash of red to his left resolved into the fox, trotting up with a herb in its mouth. Hans went down on one knee to take it. The instant its jaws were free, the fox pulled back and shook its head in distaste.

"I stole enough baskets. I should have stolen another for that." Then it eyed Hans. "You shall have to pass as a sage from a far distant land, traveling hard."

"I think I can do that," said Hans, standing.

The fox sat up. "Let all the wolves of the land hear! Here comes the great foreign sage to heal the king of the wolves of his injury!" It stalked off into the woods, repeating its proclamation, and Hans picked his way after, over hill and valley.

It seemed a long time before gray shapes shifted among the trees, and a still longer time before the shapes came forward and were clearly wolves.

"What trouble are you up to this time, Reynard the Red?" growled a wolf almost black, and as big as a pony.

The fox looked pertly up at the wolf. "What, me? I go about this out of pure-hearted benevolence. As a sign of my impeccable good faith, I myself shall come with the sage to the heart of your kingdom, where the great sage will heal your king." Its tone turned almost ingratiating. "I would not wish to forgo the reward for such a great deed."

The wolf snorted, but soon after, files of wolves to either side escorted them off, at a brisker pace than they had gone before. Hans kept his gaze on the way—falling flat would not impress the wolves with his wisdom—but he could not stop his heart from drumming, and not only from the speed. The fox had to scramble to keep up, but finally they plunged into a fir wood, dark even at noon, and wolves stood about in the gloom lamenting.

The fox spoke again. "Let all the wolves of the land hear! Here comes the great foreign sage to heal the king of the wolves of his injury!"

"Who let this insolent fox into the royal forest?" roared a silver wolf as large as a deer, gleaming in the shadows. "I shall eat both fox and fool!"

"Does your king know that his courtiers are trying to keep him bed-ridden?" called the fox.

A gray wolf came forward, of ordinary size, and nodded to them. The fox nodded back and followed as the wolf led them deep into the forest.

Within moments, they came to a clearing where a great golden wolf, the size of a horse, lay on a bed of dried ferns. Its flank was mired with blood, all the fur clumped with dried brown, and its breathing was labored.

Its eyes still picked them out and narrowed.

The fox raised its head. "Let all the wolves of the land hear! Here comes the great foreign sage to heal the king of the wolves of his injury!"

"What?" said the wolf. "Not to offer me a basket of ripe pears out of season, Sir Fox? To trick me into thinking your master a fine gentleman, fit to marry my daughter?"

"Not at all, Your Majesty," said the fox. "I leave those matters to cats, who do them so well, especially when they wear boots." It lowered its voice as if to confide. "I hate boots."

The wolf king laughed and then gasped in pain. "You did not come here in kindness."

"But of course I did. The great sage will ask you to do something to harm to the king who injured you. How could I be so unkind as to deny you such a thing? What would you desire more than that, once you are healed?"

The wolf growled. "Healing first, Sir Fox, or we shall see whether I shall desire you and your great sage eaten up for dinner. Perhaps what I need to heal me is your fat."

Hans walked carefully forward, and then around the beast to where he could most easily reach the shoulder. The fox had, after all, revived King Hendrik. He laid the herb on the flank wound.

For moments, it seemed that nothing happened, and Hans wished he could have gotten his sword back from King Maximus. The wolves looked with narrowed eyes from the wound to him, and back to the wound.

Then the wolf king moved its head. Moments later, the blood seemed to fade into the fur. A minute after that, the wolf king rose. The pack parted before him, and it stalked from the clearing. Hans started to move after, and the fox shook its head. Hans waited.

From the next valley, the wolf howled, so loudly that Hans clapped his hands over his ears.

"Now," said the fox, and they walked after. The wolves had gathered round the king, and the king glared at them both.

"Now, Sir Fox, you have already claimed a tale—tell it, and we will see if you who told the truth once, can tell it twice."

"Of course, Your Majesty," said the fox. "The king who wounded you ordered this sage to bring to his court all the wolves in the land. He did not think the sage could do it—but it lies in your power—and I do not think the king or the courtiers will like it well."

"The huntsmen will not let us," said a dark wolf.

"The huntsmen have their orders from that king," said the fox. "He wishes to see all the wolves in the kingdom."

"Not for long," said the dark wolf, lowering its head.

All the wolves laughed, making Hans step back.

#

The day was bright and mild. Grass grew greenly on the lawn, with purple and blue crocuses in bloom. The wolves all walked behind Hans with such quiet steps he could not hear them.

The silence was not enough to make him forget them.

The huntsmen sent to escort him to the forest turned pale at the sight and fled. The wolf king gave growled orders to follow Hans, and the wolves followed. Their way cleared before them. The first fleeing peasants bore the word. Soon nothing could be seen except some herds being driven off, far in the distance. When they reached the city, tradesmen and merchants had barred both doors and windows.

The castle gates still stood open. King Maximus stood there, some courtiers behind him, and called out to Hans, "You have shown your honesty, you need bring them no further."

"Go on, my wolves, go on!" bellowed the king of the wolves.

The fox darted aside, into an alleyway, and Hans sprung after. The wolves surged behind them into the court.

#

Hans felt pale as he stood in the hall, with the bodies littered about, but the fox did not comment on that as it peered anxiously about and spoke with great urgency.

"We must make haste. Not all the courtiers were eaten. Some will return. Neither you nor John nor Biancabella are safe so long as you are here."

Hans let out his breath. "The dungeon holds soldiers, too. We should free them—as long as they do not think we are sorcerers whom they should kill."

The fox tilted its head to one side.

"Free Biancabella first," said Hans. "Perhaps she will think of a plan."

"And we have to find the keys," said the fox.

Hans shouted with laughter. For only a moment, but he could not help himself.

"No," he said. "No, there is a swifter way."

#

Biancabella's breath came light and fast, and she leaned on the window frame to keep from falling.

The worst of it was the wait.

For all that she had plotted with the fox, for all that she knew of the fox's cunning and craft, still she saw the wolves—the few whose path had taken them within sight of the window—and heard their howls, and remembered Ottoline. She could not know that these were the wolves that Hans had gone to fetch, rather than some army that Ottoline had turned into wolves.

Voices at the door had her turning.

"Stand back," called Hans, and she swallowed, hard, half-sitting on the window and unable to move.

The sound of an ax hitting the door made her laugh. When Hans pushed his way through the ruins of the door, she leapt to embrace him, and the fox had not picked half its way over the ruins before she swept it up and danced about the room with it.

"Where's the musician?" said the fox in protest. "The one playing the tune that forces you to dance?"

She kissed its furry forehead and let it down. Then she forced her breath in and out. "He stopped playing—where is John?"

"We rescued you first," said Hans, his face in grave lines.

She took a step backwards. "But—the dungeons can hardly be more pleasant than this—he could *die*—"

Shortly, Hans explained about the soldiers.

Biancabella let out her breath. "I wish I still had that cloak. If they saw no one there while the door was chopped down—" She shook her head. "But we can let John out, and then ponder how we can free the soldiers."

She turned to the fox. "I think that they already think we are sorcerers quite enough. Stay in the garden."

"What?" said the fox. "Enjoy the sunlight and flowers while you do the work? *How* can you expect me to do that?" And flitted off down the stairs before she answered.

#

"You evil sorcerers!" called the prisoner. "Letting loose those wolves on the land! Feeding yourself all fat while we starve!" Murmurs of agreement came from behind him, and Biancabella kept her gaze before her. She wished she had told Hans to fetch John, and then they could confer in the bright sunlight, in a garden filled with violets and snowdrops, and not in the bone-deep chill of the stone.

The sounds died out behind them, but the heavy stone, all about, did not lift her spirits. She trudged on, and then the cell shocked her.

She lingered in the corridor after Hans had smashed down the door, and the fox leapt inside. Their voices did not carry out. She thought of going in, and even in the gloom, saw a rat scuttle across the floor. She winced. They could have been bitten by those creatures.

John emerged, pale but uninjured, and she let out her breath in a great gust. He smiled and kissed her fondly.

"But I fear," he said, "I have no more notion than Hans of how to set free the soldiers when there are so many more of them than of us."

"And," said Hans, "they still think we are sorcerers."

"They cursed us as we passed," said Biancabella.

"Whatever would make them think that?" said the fox. "When you survived without being fed and summoned all the wolves in the land?"

"Not having ever listened to a single tale?" said John bitterly. "Everyone knows that aid is not only from evil. Whatever the circle does to prevent it."

"Let's leave," said Biancabella. "To ponder how to free them in the dungeon itself is, at least, doubly unpleasant."

John blinked. "Of course," he said.

They started back, but sounds came down the corridor, and they slowed.

Finally words came clear. "Stop playing the fools. We know the sorcerers came down here to hide."

The sounds from the prisoners were less clear, but angry.

"Then we are going to search your cell—" The clatter of keys was clear.

John put a hand to her arm, and drew her back. Minutes later, when they walked up, the soldiers were all gone, having forced their way out. Biancabella did not see whatever foolish official had tried to search the cell.

"He should have known," said Hans. "That never works. Even a master sorcerer searching for his apprentice comes to a bad end when he goes searching for him."

"None of us can turn into a fox, to bite off the master sorcerer's head once he turns into a rooster," said Biancabella. "Let us be wary."

They slipped, carefully, up the stairs, into the sunlight. From the exclamation of returning servants and courtiers, the prisoners had already fled down the road. In the noise and clamor, the three of them walked from the castle and to the road. As the royal castle vanished behind them, Biancabella felt her shoulders ease.

"The Bird of Truth, then," said John. "It could have told King Maximus some timely truths."

Hans nodded. They walked through a forest where the leaves were only a haze over the trees, but snowdrops and daffodils nodded in the breezes.

After a time, Hans began to sing.

"And of this feather was made a fine bed,

The finest bed, that ever you did see,

And the bed from the feather, the feather on the bird, the bird on the nest, the nest on the twig, and the twig on the bough, and the bough on the tree, and the tree in the wood,

And the green leaves flourished thereon, thereon, thereon,

And the green leaves flourished thereon."

As the minutes inched by, Biancabella realized that the way
held no other travelers. Even the fleeing courtiers must find this
path too dangerous. Then, the three of them had no safe road.

It was full evening, and growing dark, when they saw the inn
ahead, and when they reached it, Biancabella could barely read the
sign of the Golden Gryphon. The innkeeper bustled out, full of
questions about the royal city, and Hans answered her gravely, but
always as if he spoke of someone else who did the deeds.

"Well, that's a tale and a half, and no mistake," said the woman.
"I would go ask the Bird of Truth if I didn't have to look after my
inn."

Chapter 14—Seeking the Bird of Truth

Rumpelstiltskin laughed shrilly in the night, and the sound echoed from the mountains. King Drakos pulled back from him, and Augusta Gloriana felt her lip curl. When he was the one who most insisted on meeting in secret!

"So much for all your grand plans, your ever so clever tricks," he said. "I shall have none of that."

Ottoline muttered about being busy with something else. Mother Magda just looked sullen.

"Mother Trude gone, Boney gone, Mistress Laurenza gone—I shall arrive to a meeting soon and find myself alone."

"You?" said Augusta Gloriana, contemptuously. "You with your tricks of spinning straw into gold?"

"Always wise to have two strings to your bow," said Rumpelstiltskin, hooking his misshapen hands on his belt. "For this one, I shall use the simpler. I shall do what you have so strikingly failed in, thus getting two birds with one stone, and *adding* to my collection."

"You'd best," said King Drakos. "Or I will stay in my lands to make sure of them—since none of you bother to keep them safe."

As if, thought Augusta Gloriana, he had been use to any of the rest of them.

#

Spring chased them as they went north. Rivers sank, mud dried, and more and more plants grew. Birds, in great flocks, twittered in the trees. Trees started to show leaves, but the nights were still bitterly cold.

When they made good time, and the inn appeared on the way while it was still light, John breathed a sigh of relief. He and Hans could spend time at swordplay.

Then Biancabella gasped and grew still paler. He followed her gaze. The sign bore a white bird, and it read The Bird of Truth.

"Don't get your hopes too high," said Hans, softly. "There wasn't a golden gryphon by that inn."

John nodded, but as idly as he could, after they secured the room, said, "There's been tales of the Bird of Truth all along the way."

The inn-keeper, with a thin, bitter face, nodded sharply. "They say it's at the ruins." He waved his hand at the road and snorted. "I've never seen it."

At that news, John could not stop his heart from hammering in his chest, but breathed, carefully, in and out, and proposed to Hans that they practice in the courtyard.

Biancabella came behind, with her sewing in hand. John feinted and parried and struck, and noted that Biancabella watched them as much as she sewed.

Or perhaps—watched Hans?

It cut with a sharpness. Sophia might have watched him so—or—Belsante, perhaps.

"When we meet the bird," he said, and both looked at him. He choose the words with care. "Let me speak to it alone. It is not, if tales are true, in a garden with a magical fountain, but—the mirror does not know everything. The bird might still turn us into stone for speaking."

Biancabella flinched. Hans looked at him, and snorted.

"Only if you hand over the water of life first," he said.

"We will know," said Biancabella, mildly, "to take its feather and save you. But—the statues will betray it, if it does. We can't be the first people desperate enough to speak to the Bird of Truth, not over all these years."

The fox said, "Only if you are wise enough to remember. No matter what the bird says."

"It's not going to surprise me with something about my mother," said Biancabella, bitterly, and looked surprised herself.

"What you know," said the fox, "wouldn't be the surprise."

#

Trees grew so thickly about the castle that Biancabella was glad it was so early in the spring. Grass grew lushly, flowers nodded, and both were tall enough that the fox could stalk among them, unseen. Still, the trees were still only brushed with small leaves in red or yellow or green. Never a very dark green at that.

There was no bird song to be heard. There had been none since they left the inn. No other birds would confuse the matter, at least.

John and Hans surveyed the branches. At that, it was just as well that it was not winter, with snow as white as the bird all about. They had some hope of spotting it. There would not be snow-drops sprouting in the branches.

Even the fox cocked its head and eyed the trees, and said nothing.

After straining her neck until she had a crick in it, Biancabella wondered how large the bird was. A finch-sized bird could flit in there forever without being seen, whatever its color.

"The princes had it easier," said Hans. "Even keeping silent—" He shook his head.

"We're not stone yet," said John. He frowned and raised his voice. "The Bird of Truth might yet reveal to us the truth of where it is."

The words echoed from the walls, but silence followed after, and his shoulders slumped.

A whistle struck the air. Then, a voice like a parrot's announced, "Not all spells end with the death. Death does not break all spells. Just many. Many, many, many spells." The whistle came again, and a white bird, large as a hawk, hopped on a bush near Hans. "Don't ask. Not now. Not safe. Not for *her*. Not for *him* either."

Hans blinked, but the bird pivoted its head away—passing the fox while muttering, "Untimely truths"—and toward Biancabella. It eyed her up and down. "Ninny ninny not, the name's Tom Tit Tot—and she doesn't know she doesn't control her roses, not on Anna's castle."

It popped into the air to flit nearer John and perch near him. "Water brings things besides life. Fill it up when you're done." It swiveled its head. "Also, there are things besides a swan that are not a person."

It whistled again and flew off, managing to hide among the branches before any of them found words. After moments of silence, wind rustled leaves. They turned to face each other. The wind sent shadows dancing over them from the branches.

John shook himself. "So much for who speaks to it."

Hans's face set in sullen lines.

"Back to the Four Winds?" said Biancabella, tentatively. "Perhaps—perhaps the mirror can unfold more with this knowledge."

John straightened. "I still have to venture to King Drakos's lands." He eyed Hans. "Who knows? It might make it safe to ask. Since she clearly neither married her prince and lived out her life, nor died like the Princess Petronilla, past hope of rescue."

Hans flinched. Biancabella bit her lip.

#

They walked back toward the inn. Slowly. That was his fault, thought Hans, and his folly. No matter how he lingered, that silly bird would not return and tell him that Gretel was captive under a mountain, or turned into a bird. John, the fox, and Biancabella did not deserve to sleep in the rain because he could not curb his wishes to his wisdom. They were already ahead of him, but not too far, and he should hurry.

"What's that?" said Biancabella.

"Be careful of the mud," said John.

She laughed. "And of the pond—I will. But a magical flower that could break enchantments, that would be worth some risk." She already moved into the forest, picking her way carefully among the dead leaves and the mud. The thickets of undergrowth were already leaved enough to make it hard to see, and Hans hurried forward.

"That's odd, I saw—" Then Biancabella screamed. John surged forward, and branches seemed to reach out and hold him back. The fox snapped and snarled, and the branches reached out for him as well. His heart hammering, Hans ran into the forest. Speed to ensure it did not spy him, as it had the other two.

Biancabella stood, bent, by a pond, and a hideous dwarf-like creature held her braided hair. As Hans reached the bank, the manikin cackled, and shoved his hand out to smash against the mud. The jolt knocked Hans to his knees, and the creature grabbed his hair, yanking him around to see Biancabella, also kneeling now. Hans yanked back, and his legs slid on the mud, getting no grip. A tree stood nearby—he reached—and the manikin hauled him back as easily as if he were a toddling child. The manikin did not spare Hans a sideways glance as he glared at Biancabella and showed all his teeth.

"Shall I ask you riddles? What do you have that you do not know you have?" His lips, peeled back, showed sharp teeth. "Did your mother not talk of that to you, Biancabella?"

Tears trickled down her face, but she did not answer. He yanked harder on her hair, and she still do not. Then his grip tightened on Hans, pulling him closer to the water.

"No, she did not," said Biancabella, meekly. "Rumpelstiltskin."

Rumpelstiltskin's lip curled. "If she did not tell you the truth about *that*, it's more shame to her that you've gadded about without a care in the world. Knowing not a thing and yet making a fool of her—maybe I'll let these two give me their firstborns, after I turn the fox into a collar, but you—you will not ruin anymore—"

"Ninny ninny not—" said Biancabella, and Rumpelstiltskin pulled her down, closer to the water.

"Your name's Tom Tit Tot!" roared Hans.

For a moment the only sound was his words, resounding from the water. Then Rumpelstiltskin slowly turned his head toward Hans.

"You—you—" The voice was faint, and hollow.

Hans felt the grip slackening a little. Biancabella tried to pull away, and Hans did not move except to look away from her, directly at Rumpelstiltskin.

"How did you know?" Rumpelstiltskin's voice took on strength. Then he roared. "Who told you?" He lunged for Hans's throat, and Han threw himself backward—and found himself slipping easily from the grip.

"You! You!" His face contorting with rage, Rumpelstiltskin grabbed his own two feet and pulled. He tore himself in half, into two pieces like black rags, and fell to the ground in two tiny heaps, both charred.

Hans fought for his breath. John ran to help Biancabella up. The fox limped forward.

"Out of here as quickly as we can go," said Hans, grimly, trying to rise. The fox nodded, and John held out his hand to aid Hans. He stood. He was bruised, no doubt, but he could walk.

Then another sound came. A child's wail. Hans closed his eyes. What sort of fool would bring children to such wilds?

Genoveva, he reminded himself. Perhaps the person had had no choice. He opened his eyes. Biancabella scurried by the banks toward three crying children, all of them pale as mushrooms. Utterly alone. His stomach felt like lead. Even the oldest had to be far younger than he and Gretel had been.

"The children," said Biancabella. "The ones Rumpelstiltskin carried off." Then she looked down and smiled with obvious effort. The oldest boy, still tearful, looked up at her. She crouched by him and picked up the youngest.

The oldest had pale brown hair; the next, hair almost as pale a blond as Biancabella's, and the third, hair as dark as night. With that in mind, studying their faces made their lack of kinship seem clear. They looked no more like each other than Florio and Constance looked like Rapunzel. Perhaps they were brothers—Hans let out his breath. Then, the tales the mirror had told had been of a single baby, each time.

"O my," said the fox. "The spell's broken. Because he's dead." It scratched its ear. "O my. We shall have to manage."

"We shall have to take them," said John, grimly, as if reckoning the road ahead. "Perhaps the mirror will know which one is Jill's son, and who the other two are."

"Like King Maximus's realm would rejoice to have the rightful heir back," said Hans.

"Perhaps they would, now," said Biancabella. She ushered the other two toward them, and Hans nearly groaned. Children so young would need to be carried much of the way. Her smile looked sad, and she spoke to him almost in a whisper, "Perhaps breaking the spells that do not affect us will help us, in the end."

"May Heaven grant that," whispered Hans.

Chapter 15— Curses Broken

"And that is why plans are needed," said Augusta Gloriana.

The moon was full, but the trees cast such shadows across the clearing that she could not make out King Drakos's face, or Ottoline's. Mother Magda glared at the ground, utterly hiding hers. Their silence seemed more resentful than appreciative of the wisdom of her words. They would start to complain that she had not curbed Biancabella—

"Why did you tell her his name?" snapped King Drakos.

"I didn't," said Augusta Gloriana, trying to maintain her regal dignity in the face of such childish petulance. "He must have foolishly confided it elsewhere. Or hooted it out like a fool owl in the night, thinking that no one listened. Which shows the folly of putting all the blame on me."

Silence fell. An owl hooted.

"It shows the folly of not tending to my own spells," said King Drakos. "The next thing you know, your madwoman of a daughter will descend on me and mine."

"At least you have yours," said Mother Magda. She raised her head, and her eyes were very narrow. "None of you so much as try to help—my tower remains empty."

Augusta Gloriana glared back. After all she did to pull them together, so their strengths were increased, this was the gratitude she got. The least Mother Magda could have done was *find* a girl for them to help her with—it was not help when they did all the work. As for King Drakos, his Vasilisa would have escaped and married that scoundrel without her help, but he was already departing—stalking off toward his gryphon.

The other two looked at her, not him.

"You should go back to the beginning," said Ottoline.

Hunched like a toad, thought Augusta Gloriana, poisonously. "What? Go wander about the ruined castle and the roses? At least no king has been so lacking in wit as to go back there."

Ottoline waved a dismissive hand. "The problem with Biancabella started with Snow-White."

Augusta Gloriana's lip curled. "That insipid lassie is no danger to anyone. Even you can't claim she killed one of our number. No, King Maximus is better. He did not need much incitement, and he's—" She smiled. "He is ready to destroy all that threatens us without realizing that he's doing more than salving his pride. Already he raises an army to attack and undo."

Silence followed.

"And," said Augusta Gloriana, "we should go back to meeting at the castle."

Both of them looked at her with narrowed eyes.

"Not one of us died before we stopped meeting there," said Augusta Gloriana. "Both of you should know the folly of speaking in the woods, where we can be overhead. If only by a beast—and then they go and gather to talk."

"Never," spat Ottoline.

Augusta Gloriana raised her eyebrows. "If you are so discontented with what has happened, you may amend your situation however you wish."

#

Through the night, the gryphon flew onward. The air was cold and wet, and King Drakos frowned. The best that could be said was that he did not have to conjure up an island in the middle of the sea for the gryphon to rest overnight. Not because it could make the flight without a rest, but because he did not have to pass over the sea.

The fools. The triple-cursed fools. Where would Biancabella have learned the name if not from her mother? Did she think she could fool him with nothing more than her say-so? Did Augusta Gloriana really think she deceived him when she said that Biancabella had refused to learn—had willingly cast away the source of power? What could those two be up to except trying to steal his daughters from him? No doubt they thought they could train them better than he could.

If only that fool Blaise had not been such a wretch and a knave! He remembered it like yesterday—he had gone to that master sorcerer and received a promise, to learn how to work illusions if he granted him a reward in return. Master Blaise had ordered his housekeeper to put on a chicken to roast and set out to teach him. Days, weeks, months of training, and he could work such marvels and wonders in illusion that first one kingdom and then another had fallen to his hand, and after that still more increased the bounds of his kingdom. Master Blaise had pestered him after each coronation for his reward. He would have done it, too, if the fool had realized that a king had many duties and little time and had had just a little patience. Why it was just seven years later, at his twelfth coronation, that Master Blaise had asked one last time, and when he put him off, had thundered, "Then I will have that chicken for dinner."

The next thing he had known, he was back in Master Blaise's study, knowing nothing of the magic, and being turned out on his ear, however he begged. All an illusion, he thought bitterly.

Master Blaise had not even afforded him a chance to show he had learned his lesson.

The gryphon began to sink, its wings outstretched to keep its gliding smooth. It had wisely judged the time. He would travel no farther tonight. Always, always, always, he had to do these things the hard way. He had only gotten himself one kingdom—thus far. If he had Master Blaise's knowledge, he would have left those two fools wrapped up in the dream that they were in a flowery meadow when they were at a cliff-edge, with the most beautiful flower just past the edge—and the same for that Biancabella—except that none of them would ever have been such a problem. He would have stopped them in their tracks years ago.

At least he had not told the two of them how, after the years of drudgery to find magic in place of what he had been denied, he had sought Master Blaise out and got his revenge. They would have been utterly useless and betrayed him to the knave.

When morning came, and the gryphon mounted the air and flew onward, six swans as black as midnight came flying toward him, circled around the gryphon, and formed an escort about him as he flew back. Such a filial welcome.

At the castle, the gryphon settled to the ground, and the swans settled around it and rose up again as lovely young maidens wearing cloaks of black feathers and turning their faces on him.

He dismounted. Their anxious faces—

"Your Majesty," said Noreen, bowing deeply, "there are such tales on the wind, of King Maximus's army. They speak of magic and peril—" Straightening, she looked into his face, paled, and went silent. All his daughters fled as if he had turned into a demon before them.

Wise of them—such insolence! After all the spells he had wrought to keep them safe, they thought they might be in danger! As ungrateful as Vasilisa herself!

#

The inn, the Bird of Truth, appeared ahead.

Biancabella, with the youngest boy on her shoulder, looked at it and closed her eyes.

How true, thought Hans, his shoulders slumping. Wrestling with Rumpelstiltskin—Tom Tit Tot—had been wearying, and to carry the three children after—he wished Tom Tit Tot had tried to catch them closer to the inn.

The oldest boy sat in the road and looked ready to wail. Hans sighed. That boy had walked more than the other two, which was no little help, but he grew tired.

John swept up the oldest boy and walked ahead. Minutes later, he emerged without the boy and with the inn-keeper's son, a nearly grown youth.

"Hallo, hallo, hallo, what a strange journey you had," said the son, blinking at the other two boys. "Did you find three peaches floating in a river? Mold three children out of late snow, and then find that they came to life? Chop open a tree and find the children inside?"

Biancabella wearily shook her head. John hesitated, glancing at her, and came to take the youngest from her. The middle one looked up at him, and John looked down, but the son swooped in and took the boy up. The boy merely turned his solemn gaze on the son.

The son said, "Lost in the woods so they would die of hunger?"

Hans fought down a snort. "No," he said gravely. "These three boys are orphans we are bringing to their kin." We hope. "The families do not wish the matter bruited about." Or would not if they knew.

"Huh," said the son. "I will not tell the merchants who travel your way, though some may guess." He glanced sideways at them. "Some of them have carts."

The inn-keeper appeared in the doorway, his face more bitter than before, to announce they would pay more for more guests.

#

The bear lumbered through the hills.

Still.

From a cliff, Ottoline watched it with narrowed eyes. Her hawks and crows kept a sage eye on it, but—if only Augusta Gloriana were worthy of the least scintilla of trust! All these weary months when it should have been easy to amend the spell from Zelphine and her daughter!

She might even have gotten Mistress Laurenza to help, if Augusta Gloriana had kept Biancabella under rule, if Mistress Laurenza were still alive.

Or Mother Magda, if the woman had not sulked so. She would have helped Mother Magda if ever she had *asked*. It would only be fair for Mother Magda to help her if she asked, but with the way she sulked, it was too obviously a waste of time.

#

"Now it is time for you to go," said Mistress Theodosia, looking at the spring road. The leaves shadowed the trail, but sunlight still shone through them.

Constance swallowed, and shifted Dag's weight a little in her arms.

"It will only take you a day, but you will have to stay at Theodora's house for months, as well, before she sends you on to Theophania. And, you need to take this."

It was a plain wooden box. Constance thanked her.

#

Sigurd trudged down the slope. How far it was. Though he was not roving to a far distant land, where Constance would need to win the aid of the North Wind to reach him. (She would—she would—for a moment, Sigurd closed his eyes. He had to have faith in her, and know she would.)

His paw caught a stone, and he opened his eyes again. At times, he felt certain that the spell led him in circles. He would see the same stand of birches seven times before the way finally led on. But now, the path was new: he had not seen the cottage before him, with its rose trees in front of it, blooming even this late in the year—one with white roses, one with red.

For a moment, even as he walked on, caught by the spell, he eyed those trees. He could see no chain and no key, such as Biancabella had seen.

Two girls, laughing, bore baskets of herbs from the woods. One was palely blond, and one had black hair, but still, they looked much alike.

A woman appeared in the cottage doorway to kiss them and usher them in.

He let his breath out. If Rumpelstiltskin, or even some other dwarf, gave them trouble, they would have to hope for some other bear that could speak.

He fought down a snort that would have drawn their attention. If for no other reason that not only could he not marry one, he had no brother to marry the other!

Perhaps it was just as well that he had not met them in the winter. He would have longed so much for the roof and the hearth.

#

The trees had turned to birches, all as pale as ghosts, and the sunlight was bright, if touched with green from the pale leaves. Constance walked on and reminded herself that this was a magical journey, far easier than trudging along the roads—as Florio and Snow-White had.

The moon hung overhead in the still pale sky—a half-circle of whiteness like a small and oddly shaped cloud.

Flowers grew along the way, some ghostly pale, others quite dark—darker than any flower she had ever heard of growing in a garden. She wondered if Biancabella could tell their names, or whether they were such magical flowers as might grow only on an enchantress's doorstep.

The path turned about an outcropping of gray rock, lichen encrusted, into a fir forest with its deep shadows. Constance sighed. Dag would wake soon. Perhaps she should sit here and nurse him.

She reached the rock. A snug cottage stood in the shadows, whitewashed. Smoke rose from its chimney.

Constance blinked, took another step forward, and ran. She did not want to be as foolish as Hansel and Gretel had been, having not their excuse of age, but Theodosia had sent her here.

The door opened.

The firelight was paler, the pale yellow of a moon barely over the horizon, and the woman standing by it wore a gown of pure white, and her hair was silver. A cat half black and half white blinked at Constance, and flitted along the porch.

"Why, it is Princess Constance," said the woman, "in pursuit of Prince Sigurd."

#

In the morning, Constance woke in her bed, and looked to see that Dag still slept in the cradle.

The cat sat on the coverlet, blinking at her. Constance frowned a little. The cat had been a little more black, a little less white, the evening before.

She closed her eyes for a moment and told herself not to be a fool. She had reached this cottage in a day, she should not quibble over a cat.

#

The springtime brought merchants to the road as surely as leaves to the trees. Some were kindly enough to let three little orphans—being escorted to more distant kin—sleep on the carts as the road wound on.

Lilacs blossomed along the road as they trudged on. Biancabella sighed a little. A long journey, and one where many other travelers were moving. At times the throngs were enough to make the travel worse than winter.

When, she reminded herself, they had not had to bring three young children along. It was Heaven's blessing that they did so when they could get aid.

"You sure that you will need to leave this route at Four Winds?" said the carter. "It's hard to travel alone."

"We have relatives to aid us," said John. "We can meet them at the Four Winds."

The Four Winds hove into view past the greening trees. The garden behind was filling with sprouts. Biancabella went to pick up the smallest boy. Even the oldest one could not tell them his name—she could only hope that the mirror could tell them that, as well.

Basil and Florio came out to take horses and speak of securing rooms. Basil's eyebrows went up at the sight of the children, before he mouthed at them to go around back. Hans nodded, sharply, and led the way.

Snow-White leaned against the doorway, and her belly looked as round as a peach. Rapunzel sat on the threshold, nursing her baby. Snow-White blinked and spoke in a low voice. Rapunzel looked over.

"Truly you have outdone the Four Winds," said Rapunzel.
John laughed.

"We have to see the mirror," said Biancabella, and hated how her face heated up. "After the guests are all settled and we've eaten. Perhaps in the morning, after they leave."

Hans rolled his eyes, and Biancabella had to admit he was wise. To wait that long for knowledge, when the end was in sight—but they had to see what was wise.

#

The sky was a deep, deep red by the western horizon, and a violet turning black overhead. The oldest of the three boys yawned and rubbed his eyes. Biancabella bit her lip. Perhaps she should carry him.

"It's not like he'll understand," whispered Basil. "Perhaps they should be as abed as Violetta."

Biancabella laughed a little. The baby, secure in her cradle, was the only one not trying to press into the room. But—"The mirror has her limits. Seeing the boys may reveal more than knowing they are here."

They eased up the stairs. Hans and John had crossed to stand by the window, Snow-White sat on the chest with the two younger boys by her, both asleep, Florio waited by the door, and Rapunzel spoke in a low voice to the mirror.

Biancabella came in and sat by Snow-White, but the boy's eyes widened at the mist, and he slid down and walked toward the mirror. Then the face began to form. He stopped, and blinked, and stared. The face looked down at him, and he ran back to Biancabella, clutching her skirts.

"That one is Jill's son," said the mirror, sounding amusing. "His name is Sylvio, and King Maximus has usurped his throne."

Sylvio looked back, with one eye, for a moment, before hiding his face in Biancabella's skirts again.

"The next oldest is Roland," the mirror said. "Also a prince. The rightful king of the lands that King Igor holds."

Biancabella blinked. It took her a moment to remember—Princess Silverhair's father. Roland sprawled on his back without stirring.

"And for the youngest, his name is Giorgos, and—"

Giorgos grumbled and stretched his arms, without waking.

"I told you of Prince Sigurd's realm, and how Zelphine's son had his house, and those sisters Rhode, Leocadia, and Anthia. That was another realm. Lacking a king. After Giorgos was taken, the king repudiated his wife, and went to marry his own daughter, the Princess Preziosa—and she fled, and then he had neither son nor daughter. It was not well with them, any more with Princess Anna's realm."

Snow-White shifted. "Didn't he reconcile with his daughter? Ever?"

"Ah," said the mirror. "Augusta Gloriana muddled her path so that she did not find her way to a royal castle. Meanwhile, her father looked about for a princess to marry. He heard of a lovely one, Isabella, who lived far to the north."

John shifted. "Belsante had a great-grandmother of that name."

The mirror chuckled. "The very same. But the king did not want to go find her, let alone woo her, and his courtiers assured him that to go wooing like some young prince did not befit his dignity, but he should send a young man in his service. Whose name was Alexandros. The king considered him for a time, and decided to test him first. He ordered him to steal the ogre's horse. Alexandros went to the ogre's house and snuck into the stable, and tried to steal it three times. The horse neighed each of them, but Alexandros hid so well that the ogre did not find him, and the third time, the ogre beat the horse for keeping on waking him. The fourth time, the horse did not neigh, and Alexandros rode him off. So the king ordered him to steal the ogre's coverlet of gold. Alexandros went to the ogre's house, and called that the thief of the horse was riding by, and if he made haste, he would catch him. While the ogre hurried off in the direction he pointed, Alexandros stole the coverlet.

"The king resolved to send him after the princess, but his courtiers said that he had to be sure Alexandros could bring her back alive against her will. So the king ordered him to steal the ogre. He went near the ogre's house and started to build a coffin. When the ogre came to suspiciously ask what he was doing, he said that he built a coffin for Alexandros who had stolen the ogre's horse and the ogre's coverlet.

"The ogre said, with pleasure, that having died suited Alexandros well, and Alexandros confessed he was not certain he had made the coffin well. But the ogre was just Alexandros's size—if he got in, he could test that it was just the right side. So the ogre did, and Alexandros slapped the lid on and brought the ogre's coffin to the king's court. The courtiers wondered if it really was the ogre, and Alexandros had the wit to flee, but the king opened the coffin to be sure, and the ogre sprang out and tore them to pieces. The ogre lives in the royal castle now."

"One would think," said John, "that a cat would have aided some peasant lad to claim it as his own by now."

"The circle can bewilder things even for cats," said the mirror.

"Did Alexandros get away?" said Hans.

"Yes," said the mirror. "Indeed, he walked into the same spells that had led the Princess Preziosa astray and met her, and they married in due course and lived as farmers."

"Better than some," said Basil, under his breath.

"What a fool the king was," said Biancabella. "For all he knew, Isabella would have said that she could not marry so ugly and old a man and made a bath that would make the one who went in young and handsome—and then he would have had Alexandros test it, and come out young and handsome, only to realize when he jumped in that it would make only one, and it was the death of him."

"I always wondered about those young men," said Rapunzel. "Happy to marry the woman who had put the king to death."

"He hated the king too, by that point," said Basil.

John swept the air with his hand. "So, three princes," he said magisterially. "Not one of whom we can deliver to his throne."

The mirror paused for a moment. "Yes."

John sighed. "At least, I know my journey should be toward King Drakos's land. That will do something."

"That may be best," said the mirror. "But Hans and Biancabella might help by taking the children away. Have you ever heard of the Daughter of the Skies?"

"She tried," said Snow-White, "to steal a bride from her bridegroom." She hesitated. "The bride had stayed at her father's house three times when she was far gone with child, and given birth, and each time the child had been stolen."

"That is the important part of the tale. The children were given succor by enchantresses. There are three, their names are Theodosia, Theodora, and Theophania, each of whom lives in the kingdom where one of these is the rightful king."

Hans looked up attentively.

"I fear that the circle has seen to it that they will be of little help. To Constance and Sigurd, because they were already involved in that spell—"

Hans's face contorted, briefly, but he wiped the expression away.

"And to take charge of the boys."

Biancabella groaned. "Back all the way across the kingdoms we have taken all winter to cross?"

"Ah, there are magical ways to their cottages," said the mirror, thoughtfully. "Augusta Gloriana hid them but gave Biancabella the power to see through her spells. You may go and return even before your sister gives birth, Biancabella. Then you may work against them by staying here. I—it is not clear—but—" Then the mirror shook its head.

"Giving birth for the first time," said Rapunzel, and her face was like granite, "is always a danger. All the more so when sorceresses might use that time to imperil you."

John froze like a statue. His gaze went to Snow-White, and his hand went to his sword.

Snow-White, looking paler than usual, said, quietly, "There will always be evils that sorceresses are up to. Leaving Vasilisa and Ian to suffer—what would have happened to *you* if Biancabella had lingered forever to ensure the dancing princesses and their princes did not suffer?" Her hand rested over her waist. "Or to me, or to Basil or Florio—and the princesses were not safe from them— you were there when the youngest brother had to learn where they were."

Hans snorted. "It's not like you have to cross thrice nine kingdoms, only a desert. You might be there and back before the babe is born. Then Vasilisa might aid us against them."

Sylvio sat with a bump, and started to wail. Rapunzel rushed to pick him up.

"The boys need their beds," said Basil, firmly. He picked up Giorgos. "Let Biancabella, Hans, and John tell the mirror all that befell them. Perhaps that will free some knowledge."

Florio picked Roland up.

"Let the boys rest for a day or two," said Rapunzel. "After that journey, even a magical one will be difficult."

"I will leave in the morning," said John, his voice toneless and his face like flint. "Since I will not carry the children."

"And Heaven prosper your path," said Rapunzel.

\#

John adjusted his pack.

"The merchants are gone," said Florio. "And the morning mists. You will have a hard day's journey reaching the next inn in time to not be taken as a sly talking wolf trying to sneak in."

"When I have already eaten chalk to sweeten my voice and put flour on my hands?" John tried to smile. "I shall walk briskly. I do not think we want news to get back to Augusta Gloriana, or Otto-line, that some mad traveler reached this inn, turned around, and went back the same way. Dangerous for me, dangerous for you, dangerous for Snow-White—it's just as well for the boys that they will be elsewhere."

He walked out the backdoor. Biancabella, wearing a straw hat and rough clothes, straightened up in the garden and waved a filthy hand full of weeds.

"Heaven protect your path!"

He smiled. "And yours. And bless your staying put!"

Biancabella laughed.

\#

Beneath the sunset, Violetta shifted in Snow-White's arms.

Tiny little clothes, half-made, lay next to her, though they still needed to be sewn; the months would pass quickly. At that, with all the people about, there was much that could be mended, and more that could be sewn new.

She did not put down Violetta. Her own baby wriggled a little, and she smiled a sad little smile. Months yet—but not that many.

Biancabella, her arms and skirts splattered with water where she had washed off the dirt, came over to smile down at Violetta. It eased her face. She looked almost as beautiful as Augusta Gloriana—and, thought Snow-White, one day she would be more beautiful.

Violetta sighed and slept. The baby wriggled again, and Snow-White drew in a deep breath. Perhaps Biancabella had been prudent to put off thinking of marriage. But then, Snow-White told herself, Biancabella had not needed to disenchant a prince. Constance had married quickly enough. And who knew? Perhaps Biancabella could not stop Augusta Gloriana and would have to either marry with the danger or never marry.

"I hope you are back before the baby's born," she said.

"It would be a hard journey for that to be difficult—" began Biancabella idly, and then winced.

Snow-White blinked.

"Those six princesses and princes thought they had an easy journey, so yes, I hope so."

The princes and princesses frozen into statues by Boney. Snow-White looked down. Seeing through Augusta Gloriana's spells, and that Boney was dead, would not ensure that Biancabella would slip through every spell.

"I will ask the mirror if you are late," said Snow-White, but her voice sounded odd in her own ears. At least, if she could not learn what happened, John could chase after Biancabella when he returned.

If he returned.

"As you so sagely reminded me, princesses have always lived in peril," said Biancabella, but her voice was sad.

Snow-White hesitated. "Could you take Violetta in to her cradle?"

Biancabella carefully gathered the baby up. Snow-White looked after her.

If Heaven granted that Biancabella could destroy the circle, Rapunzel and Basil would insist on returning to his father's kingdom.

She and Florio had to go; Florio was his father's heir, and her children, Florio's.

She picked up the sewing. She had been seven when she left the castle. She had learned enough to help Florio be a prince, even if living here at the inn was so much more like the life she had lived since.

The baby squirmed. She sighed and sewed. At least she was not trying to sew seven shirts from nettles in silence, she told herself.

#

The last stars had melted from the sky, the moon shed no light—and the cat was entirely black—and the sun had not yet risen. Dag slept as soundly as the day, but he would wake with it.

"There is still a wait ahead of you," said Theodora. "You will have to bide at Theophania's, even if you reach her earlier."

"It was late in the day when I reached here," said Constance. "I hope to reach her earlier, for fear that if I am slowed for some reason, I may break my neck in the dark."

"At least the summer will give you long hours," said Theodora. "But for now."

She held out a plain wooden box. Paler than Theodosia's, but otherwise they could not be told apart.

#

Biancabella rose with the dawn, but Hans already awaited her in the kitchen. At least she had brought down her pack when she came. She let it down on the table when she sat for breakfast.

"Eat up," said Rapunzel. "You won't have a chance to eat a hot meal on the road, and you will need to keep your strength up."

"A long day and a slow journey," said Hans gloomily.

"Very much so," said the fox, springing up to put its forelegs on the table. "Might as well enjoy the breakfast."

"At least the boys are early risers," said Biancabella.

A wail from behind her made her roll her eyes. At least she told the truth.

"At times, being a scullery maid would be easier," she muttered.

"A pity they would not hire you as a gardener's boy," said the fox. "It would suit you better."

Biancabella sighed and wondered what happened with her own garden, after the years of work she had put into it.

The circle first, she told herself, primly, and ate porridge. The problem with Anna's castle was not how the roses had overgrown it.

#

With servants fleeing the corridor as soon as she came into sight, Augusta Gloriana swept down the castle corridor. Mother Magda off on her handiwork as if nothing had happened, or she expected Augusta Gloriana to do all the work—probably the later. Ottoline smug and silent. King Drakos never putting his nose out of that *kingdom* of his—as if you could have a kingdom without a single subject!

It was up to her alone. Again. Not that any of them would hesitate to profit from her labors.

At least Ogier and Herbert would not be a problem—

She came around a corner into the great hall. The two of them sat at the table, drinking away. She stood and stared. They *would* have to stay out of the tavern the one day when it would be useful to her.

"Ho, my dear!" Ogier raised a cup. "Have you tasted the new beer? They just brought it."

"Have you heard the news?" said Augusta Gloriana.

Herbert rolled his eyes. Ogier smirked.

Augusta Gloriana swept on. "Your brother John has appeared, alive and well."

For a moment, Herbert blinked, and then he started to laugh.

"Suit yourself," said Augusta Gloriana, turning away. "I heard it from good witnesses. He's coming with an army of wolves to eat you up—the way they came to eat up King Maximus."

That seemed to penetrate their fatuous contentment. Their gazes shifted back and forth.

"There's a fox leading them," said Augusta Gloriana.

"Horses," said Herbert, unsteadily. "We can ride the horses away."

"Until you reach the sea," said Augusta Gloriana.

Ogier put down his cup. Wine slopped over his hand. "Then we'll take a ship."

Augusta Gloriana fought down a smile as she planned the proclamation that the king and the prince were on a quest for the good of the land. Being queen and serving as the regent would exceed what being queen mother would have been, even if Biancabella has not been so unfilial. Furthermore, her regency would not end when Biancabella came of age.

And no more of these fools!

\#

Between the pine forest to either hand, goldenrod grew on the wayside, as thick as a wall in a garden maze, and blazed golden. Roland stared at the blossom, and Giorgos slept on Hans's shoulder, but Sylvio dragged his feet. The fox had gone ahead, a little, as if to scout out the way—as if they had seen any way but this the entire day.

Biancabella closed her eyes. If only they could have gone to Theophania's first! So much easier if they could have left the largest, not the smallest.

"Speedily a tale is spun," said Hans, softly. "With less speed a deed is done."

Biancabella winced. Even if Hans had found it as wearisome as she—he had not sung at all after noon.

"If I found a shoe on the way," she said softly, "and then another one just like it a little farther on, the master thief could still not steal anything from me, because I would not go back to find the other shoe."

She sighed.

Hans smiled, wryly. "Now, if I found a blue belt that would make me strong enough to carry all three boys all day long without any effort, and then kill all the bandits but one in a bandit camp so we could spend the night there—"

"I would insist that you track down and kill the one," said Biancabella. "Or he would threaten me in your absence, and then I would betray you and get the belt from you. Having fallen in love with him—somehow."

"The bandit captain who could threaten you badly enough to frighten you does not exist," said Hans.

Biancabella held her tongue. She thought she would insist on their leaving in the middle of the night and sleeping elsewhere for fear of that last bandit, because she would be as afraid of him as of her own mother.

They came around a bend. The fox sat in the way, looking ahead. A snug little cottage stood among golden lilies. Rose vines clambered over it and bloomed with golden roses.

A woman on the porch nodded to them, and an orange marmalade cat looked indignant, and distinctly on the yellow side.

"A surprise," said Theodosia. "It s been a time since I had one of those—though—" Her gaze went to Giorgos. "—it does explain itself readily."

She walked down the stairs and picked up Sylvio without a glance for his whimpers, and he was startled into silence. With weary gladness, Biancabella climbed the steps. The fox eyed the cat warily and kept Biancabella carefully between the two of them. Then, thought Biancabella, it would be more odd if that were an ordinary cat, here.

"You might meet Constance on the way," she said.

"A slow journey for her, then," said Hans, half dubious.

"Princess Biancabella can move more swiftly. And it profits her more. Queen Constance does not want to arrive too soon and work as a scullery maid." She smiled. "Come, sit, rest your feet."

She produced a dinner of milk and of porridge with honey for the children, with remarkable swiftness, and then, as the children ate, a cradle and trundle beds.

Then she sat by Hans and Biancabella, with the fox between them, its head already resting on its legs.

Her voice low, she said to Hans, "I do not know anything of her whom you seek."

Hans winced.

"I will of course send you on to my sisters, but I do not think that even Theophania will know. And I—you know the tales, but I have nothing to give you in the morning."

Biancabella looked into the fire. She knew better than to ask whether the woman knew a way to stop Augusta Gloriana forever.

"My mother would not let me bribe her, anyway," she said, her voice soft and sad.

A log cracked, and a plume of sparks flew up the chimney. The cat, purring by it, looked more red than it had earlier. Biancabella frowned. She was almost certain that was not the firelight.

Theodosia glanced over at the boys. Biancabella leapt up to help put them in the beds.

And Giorgos would stay here in the morning. She pulled up the blanket. For a heart-sick moment, she longed for a baby in her own arms. Then she turned her face sharply away. Was she not in peril enough? Would she woo more, and so that she could not search for an escape? Constance, at least, had not *intended* to trudge over hills and valleys with her infant in her arms.

#

The road grew more and more dusty, and less and less broad, until John thought he could only call it a track. Cliffs of red-touched brown, like clay pots that decades had weathered the color from, sometimes had scraggly trees, in the most sheltered spots. Tough, wiry grass grew here and there—or had grown, it was generally yellow.

In a cliff's shade, John stopped. The track wound on through hills that hid the horizon. Whatever met his gaze was the last thing he could see in that direction. The sky burned blue.

John drank some of the water of life, and walked on. Filthy was hardly as hard as trudging through snow. It would, he thought, have been wiser to seek out Belsante's land in the summer, and this in the winter, but he could hardly turn back now.

The track came about a bend. He looked down on a view: hills grew lower, and rolling, and not one whit less dry or more green. No lakes, or ponds, or streams, as far as the eye could see. Or travelers, or birds soaring on the desert air.

"A well-kept track, considering how little it is traveled," he said. The words echoed more than he thought they would. He straightened the pack on his shoulders and went to become the first traveler to walk on it since Ian.

\#

The forests about Theodora's home were not so thick and dark than the ones before her now. All firs, and all towering, and the path itself went deep into a valley, so that the hills shadowed all the way. Though not enough to greatly cool it—it had been a hot day, and would be a hot night.

Constance held Dag tightly to her. Wrapped in a white blanket—he must be visible as a star through all this gloom—any wolf that wanted a tender scrap of child's flesh could see him for miles. And though she had left Theodora's house while it was still as gray as charcoal, she feared she would walk past Theophania's. So dark it was here—

Light glimmered, off to the side. Warily, she turned to look. It could be the fire of a bandit camp—and she carried no letter that they could, in a fit of amusement, change from ordering her death to ordering her marriage to Sigurd.

But she saw the window it was in, and then the house about it. It was like Theodosia's, and Theodora's. Darker. Slowly, she inched toward it. She was almost at the steps when a glint from its eyes let her see the cat, black but for single silver hairs in its coat.

The door opened, and the silvery light came out. A dark woman stood in its path.

"Ah, Constance has come, with her son in her arms, and in search of her husband," said Theophania.

Constance closed her eyes a moment, before climbing the stairs. On the porch she saw how Theophania's hair had sparks of light about it, like dew drops from a morning mist, but glowing.

\#

Snow-White sat at the kitchen table, binding together bunches of herbs to be hung from the rafters. Rapunzel finished washing the last of the breakfast dishes.

Basil came in. "The guests have left."

Rapunzel raised both eyebrows. "I thought the merchant would insist—but that his companions might respond by insisting that he stay. With the way he coughed, I'm surprised they didn't overbear him."

"So that he could die here, and I beat the corpse for his failure to pay?" said Basil. "He had money enough and paid enough."

"Shocking," said Florio, coming in with a load of firewood. "He should have died, penniless. Now you will not beat his corpse, and then some young prince will not stop you by paying off his debt so he can be buried, and then a mysterious white knight will not help him win a princess—*how* can tradition go on?"

"He can wait for the fox to return," said Basil.

For a moment, there was silence.

"It is possible," said Rapunzel, slowly, "that the fox is the dead man seeking to reward John for the good deed of arranging his burial."

Snow-White looked at the herbs. "No doubt," she said softly, "all will be revealed in due course if that is so. Certainly we have nothing to blame the fox for."

Rapunzel turned her face away, and then shook as if throwing something off. "No, no. The mirror told us nothing of the fox before it met John, but it told John's story. It would not have left out burying a dead man."

"And if it had," said Basil, "John would have spoken of it."

Snow-White nodded. So he would have.

#

The garden flourished magnificently. By sunset light, Mother Magda looked about and felt smug at the radiant, rosy color. Peaches, plums, and pears in full fruit and with branches leaning over the garden wall—rows of lettuce and radishes and carrots—pole after pole of beans—garlic and onion and all sorts of herbs—the pumpkins were not ripe, but she had much to tempt, and could sit and ponder what she would name the daughter.

Mother Trude had not managed something so fine in all her years of tending her garden. As for Augusta Gloriana and Ottoline, they had wasted—wasted!—their garden on flowers. Did they think to catch a girl by having her father pick a rose?

At the market, she had heard the whispers and seen the glances. This time, the women would brace themselves to all raid the garden together. In earlier days, she would wait to see the damage and know they would always return. Now, she had grown keen enough to tell them at once.

The sky darkened toward crimson and violet.

She would have to take care to seize the pregnant one. The others could escape, it was hardly as if she wanted to raise a castle filled to overflowing with daughters, and the other ones might prove barren. Bargains for impossibilities went badly.

She walked across the garden to sit under a trellis, taking advantage of Augusta Gloriana's spell—the women would not come in here.

Which was the extent of Augusta Gloriana's help. A spell with some limited use, far less than she had done for Augusta Gloriana and the others. She had caught many a thief, to give her daughter the honest upbringing that her mother and father could not. The thieves were less of a nuisance than the demands of the rest of the circle.

Stars began to shine in darkening sky. Below, among the trees, fireflies flashed on and off, and looked faintly greenish.

Before stars filled the sky, the whispers came, and the sounds of feet futilely trying to be silent as they crept into the garden. She smiled in deep satisfaction. They had even brought lights that illuminated their faces as they sought out the rosemary plants.

That was simple enough for the name, and her rounded belly marked out the pregnant one. Mother Magda rose and walked toward them, actually silent. She was upon them and seizing that thief and mother before they knew she was there.

The other women screamed and fled—most dropping their stolen rosemary—but her captive's struggling only had her tightening her grip. Did the fool woman not know that a witch had a grip of iron?

"Have done, you thief," she spat. "Or I will tear you to pieces and cook my soup from your bones!"

The woman paled and stared wide-eyed at her.

"I will give you all the rosemary your heart desires," she added. "While you bear the child and for seven years after—and you will name her Rosemary, and when she is seven years old, you will give me her."

#

The cat had been black last night, Biancabella knew. Now it had a spot of white.

The fox still stayed away from it.

As Sylvio stared about, and Roland looked down from the porch, Theodora wished them well, said she could give them nothing to aid on their quest, and concluded, "Unless things have gone very ill, you will find Constance at Theophania's."

So many things had gone so very ill that that brought Biancabella only discouragement, but she said nothing. She had found nothing. Snow-White and Florio had found each other, and those silly dancing princesses had found their princes, and Kari and

Pierre, and Basil and Rapunzel, and—she forced her breath out. She had done little enough for many of them.

Hans took up Sylvio, the fox leapt ahead, and Biancabella turned to trudge down the road. If she wanted to spite anyone, she could remember how much she must frustrate the circle.

A thought came, nagging her, telling her that she had not been so fearful, she might have a husband and a child, like Snow-White and Constance. She had hidden under a cloak of invisibility as long as she had one.

She forced her breath in and out and tried to study the trees. If she had married one of the princes she had freed, Snow-White would not have found Florio, and likely not Constance, Sigurd.

Or, for that matter, Rapunzel, Basil.

The wind rustled the leaves. Flecks of sunlight danced over the way. Hans started to sing.

"And on this bed was laid a fine mother,

The finest mother, that ever you did see,

And the mother on the bed, the bed from the feather, the feather on the bird, the bird on the nest, the nest on the twig, and the twig on the bough, and the bough on the tree, and the tree in the wood,

And the green leaves flourished thereon, thereon, thereon,

And the green leaves flourished thereon."

Sylvio crowed. Biancabella tried to sigh quietly. Singing would wile away hours, but it would be a long day.

#

The fox sniffed the air and ran a little ahead.

"There," said Hans, pointing over the fox's head.

Except for the red that was the fox, Biancabella could see nothing. The trees were too thick, the branches too all-encompassing. Shadows lay everywhere, without—

No, two spots of light looked at them—like the eyes of a cat.

Her shoulders slumped, and she walked toward the cottage. It still was hard to tell from the forest, but then a baby's wail pierced the air.

Sylvio stared ahead.

The door opened.

#

"We should have made you to go to the mirror, first," said Biancabella. "We went, after, and it told us about the castle."

Constance smiled. "It would have slowed me. The faster I reached the castle, the better."

Biancabella's mouth pursed. Hans looked at her with narrowed eyes.

"And there was nothing I needed to know that I did not find out there."

Neither one spoke to that, either, but Biancabella turned to admire Dag.

Constance sighed. "I suppose that Snow-White will have her baby about the time that I reach Sigurd's lands."

"The time would fit," said Theophania.

"We can return for those days," said Hans. "And hope that if the circle does anything, we can be of aid."

Constance nodded. "A pity Biancabella could not show me the path."

"She could," said Theophania. "But what would it profit you?" She spread her hands. "Had Ottoline brought Zelphine into the circle, worked with her on the spells—perhaps she could have done a better job of it. But now it will take Sigurd a year and a day to reach the castle."

Constance looked so wan that Biancabella said, "Doesn't the spell protect him on the way?"

"So it does," said Theophania. "He will surely arrive safely."

Constance's breath came out in a gush.

"The bird did warn us," said Hans. "That spells would last after the death—but—was Ottoline already involved?" He scowled. "She might have tried to draw Zelphine into the circle."

Theophania shook her head. "I do not know. Perhaps. Perhaps this is one of those spells that the Bird of Truth warned you of. The effect, to Constance, is little."

Dag snuffled a little and then sank back into sleep.

Constance glanced over at the bed where Sylvio slept. "Then there is little profit in talking more of it—and you have to tell me about this Sylvio."

"And Giorgos, and Roland," said Hans with a groan.

Theophania served up bread and honey, and cheese and peaches, while they talked, and at the end, said dryly, "The ogre had the wit to not enchant a princess into a cat, then."

"Isn't that when the ogre wants to claim the castle?" said Biancabella. "And she's the rightful heiress? This one did not need to."

The fox looked up. "When do they *need to* enchant princes and princesses?"

"That ogre is not in the circle," said Biancabella. "Perhaps the ogre has a degree of sense that is not found in their number."

"Let us hope," said Theophania, "that Prince Giorgos will have the sense to realize he can build his own castle and need not send knights to perish at the ogre's hands."

She smiled. Biancabella felt a little unnerved.

"And he is likely to have to know that," Theophania went on. "The Bird of Truth has flown far. It flew to the lands that are called King Maximus's, and told of how Queen Jill's son had been taken—and recovered." Her smile deepened. "Perhaps now they shall hear to speak with me."

"King Maximus," said Hans, "does not seem likely to give up his throne without argument. We were lucky to escape with nothing more lost than an enchanted compass."

"He has raised an army," said Theophania. "He managed only because of the many kingdoms he rules, and still the army is small. At that, other nobles may also raise armies in support of young King Sylvio. Still, it will be a danger to travelers."

#

A few aspens, among the green trees, had turned as yellow as a dawn. The fox, running down the way, was bright red among them, and it playfully snapped at orange butterflies.

Biancabella sighed. "I wonder how John is doing."

Hans pondered that. There was good reason for John to go alone, they had no reason to think the water would suffice for him and even the fox as well. Still—

"I wish we had a knife in tree," he said. "One where we could inspect it, and know if it were dim, he was in trouble, and black, dead."

"A silver knife, a silver fork, or a silver spoon, which we could carry with us, would be easier," said Biancabella, looking mischievous for a moment. "Along with being a way to remember him." Then that humor slid away.

"I am certain at least that no peril will stop him," said Hans. "A nobler man than I am—he just wants to end their evil, while I am looking for Gretel."

"You are trying to save someone else," said Biancabella. "I am just trying to save myself."

Hans looked at her wan little face. "You would not have rescued so many people if you wanted to rescue only yourself."

She looked at her hands.

"You could have rescued yourself by returning to your mother and claiming you had learned the error of your ways. Aviette's sisters joined their mother."

Biancabella froze, and her face was a mask of horror.

"See, your noble nature did not even let you think of such an evil."

Biancabella looked down again.

"Though, I grant you, none of us for nobility match the fox, which has aided us all without reward."

"Perhaps it'll ask for one yet," said Biancabella. "It has earned one of great magnificence."

The fox yipped in excitement, and Biancabella realized that the Four Winds was in sight. In the back, Florio chopped wood, and Rapunzel's voice raised in song floated out of the kitchen.

#

The day dawned in shades of dusty rose and yellow, and bitter cold. The stretch of sand and rock was still colorlessly dark in shadow, and bore no dew.

John drank.

If the bottle was endless, the water poured into it was not. Nevertheless, he could not sip at it. There was no point to having ventured all the way to Belsante's kingdom to spare the water that he brought to bring him through this land alive.

He stood. His journey through these lands would be less time than the winter months he spent in Belsante's lands. Far less than when he lay, dead, in that field.

Still, months were possible. King Drakos had set the desert to make it hard to reach his kingdom. He thought he had already drunk more water than he could have carried in the ordinary way of things. He should have counted days as soon as he reached the desert, he had no notion now beyond weeks.

Then, what did it matter? He would endure as long as he needed to endure. He was already ruddy from the dust.

He slung on his pack again and capped his water before hooking it to the belt. It was not as if he had other things to do. Belsante would be prudent to bring water if she came for him. The road lay before him.

Around the next bend, he saw a swan in flight, as silent as any swan, and below it, he could clearly see the body of a young man, slumped face down.

John let out his breath slowly. He took up the bottle and edged toward the body. The swan could not attack like a hawk, but those wings could strike hard indeed.

The swan eyed him and turned its flight. It circled about him, and he hesitated. The wings had come nearly close enough to touch him.

"I have come because I wish to destroy Augusta Gloriana, and your father is her ally. I need to prevent his triumph."

The swan circled him again, twice, and thrice—like a wolf deciding what it faced—but then it flew to the body and landed beside it. Little puffs of red dust rose up about its feet. John walked over and knelt in the blood-red dust, keenly aware of how close its beak was to him. Kneeling, he realized that some of the clothing's red was the dark red of a heart's-blood wound. Though he could not tell how deep the wound was, the redness of the dust could not hide how pale the corpse lay, and he thought the man's hair was auburn even under the dust.

He himself had bled like that, John reminded himself, and had lain the same on the earth, dead but undecayed. He poured water over the wound.

The water made rivulets over the cloth, in the dust, and started to turn it to mud, caking on Ian's clothing. It dripped to the ground, which drank it up in a moment. The swan stared, mournfully, and his tongue froze in his mouth. The mirror had warned him that it did not know everything.

Ian sighed. John started and looked down. Ian's breathing began distinctly, and the wound in his side—when had it disappeared? There was still blood, but John could not have sworn to its being as much as there had been moments before.

Ian's hand started to move. John held his breath and thought the swan did as well.

Then Ian opened his eyes—gray as mist and looking wondering for a moment. John pulled back with a jerk. Let him see Vasilisa at once, let him know she was well.

He felt more heartsick than he had when the mirror had told him how Sophia had perished. At least Ian's gaze went to Vasilisa, and his face, as it regained its color, lit up with delight.

For a minute. Then his voice, strained, said, "My love? My darling? Must you remain a swan?"

The swan stood there. Its head moved a little. It could not even, like a duck, quack.

John cleared his throat. Ian blinked and looked at him, and scowled.

"I have spoken with the Bird of Truth. It told me, cryptically enough, that there are things that are not a swan that are also not a person—"

A moment later, a dove sat in the dust. It looked at them quizzically. Ian winced. It flew into the air and toward him. Ian reached out a hand, and it landed and cooed. Ian's eyes closed.

After a moment, it turned into a parrot of blazing blue, and Ian's arm for a moment faltered under the new weight before bearing it up again.

The parrot flapped its wings. "Yes!"

Ian's face almost lit up again, but it could not fight off his expression of consternation.

"Let us make haste," said John. "We can speak as we go."

Ian drew a deep breath. "You can tell us your name, and let us thank you."

"We have not escaped her father yet," said John. "Walking will not silence us."

The parrot launched itself from Ian's arm to become a swan again. They followed her down the way.

#

Hans feinted with his sword. The sunlight glinted from it, over the inn. Not so good as working with John, but if they faced a dragon again, if Ottoline threatened Biancabella—

"You should learn swordplay," said Basil, his voice deep. Hans looked over and saw Florio standing with him.

"I know some," said Florio, hesitantly. "For fear of robbers."

"I knew rather more," mused Basil. "As a prince. But being a beggar for years rather leaves me lacking."

Hans spread his hands. "I knew nothing before John undertook to teach me. I can not fight a master swordsman, and probably not a dragon less foolish than Ottoline's, but I did fight one."

"I could offer only to teach you, for what help it would be," said Basil.

"I'll get the sword," said Florio, and Hans nodded.

The breeze sent a plume of yellow leaves flying over the yard, and Biancabella came out, no more than nodding to them as she went to the garden and gathered some of the late herbs to bring back to the kitchen.

When Basil cleared his throat, Hans realized how long he had stared at the kitchen door. His face heated as he turned away.

"She—is finding that waiting for some way to fight her mother is very hard," he said.

"You think so?"

"She was more beautiful when she led Florio to Snow-White," said Hans. "Her anxiety is wearing on her."

Basil, his eyes narrowed, studied him in silence, until Florio emerged with a sword.

#

The sky had turned as fiery red and orange as the forest below. The swan looped overhead, as it had many times after they had heard his tale, but not very high. It could not see past the cliffs about them.

Or, John reminded himself, be seen. He wondered how far King Drakos's gryphon could see. But no matter what the danger of pursuit was, they had to rest. He wondered if Vasilisa could wake all night as an owl, keeping watch, and let Ian carry her as a sparrow the next day. Then he wondered if that would do any good. Even if she could become a pond and the two of them drakes on it, King Drakos had shown that he could know them in their new form. He sighed.

"In the tales," said Ian gloomily, "the evil sorcerer father sends servants twice, who do not recognize the daughter and her beloved, and then comes himself and is tricked."

John nodded. "How true." He watched the swan. Perhaps King Drakos would think that Vasilisa still did not know she could take other forms, just not her own.

If not—perhaps Biancabella would find him again. He had survived many years. Ian had survived with the water.

A fugitive thought said that Belsante would bring water when she came in search of him. She was prudent in that way.

Then the swan, gilded by sunset light, plummeted, turned into a falcon once in the shadow to plummet the faster, swooped down upon them, and turned again into a parrot.

"Don't fight it," she said.

John opened his mouth to ask what it was, and found he could not speak, or close his mouth again, because he was made of stone. He thought he saw Ian, just barely, and that the other man was also stone. Gray, not the ruddy shades about them.

No bird, either swan or falcon or parrot, could be seen. For a moment, he thought she had turned into another statue, one he could not see.

A gryphon plummeted, more swiftly than the falcon. The beast towered over both of them—no lion was that large, thought John—and King Drakos descended from it.

"Do you think I'm such a fool?" he said, drawing his sword.

John wished he could hold his breath. If whatever Vasilisa was trying failed, he could only hope that Belsante followed—

King Drakos's eyes jerked back and forth—searching, or nervously. "I know your tricks, Vasilisa—that these fools could free themselves if it came to that, from this spell—and you know that I have only to stab them for them to be trapped—but you—"

A gryphon leaned over the statues and bit. Blood spurted red.

And within moments, was red on green grass. A woman stood over the dead man. Her pale face was stained with blood. About them, the grass ran along the road, but green forest spread behind, and unseen streams gurgled.

The gryphon—King Drakos's gryphon, the first gryphon—screamed.

Ian stepped forward. John blinked, and tried, without thinking, to follow. And did. King Drakos's gryphon reared up, screaming with rage. John drew his sword and kept all his thoughts on the beast.

The gryphon screamed again, and its wings beat the air. John charged forward. The wings—get the wings before it could fly off and attack at whim—a plummet like a falcon—

Ian's sword caught its heavy, leonine paw. With a vicious cry, its head darted toward Ian's throat, leaving its own throat naked and exposed. John raised his sword and brought it down as if chopping wood.

The blade cut through it. For a moment, it seemed to grow harder to cut, and then, oddly, easier. And moments after that, the gryphon's outstretched wings no longer cast shadows on the earth. Its body did not fall, or even exist.

John drew in a deep breath. All the blood was gone, not bespattering the road, or his clothes, or Ian, who stood and stared.

"I will go see the road," he said, and hurried on. He was *not* jealous, he told himself. He could rejoice in this much, that Augusta Gloriana's aid had, in this case, not been the end.

At the hilltop, the rolling hills spread before him. Green, yes, but he could pick out golden trees by the dozen, and some were flaming orange or ruby red. A river ran down the valley, and on its dark waters, little golden leaf boats already floated away.

He let his breath out. At least the road ran along it. His gaze went up, reckoning the hills. Speedily a tale was spun, with less speed a deed was done. He would be fortunate to reach the Four Winds before Snow-White's child was born.

A voice rang from behind him. "Let my sisters hold his lands. We shall return. If not to your father's lands—I can sew. You can sell what I sew. There's many a princess who had to live off her needle."

She smiled radiantly at John as the two of them reached the hilltop, both of them looking mussed.

"You can not fly us from these lands?" said John. "As a gryphon?"

She laughed a little. "Father conjured so many spells on that gryphon that I'm not surprised it dissolved with them. It could have crossed the sea without an island to rest." She looked over the way and grew more sober. "And to fly means to draw the eye of monsters."

"Walking it is, then," said John. "But first—"

He walked up to the river. Then he shed his boots and stockings, and walked into the cold water, with the emptied bottle. He walked until it was waist deep, and pulling at him with an icy touch. Then he uncapped the empty bottle and held it down, under the surface, facing the flowing current.

Vasilisa looked at him, from the shore. "We can use spring water, it would be better, and I am quite capable of that."

"I was told," said John, "that it was wiser to keep the bottle full if I could. By a little old woman. And by a white bird."

"How long will it take?"

John hesitated, and said, "Three hours."

Both of them looked at him. He managed a shrug.

Vasilisa rolled her eyes and sat on the bank.

#

By the window's light, Biancabella sat and mended. The autumn leaves sent golden light over her.

She stitched neatly enough, thought Snow-White. She could make her living as a seamstress if it came to that, though she would not win the eye of a king by her supreme skill.

Hans, rosy-cheeked from the cold, came in with logs to heap up by the fire.

"At this time," said Biancabella, dreamily, "I would plant bulbs and watch the garden plants have their leaves turn as red as the forest."

Hans laughed, shortly. "It was a busy season. All sorts of folks left off buying their wood for winter until the latest hour. Sometimes they even got caught by the snow. Which made it hard to spend the money and get the supplies back for the winter."

"The dwarves had it easier," said Snow-White. At the castle, she and her mother had just spent more time inside, sewing, but at the dwarves'— "Still, it was harvest time. All the food had to be put up against the winter, even if they could buy it more over the months than in a great burst."

Leaves blew by in a great flock of yellow and orange and red. Snow-White watched, and she gasped.

After a moment, she said, carefully, "Hans, you may want to go tell Rapunzel—and let her send you for the midwife."

\#

Oaks towered, higher than castles. Their leaves had all turned to a deep red, like heart's blood. The way led up a slope, and the path it took was steep. Sigurd trudged on. The sort of tree that a bear could climb, chasing a squirrel. He peered up the nearest tree to where the leaves clouded his vision like a sunset cloud, and shook his head. He doubted that even a squirrel could leap from tree to tree, to lure a bear to leap after it, fall, and split open.

That bear deserved it—chasing that hard after a squirrel when it had already eaten a boy, a girl, an old man, and an old woman, gulping them down so fast they came out when it split.

He trudged on.

The way reached the top—first he glimpsed the sky blue between the trees, and then he reached the height—and descended again, even more steeply. Between the trees, he made out bits of a castle. Enough to see little more than its presence, enough to know his journey would end there. It gleamed silver.

He sighed and looked about.

A man stood like a statue, as if trying to avoid his notice, but flinched from Sigurd's gaze. He scrambled through the dead leaves and climbed a tree.

Sigurd walked by and hoped he was not a prince. He could not coax him from the tree, and if he did, he could not help him on his quest.

The castle came slowly clear, and the village below it, and the firs in the forest behind it. Had he been the one who failed to break a curse on Constance, the sight would have delighted him. His only fear would be that she would be forced to marry again before he could arrive. Now, he could only hope that she could follow him, and reach him before he was forced to marry again.

He trudged down the slope as slowly as he could.

#

Constance looked up at the silvery castle, up the slopes where green firs formed great swathes of forest. So did Dag. Then he wriggled about, his breath forming white clouds before his face.

Constance sighed. A village lay below the castle. She could find service there. She trudged on. At least growing up at the inn had her accustomed to the work, and she could hear the rumors from the castle.

It had to be the right place. The path wound upward, and she bent her head. Sigurd had told her of Theodosia, Theodora, and Theophania. Biancabella would have seen through any trickery on Theophania's part. It had to be.

She swallowed.

Night approached. Though the sky had not grown darker, it showed tinges of pink and orange. She needed shelter at any rate.

A sign swung outside an inn: The Three Birds. She thought they were meant to be a raven, a falcon, and an eagle. Or perhaps she merely guessed that from tale after tale.

She wondered if they were three princes, or three birds who aided some prince. She hoped the latter. Princes, like princesses, needed all the aid they could get.

The inn-keeper's voice rose in fury ahead of her, and she cringed. Slowly his words came clear.

"Every servant! Every one! She says she needed to hire them *all* for the wedding! How am I to run this inn when she claims them all!"

Someone else spoke, more softly.

"She isn't even our lady! He's our prince, but her!"

"The eye may not be her fault," said a woman. "There's many a princess whose hands have been chopped off, or eyes torn out, to prove to some monstrous stepmother or mother-in-law that she had been executed when in truth, she was suffered to live."

"He wouldn't sit about then," said the innkeeper. "He'd be off tricking the witch into giving the eye back, so he could restore it. It's not like some enchantress will bring it to the christening of the newborn."

Constance winced and inched forward. The man and woman, both middle-aged and a bit stout, came into view. The woman, with brown braids down her back, turned.

"Have you come for a room?" she said.

"I have come to see if I can find a place," said Constance. Perhaps, she thought, the only time an innkeeper would be more glad to hear that.

The inn-keeper snorted. "Not afraid to work here?"

"Not unless your wife asks travelers whether they have ever seen anyone more beautiful than she is," said Constance.

The woman laughed. "That's folly in a queen, let alone an innkeeper." She sighed. "Besides, we have no daughter." After a moment, she gave Constance a sharp glance. "Not one who vanished one day. No daughter at all."

#

In the mid-morning, Violetta crawled at her in a determined manner, and Biancabella put aside the mending with a sigh of relief. An excuse better than that she would have to tear out half the stitches as misplaced. She bent over and swooped the girl up.

Violetta squealed in delight. Biancabella made a funny face at her.

Basil and Florio walked in.

"The last guests are off," said Florio, sitting down.

Violetta squealed again and reached for her father. Basil took her and said, "Hans may cut more wood than the inn will need."

Florio groaned. "I envy him."

The fox trotted in. "Envy is a sin. It brings the wrath of Heaven—what do you envy him?"

"The wood cutting. It distracts."

The fox hopped up on a bench, carefully far from Violetta. "You evil soul. Now I envy him too." After a minute, it added, "I should go chase a rabbit. More meat for the table."

Another wail sounded, not from Violetta. For a minute, they all sat still. Biancabella realized after a moment, that she was not breathing, and forced the air in and out. Moments inched by without the sound of footsteps on the stair, and Biancabella reminded herself there was swaddling the baby and delivering the afterbirth—and there was something odd about the wail—

Minutes later, Rapunzel came down the stairs, looking weary, and smiling.

"Snow-White is doing well. As are the babies."

Florio blinked, sat back so that he leaned against the table, and said, "Babies?"

"A boy and a girl, so your names are all picked."

Basil lifted Violetta up. "You hear that, Violetta? Not a year old and you're already an aunt thrice over!"

Florio's eyes were closed, and he drew deep breaths—Biancabella said, quickly, "Can we see them? Or at least Florio can?"

"Someone should," said Hans from the doorway. "Given Ottoline's—history."

Silence fell so quickly that Violetta looked from face to face, and started to whimper. Basil whirled her around again, singing, "Sally go round the sun, Sally go round the moon—" and Violetta laughed again before the first two lines were complete.

Florio, looking pale, stood. "May I see her now?"

Rapunzel nodded.

#

Dag slept in his cradle. Constance chopped carrots. There was much to do; the servants must have been hired away weeks ago.

Deal with Ottoline, she told herself, and they can come back. She did not look over at her bag. Master Quentin and Mistress Septima needed servants, but they would know that a woman who was preoccupied with what she owned would be worse than nothing.

She scrapped the carrots from the board into their bowl and reached for the celery.

"Ho, Constance, what's that bag of yours?" Master Quentin smiled jovially as he dropped the wood by the fire. "Did you bring a tablecloth that spread out brings marvelous food? Or a bag ever filled with gold?" He straightened. "Or did you jump straight to the stick that would beat me black and blue for stealing from you?"

"Perhaps I have the box the cats gave me after I left their service," said Constance. "Perhaps they were so angry with me that it will burn the inn down if you open it early."

Mistress Septima laughed. "You have neither donkey ears nor a gold star on your forehead. Were you in service before, it was not to the cats."

She stirred the stew again. Constance cut more carrots. When she had finished the heaps and thought that her mother had never had her cut so many this late in the year, Master Quentin walked in.

"Done with your work? Come see the procession. The prince and his bride are riding down the street."

Her heart started to hammer harder, and she agreed. Her cloak about her, she scurried with him down the streets to the grand road. Clouds cast shadows and yielded to sunlight, but the crowds, without heed to whether they had light, shouted in welcome, and the couple rode. The woman, on her milk-white steed, had a veil on her head that left her face in shadow, but Constance could still pick out the missing eye. And—she swallowed—Sigurd rode beside her on a blood-bay. For a moment, she drank in the sight of him, fair-haired and kingly—her first sight of him as a man—as he nodded and waved to the crowds, but his manner slowly unnerved Constance.

After a moment, she realized that he reminded her of the tales Biancabella had told, of those clockwork wonders in the lands of King Hendrik and Queen Genoveva. She shuddered. A break in the clouds sent sunlight pouring over them, and Sigurd's gaze passed over her without a glimmer of recognition. For all the earlier chill, that cut like a knife.

Moments inched by her before she heard the talk surrounding her, and a herbwoman recounted how the poor prince needed a sleeping potion every single night.

Constance let her breath out again. A cloud passed over again. If Biancabella were here, she could have, perhaps, have pushed her way through the crowd, and pointed her out to him. Then Sigurd could have seen her.

Biancabella was not here. A princess had to rescue her prince without aid. Constance turned away. She had aid. Theodora, Theodosia, and Theophania had all given it.

There had to be a purpose to that potion. Ottoline would not be distressed by her bridegroom being unable to sleep. Her eyes narrowed, and when the crowd started to move about her, she barely managed to move with them, back toward the inn.

At the inn, Mistress Septima gave her a bowl of stew, and she ate, hoping she looked outwardly calm, before she withdrew to the small chamber they had given her, with Dag. Who looked very like his father.

There, her heart hammering, she opened the first box, which Theodosia had given her.

A ball sat there, so gold it seemed to shine. She took it up and turned it back and forth.

Then she scowled. When she had held it over to the left—

She shifted it back and forth, and then she closed one eye. It seemed oddly alluring. She winced and opened her eye, and tried again. Whenever looked at with one eye, it seemed beautiful beyond belief.

Her heart began to drum. Not faster than usual, but harder. Whoever looked at it with one eye would want it.

She sat back. She had heard all the tales, and the castle did have windows. She might have to ask where the bride would look out.

Her hands shook as she stood. But first she would ask the way to the herbalist.

She swallowed. First, she would ask if there were one. She did not want anyone to notice that she had noticed that there was one, instead of watching the splendor of the procession.

She checked the blanket on Dag and went to the door to ask Mistress Septima.

Cheerfully, easily, the woman said, "Turn left, go down three streets, you will find it before the next street." She stirred the pot. "By its scents, if nothing else. Buy some thyme and rosemary while you are there."

Moments later, with measures in her thoughts and coins in her purse, she headed out. She needed her cloak against the chill, but the herbalist was close enough and had little business at this hour. The herbs for Mistress Septima were easy enough, and then she drew a deep breath.

"Do you have any herbs to help against sleepiness? to let you keep wakeful?"

"Why, many," said the woman, and briskly talked of this one and that, and how many of them worked by smell.

All to the good, thought Constance, her heart pattering faster in excitement.

The woman said, giving her the final bundle of herbs, "It works better if eaten, but even the smell is potent to wake. That will last you for a week."

A night will suffice, thought Constance, but she bought it all.

#

The window opened on the hillside, dingy now with fall.

She would have a garden there, Ottoline told herself. Mother Magda owed her that much help. It would outdo Mother Trude's entirely. It would be a mighty marvel of magnificence. As was only fitting for a *queen*, not some peasant witch hiding in the forest.

It would outdo Biancabella's—a silly little princess who would never be queen now. She wouldn't need to send men hunting for a gardener whose father and grandfathers had been gardeners before him.

She looked over the slope again and froze.

A woman sat there, bold as brass, with a little boy. She let him play with a marvelous golden ball—obviously magic. What did such a grubby little servant and her brat do with having magic?

Light glanced from the ball as the boy squealed in glee, batting it about. Then, abruptly, he sat and let his mother take the toy, as if a gleaming ball of gold were some commonplace *thing*.

"Woman!" Ottoline shouted.

The woman at least bowed her head in suitable meekness.

"What will you sell me that ball for? Gold? Silver?"

She bowed her head still more meekly. "Neither gold nor silver, my lady. I will give you it only for the right to sleep the night outside the prince's chamber."

Ottoline felt her face freeze. After a moment, she eyed the woman, but it hardly mattered—the marvelous ball drew her eye, and she knew who the woman must be. Which meant she know how to deal with her, and with her brat. She would show him to try to evade the spell, and what it would mean to those two. And she would get her long-merited crown.

How the golden ball would glow for her.

#

The servants were soft-voiced, deferential, never speaking except at need. Dressed in dust-gray clothes, they moved around the castle like ghosts.

Even the one escorting her.

Constance wondered if the spell would break if—*when* she freed Sigurd. If so, it would not be the first time that freeing the prince had freed other prisoners.

She forced her breath in and out and turned her attention to the steps. So faint was the lamplight that she needed to, to avoid breaking her neck.

Her heart hammered. She took a deep breath, and another. She did not want Ottoline's one-eyed attention on her. She climbed the last steps of this flight. Not that Ottoline did not know. She would not drug Sigurd every night except that she knew how the tales went.

As long as she did not realize that Constance had come with the herb to break the spell. The bag was tucked carefully in under her mantle, her tunic, and her shirt, but she still wondered whether the shape could be seen and fought to keep her hands away. Reaching for such a thing would make it seem important.

The servants might not guess, and if they did, might not tell Ottoline. Still—Heaven guard it from their gaze!

"My lady," said the servant in that soft voice, as if muffled by dust. He bowed toward the door.

Her heart hammered so loudly that Constance thought the servant might hear it. She inched forward and opened the door.

On a side table, a candle burned. Its golden glow reached the bed, where the bed hangings were far back enough to her to see the blankets, and the sheets, and Sigurd asleep in them.

She fought down a squeak and pulled the door shut behind herself, though her heart hammered every moment. Then she ran across the room—the breeze of her passing making the candle flame stir and the shadows dance—and threw herself between the hangings, unable to suppress herself at the sight of that dear, dear face.

"Sigurd," she called. "Sigurd, wake up, I'm here, I'm here—wake up, o Sigurd—"

Minutes later, she tore herself away and sat on the bed, staring at the wall so that she could not see Sigurd at all. She forced herself to breathe in and out, slowly, though her heartbeat hammered in ears.

When, finally, her heart and breath were calm again, and the room silent, she reached for the bag. She had known that it would come to this. To merely call had been her folly.

She turned and studied his sleeping face a minute longer. So calm and peaceful, as if he were happy here, but she knew without consulting the mirror that the rumors were true, that Ottoline drugged him.

The herb, crushed beneath his nose, produced not a bit of wakefulness in him, not so much as stirring under the blankets. She pulled out more, and crushed, her heart beating harder by the moment.

Then she bit her lip, and carefully put the herb away, lest it betray her to Ottoline, and turned to shake Sigurd's shoulder.

"Sigurd, Sigurd, wake, it is Constance, I have reached you, wake for me—"

The sky was still black when the guards came to escort her out, though it was dark gray when they sent her out the gates. She walked so slowly that it was red and pink before she reached the inn.

Dag still slept. She collapsed by the cradle and wept.

#

"Mirror, mirror, on the wall," said Biancabella, sitting on the chest.

"How odd to see you all alone, Your Highness," said the mirror.

Biancabella looked out the window at the barren branches. She could not see the road for here, but she knew. "Few travelers. Less work. Even sewing for Sophia, Giovanni, and Violetta does not fill up all the hours."

Her hands still ached. Even though they used Violetta's outgrown clothes for the new babies, more had been needed. She would not sew more than was needed.

"With so little work in the kitchen, Rapunzel can do it all. Easily. I was just underfoot."

"And what do you wish to talk about?"

Biancabella's touch touched her lips. It was unlikely that she would learn how to defeat her mother here, when so much else had failed, but she had nothing else to do.

At least she could console herself in her misery that she made her mother miserable too, she supposed.

"Nan. And Ned, too. What happened to them?"

"Ah," said the mirror. "That was back then, before Augusta Gloriana found Snow-White with the dwarves. With Nan, even before Rapunzel found the Four Winds—but still, after Ottoline married your uncle."

Biancabella winced.

"She had a cottage where she had lived before the marriage, and she still went, and goes, there from time to time. It is filled with caged birds. They used to be maidens and youths, but she turned them into birds and caged them for spite. Anyone who wandered too close."

Biancabella let her breath out. "Only Nan, or Ned as well?"

"Both of them, both of them."

"Is—was there a way he could have freed her?"

"Oh, no," said the mirror. "Sometimes, in old days, she would free a man whose beloved was trapped, to taunt him, but Augusta Gloriana pointed out how foolish it was. Always the chance he might find something to break the spell—some magical flower, or something. She kept them all birds, and all in cages as well."

"He couldn't find an enchantress to tell him," said Biancabella slowly.

"There was always the chance that he might dream it, or merely have a lucky guess. No, she turned him into a bird and caged him and had done with it."

Biancabella's tongue touched her lips.

"It was a flower," said the mirror. "You can not find it in the dead of winter. It is an ordinary flower in that much, at least."

Biancabella blinked and wondered whether the mirror could see that—and if it just meant that she was so transparent. Then she scowled. "That woman—the one who was turned into a flower without dew—"

"That woman," said the mirror, "was a trap."

Biancabella blinked.

"Your mother meant to find you, and she did. It is Heaven's blessing that you escaped your peril then."

#

The ball gleamed silver in her hands. Dag squealed with glee, and Constance convicted herself of folly. What could she do that she had not done?

Feed him the herb, said a cold thought, and she blinked. Slowly, she let her breath out. She had three tries. Only a fool would not try all three, even if the tales could not go as when her mother had told them. She did not want to end up a beggar at the castle door, as her father had been for so many years at the inn.

And she had been a fool to not try it the first night. Doubly so if she did not the second.

At least Mistress Septima and Master Quentin merely whispered and laughed softly about her. She could sleep again in the afternoon, since the travelers were now few enough for her work to be less.

#

"No dinner," snapped Ottoline. She glared about the kitchen. A good thing she had come down here to oversee it herself. It almost made having servants pointless, the way she had to watch—but (she reminded herself) this was the important part of the spell.

The servants looked carefully blank, and Ottoline nearly sighed before them. From the morning to the evening, to keep watch and ensure that Sigurd could never speak to a servant, was a task in itself, before the watch for the woman, and seizing the second treasure. Her eyes narrowed. She had no need to forfeit the treasures meant to bribe. She could outwit her, and both gain the treasures and keep Sigurd from her.

For such a crafty sorceress, the judgments of servants mattered not at all.

"Make a tray. I will bring him it. We must speak of matters of import."

She turned away. If they muttered to themselves about how she still ate in state, in the great hall, they did so out of her hearing. It was not as if she had to take special care about the sleeping posset. Sigurd had slept through her first try, he would sleep through the second.

That silvery ball, as fascinating as the first, golden one—

"My lady?" said a hesitant voice.

Ottoline blinked. A cringing servant held a tray, and she realized she had already turned toward to her chambers, where those trinkets lay.

She forced herself to take a deep breath and then took the tray. There would be a third, as fascinating as the first two. She could have all three and show that every sorceress who had ever failed to keep a prince had done so because she was a fool—because of, not greed, but lack of care.

None of the servants followed her, of course, not even on the first part of the hallway where they might have other business, still less on the stairs to the room.

Sigurd sat by the window. In broad daylight, looking out—at least the shadows hid him from sight of those outside. What a fool Zelphine had been, letting him slip through her fingers to indulge her son.

Then, she had only tried to catch him for her daughter. A fool twice over.

Ottoline put down the tray and said, cheerfully, "There is much to discuss."

Sigurd slowly looked at her, and his face was blank as that of the servants.

#

Propping up Sigurd did not help at all, realized Constance, as the crushed herb fell from her fingers. Her eyes closed. The air stank of the bitter scent, but Sigurd had not roused at all.

Every tale had the princess having to come for three nights, but she could not see how the third night would help.

The servants, she thought, drearily. The servants might tell him of her visits. She could hope. It would be no different than many a tale.

#

"Is that a town?" said Ian, looking at ahead.

John frowned. The hillside was golden with autumn leaves, and below it stood a tower. "I—doubt it. I did not see it when coming this way. Which is more plausible for a lone tower than for a town." He pondered a moment longer, and spoke with more confidence. "And there was no road there."

Vasilisa nodded.

The tower became clearer while they crossed the valley, and slowly it dawned on John that it had no door. There was only a lone window, which had a hook beside it. A large hook, one that a prisoner maiden could wrap her hair about to lower it, and let a wicked witch, or a handsome prince, climb up.

He swallowed. Rapunzel's prison.

"Is there something wrong?" said Ian.

Briefly, he told them. They looked suitably shocked, and then Vasilisa eyed it.

"I do not think she has another prisoner," said John. "I think the mirror would have told us."

Ian scowled. "If it could. But you said that it did not know everything."

He had, and it was still true, he had to admit.

Vasilisa shrugged. "It's not as if we have to trick her into revealing herself after she's been warned against us." A dove appeared where she stood, and flitted upward.

John stood, feeling a fool. Vasilisa could look more quickly than he could hunt about. Ian stared after her as she flitted about the tower, rising in her flight. Then, she swung into the window, vanishing into the shadows. Minutes inched by, and Ian started to shift where he stood.

How long did it take for a bird to search a tower? John swallowed. If there had been a trap inside, how could he and Ian discover that? Perhaps Ian had already thought of that, from the way the other man peered up, his face dreadfully set.

Minutes later, the dove flitted out of the window and down the height of the tower. Vasilisa, smiling, stood on the ground again. "Empty and cold. No food in the pantry, no sheets on the bed, no ash, even, in the fireplace. She has not had a maiden prisoner here for a long time."

John wondered if Mistress Magda was growing angry about that, but they had nothing to do but go on.

#

The candle flame could not be seen from the stairs, but the candle-light was enough to walk by. Biancabella slipped over to join them at the sewing.

Rapunzel looked up. Snow-White glanced over only briefly before turning her attention back to the nursing Sophia. Giovanni lay soundly asleep in the cradle.

"Ready for the night?" said Rapunzel.

"For all it may bring," said Biancabella. Even a ghost, and managed to choke that down. Snow-White had not been murdered, and Ottoline had not taken her place, or the babies would have noticed.

"At least there is not a dead body here to come back to life," she said as solemnly as she could muster, while Rapunzel stood, gathering her own sewing.

"All you have to do then is hit it with a stick," said Snow-White.

Biancabella shook her head. "As brave as a bee I am not." She took the seat and pulled out her sewing. Or rather, her mending. "Not a patch on what you do."

"Oh," said Snow-White, laying little Sophia next to her brother, "I was not that fine a hand at sewing when I was still in the castle." She pulled up the blankets over her daughter, and then over herself. "Whatever tales Lady Regina told me about princesses who had to make their living with their sewing at best were enough for me to learn to embroider. And whatever tales I told myself, I do not embroider so well that some king would see it and demand to see the maiden who embroidered it, and want to marry her."

"Just as well now," said Biancabella.

Snow-White rolled her eyes. "True. I do not want Florio sent off to I Know Not Where, to bring back I Know Not What. But my ordinary sewing—it was working for the dwarves that taught me mastery."

Biancabella sighed. "I hope—" She might indeed spend years sewing for her supper, she thought, spreading out the cloth. "A greenish bird would be better."

Snow-White giggled. "So that the prince, no longer trapped as a greenish bird, will claim to take the cup from the hand of the woman who made it best, but will actually look at their faces and take yours? How Lady Regina hated the maid who told me that story—she had to go work in the kitchen, and no one ate her food unless it was well made."

"Would you rather have to wash out a shirt? One that a troll-wife could not clean?"

Snow-White frowned in mock-thought. "Now, that depends. Is it one enchanted to keep trolls from washing it?"

"If you could tell in advance, that would be so much easier." Biancabella took a stitch. "There's a great deal to be said for sitting about sewing and supporting yourself and your little son until your king and husband shows up to bring you home."

"When you get exiled like that," said Snow-White, "there's always the chance that they will chop off your hands—as they did to Genoveva—and then there's no sewing at all."

Biancabella winced, but said, "Hands always struck me as foolish. Hearts are worse—the huntsman gave her a false heart for you. Why do they not tell them to chop off the *head*?"

"Too dangerous," said Snow-White. "If someone sees the head, the murder will out."

"It can't be more dangerous than for the victim to show up alive again. Though—I suppose Elinor shows the limits of that."

Snow-White nodded. "So she does, so she does. Hans more so, since some witches will leave less to prove the death."

Biancabella flinched.

"But, hands or no hands, to have a white deer come to help is far more marvelous than merely sitting about sewing—" Snow-White shook her head.

"You could kill seven with one blow," said Biancabella. "In the summer, of course. No flies now."

They looked at each other. Snow-White giggled. And they both started to laugh, far beyond the humor of the jest.

#

A ball as black as night and glittering with lights like stars. Dag had still marveled over it, but it had left her cold. She had surrendered it as easily as the others—more easily—than the others, with no hope in her heart. Now she walked alone up to the door, through a corridor almost as dark, and entirely silent.

The door loomed before her. Constance drew in a deep breath. This was the final night. She had spent the last gift. If she did not win back Sigurd tonight, Ottoline had laid claim to all three gifts and to Sigurd as well.

Constance pushed the door open. Sigurd, lying in the bed, looked over at her and smiled.

#

The door securely shut, and both of them warm in the bed, Sigurd said, "I did not know when to stop drinking it—I could not stay up every night until I perished from weariness—until Ottoline did everything she could to keep the servants from speaking to me. She even brought my meals on a tray with her own hands."

Constance giggled. "She would hate that. When she hated being a mere princess with Augusta Gloriana as queen—to act as your maid servant—"

His smile slowly vanished. "I tried to not drink the next night, but—she used magic. The third night—you had left some herb here, and I washed it down with the posset."

Her eyes closed. So that was what it took to work. She shivered, and his arm tightened about her. If anything had gone wrong—

Sigurd's mouth touched her eyelids. "Hush. It's done now. We have only to rouse early in the morning. You know as well as I that this is the moment at which the spell is weak."

#

The morning came, gray as a dove. Snow-White yawned and shifted. Biancabella no longer sat in the chair. Snow-White blinked and looked about, to see the pale hair by the window. Biancabella stood looking out, but she turned, her pale face severe.

"There were owls in the night, though they showed no signs of enchantment." She shrugged. "And some twittering birds this morning. They could be spies from Ottoline."

Which, thought Snow-White, will be Biancabella's constant thought unless the circle all died, and Biancabella knew it. She took up her sewing and half-hoped that the witch attacked them and ended the matter. Then she scowled. She could not be certain that Ottoline would die. Not when John had lain dead for so long—and Biancabella needed no encouragement to think on that.

Snow-White said, "Or perhaps not. Ottoline no doubt has many things to do."

Giovanni started to grumble, and Snow-White reached for the cradle. Biancabella yawned.

"Best to stay up all day and sleep only at night," said Florio from the doorway.

Biancabella nodded. "It—I felt more sleepy in the wee hours, before the moon set, and less by now."

"Breakfast will help," said Florio.

She nodded and went down the stairs.

"Were there many birds this morning?" said Snow-White. "Biancabella talked of them—she was by the window when I woke this morning."

"I did not notice," said Florio, sitting down. "But—Hans was in the yard just now."

Snow-White winced. Hans would search as faithfully for his sister as ever a sister was for her seven brothers turned into ravens—and the Bird of Truth had warned that not all enchantments were broken when the witch died.

She should tell Biancabella that only she could lure Hans from his futile quest. Except that while that would require Biancabella to give up stopping the circle, it would set her to trying to persuade Hans to stop searching for his sister.

#

The murmurs began as soon as they appeared in the morning gray. Mists slipped down streets and alleys, veiling those about this early, but enough were in the square to see.

Constance drew a deep breath. She was dressed no worse than she had been when first she met Sigurd, as an innkeeper's daughter. She should not be ashamed of herself.

Sigurd's voice rang clearly over cobblestones. "Let my subjects gather! A question of great import must be put to them."

The crowd gathered quickly. Constance fought to keep from shifting on her feet. That would be unqueenly, and to see how fraught she was could only encourage Ottoline. She glanced back. No sign of the other woman appearing to cut off her hopes in the last moment.

Mistress Septima smiled up from the middle of the crowd, with Dag in her arms. Constance swallowed.

"My people, I had a key to my chest, but I lost it. So I had another key made. Since then, I have found my old key. Which one is better, so that I should keep it?"

"The old key!" called someone, and the voices joined in a ragged cry, all praising the old key as better than the new. As if, thought Constance, they had heard all the old tales. Then Sigurd took her by the hand and drew her out onto the balcony. In her plain clothes, like a beggar's brat—

Cheers rose, loud and passionate, and hails to the king's old bride, who was better than the new.

The voices must have roused Ottoline. She staggered out the doorway and stared at them. The crowd murmured, angrily, and she turned and fled, past the castle. Soldiers, without even orders, turned to chase her.

Mistress Septima and Master Quentin came up to the stairs, him bowing, and she trying to curtsy despite her armful, and Constance went down to take up Dag. Many minutes later, after the crowd had roared their approval of the fine young heir to the throne, soldiers returned, calling that the witch had lost herself in the woods.

"I hope the wild animals eat her this time," said Constance.

"That," said Sigurd, "is probably too much to hope for. But she can not strike here."

#

The window showed a cloudy day. Not so dark as night, not yet, but with winter approaching, the travelers were fewer, and every now and again, she finished all her work, and had time to think. And to climb the stairs to that tiny room.

"Mirror, mirror, on the wall," said Biancabella.

"A question?" said the mirror. "Or have you just come to chat?"

"I can chat, if you like," said Biancabella, "but I was wondering—will Ottoline seek out Augusta Gloriana's help?"

"I can not tell you," said the mirror, gravely, "but this I know, they are angry with each other and do not talk often. Mother Magda is angry, also. They all plot and plan. Alone."

Biancabella nodded. "And King Drakos?"

"Is dead."

Biancabella blinked.

"John killed him. But, you must remember, he did the least for the others in the circle and was the least danger to those outside. The three left will be trouble enough, and King Drakos's death will make them angrier.

There was that. She sighed. "As if my mother could be angrier. I was looking at my reflection in the pot when I polished it," she said. "I am in no danger of being fairest of them all, but I suppose it does not matter now. Though I ended up with a sheep's head instead of my own, she would never forgive me."

"Perhaps if it were a calf's head," said the mirror, dryly, and Biancabella laughed.

A moment later, sober again, she said, "If they plot separately, it will be harder for us to keep watch. One might strike while the other distracted us, without even intending to do so."

"Mother Magda is concerning herself with a tower for a new baby," said the mirror. "But—Ottoline—Sigurd and Constance have undone the spell—and she is angry."

Biancabella felt the color draining from her face, but managed to croak out, "Sigurd and Constance—they're well? And Dag?"

"Very well," said the mirror.

Biancabella stood, thinking of what Ottoline might do in her fury. Too much to hope for, that she would rage at Augusta Gloriana, or Mother Magda. "I should bring the good news."

The mirror's voice turned severe. "If you wish news—there is the matter of whether it is good or evil."

Biancabella's eyebrows went up. Unlike the mirror to vacillate.

"Your father and your uncle both are dead. Their ship was caught in a storm and sank to the bottom of the sea. Some sailors escaped, but those two were drowned."

Biancabella's tongue touched her lips. Heaven help them, she thought, feeling numb.

"None but mermaids can reach them now."

Biancabella found her voice. "Was—did Augusta Gloriana drown them? Or Mother Magda? Or Ottoline?" None of them had done storms before, but they might have mastered a new spell, or found a new ally, or merely never used it before. They had to know.

"No," said the mirror. "It was just a storm. Such things happen."

#

The cottage was dark, and Ottoline was too angry to light the lamp as she surged about, seething.

The birds did not need the light. Her presence was enough to make them give frightened cries, as if they realized that she glowered at them.

As if they feared harm. As if their little lives were anything of importance to be cut off—and she had harmed them not at all—the fools had no grounds to lament being birds—and if they would wail like this, she could give them something to wail about.

Ottoline poked a stick in the cages with the most mournful cries. As if they had a right to pity. Not one of them had done a tenth—a hundredth part—of what she had done to win Sigurd.

One dove even cried more mournfully when she prodded it to keep silent. For a time.

In the new silence, she pondered a while. Augusta Gloriana had failed her. Again. Her eye narrowed. She could just see the crowds rejoicing over the simpering bride and pompous bridegroom, and then crowning them both.

It was not as if going to Augusta Gloriana would help. She had not even done anything with the knowledge of—the Four Winds. Told the very thing she needed to know, she had done *nothing*.

After a moment, Ottoline smiled a little.

She would tell Augusta Gloriana. After she showed her what a well-cast spell could do. She would find an opening at the Four Winds, and strike.

Another bird called sorrowfully. Her smile deepened. She should start a rumor that this cottage held the Bird of Truth. That would attract many a fool and fill up the cages.

Do the world some good, removing so many fools from it. Once she had removed the fools at the Four Winds.

#

At the kitchen table, Biancabella mended. She eyed the doorway again and again, but no travelers arrived. True, these days, not many did, with the fall advancing. Trees bore bare branches already, with only a scattering of brown leaves left, and the bite of cold was in the air. Especially now, in the early evening. Now, they needed every moment of daylight to travel, if they did.

Florio and Hans practiced their swordplay out back. Basil and Rapunzel spoke in a low voice. Perhaps considering whether venturing to Sigurd's kingdom would be wise. And, Biancabella told herself, that there was such a kingdom was good for them.

Rapunzel waved her hand at the door, and Biancabella looked down. But most likely of how many travelers would stay that night. Life went on despite the peril of Ottoline and Augusta Gloriana and Magda.

Things still needed mending as well. She spread the cloth over her lap. The mending did not advance quickly, and she doubted that Ottoline would seek out Augusta Gloriana's help for hiding her approach.

The fox frisked about, around the road. Every now and again it sniffed the air. Biancabella smiled, sadly. She wondered if the fox had learned Ottoline's scent.

Then the fox stiffened as if ready to pounce, and darted off, around the back of the inn. Biancabella shoved aside her sewing and hurried after. Running would draw the eye—

The fox stood with its nose pointing over the land, toward the road. Travelers came. Among their number, a woman in a drab dress had her hair covered in a drab shawl, which shadowed her face, and hid her left eye.

Or where her eye should be.

Biancabella turned. Florio and Hans had lowered their swords and looked intently at her. Mutely, she pointed, and they turned to face Ottoline.

Ottoline ran toward the forest, pushing people aside without the slightest concern, making travelers about grumble about the nuisance. She fled into the woods without even a poisonous glance at the travelers.

"That," said Basil, his voice low, "was too easy."

"Perhaps wild animals will eat her up this time," said Hans.

"She has escaped too often," said Basil. "She could slip inside again and turn Snow-White into a duck and the twins into ducklings."

"Or Giovanni into a swan," said Florio. "So that Sophia has to disenchant him."

Heaven help them all, thought Biancabella, and anyone whom Ottoline met on the way.

#

Songs or tales could only do so much to alleviate the weariness of the way. They plodded along the road and reached the top of a slope. Before they descended, John looked back.

The trees were bare, but the top of the tower had come back into view. Though a rainstorm had sent leaves falling the day before, John shook his head.

"I would have thought it long behind us," he said.

"I think," said Vasilisa, slowly, "that my father's enchantments are not quite gone. That the way is longer not because it must cross more distance, but because he worked it so that many days' journey does not actually take you the seven leagues that each day's travel should cross."

Ian said, slowly, "It was long—but many journeys are long."

"Past thrice nine kingdoms," said John. "Over thrice ten kingdoms."

"Many are," said Vasilisa, "but I do not think my father would have moved that far when he could set spells again."

"He's dead," said Ian.

John remembered the Bird of Truth, but before he could add that did not break all spells, Vasilisa said, "There are the others. Perhaps it was Mother Magda's all along—it was her tower, after all."

"That was their purpose, after all," said John. "To aid one another in their wickedness." He could hear how flat his voice grew. "Sometimes they succeeded."

Vasilisa took a step back, her hand going out to Ian's. John looked away, sharply, and forced his breath in and out. Ian had died, and Vasilisa been caught in her swan form, before he had ever met Sophia.

"What's that?" said Ian, sharply.

John started, and looked where he did. Something like a cloud on the horizon—

"It can't be your father," said Ian, his disbelief fighting with horror. "You killed him. And he didn't keep his heart outside his body—you knew his spells well enough for that."

Vasilisa, pale as a ghost, leapt into the air as a swan.

"Come down the hill," said John, his voice low. "Where we can not be so clearly seen."

After a moment, Ian followed him, and moments after, Vasilisa swept down after them. She stood on the way.

"Flee," she said hoarsely, panting for breath. "It's not my father. It's—" She waved her hands. "The witch. *A* witch, I do not know them, I can not tell them apart—it does not matter! I have nothing to stop her!"

She leapt to the air again as a swan and flew down the road, low enough that the trees would hide the whiteness. John and Ian tore after. His heart hammered, his breath came harshly, he tried to imagine—it could be Augusta Gloriana, or Ottoline, or Mother Magda—he would know Ottoline—

They went about a curve, and he risked a glance back. They were pursued by a great dust cloud, furiously raised about the running woman. He could not tell one-eyed Ottoline from the others in that.

The road sloped upward, and he nearly groaned. Vasilisa was right, her shape-shifting would not stop any of those three—

Then he remembered the water.

At the height of the hill, he stopped.

"Flee, you fool," shouted Ian. "She'll kill you!"

He turned and looked down into the valley. A woman glared from the dust as she reached the bottom. Her voice rose with inhuman strength.

"Already you plot to steal her! But you won't—you won't! She will come to the tower and stay *safe*!"

He took the bottle from his pack and upended it. The river water trickled out as he tilted it, making the way muddy, and the woman ran faster at the sight of him. He thought, for a moment, he could see her teeth flashing pale like fangs, as the water slowly grew to a stream.

Then water flooded out. Within moments, it was a true flood, thundering down the way, gouging into the road's dirt, tearing up brush, and bearing off deadwood. The witch—Mother Magda—gaped for a moment, took a step backward. Water reached the ground at her feet, like the lapping wave of a lake. She turned and ran. A moment later, the water struck her down and bore her off in its brown waters. She bobbed among it like the wood, but then she went down and did not rise again. Within moments, he could no longer see her.

His breath still had not eased, and his gaze went restlessly over the water, searching for any sign of her rising, ready to tear into them.

"John," said Ian. "There's a village. Just down below. One Vasilisa could not see before."

John turned to face him. The water had yet to subside, and the trees hid everything except the scrap of the road they were on.

Ian swallowed. "She says—a spell must have broken. As a witch died."

#

Biancabella walked around the Four Winds. The wind bit at her, sharply cold. As if she could happen on the moment when Ottoline attacked, or stop it alone, if she did.

Basil and Florio sparred by the garden. Her gaze drifted over to the inn, where Hans stood in the lee of the inn, inspecting his own sword.

He saw her looking and smiled. She felt the heat creeping into her face.

"Easier to wield than a wood ax," he observed lightly. "At least for weight."

Basil shook his head, and lowered his sword. "Enough. At my age, I can do only so much, should they send force against us." He glanced at Hans. "A battle ax is lighter than a wood ax, just as a sword is—not only because flesh and blood yield more easily than wood, but because you need to wield it longer in battle."

Biancabella looked away from Hans, but her face still burned. She looked at the trees. The leaves had fallen but for a few tenacious oak saplings, the bark was brown and gray—but some of the brown moved—

She screamed. Wolves and bears and pards and—her darting gaze finally picked out Ottoline, in the midst of the bestial cavalcade.

Hans stepped forward, seized her arm, and pushed her behind him. "Into the inn."

His voice brooked no dispute. She scrambled for the door. The men followed after her, only a little slower—Basil had raised his sword again—and inside, Rapunzel, pale as snow, bolted the front door.

Enough for one bear, perhaps, that bolt, thought Biancabella, but against that force?

Hans slammed the backdoor shut, and Florio threw down the bolt against it. For a moment, they all stared at each other. Violetta sat on the floor and wailed in abject terror, but the peril was too great—spending time to comfort her might endanger all their lives—

Biancabella opened her mouth to speak, and a sound like a coo came out, before she found it was a beak, and that she sprouted feathers. Pale gray-brown feathers—and Hans was growing into a bear, and Florio sinking into a wolf—

Cooing frantically, she flapped her wings and flew up the stairs, fearful that one of them might turn into a cat. Wails came from ahead, and she found another dove perched over the crying infants, unable to soothe them.

Time enough for that later, thought Biancabella. Cooing still more desperately, she waved her wings at the window and flew to it herself. Ottoline laughed outside, waving her hand about to have the beasts flood this way and that, her single eye glittering as she surveyed all before her.

Biancabella flew down. She could not dive like a hawk, but that single eye stood before her. Moments later, she heard Snow-White's wings behind her, and she swooped in, to perch on Ottoline's shoulder. And peck.

She drew blood at the first blow, and Ottoline screamed as Snow-White settled in her hair and joined Biancabella, pecking at that eye. Moments later, Ottoline was screaming in agony, her hands pressed to the bleeding eye.

"Kill!" she screamed. Biancabella leapt to the wing and flew for as high as possible, her heart beating faster than she had known a heart could beat.

"Kill!" screamed Ottoline again, and the leopard near her lunged—not into the air, but at Ottoline herself.

For a frozen moment, Biancabella felt too terrified to move. Then she plunged downward, toward the inn, over the beasts streaming to slay Ottoline.

It was still a jolt when, while she still flew a foot over the ground, she became a woman again.

"Snow-White!" called Florio, tearing open the door.

Biancabella stood and breathed hard.

Hans came up to her, his face grave and anxious, to ask if she were well.

"Yes, yes—" She put a hand to her face. It found nothing splattered there. "The blood didn't even—"

Hans put a hand to her arm to usher her, firmly, inside the inn, after Florio and Snow-White. She glanced back. Wolves and bears and leopards, many blood-splattered, fled for the woods, and feeling light-headed, Biancabella laughed a little.

"She must not have changed them all, or any of them, she must have summoned them all somehow—I did not know that she could do that—"

"Perhaps," said Hans, "she learned it from one of the others and did not know perfectly how it worked. Or perhaps this is the spell the bird spoke of."

#

Watery sunlight came into the upstairs room, with all the work of the inn awaiting, ignored, below.

"No," said the mirror gravely. "Ottoline in fact knew more than one spell. She favored the transformation, except that it had failed her so often of late that she fell back on enchanting beasts. She did not think that they would obey her commands just as she spoke them."

Biancabella looked at her hands. That was the end of that, then. She shivered.

#

Clouds glowered at them, threatening rain, or perhaps snow.

John shivered. Snow would be better, in this cold. Rain drenched a man, and then leached the heat from him.

"I am afraid," said Ian to Vasilisa, "that I have rescued you for a fate worse than you suffered in your father's land."

Vasilisa lifted her head. "We will go to this inn that John speaks of. There we will consult the mirror that told him so much. It guided him to restore you to life. It can guide to us a new place where we may live."

I hope, thought John, but said nothing. A village came into sight ahead. One where they would have to haggle for room in a barn, there being no inn.

But as they came closer, he realized that one building was an alehouse that might offer beds as well. A gaggle of women gathered at it, lamenting over a newborn—the poor lass!

"You didn't *have* to name her Rosemary," said one. "The witch doesn't even live near here! She would never know!"

"She's a witch," said an old woman, wrapped in a black shawl. "She would know. They always know."

"The witch in the tower?" called Vasilisa.

Hisses spread from the women, and they pulled back, staring at the travelers.

"She will not know," said John gravely. "She drowned. She is dead."

After a shocked moment of utter silence, one ruddy and rotund woman lifted her cup. "Drink to that, good gossips! The greedy old witch is dead, the child is safe, what we gathered we hold!"

"We beat Bob Tail!" cackled an old woman, lifting her mug. "And Bob Tail beat the Devil!"

Several women exclaimed, What, what? and when the old woman said that they were more crafty than Bob Tail, one sulked.

"I never heard of any such man," she said.

"Why he was a blacksmith, and one day, a strange rider came to have his horse shod and told him that he could have a wish for it. So he wished that whoever sat in a chair could not get out of it without his leave. He was a wicked man, and one day a little imp said to the Devil that he should carry off Bob Tail to Hell.

"So the Devil came to bear him off to Hell, and Bob Tail said he was shoeing a horse and wasn't going to leave off just for the Devil, but as soon as he was done, the Devil could do as he pleased, and he could sit in the chair for the time—"

Laughter resounded, raucous.

"So the Devil went off without him! It was the price of his freedom!"

Their mugs went up to toast Bob Tail, and they started to brag that they were more crafty.

"The garden is growing," said a skinny woman, thoughtfully. "Where she planted it. And if she drowned—"

They started to babble of the plants as if they were utterly alone. Moments later, the three travelers stood alone in the alehouse.

The sour-faced alewife told them that they could indeed hire the floor for the night. It was not until they readied themselves for slumber, with the lamps quenched and the fire banked, that from the shadows, Vasilisa said, in a low voice, "The garden is no doubt dying away."

"Oh, none," said John. "Let there be no doubt. Even if the magic let it bloom and grow all winter. Mother Trude's did not last until morning." He stared at the ceiling, invisible in the dark. "And Bob Tail did die in the end. Went to Heaven's gate, and they turned him away. Went to Hell's, and the Devil ordered him out for the trick he had played, giving him a coal of hellfire but nothing more. So he put that coal in a lantern and wanders the waste."

Ian shifted.

"Or so the tale goes," said John.

#

The stream had sunk, and merely gurgled among the stones. On the bank, Hans looked at the mud. Among the crystals of ice, it showed such tracks from wild beasts as it had shown before. Ottoline's beasts had dispersed—his mouth flickered into a smile for a moment—to the four winds. He stood, hearing none of those winds, but he did hear voices. He did not move except to tilt his head.

The voices were low, hushed, but they carried over the stream. Hans looked over. Odd to arrive at this hour—it was barely past noon—but odder to arrive through the woods. It was a day's journey from the inn before, on all the roads, and it would be harder in the trackless forest.

Hans slipped up higher on the bank, away from the muddy footing. Not one of Ottoline's beasts, but who knew what Augusta Gloriana might have mastered? And other perils lurked—robbers if nothing else.

Though if a robber came to woo Biancabella—he forced his breath out. If a robber came to woo Biancabella, she would refuse to go into the forest to his home, and he would not have to lift a hand to defend her from him. He edged along the stream. He should have asked the mirror what other perils threatened.

"It's over here," said the woman, her voice almost despairing. "I know it is. I have walked here so often—even with how the trees have grown—and fallen—"

"You don't know what's happened," said the man. "Years have passed. You said that the trees had grown. Heaven help us—"

"There it is, and it is still the Four Winds—" Then she scowled. "Father did not plant the garden like that."

Hans sighed and walked forward. A doe-eyed young woman and a lean young man looked at him. The woman edged behind the man.

"You are Nan and Ned, aren't you?"

\#

Rapunzel eyed them carefully, concluding more cider would not be needed. Nan, red-eyed, huddled under a cloak next to the fire. Ned held his cider while he told his story. Only a sharp eye could see how white his clutching fingers were.

"I dreamed of a flower," he said. "One that would let me break the spell on Nan and all the other birds. So I searched the forest for it. Except—" He shook his head. "—the forest did not seem to let me walk a straight path where the dream had led me. Until that one-eyed witch found me and turned me into a bird as well."

He drained his cup and put it down.

"Then one day it was just as well that the cages were all flimsy things. We smashed them to smithereens as we—" He gestured at himself. "Then we all set out to find our homes."

The fire crackled.

"I wonder if any of them managed to return home in any way," said Ned, meditatively.

Nan sniffed. "I—am—glad that my father had your help, and it's only just that he leave you the inn." She sniffed again.

"It is just as well," said Rapunzel, gently, "that the spell was broken now, and you returned to your father's inn. The inn should hardly be left deserted where bandits could take it up and kill the travelers as they come. I watched it for a time, but certainly, it is rightfully yours."

Nan gawked.

Ned frowned. "What will happen with you?"

"Magic is afoot," said Rapunzel. "We will stay the winter long, but in the spring, it may be wiser of us to leave and seek our fortune." She smiled a little. "The winter lies before us. There will be much time for us to tell our tales, and for you to learn what happened while you were gone."

For all the tales she had heard, thought Rapunzel, it wasn't as if she had learned a thing while she kept the inn. If Biancabella had taken a different road, Basil would still beg outside. Hunting down the Bird of Truth would prove more profitable, even if they had yet to learn what magic would last longer.

"Your father would have been glad to know that you had returned safely." She cast a sideways glance at the young man. "He told me, also, that he thought Ned a fine young man."

Nan sat still for a long minute before her gaze crept toward Ned.

#

Snow drifted from the sky as Biancabella watched.

On the brown earth and leaves, and the road where ruts were frozen as hard as diamond, it was a tracing of white too slight to hold footprints, but in the air, against the pale gray sky, it flew as black flecks. Her breath came out in a gust of white. Pale gray clouds, but without any break in them. It might snow for days.

After a trickle the days before—some of them exclaiming that the rumors about Nan were true—no travelers had arrived that night, which had left little for the morning to do, and nothing for after noontide. Still, Biancabella stood outside for only a moment before going back in. The air was cold enough to encourage that, and she pulled the door shut. The common room was shadowy as she walked through it. All those staying at the inn were firmly ensconced in the kitchen.

The fire crackled, and Violetta yawned next to it, with Hans whittling and watching her. Curled up next to the sleeping fox, Giovanni and Sophia slept, their arms about its red pelt—at least, Giovanni slept, and Sophia stirred. For a moment, her eyes opened and looked solemnly at Hans.

He smiled softly at her, and sang, no louder than a whisper, "There was an old woman, who lived under a hill, and if she's not gone away, she lives there still. Baked apples she sold, and raspberry pies, and she's the old woman who never told lies."

Sophia yawned and settled again.

"Travelers on the road," called Basil from the front room. Violetta grumbled, but Rapunzel looked up, pale and anxious, from making bread, and Nan said sharply, "This early?"

"Even we were later," said Ned, looking over from chopping carrots.

"It's a few hours in," said Basil. "And they seem to be coming from the western road."

Biancabella went into the front room and looked out the window. Three travelers indeed, two men and one woman—

She threw open the front door and ran, shouting, "John! John!"

#

Snow muffled the trees and covered the hollows with treacherously level footing. Near the horizon, the sky still shone with orange and peach, but the deepening blue overhead already showed a gleaming star. Biancabella's breath came out in white gusts.

The thing about winter was not only did the night come quickly, the travelers might come late, such was the difficulty of the roads.

Biancabella turned back to the main room where they had half a dozen travelers drinking mulled cider. Pleasant though the winter with Queen Genoveva and King Hendrik had been in some respects, working in the inn meant that spring would let her act more swiftly.

Snow-White and Nan were nowhere in sight. No doubt sewing industriously on Nan's wedding gown.

Her gaze drifted over to where Hans fed up the fire. She ought to feel less anxious. With Hans rescued from Gertrude's spell. With Snow-White and Florio's twins flourishing—and Violetta as well, though she had never heard a tale where a witch came after the third child at birth. With Nan and Ned free and bold enough to talk of marrying—

With her mother still loose and no doubt angry.

"Oh, there has been trouble in the lands," said the woman among the travelers. "An old wise woman came out of the woods with a boy. She said he was Giorgos, the missing prince from years ago. Half the land said that he could not be *their* king, only the princess his half-sister could be queen, because that half came from her mother, and then an old woman came forward and told how she was that princess, the Princess Preziosa, and too old to be their queen, but she had three daughters, Leocadia, Anthia, and Rhode— already married and with their own children."

She shook her head. "Everyone said that Rhode ought to be queen because she had saved them all from an evil sorcerer. Imagine that!" The woman leaned forward. "She had killed a sorcerer and gone back to being a commonplace peasant woman."

All her companions shook their heads and agreed that that was the story, however strange it sounded.

"They had helped her burn down the sorcerer's house," said an old man. "They knew she had done it."

"The next thing you know," said the woman, lifting her cider, "they were crowning her for half and the other half was proclaiming Giorgos king, and they even dug up the crown that was much too large for him."

"Did they find a regent for him?" said Basil.

The travelers seemed not to know, their talk breaking into confusion about this man and that one. Minutes later, one said, "And

King Maximus's lands! Half the kingdoms say they are going to wait for their old kings to reappear, and not obey King Maximus!"

The old man said, "They say the Bird of Truth flies about telling this man or that woman that their king or queen is here or there, and they just have to wait—and fight off King Maximus."

#

Snow fell in great swathes of white, wrapping the forest outside, beneath a dark sky. Only the most careful look saw the deep, dull red traces in the west, the little of the sunset that reached them.

Rapunzel still listened with half an ear for the door. Any traveler arriving now would be desperate to get in, and the very fact it snowed so thickly meant that the late hour could still yield travelers.

Still, all had gone smoothly for the wedding.

Nan and Ned sat at the head of the table. Nan, rosy-cheeked, could not seem to sit still, and Ned did not seem to stir, he watched her so intently.

Except that as the last of the sunset faded, he rose and reached for Nan's hand.

Cups went up about the table for a final toast, and they turned to the remnants of the meal as the couple hurried up the stairs.

Ian sighed, theatrically. "Almost I wish that a king did not have to consider his kingdom." He drained his cup. "But with the trouble it has already had, my dear, I suppose it is worth the wait."

"After what happened to Anna's children when their father hid her and them?" said Vasilisa. "Fortunate that there is little of the circle left."

"There will always be witches and warlocks, out to ruin your life," said Snow-White. "Remember that."

"Oh," said Ian, "we must live with such knowledge. That is why we do not want to talk to your mirror about this and that until spring comes, and we can act upon our knowledge."

Rapunzel contemplated her reflection in her cup. Would she have been happier to have known that she could not find Basil, that a curse kept her from seeing him, for all those long years? She doubted that she would have refrained from asking the mirror about him.

She drained her cup.

#

The snow was half water, heavy and clinging, and leaving vast spreads of muddy earth. Of all winter weather, the worst to travel in. Especially, thought Biancabella, looking at the watery sunlight, because it would freeze to ice, not snow, overnight.

"What we need," said John, sitting at the kitchen table, "is a ship that can travel through the air over sea and land. Given the size of our company, it would be best."

Biancabella nodded. All the more with three small children. "A grave mistake, not having it. So who among us was rude to an old man when going to build it?"

"Ah, going to build it! I knew we missed something!"

"You also missed that its crew holds men who can run like thought or freeze a great furnace, not mere princes and princesses."

Hans's voice came from the kitchen door. "We do have a princess who can see sharper than ordinary eyes."

Biancabella felt the heat in her face, as if it were not just an observation.

#

Snow sifted down. John thought he ought to go and sit by the fire. The fox was sensibly asleep, and all the children as well, gilded by the firelight until they looked the same fiery shade. Some of the others might be drifting off.

Prudent. Once spring came, they would get little rest.

In a low voice, Vasilisa told Nan and Ned how she could turn them all into other shapes—perhaps the inn into a bush and all of them birds in it—but it was not something she would do lightly.

It would not protect them from Augusta Gloriana, he thought, and looked out at the snow.

"Thinking of something as white as snow?" said Biancabella.

"Paper," said John. "And ink as black as a crow—though nothing red."

She cocked an eyebrow.

"I was half thinking of it when I read through Belsante's library. A book of what happened to us would have proven a wondrous find. If I wrote one, who knows how useful it might prove to another prince, after me?"

"I didn't know you were so studious."

"I wasn't," he said. "I was the despair of my tutors. I would rather ride my horse around the kingdom seven times than read a book. Or walk about it on foot." He turned away from the snow. "But what use would that be?" His riding, even on a wondrous steed, had not saved Sophia.

"So, red as a fire to write by?"

"Firelight is not bright enough," he said. "I would need yellow candlelight."

He looked at the fireplace. "No doubt it would be wiser to wait until Augusta Gloriana is dealt with. Who would read a book written by a prince whom a sorceress slew out of hand?"

Biancabella's smile was sad. She looked, thought John, not half so beautiful as Snow-White—not when she looked so worried.

Chapter 16 — A Curse is Laid

Augusta Gloriana sat alone. Candles formed a circle about her, and their golden glow was steady. Pale shadows crisscrossed the floor, and beyond the candlelight, darker shadows loomed. Her breath going in and out, she barely noticed the light, or the darkness.

All the ladies-in-waiting had gone off, however flustered they had been, and Augusta Gloriana sat in the room, where she had kept her magical mirror, and brooded over how ill-served she had been by the circle. The idea of it had been brilliant, if only they had done as they ought to have. Between them all, at least one should have left a single *useful* spell. No doubt they had left spells enough that would last long enough to cause trouble, or break when it would be ruin, but none that would help her.

Already, they talked about the deaths of King Ogier and Prince Herbert. Without the mirror, she could not know that their bodies had been lost, and her crown was in peril from the knowledge.

And her impudent rascal of a daughter had not only gathered a company, like an idiot third son with a ship that could sail over land as well as sea. She and the lot of them had murdered every other member of the circle. As if they were any match for knowledge and power of the least of the circle! Yet they had struck such wonders from the world, merely to let their own commonplace selves prosper.

Her hands tightened into fists, and then she smoothed them out again.

She should have married off Biancabella. Surely, she could have found an ogre or a wizard who would want such a bride, even one so lacking in loveliness. Boney might have done, if she had gotten to him before he abducted that Katrina or Karla or whoever she was. After, of course, he would be far too negligent—

She twitched. No, Boney would not have done. That peevish
princess he had prisoner had turned out to be the death of him,
and she was just a commonplace princess. Biancabella would have
worked more swiftly, and once she had murdered Boney, she would
have been free to attack her own mother. And Biancabella would
have.

One candle flame wavered, as if it felt the breath of a draft. The
faint shadows danced and whirled.

Augusta Gloriana forced her breath out. Perhaps she could use
new, more useful allies, but she would need to find them. King
Maximus had done many marvels, and even imprisoned her daughter for a time, however short, but he was not fit for the circle.
He had not mastered magic or even sought it out. Kingdoms here
and there held a few who had worked a spell or two, but they
were not the true masters. A spell of forgetfulness did not a witch
make. As for King Drakos's dutiful daughters, they were such colorless, spineless, savorless creatures that she was astounded that King
Drakos had not driven them into exile before his death.

Her lip curled. Then there was that witch who had cursed the
prince—so that the *prince* ended up happy, and Mother Madga's
sister ended up drowned. *She* could enjoy being trapped in the forest and protected from all princes who could offend her.

She looked at the wall, where the mirror had hung. She did not
have the time to look farther and longer. Biancabella was a peril
who could not be ignored, and the insolent knaves she had gathered around her were worse, but they were all of them fools. Not
one of them, not even the mirror, had realized that she did not only
hide places from prying eyes, or things. She hid people.

She contemplated the spellwork for a time, considering what
she could do. Those childish brats, always thinking and acting as if
a sorceress could toss off a spell as easily as a country chit could spin
a bit of thread. This one needed time, and work, and prudent judg-

ment. If she did it with enough care, she could hid each one of them from the other, so that Biancabella would be alone, and all the others, too.

The time was too great. The peril was too high. If she tried that, she would have to do something to keep Biancabella from seeing through each spell.

She nodded. She could hide them all as a group, and then they could take counsel with each other and realize that they could do nothing against her. With them thus weakened, she could—she would—turn them into statues that could see all that passed before them. Then she would install them in her courtyard so they could watch all she did.

For a moment, she pondered the kingdom. Her crown was in danger. You could not hide a death like her husband's forever. Sooner or later some sailor would appear with a ring from King Ogier's finger. She did not have to worry about a harp made from his bones that accused her of his murder, he had gone of his own free will, but his subjects would not accept her except as his consort.

She straightened. There were other kingdoms, other kings, other crowns, other thrones. What courtyard the statues stood in did not matter.

"And it serves you doubly right, Biancabella," she whispered. "Making me give up the throne I worked so hard for, just to stop you."

She stood. The wind of her abrupt motion made the candle flames dance wildly. Some winked out, unable to endure it.

#

Snowdrops blossomed outside, and a few trees showed buds of yellow or red. Basil and Rapunzel prepared for their departure below, but Vasilisa sat before the mirror, her hands folded in her lap. Ian stood by the window, shifting from foot to foot.

John stood in the back, by the window. He was not really needed, having shown them the mirror, but Basil and Rapunzel did not need him underfoot, and they did have to take the mirror down.

"What of my sisters?" said Vasilisa, her voice carefully mastered. "Olga, Ludmilla, Elena, Marina, Irina, and Raisa."

The mirror said, gravely, "They still live at your father's castle. They have yet to fly beyond the bounds that he set or look at the spellbooks he owns."

Vasilisa shivered. "If they gain their boldness yet—"

"Every princess," said the mirror gently, "and every prince, has always known that there were witches and sorcerers who did not wish that anyone be happy. To let fear of them stop you, will stop you forever."

Vasilisa looked up at Ian, who stepped forward.

"My father's kingdom," he said, briskly.

"It was conquered by King Maximus. Your cousin inherited when you did not return, and his sons for a time, but King Maximus slew the last king and his sons."

Ian closed his eyes.

"King Maximus's kingdoms are in open revolt, and an enchantress has told your father's kingdom that his heir has returned. You could return now."

Ian shook his head. "Augusta Gloriana must go first. Biancabella is right in that. We can not invite her to the wedding and force her to dance to death in red-hot shoes. We must deal with her beforehand, lest she come and curse the child in the cradle."

"I can not tell you how to do that," said the mirror, "but I can not say that you are wrong."

John nodded gravely.

"And you, John?" said the mirror. "Have you no questions?"

John stood straighter and squared his shoulders. "All that lies before me is to defeat Augusta Gloriana and avenge Sophia. Then perhaps I might have more questions. For now I have none—unless perhaps whether Biancabella has grown more beautiful."

The mirror blinked. It was a silly question, he supposed, but he did wonder.

"That was what began this all—the fond nursery maid's telling her she would grow more beautiful than her mother, and her fleeing for fear of it. She is lovely, but too worn and anxious for true beauty—if the nursery maid was just fond—"

"Yes," said the mirror, without a hesitation. "Yes, the nursery maid was just fond. Biancabella in her mother's castle was a pallid and anxious ghost. Her beauty sprung from such freedom as she found on the road."

John blinked.

"I can not tell you whether she will be more beautiful than Augusta Gloriana if you put an end to her mother."

"It won't matter," said Vasilisa, low-voiced. "Hans will marry her anyway."

"If," said Ian, "he can be persuaded that his sister can not be found and would want him to be happy. Or, of course, if she is found." He glanced at the mirror.

"With that, I can not aid you," said the mirror.

Silence prevailed. John shifted his weight.

Nan's voice rose from outside with sudden sharpness. "Ned, Ned! Have you seen them?" She ran toward the woodpile. "I did not think they would leave without saying farewell."

"Neither did I," said Ned, sounding thunderstruck. "He—Basil—was helping me with the wood. But—where are they?"

"I'm here," said Basil, sounding startled. John looked down. Basil stood, clearly in sight by the woodpile, and Ned and Nan looked frantically about.

Nan's voice rose in fright. "I don't see any more footprints—and this morning's travelers did not leave too many in the mud and snow. It ought to show."

Ned scowled. "If some whirlwind had swept them, we would have felt it."

The two of them scrambled inside. Basil looked after them with narrowed eyes. Then he looked up toward the window, and raised an eyebrow.

Moments later, Nan's voice rose up the stairwell. "Even Ian and Vasilisa are gone."

"They did plan on leaving," said Ned, slowly.

John felt the blood seeping out of his face. Heaven help them all. A whirlwind might have been easier.

"A new question," he said, turning back to the room. Vasilisa bit her lip, and even Ian seemed not entirely cheerful.

"Augusta Gloriana," said the mirror, with uncommon gravity, though great calm. "She had to work a great spell to do it, but she has made you invisible as she made Basil invisible to Rapunzel."

"We can see each other," said Vasilisa, anxiously.

"So you can," said the mirror. "It was a single spell, and she would have needed to cast one for each of you to keep you ignorant of each other, but others can not see you."

"Augusta Gloriana thinks she can hunt us down at leisure," said Ian, fiercely.

"Oh, she can't," said the mirror. "She plans to, she thinks she can, but she can't. You are, of course, invisible to her."

Ian grinned.

"The spell is much more powerful than the one on Basil," said the mirror, as serene as a forest pool on a windless day. "When

Biancabella led him to Rapunzel, Florio and Constance could see him as well. Indeed, when Biancabella merely told Prince Thomas of the marvelous rose that was the enchanted Elinor, he could find it. This will not be so easy."

John felt more chilled by that thought than by the snowstorm. He glanced down to the ground and saw Biancabella picking her way to Basil. He called down to her.

"Bring the bag up, will you? We need to pack the mirror."

Her pale face peered up at him, and for a moment, he wondered if she had looked that anxious living at the castle. Still, she nodded and hurried off.

The fox came around the inn and eyed the window and him. John let his breath out. They would have to ask the fox as well, though it had not yet known anything the mirror had not.

He would truly feel a fool if this were the one time that were false and did not ask.

#

They left scores of footprints in mud and snow, and yet Nan looked at them as if they did not exist.

Hans shifted the weight of his pack. Violetta wriggled in Basil's arms. At least Sophia and Giovanni slept for a little while longer, but he could only remember fetching those three boys—and two of them had been old enough to walk.

John walked up to the fox. "Sir fox," he said, "can you tell us anything about the spell on us?"

The fox looked sharply at him. "No. Could the mirror?"

"Only that this one is harder than the one on Basil had been."

Biancabella said, abruptly, "Will the Bird of Truth be able to see us?"

A breeze sighed by them.

"Perhaps it will sing its words without realizing we are there," said Hans, roughly.

"Perhaps it will know we are there without seeing us," said Vasilisa. "That magic would make more sense, and it would be true that we were there."

At this hour, thought Hans, he would never fathom any such sense.

#

How few days of walking were needed to make her regret this journey, thought Biancabella.

The wind was chilly from a cloudy sky, and might bring snow, or worse, rain. They trudged along the road. Shelter would lie ahead, not here, if they had to slide into a barn to spend the night, and none of them were fool enough to stop.

Biancabella wished she did not already feel weary of traveling.

In the lead of their company, Hans carried the mirror, once again in the bag she had sewn.

Biancabella supposed it was just as well. She had found the burden heavy many times on her journey alone. Her foot slid a bit in the snow, but caught a moment later, and she let her breath out.

They had not known that Nan and Ned could not see the mirror.

Mud squished underfoot, and Biancabella grimaced. Then, they had not known that Nan and Ned could, and they might never have returned. Every hour on the road, it seemed less likely to her.

Hans sang, lightly, as if someone outside their company could hear him were he louder.

"In the arms of this mother was laid a fine babe,

The finest babe, that ever you did see,

And the babe in the arms, the mother on the bed, the bed from the feather, the feather on the bird, the bird on the nest, the nest on the twig, and the twig on the bough, and the bough on the tree, and the tree in the wood,

And the green leaves flourished thereon, thereon, thereon,

And the green leaves flourished thereon."

Then he stopped, looking down the road.

"Inn ahead," said Hans. "The Dove and the Ivy."

Biancabella looked up. A company of travelers had already reached it and milled about the door. Exclaiming voices reached them.

"Only a fool would risk it. That way lies King Maximus's forces. And Lord Colin's. Would you believe that a man would actually go to war to fight for some heir that a bird told him about?"

They stood and waited. The air was colder without the effort of the walk to warm them. Slowly, the milling company filed into the inn as one by one they choose shelter over their chatter. This left the road open for them, but for a moment, none of them took a step forward.

The fox whispered, "Go. Find shelter. I will spy on them and learn the way."

Biancabella nodded with the rest and bit down the urge to observe that the armies would, of course, block their way toward the Bird of Truth. Where else?

She wondered if Augusta Gloriana had set them there. As soon as she had learned of how the spell had worked, no doubt. Bianca-bella shivered.

#

"Yes, you could go around," said the mirror softly, in the stable's gloom. "But, the armies are not fixed in place. Flee them, and it is likely that your new path will only find theirs again."

"Does Augusta Gloriana guide them?" said Hans. Minutes ago, the faces of the others were pale blurs. Now, the night utterly hid them.

"She knows that you are going to the Bird of Truth," said the mirror. "She has—influenced what chances along the way."

Hans closed his eyes. Stupid, useless bird. He ran a hand through his hair. They should—they should take to the high seas as John's brothers had. Those two had drowned, but the mirror had said it was a storm, not malice, that had done it. If they sailed away for a year and a day, they might find a land beyond Augusta Glori-ana's interest.

It was not as if he had, in over a year, found anything that would be of the least use to Gretel. He had failed her utterly.

"We should sleep," said Rapunzel, gently. "Remember how awk-ward it has been to escape from a stable with all the guests and ser-vants about, and not a single one of them able to see us."

"And," said Basil, his voice very deep, "we can not expect the road to be easier tomorrow."

"You will go past a castle on this way," said the mirror, "but it will be the castle where Anna slept."

Hans sighed. Fortunate Anna.

#

The day was uncommonly warm, and in the sheltered hollows, spring flowers were bright in delicate shades of blue and yellow. The road wound through the hills, so that forest and hillside protected them from the wind.

Biancabella still felt cold.

Violetta fussed, and Biancabella closed her eyes. Reminding herself that they had brought Sylvio, Giorgos, and Roland down this same road only brought to mind that many other travelers had aided them on the way, and that no army had gathered, let alone fought, on the way.

The fox, a flash of copper, appeared again at their feet. "Over the hill. The armies. They look ready to fight."

Basil scowled, and the others pulled back.

"I think there is a path around, we could try that—"

"We will!" said Basil. The fox darted off, and Basil followed. The rest of them hurried off. Her heart hammered, but, Biancabella told herself, speed was of the essence, now.

At the hilltop, the wind was sharper, and she pulled her cloak more tightly around herself. It was hard to remember that no soldiers could see them against the sky. For a moment, she glimpsed the tower of the castle, green and colorful with roses. Fortunate Anna, to escape.

Biancabella gladly followed the fox down the slope. Even if the Bird of Truth flew there, and happened to fly past the towers in this direction, she could not see it at this distance.

The sound of horses came from ahead of them, moving to graze, and soft whinnies. The fox slowed, and Basil came to a stop beside it, staring at a thicket as if that would give him the power to break it to pieces.

For a moment, Biancabella thought of merchant caravans, but the ringing of metal made unlikely. At that, what merchant would be fool enough to venture this close to these armies?

Her fingers closed on her skirt. It was folly enough for those who could not be seen.

"Who is here?" said John, sharply. "Not King Hendrik, he has no desire to fight King Maximus again—"

A bird sang overhead. Biancabella blinked and glanced up. An odd note, though she was almost certain that it was not the Bird of Truth.

Something bright flew through the air. Too small, if all the tales were true, to be the firebird, but bright enough if rather yellow—

It flitted down behind the thicket.

"Cast around north," said the fox, "there is less of an army there—I think."

But before they could move, horses came around the thicket. Soldiers, about a rosy-brown woman with long black hair, and a bearded man with nut brown hair, and a woman with bright copper hair. All of them looked baffled except for the copper-haired woman, who pointed at them. Biancabella glanced at her own company

John had not glanced at that gesture. He looked only at the rosy-brown woman, and his face was paler than snow.

"Belsante?" he whispered.

Belsante followed the woman's gesture. "John?" she said.

#

In the forest, Belsante had the soldiers draw up about them, with Aviette pointing them out to each man. Then Belsante listened gravely as if they stood in her court. She nodded when they told her why a castle overgrown with roses stood by the road, and then the tale finally ended with their meeting. The wind blew through the bare branches, and she turned to Karl.

"Arrange for scouts."

Karl nodded and went.

Belsante turned to them again. "We keep camp over there, it is not far."

Basil nodded, and Biancabella had to agree. She wondered if Belsante's force could take on King Maximus's, and prove victorious, and if he were wise enough to avoid the fight with all that he had before them, and whether they, even unseen, might perish if her army lost—or won.

But better with an army that could see them than one that could not.

The guards glanced over their company as if they did not exist, and Aviette called out to the guard and pointed them out. The guards blinked, rubbed their eyes, and called back into the camp, to other soldiers who could not see them until Aviette pointed them out. She tried to tell them, alone, but that did not suffice.

Elinor would still be a rose if Augusta Gloriana had cast this spell on her, thought Biancabella.

"Here's to hoping," said Hans, "that this is one spell that will end with the death of the sorceress."

Biancabella winced. That death would not be easy to encompass. She did not want to think about needing to break this spell on top of it.

It still did not take Belsante long to usher them to the middle of the camp and have them fed such bread and cheese as could be quickly served up—the fox graciously agreeing that cheese would be fine. Sophia and Giovanni stared about, and Violetta ran hither and yon and had to be shepherded back to where they sat on camp stools.

"To think," said Belsante merrily, "that I thought myself foolish, because in the wide world, there was no way that I could find you, John, and I was only bringing war onto my principality."

"It is a danger," said Biancabella. "Now that your principality can be seen."

"King Maximus perhaps would be so rash," said Belsante, more thoughtfully, "but perhaps not."

She swilled her mug of water.

"You must have that spell broken," she added. "Aviette can not live out her life dancing attendance on you. Karl would object, if nothing else."

"It would hardly be prudent," said John, "to let the fate of king-doms rest on such a thing. If it were even safe to let Augusta Glori-ana cast more spells."

Raised voices in the camp made Biancabella blink and look over. Karl strode across the ground to Belsante.

"Your Highness," he said, with a curt nod. "King Maximus had fewer soldiers before the armies came close, but—" He drew a deep breath.

Belsante's eyebrows rose.

"His men are deserting now. Fleeing to Lord Colin, many of them, though many are just fleeing altogether." He glanced about. "Not toward us."

Biancabella bit her lip. They would have to keep watch on the way, as well. She hoped that none of the deserters made a deal with a dragon to escape. If three happened on an enchanted princess, and one rescued her, that was just as well—she supposed that with six of the circle dead, many enchantments must have weakened. Better for the soldiers to break them entirely than to return home and find no place—and then go make a deal with some evil wizard.

"Some are saying that the Bird of Truth is at that castle." He waved down the road. "Where the roses are. With the news."

Biancabella felt cold.

"The bird flies about enough for that," said Basil. "By all reports. And may fly off. The important thing is that the soldiers are desert-ing."

Belsante nodded in thought. "It is a good thing. I think Lord Colin is mostly like to serve as King Sylvio's regent. It may be wise of me to come to cordial terms with such a power in the land."

John leaned forward. "You heard what happened to King Hendrik's forces."

She inclined her head. "Care is needed, but it is needed in order to avoid his attack. If kings and queens had allied against him, few kingdoms would have suffered under his tyranny."

She rose to her feet to choose her messengers.

#

Charcoal gray clouds billowed in the east, blotting out the sky. To the west, the cloud blazed in bloody scarlet, perhaps enough light to walk by, but the light on the battlefield was mostly the torches in the soldiers' hands.

The fox stayed closely beside John.

Hans and Biancabella were what was needed, here, to tell of Sylvio and how he came to claim the throne, but—John grimaced—the rest of them could hardly let the two go alone. Once parted, they might never find each other again.

His gaze went over the field again.

The news that Princess Belsante's forces had joined Lord Colin's had encouraged the deserters still more, to judge by the fewness of the corpses. Still, some of King Maximus's guard had died defending him to the last. John looked away.

Florio, Snow-White, Basil, and Rapunzel stood together, with the children, beside the field—in the shadow of the trees, where it was growing difficult to see them. John sighed. Wise and prudent, and he should join them, and the fox as well. Even Hans and Biancabella merely stood aside from the discussion, and soldiers and nobles looked odd as they stepped about them, not quite realizing how it was that they had to move. Aviette could not tell them all.

"We have to bring back King Maximus's body," said Lord Colin, talking gravely with Princess Belsante. "To prove he is dead."

John turned to the fox and said, "Could he be revived yet?"

The fox shook its head. "You and King Hendrik both were fortunate in where you fell. Not everyone can be revived that way. Most can't."

"Better to be pushed down a well?" said John.

"Much better," said the fox cheerfully. "A longer journey, you might have to bribe an eagle to fly you back, but still better."

John walked toward the side of the battlefield, and the fox frisked along. It was still awkward, with all the soldiers who could not see them. From the northern side, those who looked down the road could see the castle overgrown with roses.

Ian looked down at it in amazement.

Its walls were overgrown with roses, after all, even in this season. John supposed that Augusta Gloriana had had no wish for a prince to make his way in during the depth of winter. And what enchantments Ian had seen had been barren desert.

Rapunzel held Violetta against her shoulder. "We must ask Princess Belsante that we might have tents to sleep in, for the night. To venture down the road at night would be folly in fair weather. With that storm—we would break all our necks in the mud and do Augusta Gloriana's work for her."

"I can see the bird," said Ian. "Pale enough even now."

"We can see it in the morning," said Vasilisa. "Unless it does not wish to see us. Then going this night will not force it."

Ian scowled.

"It's not as if *the Bird of Truth* were ignorant of who we are, and why we come. No doubt it knows every traveler, and every soldier in each of these armies."

"It let Hans and Biancabella see it," said the fox, gravely, "but even that did not help when it did not wish to say what they wished to know." It scratched its ear. "Not that it did not help at all. I wonder if it helped when people came for it, and it did not show itself, by not showing itself."

John rolled his eyes. "We can not go without Biancabella and Hans—but, here they come. Perhaps they have news."

Biancabella looked pale even for her, drifting across the field. They should sleep, thought John, if only to keep their wits about them when listening, and asking when they could.

Lightning crackled, vividly white against the clouds. Biancabella and Hans walked a distance before the thunder rumbled after.

Hans nodded as they reached the forest edge and said, "Lord Colin said that until the woman brings Sylvio out, there's little he can do but keep peace in the land. He offered to send an escort for Ian and Vasilisa—soldiers from your father's kingdom, Ian."

Biancabella's voice was soft. "They were already determined to have you, Ian."

Ian shifted his weight. "But—' He looked up, and looked frightened. "Aviette won't go with me. No more than Biancabella. And Vasilisa can't help as Aviette can."

"I talked with Aviette," said Vasilisa. "The spell was cast on her in a way to keep her from learning it."

Biancabella grimaced.

That would complicate everything, thought John. The evening breeze picked up. Branches rattled in its chill passage. That kingdom would have to manage, as Sylvio's would. Perhaps Ian could appoint Lord Colin to act as regent.

Ian's gaze went over the field and its crowds. "Who's that woman? The one speaking with Aviette? I thought we knew at least all the nobles here—is she one from my father's kingdom?"

John looked over, sharply. The torchlight fell on the woman, tall and elegant in violet. Between the fineness of her clothes and the command of her presence, Ian had to be right: only a noblewoman would walk like that. Only one both foolish and rich would wear such finery on this field.

Aviette nodded to her with respect, and they spoke. Aviette started to gesture.

Biancabella gasped.

Aviette, looking at the noblewoman's face, pulled back and stared about wildly. Karl called out something, his face set in angry lines. A moment later, Aviette leapt into the air as a brilliantly bright bird, but the woman scowled and looked in their direction. She could not see them, that was clear— her face was contorted with rage—

With a note of panic, Biancabella called, "Run!" and she did not tarry to see if they listened. Skirts in hand, she ran over the rough ground without any heed for crowds or soldiers.

She ran, in fact, as if the woman was—

He ran after before he finished the thought. Not a noble-woman, but a queen.

And not just any queen.

Augusta Gloriana.

#

Her heartbeat hammered in her ears. How could John not have known? thought Biancabella, and cursed herself for a fool even as she ran on. Of all of them, only she and Snow-White knew what Augusta Gloriana looked like.

Until now.

She glanced back. Augusta Gloriana's head turned, and she looked across the battlefield. Directly at them. The *rage* on her face was chilling.

"Toward the castle," shouted Hans. The fox rushed after. Basil snatched the wailing Violetta from Rapunzel's hands before they all fled down the road. Thunder rumbled behind them. Flashes of lightning lit up the sky and the way—brilliantly but too briefly to be of use.

Soldiers shouted, and their shouts spread. Anger and distress—but shouts could do nothing against this foe, and neither could their swords. Biancabella ran onward, with the others, and looked back no more.

Winds buffeted their backs, hard enough to stagger them. She grabbed Snow-White, steadying her with Sophia in her arms. Florio looked anxious, but his arms were too full of Giovanni to help.

Hans slowed, until he, Ian, and John brought up the end. As if the three of them could hold Augusta Gloriana off—and too many people had seen them flee, people whom Augusta Gloriana could question—

"Do you take me for a fool?" The voice resounded like thunder. Augusta Gloriana rose against the storm clouds, as purple-dark in shade as them. Lightning flashes illuminated her. "You are such fools that you think you can gain help against *me* from a silly bird—but I am not such a fool that I can not find you there!"

Biancabella forced herself to look ahead again and run. Despite how her heart sunk. Augusta Gloriana was so certain that she could strike them down.

Lightning, realized Biancabella in despair. She did not need to point it at them like arrows. Augusta Gloriana would strike about with lightning until they all perished, if she had to burn the forest down to do it, and slay all of both armies, and every other traveler for leagues, to boot.

Unless the Bird of Truth could tell them how to escape. Heaven grant that it could.

She ran harder. For all the gloom and the slightness of the sunset glow, the pale glint of something white flew ahead.

Her breath labored and her heart hammering, she out-raced the others and reached the castle. She could—just—make out the bird flying overhead, in and out of the roses. The air was sweet, but she did not come for the flowers.

She tried to catch her breath and call to it, but it did not by so much as a twitch of a wing show that it had heard her. She stepped closer, toward the arched doorway.

The rose there reached a bramble out toward her. Thorns scratched at her hand. She leapt back, and the bramble stopped where it was, without pulling back. Her heart hammering again, she walked in through the center of the arch. If she stood far enough away, the vines did not reach for her.

She called back that warning to the others, but—what was the point of it? Augusta Gloriana could strike them all down, and it was not as if there were any safety for them here, with the bird indifferent and flitting about.

Ian cursed by the arch. Blood showed on his hand. Vasilisa looked about them, her face growing pale and frightened.

Biancabella sighed. A danger to them, but they were Augusta Gloriana's roses.

She froze. Just as the spell hiding them was Augusta Gloriana's.

"Biancabella!" said Vasilisa. "Do you not know what these roses *are*?"

Biancabella took a step toward them. "Everyone, near the walls. As far from the roses as you can find a spot to stand."

They all looked blankly at her.

"And you, Vasilisa, turn us to roses among these roses. Rose vines, of course."

Vasilisa looked the blankest of them all for a moment, and then she smiled. She seized Ian's hand and ran toward a patch of gray stone.

The others dispersed, standing here and there. Biancabella watched for a moment and felt Hans's hand close firmly on her own, drawing her over by the arch and pulling her close to the wall.

Augusta Gloriana screamed outside the wall, and lightning arched over them. Biancabella glanced up, and Vasilisa's enchantment seized her. She felt it drawing her long and thin and green, blooming with pale gold flowers, clinging to wall, and entwined with another rose, beside her, with brightly gold flowers.

With no eyes, somehow she could see more clearly than with them. See the red and pale gold roses where Vasilisa and Ian grew—the dark red with Florio and Snow-White, Basil and the children, with Rapunzel alone golden, and John also gold with the fox a rusty red beside him.

With no mouth, she could not laugh. Or even smile.

Augusta Gloriana swept into the courtyard as she had, from time to time, swept into Biancabella's chambers at the castle, and her look about was more dismissive.

"I have you now," she said. "Every soldier in the army was ready to betray you all. Now you are trapped here. You can not set a foot without peril."

Augusta Gloriana turned and lifted her hands. The roses grew over the doorway. In odd corners, other roses twisted and turned, and grew about what had to have been other exits.

Biancabella felt keenly that her heart should have hammered. But she had gotten her mother inside the castle.

She felt as if she were biting her lip. Her leaves rustled, though the sound of the leaves on the growing vines hid it. It certainly seemed that Augusta Gloriana controlled the roses. Biancabella wished she could close off how she saw, as she could close her eyes. Proposing this transformation, she had trapped them all, and she had to watch every moment.

Perhaps, she told herself, that motion was the original spell itself, having nothing to do with her control, but it gave her no hope.

Augusta Gloriana laughed. "And—you brought me directly to
the means! There is no way, having the Bird of Truth, that I can not
find out the truth!"

The bird flew down, docilely. As it came within a stride of her,
she raised her hand, and the bird darted up and away, through
a window surrounded by blood red roses. She laughed again and
reached in.

The vines surged about her hand, seizing her. She stared, and
pulled back. Blood seeped down her arm, but she could not pull
her arm free.

"You foolish sprouts! I am your mistress!" She reached with her
other hand to pull free. Roses encircled it as well and reached out
for her.

The scream was mercifully brief.

Shouts rose from outside, full of bewilderment and cursing the
curse, and footsteps sounded as boots of running soldiers hit the
ground.

A breeze stirred the leaves, and the roses withered about them.
One by one the vines fell from the wall. With the courtyard as barren and leafless as any early spring garden, soldiers pushed their way
through the last brittle branches across the doorway. There, they
stared about with wild eyes and talked of madness.

Vasilisa's enchantment broke, and she appeared beside Ian, and
perhaps she looked a little smug. Biancabella found herself standing
by the wall, with Hans's arm about her waist, and the soldiers blinking and wondering how they could ever have missed seeing them
before. There had been roses here, had there?

Biancabella laughed aloud, and Hans swept her up and kissed
her. She laughed again, put her hands about his face, and kissed
him.

Thunder rumbled. Moments later, raindrops splattered on the
courtyard, leaving dark marks on the dry stone. Hans put his arm

about her and drew her through the nearest doorway. Under the roof, they watched as their company, and the soldiers, took shelter in the castle, against the spring rain.

Chapter 17—Happily Ever After

The thunderstorm passed swiftly, leaving puddles in the courtyard and damp stone walls. It washed away much of the dead vines, and all of Augusta Gloriana's blood. Stars gleamed, and torches moved about the courtyard, making this puddle and that one flare orange. Half a dozen soldiers stood watch over Augusta Gloriana's body, but John still waited. The fox sat at his feet, as watchful as he was.

Or rather, thought John, he was as watchful as the fox. At least—the fox's head turned a little, eyeing the archway—he aspired to be.

Outside, a bonfire burned. The firelight cast sharp shadows through the archway whenever no torch was near, so high and so fierce the flames were. The soldiers had needed no instructions on how great a fire was needed.

He could hear voices, some by the bonfire, some farther away—where Ian spoke to the men of his father's kingdom. Vasilisa and Ian would, no doubt, spend their night in the camp among his men's tents.

More soldiers came through the arch and bowed to John, before they went to take up the body with the guards.

The fox stood, gleaming in the torchlight. "I'll see to it that nothing goes awry."

John nodded. After what had happened when she had fallen into the pit of snakes and toads, burning her body was the wisest.

Lord Colin and Princess Belsante came through the arch and stood looking about. Moments later, shouts rose outside, but John turned all his attention on the two of them.

"So this is where Augusta Gloriana began her evil," Lord Colin mused.

"King Sylvio has the right to it," said John, "with his being descended by right line of blood from Queen Anna, and its being part of the kingdom that he inherited from her."

Belsante laughed a little. "He will need the last claim. How many kings and queens come of her blood?"

"Most of us, I think," said John.

Lord Colin looked about gravely. "It looks more useful than a mere ruin—indeed, better than a tent."

"The Princesses Rapunzel and Snow-White," said John, "are already taking advantage of that to impose on King Sylvio's hospitality. The children are asleep."

Prudent children, he thought. Most of them would wish they had joined them, come the morning.

#

Lord Colin spoke gravely to Basil and Rapunzel, without bothering to find an out-of-the-way corner. Enough words drifted out to tell that one kingdom that King Maximus had conquered had lost its royal family during the conquest, and that the closest heir was Basil, through his grandmother, and that Basil was mildly telling them that his father was still alive.

In the shadows of the castle, John thought that he had to do a few things, even if Belsante's principality were safely guarded by mountains, and his father's too far off for King Maximus to attack.

He turned to Belsante. "There is something that we should do this night."

The bonfire's stray light made her eye glint as she turned toward him.

"Speak with Snow-White and Florio before we sleep." He gestured across the courtyard, to where Snow-White stood. Watching Biancabella, if he judged rightly. "In the morning, we can speak with Biancabella."

He thought she nodded.

"And Hans," said Belsante.

He sighed. "Let us hope. Perhaps the bird will be less—elusive tomorrow. And clearer of tongue."

Snow-White already had two children who could inherit separate kingdoms, if heirs were needed— but he should not reason as if Biancabella's love was forever doomed.

He walked slowly across the courtyard, not to draw Biancabella's gaze. Snow-White turned to him.

"She looks more beautiful already," she whispered. "Without the dread of her mother. She may yet be happy." Her mouth pursed for a moment. "She could tell travelers they had to tell their stories. It would work better for her than for Rapunzel, without the spells to hide things. And she could do it in a castle, not an inn. She might learn about a sister that way."

#

Dawn drifted through the windows.

This inn, thought Biancabella, had harder beds, and colder, than any other she had stayed in, in all her journeys. She shifted her weight a little, and blinked as she remembered it was not a bed but a stone floor, not an inn but a castle in ruins. Her blankets lay in a mess about her, and the window was filled with rosy light.

She pulled on her mantle before she stood. The morning was cold. At the doorway, still in shadow, she saw she was not the first riser. John and Belsante walked together, and talked, and Belsante laughed.

Biancabella turned toward another door, which led her outside. The sky still gleamed with pinks and oranges on the last rags of clouds left from the storm, and a few bushes about the castle had barely green leaves. In the forest, flowers bloomed white and pale blue between the dead leaves.

She sighed.

Hans spoke behind her, his voice deep, "Sad at this hour?"

"Melancholy, perhaps," she said. "The first flowers will be gone by the time I reach the castle of my kingdom again." She looked at the dead leaves for a moment. Her nose was not a foot long, but she still might never marry. "Since I will most likely go there. Perhaps I could help look about and see if Augusta Gloriana left any vicious enchantments in the castle."

For a moment, she wondered if Greta was enchanted and hidden there.

"Perhaps the mirror will help there," said Hans. "Or the bird." He tilted back his head, and she followed his gaze. If the Bird of Truth flew about, it did not do so here.

"There you are," called Lord Colin. "The cooks have nearly finished cooking breakfast."

And, thought Biancabella, there was much to be done.

Hans bowed deeply and offered her his arm. She took it, and a trill of notes filled the air. Whiteness flitting through air turned into the bird perching on the bush.

Biancabella realized, with a start, that the song had caused everyone else to move, and they gathered round before the bird perched. Even Lord Colin peered at the bough and the bird. She bit her lip. They did not need to ask how to defend themselves from Augusta Gloriana, not now.

"Cut off the fox's head!" declared the bird, flinging out its wings. "Break the mirror! Let all be concluded!"

A moment later it flew off, and Hans stood there with his mouth half open, giving it a baneful glance. Biancabella chided herself for forgetting his sister and felt the heat rising in her cheeks. That question might mean her grief, Greta might be prisoner past thrice ten kingdoms from this land. But—

"I think I could break the mirror most easily if it were on the wall," she said. "With a hammer." For a moment, Snow-White and Rapunzel looked at her, but John had come to grief through not listening to the advice of a magical beast. She would not ignore the bird's.

The fox looked brightly up at John. After a moment, it said, "If you do not wish to do it—"

"No," said John heavily. "No—I am sure there are others here who would do it—but I will."

"There's firewood for the camp fires," said Lord Colin. "Enough for a block."

"I'll get the mirror," said Basil.

It seemed like mere moments before she had the mirror on the wall and a hammer in her hand as she told the mirror what the bird had said.

With it hanging on the wall and the face looking solemnly at her, her mouth was very dry, and the hammer felt very heavy. She swallowed. It did not settle her stomach.

"What do you dally for?" said the mirror.

Biancabella remembered tales when someone had arranged for a stranger's funeral, and learned in due course that a good friend had been, in truth, a ghost of that stranger—and now would leave forever.

She stood to one side and swung the hammer round. It struck the mirror hard. Glass splintered. Shards cascaded from the frame, flying out into the room like silvery birds, falling far too closely together, as if in a silvery arc—and was the mirror's face forming again on it?

She watched, the hammer falling to her side. Before her eyes, the falling glass formed a woman's shape, all silvery bright, and as the light shifted about, it shifted again, taking on color. For a moment, Biancabella thought it reflected the room, but a moment later, that was madness. A woman stood before them, wearing drab gray, but her bright blond hair fell in a braid down her back, and her cheeks were touched with roses. She looked oddly familiar as she looked about, her eyes large with wonder.

Hans made a choked noise. Moments later, he had swept the woman up in his arm and swung her about him. Biancabella bit down on the stab of jealousy, telling herself what a fool she was even before Hans choked out, "Gretel—Greta—"

"Hans!" Greta kissed him. He swung her about again, and Biancabella stepped back to lay down the hammer as quietly as she could. Then her gaze drifted toward the door. John had cut off the fox's head by now.

Greta laughed, and her gaze fell on Biancabella. She froze in place, looking abashed.

Biancabella said, quickly, "Is this one of those things that you knew and could not say?"

Her laughter pealed, again. "No, no—I guessed that something would happen after the Bird of Truth told you—but I did not know—" Her hand loosely in Hans's, she leaned forward and kissed Biancabella's cheek.

"Though you were right in one thing. I would have been glad to have Hans happy."

Biancabella kissed her cheek, and drew a deep breath. "We should see what happened when John cut the fox's head off."

Both of them looked puzzled—as if it were not obvious. Biancabella walked over. John stood by a block of wood, which showed not a spot of blood, talking with a young man with red-brown hair—much more brown than the fox, thought Biancabella. She stood carefully to one side.

Greta squealed behind her. "Carolus!" she called, dropping her brother's hand, and running. "Carolus!"

Hans walked up behind Biancabella, more slowly. His sister threw her arms about her prince and kissed him thoroughly.

"So," said Hans, "Heaven has granted everything that I hoped for—in the end."

Biancabella glanced up at him, through her eyelashes. "Everything?"

He looked down at her face. Then, abruptly, he blushed. "You will have to assure me on that one."

For a moment, Biancabella stood halfway in the castle, and halfway out, and marshaled words, but then Greta and Carolus pulled apart, and Carolus said, "I have to speak with Snow-White."

Greta blinked. Then she nodded.

"Snow-White," said Hans, carefully.

Carolus ran a hand through his hair. "My sister Sophia told John—she had a brother who vanished—" He glanced between them. "Greta was not the only one who did not know all, and could not tell all that she knew."

#

Lord Colin stood back as Carolus and Greta told how they had fled Mother Trude, and been bewitched, how Greta had served Augusta Gloriana as her magical mirror, and how Carolus had managed to find John and help him, and Sophia. Carolus's sister.

At the end of it, Lord Colin said, "I have heard of King Helias and his kingdom."

Their father, thought Biancabella.

Carolus looked sharply around. His expression grew steadily graver as Lord Colin told how King Maximus had never tried to conquer it, but that the king was so old that he could barely rise from his bed.

"Too old for any magic to aid him," said Lord Colin. "Not even the water of life, or the golden fruit of a firebird's tree."

Snow-White sadly shook her head. "He already has great-grandchildren," she said. "That many years can not be shaken off."

Carolus nodded. "I will go at once." He hesitated. "Greta? It will be a hard journey. You could—"

"No," said Greta. "I do not know how to conjure doves that will jog your memory of me free again when some witch bewitched you. Let alone how to prevent such a witch from turning me into a canary. Aviette was trapped so; I would be trapped all the better. Even if your father set me to work as a goose-girl—I am not letting my bridegroom leave me."

"And there is no talking fox to save me," said Carolus, "if some knave decides that he can steal my place as well as my brothers could have, if I had them."

Hans shifted closer to Biancabella. Lord Colin laughed, shortly.

"Such prudence. It is close, and King Sylvio will have need of good will on his borders—" Then he blinked and stared over the field.

Biancabella followed his gaze. An old woman, dressed in black, came walking out of the woods. A small boy peered about her skirt, but held it with both hands.

"Mistress Theophania!" she called, and Lord Colin started.

Sylvio hid his face in Theophania's skirts. Theophania laughed aloud.

"This is the young King Sylvio!" she called to the soldiers, and walked toward the castle. Lord Colin's face slowly took on a look of panic.

Sylvio peeked out at the castle. Violetta ambled out and looked at him curiously. His nose wrinkled, and she thought he said something about a *baby*. Theophania smiled and, when Rapunzel went to pick up Violetta, turned back to Lord Colin.

"Good Lord Colin," called Theophania. "They tell me you have not wed."

Lord Colin shook his head. "Heaven grant that I may."

She smiled. "And soon. When you are wed, I will bring King Sylvio to the care of you and your wife."

Sylvio tugged on her skirt and whispered.

"Many of them are princes and princesses," said Theophania. "That is why they can speak so freely with your regent, and even with you."

Sylvio peered at them. For a moment, Biancabella wondered whether he knew her, or Hans, but then he said, dubiously, "All of them?"

John laughed, deep in his chest. "Most of us." He waved his hand at Biancabella. "She's a queen."

Biancabella blinked. "But—John—you're the one who found the golden bird, and won it. My—your brother got it from you only by treachery that should not be rewarded—"

"And he's not going to receive the reward," said John. "Drowning was only fit for him. But even with a horse of power, to reign over both the kingdom and the principality, would be hard indeed. I would spend much of the year traveling."

She opened her mouth and shut it again.

Snow-White nodded. "And it would be simpler for me, but still—two kingdoms! No, no, let the crown go to you." She straightened. "You saved that kingdom, and many more. The kingdom by itself—that would be the point at which elder brothers declare that the youngest should inherit."

"Having saved all these kingdoms? Why should you *not* receive the crown?" said John.

"It is only fitting at that, that the one who rescued both John and myself should be rewarded, in itself," said Snow-White. "There is many a maiden who won the prince merely by healing him."

Sylvio said firmly, "Queen." Then he peered up at Hans. "And you—prince?"

Hans shook his head and spoke gravely. "No. They all are princes, but I am a wood-cutter."

"Wood-cutter?" Sylvio looked at him with large eyes. "I never met a wood-cutter before!"

#

Plans moved so swiftly, but really, thought Snow-White, it was the wisest route. In the shadows of the castle, she hoped that she just found it hard to read Biancabella's face.

"It's safest if you come with us. It's not as if it's out of your way, except as the crow flies, and these soldiers are, after all, in Basil's service."

Biancabella frowned a little as if in thought.

"Once at his father's castle, we can send more soldiers to escort you, or summon soldiers from the kingdom."

"The second might be better," said John. "So that Snow-White can assure them that neither she nor I will claim the throne. Then they can proclaim it at the castle, so that all the kingdom knows."

Snow-White bit her lip. The walls were gray about them. This was no place to stay long, in the snow and the wilderness, and they wanted to reach shelter before nightfall. Belsante's army had already gathered to return, and the soldiers escorting Carolus and Greta were barely visible in the distance.

Biancabella nodded. Snow-White tried to keep her sigh of relief small. The land still had bandits, and if Hans would never be such a fool as to leave her side, there still might be a man who would try to murder him and force Biancabella to claim he rescued her.

Hans strode toward them, and Biancabella's face turned radiant with her smile.

"Are we going with Basil's forces?" he said.

"Yes," Biancabella said, and took his arm.

As they walked off to tell Basil, Snow-White turned to John and said, "Meg was right. She is more beautiful than Augusta Gloriana."

"Much," said John. "Or at least—" He waved a hand. "Her face as she chased us was not a marvel of loveliness."

Snow-White's laughter rang.

#

The castle stood visibly ahead, but the forces waited.

A wedding procession came down the cross way. The bride and bridegroom, both white haired, walked with measured step among the flowers and the mirth.

Biancabella asked quietly. She felt unsurprised when she heard that the two had sought each other for many years, only to find each other in the last week.

She watched them go by. Their steps were measured, but they both smiled as they walked.

She smiled.

#

The court gleamed with gold and scarlet. King Ivan, though his hair was utterly white, sat on his throne, and the courtiers murmured how hale and vigorous he seemed with his great-grandchildren, and his smaller granddaughter, before him.

Enough that she could hear it, thought Biancabella, though she sat beside them as befit a queen, however uncrowned. All about the crowd, as brightly clad company murmured the news about this and that, the wedding clothes that Rapunzel and Snow-White sewed for their guests, and how messengers had come from King

Sigurd and Queen Constance, promising they would visit with Prince Dag.

Basil emerged from the crowd and bowed to his father before he straightened and said, "There came news about King Igor. Theodora went there. With Roland. King Roland, I suppose. King Igor and Queen Jacintha and Princess Silverhair were driven out before the sunset."

"Was Red Ritter sent with them?" said Biancabella.

Hans laughed aloud.

"Rumor," said Basil, mildly, "did not go so far as to mention him."

"They did not marry," said King Ivan, with authority. "I believe that Red Ritter left even before this—matter."

"And now," said Hans, "he is no doubt praising himself for his prudent departure."

A messenger hurried through the crowd to bow and announce that the watchmen had seen a company on the road, with a banner that proclaimed they came from—Queen Biancabella's kingdom. He glanced sideways at her as he spoke.

Snow-White, agleam in white, stood.

"We must go. To greet, and to speak with, them." She offered Biancabella her arm.

So soon they stood at the gate, arm in arm, and drawing many sidelong glances and mutters from the arriving company. Florio and Hans stood in the shadows behind them, and rather more of King Ivan's soldiers than struck Biancabella as necessary.

"Good morn, my lords, my ladies," she said, pitching her voice to carry. "This is indeed my sister Snow-White, as you have heard from King Ivan's messenger."

The lords bowed, and the ladies curtsied.

The leading lady straightened. "Two fair flowers from a royal branch. We have come to escort our—sovereign."

Her gaze darted toward the archway, dismissed Florio, and settled on Hans. She frowned a little.

"The tale you heard," said Snow-White, "that Prince John is likewise alive, is also true. You will not, however, see him here because he would not leave his bride's side when she returned to her principality."

She raised her head. "Therefore he charged me to bear you the news that because Princess Biancabella rescued him, as she rescued me, the throne is to be hers. Prince Basil and Princess Rapunzel can swear to the truth of that."

For a moment, a ripple of talk ran through the company. Biancabella stood in silence. She was the daughter of the usurping prince who had killed their rightful prince and the evil sorceress who had killed their rightful queen. She and Hans might yet have to live on the generosity of those they had aided.

Then they turned toward her again.

The leading lord bowed to Snow-White. "Your Royal Highness." He shifted a little to face Biancabella. "Your Majesty." His bow was much deeper, and all the lords and ladies and soldiers escorting them bowed and curtsied like a field of flowers bending before the wind.

#

The morning sky was still gray, if not the charcoal shade of earlier. With the grooms drawing up the horses, they gathered in the courtyard.

"This is a shorter ride than to this kingdom?" said Hans, his voice low as he eyed the horses.

Biancabella fought down the laugh. It had not been an easy ride for her, either, after all those months going everywhere afoot. "Yes, far shorter. Snow-White told the truth when she said this castle was on our route."

Without looking much happier, he nodded. Snow-White and Florio emerged from the castle, coming toward the two of them. Snow-White took Biancabella's hands and kissed her cheek.

"Heaven bless your way. Rapunzel and I will have to come before the wedding, to ensure the wedding clothes fit."

"Of course," said Biancabella. "Though I am beginning to dread the time it will take, and think of how much more swiftly it could be done at the Four Winds."

Hans shook his head sadly. "And if we came to your home wed, it would be no more than many another princess has done—and prince, too, as well."

A guard called from the gate. About a rider from the North.

"I hope nothing's happened to John," said Florio, frowning. He pressed toward the gate, but when the sound from them reached them, Biancabella heard rather Carolus—

Florio looked grave as he escorted the travel-stained messenger back to stand before Snow-White. The man bowed and told how King Helias had rejoiced to see Prince Carolus return, and with a bride, and in the news of Snow-White and her children.

And how he died that night.

Snow-White stood still and was paler than a ghost. Her head bowed.

"May Heaven grant him peace," said Florio. Biancabella echoed him.

#

Every now and again, a glimpse of the castle could be seen ahead, between the hills.

The cloudless day was bright and still as they rode toward it. The barely leafing trees cast little shade, and the birds chirped and twittered and cheeped from every corner of the forest.

Hans caroled after them.

"And the babe he grew up and became a fine boy,

The finest boy, that ever you did see,

And the boy from the babe, the babe in the arms, the mother on the bed, the bed from the feather, the feather on the bird, the bird on the nest, the nest on the twig, and the twig on the bough, and the bough on the tree, and the tree in the wood,

And the green leaves flourished thereon, thereon, thereon,

And the green leaves flourished thereon."

Light glinted ahead of them, from some body of water. A river, remembered Biancabella, rather than a lake. The captain of the guard drew up and bowed to her.

"Your Majesty. There's a ford here, and a merchant caravan half way through fording it. Going down another road, after."

"Then let them ford," said Biancabella. "It will be more time and trouble for them to yield to us than to let them pass. Unless you think we shall not reach the castle today?"

The captain shook his head and rode off, giving orders. Biancabella drew up her horse, and looked out into the forest.

"I wonder if the spring flowers are blooming still," she said, softly.

"Probably not the early ones," said Hans. "Mother always had us watch so she could gather as soon as some of the greenery was edible. Perhaps we should look." He dismounted and came to hand her down.

"Do you have notions about the trees?" she said.

"Father had us plant acorns, and other seeds. He said the forest grew too thin." He smiled and spoke in an airy tone. "I shall pester your ministers for not giving orders to replant the woodlands."

His hand swept the air, and she giggled. His voice rang out to the trees.

"And the boy put an acorn all into the earth,

The finest acorn, that ever you did see,

And the acorn in the earth, the boy from the babe, the babe in the arms, the mother on the bed, the bed from the feather, the feather on the bird, the bird on the nest, the nest on the twig, and the twig on the bough, and the bough on the tree, and the tree in the wood,

And the green leaves flourished thereon, thereon, thereon,

And the green leaves flourished thereon."

The leaves were still stirring, not yet to flourishing, thought Biancabella as she looked about.

Something moved in the woods, skulking among the trees. Not golden like Sigurd had been, closer to Florio's brown—more reddish and not fur at all—and something glinted in his hand.

Hans followed her gaze, and drew his sword.

Her wits stirred. "Guards!"

The figure in red garments, dirty from travel, tried to dart off, but the soldiers swept round and brought Red Ritter before her, still with his sword in hand. His gaze darted about, and he muttered, madly enough, that if he had killed Hans—and then he lunged, and the captain of the guard struck him down. He groaned where he lay on the earth, more red than before, but did not open his eyes.

"Madman!" said Hans.

"Quite, quite mad," said Biancabella, feeling the color seep from her face.

"Your Majesty!" called a young soldier. "The merchants are gone."

She raised her head.

The ride over the river, and up the hill, did raise her spirits. The street to the castle was adorned with flags in every color and garlands of spring flowers. Crowds pressed around with many cheers, and small children were lifted up to see for themselves that the queen had returned, so lovely, and her handsome bridegroom.

The castle gates stood wide open, with servants and courtiers bowing and curtsying everywhere. After Hans handed her down, and the stable boys took their horses, the housekeeper, old Willa, and the butler Hal came up, speaking of how they would arrange their dinner.

"Save the grand feast for the morrow," said Biancabella. "It has been a long journey."

Lizzy, curtsying by the kitchen, shouted at the kitchen maids that if she had to harry them all night, they would manage a feast by then as well as a dinner this night. The ladies in waiting twittered about her, taking her up toward the royal chambers, which, they assured her, maids had prepared, and a chamber for Master Hans as well.

In the great chamber, outside the private ones, the window looked down into the garden. From a glance, it did not seem to have suffered much, green sprouts everywhere and flowers blooming in red and gold.

That meant little, she reminded herself. Many of those could be rank weeds. The kitchen garden would be better, with Lizzy insisting on it for the table, but the flower beds might have suffered.

Hans came up behind her. "Is there a private way down to the gardens?"

She blinked. "Yes. Yes, there is." She walked over to a door near the back. "Not secret, the castle has no secret doors, but private."

Minutes later, they walked down the path there, and she talked of how the heartsease must have been planted in the autumn, to have grown so—and thought it did ease the heart. Gardeners had tended it, and she saw no plants that had to be rooted out as a sorceress's garden.

At the end of the path, she looked about and blinked. A shed stood off by the woods.

"I always thought that was a gardener's shed," she said, "but the gardeners always had their tools closer to the castle."

Ted emerged from the woods, lugging branches. He nodded, making a gesture toward his cap.

"Ted," she called, waving toward the shed, "is that for work in the woods?"

"Not at all, Your Majesty, not at all," said Ted. "No servant would dare go in. I dare say we'd stop you, because the que—"

In the silence, he looked between them. Then he licked his lips and spoke again.

"Because your late mother forbade anyone to go in."

Biancabella's gaze went over to it.

"Even when the evil sorceress forbids entry," said Hans, "it can be a danger."

"Oh yes," said Biancabella, "but you know that someday, someone will go in. Perhaps our child. And—" She tilted her head to one side. "Perhaps it will not be evil. Perhaps we would find a master maid, who could have unraveled in a day all that we took years to undo."

Hans scowled.

"But if it's someone who asks you for water, do not give it."

His laughter came in a short bark. "I will open the door."

She bowed her head. Reasonable enough. She stood aside as he pulled.

The burst of gold came out as brilliantly as a crown struck by sunlight, and Hans stepped back. Moments later, its wings outstretched, the golden bird brushed by them both, and took to the wing, gleaming like the sun itself. Biancabella watched its flight over the garden, past the wall, and above the city. She could hear the cries of wonder, and only as a church tower hid it from view did she let her breath out.

She still could not speak. How had anyone managed to cry out?

Hans went down on one knee. She blinked. Something glinted before him, and she turned. A golden feather lay on the ground before it. He picked it up.

"John, perhaps, had a good claim to it," he said idly.

"It would not heal his father," said Biancabella sadly. "Perhaps it might have aided King Helias, but not for long. Old age can not, in the end, be healed."

He stood. "Perhaps we should put this in the treasury."

#

Outside, in the sunshine, the flower beds bloomed, with bees and butterflies flitting about flowers. Roses blossomed in red and white, and birds chirped and twittered, each one in its own tree, by its nest. Biancabella stood still in the shade of her chamber.

Looking severe, Snow-White walked around her again.

The green skirts swept out much farther than Snow-White's own, and under Rapunzel's hawk-like gaze, the maid servants had embroidered the gown with flowers—and also the clothes for Hans, now being severely overseen by Rapunzel.

Both Snow-White and Rapunzel, thought Biancabella, could gain a job as a seamstress in exile.

She sighed. "It was easier to wait even a week ago. Hans and I were walking in the gallery—"

"Putting faces to the tales the mirror told us?" said Snow-White, with amusement.

"We got through those quickly," said Biancabella. "In the gallery it does not seem like such a long time. No, I told him the tales of the older kings and queens, and we considered names for a son."

Her eyebrows went up. "Have you meet an enchantress you did not tell us, to have such certainty which name you need?"

"A daughter we will name Isobel, for his mother."

For a moment, silence reigned in the room. Sophia, like Giovanni and Violetta, stayed with the nurse back in King Ivan's castle.

"Did Florio take you down the gallery to show you that Giovanni was also a namesake?"

Snow-White smiled again. "Of course. But you and Hans still have time—"

"Oh, we will name him Per."

Snow-White frowned a little. Then—"The miller's son, whom the talking cat helped reclaim an ogre's castle that was hers—he cut off her head in the end, and she turned out to be a beautiful princess—he was a little simple, and she did most of the work—"

Biancabella's breath came out, half laughing. "At times both Hans and I would have been glad of a talking cat to manage things. Carolus did his best as the fox, but much was beyond him." She tilted her head. "Wouldn't you and Florio?"

"When a princess aids me, does all the work, and ends the evil spell—why would I insist that she be a cat at the time?"

Biancabella opened her mouth. Then she shut again. Then she hoped she did not blush impossibly.

A lady in waiting reported, in a mild voice, that the last of the carriages had arrived at the church, but the guests still descended to take their places.

"And no wonder," said Snow-White, "with the brave show they are making. Even Greta and King Carolus are fine in their half-mourning."

"I was surprised that so many accepted," said Biancabella.

"You went to John and Belsante's wedding, with us," said Snow-White. "And that was only a wedding and his coronation as consort. You will go to that for Greta and King Carolus as soon as they are out of mourning, and that will be as grand as this one, a wedding with a double coronation."

Biancabella gave a little laugh. "But—King Heinrich and Queen Genoveva I might have guessed, or even Prince Thomas and Princess Elinor—but Princess Kari and Prince Pierre—and all twelve of the dancing princesses—they don't even know I had a hand in their disenchantment—and so many others—even Queen Rhode and her King Yanni—"

Snow-White's laughter rang. "As if the tales did not spread over the lands! If you saved one kingdom, you would have many guests. When you saved so many—"

Biancabella let her breath out. "The news barely reached us in time," she murmured. "We were going to invite Lord Colin."

Snow-White raised an eyebrow.

"We were about to send off the messengers when we heard about how he held balls to meet a bride, and how a marvelous lady appeared at each one, and turned out to be a scullery maid, who was a noblewoman who had fled her home. So we needed to invite his bride as well."

Snow-White smiled. "Just such a ball as the late queen would happily have destroyed. No, you will just have to suffer through the burdens of our gratitude."

"Your Majesty," said the maidservant, "the last guest has arrived. And Master Hans is inside the church."

Hans—she felt the smile take over her face.

"Come," said Snow-White. They descended the stairs. In the courtyard, the carriage awaited, and John as well. It was as well that the procession was meant to be slow, the crowds gave it no chance for speed, and flowers and cheers engulfed the way. More loudly than when John had arrived for the wedding, or Snow-White.

The cheers redoubled as she alighted, went up the stairs, and entered the candle-lit church, with its glittering gathering. Her gaze went past the congregation, and to Hans, standing with Greta and Carolus, and looking solemn, until his gaze lit on her.

#

Great white flakes drifted down, so large that she could see them from the bed, and settled over the garden.

In his cradle, Per snuffled a little. Hans stood by him and sang.

"And out of this acorn there grew a fine tree,

The finest tree, that ever you did see,

And the tree from the acorn, the acorn in the earth, the boy from the babe, the babe in the arms, the mother on the bed, the bed from the feather, the feather on the bird, the bird on the nest, the nest on the twig, and the

twig on the bough, and the bough on the tree, and the
tree in the wood,

And the green leaves flourished thereon, thereon, thereon,

And the green leaves flourished thereon."

Biancabella smiled. And so it would never end. Per settled
back in his blankets, sleeping more deeply. She yawned, and Hans
looked over, and smiled.

"And to think," said Hans, "that I had hoped to bring you back
news from the garden, about the green sprouts."

Biancabella smiled drowsily. "It will melt soon, at least. The
sprouts are sturdy, this early in the spring."

A lady-in-waiting—Karoline, she thought—appeared by the
doorway to say they had a visitor.

"In this weather? He must be desperate," said Hans. "But he will
be hard put to get back with whatever he petitions for."

Karoline shook her head. "It's a woman, an old woman, very
plainly clad, and—" She glanced between them. "We showed her to
a room with a fire where she could warm herself."

Biancabella's heart seemed to stop, and then to hammer in her
chest.

"Show her in," said Hans, but his voice sounded constrained, as
if he too remembered Anna and her long sleep.

She heard the halting footstep in the hall, and then the old
woman peeked in. Biancabella blinked. She had seen this old
woman. Once. Far back, when first she left the castle, when she had
not even won her way to the castle where the twelve princesses had
danced in their underground prison.

The enchantress smiled. "What a charming scene." She
stumped into the room. "How glad I am that none of you need fear

a curse in this hour, with all who are so grateful to you for all the spells you have broken."

"In this hour," said Hans, gravely.

She raised an eyebrow. "You can not undo the world itself. Those who come after you must win their own way to their own happiness."

Per yawned.

"Such as you, little prince. Because your parents freed the golden bird, you were born to them much earlier than you would have, before your mother bathed in a forest pool and heard a frog telling her she would bear a child."

Per opened his eyes and looked at her.

"And you would have no sister in due course, then. But—for what you will face—I have a gift for you. You will see through spells as your mother does."

Per chortled with glee.